Praise for *Still Alice*

'An incredibly compelling and engaging insight into a world of which we know so little, full of emotion at every turn. I was utterly engrossed from beginning to end'
Natalie, Newcastle-upon-Tyne

'Absolutely beautiful, heart-breaking and haunting. I loved this book and was still talking and thinking about it for months afterwards'
Sara-Jade, London

'Illuminating and gripping. It arouses such powerful emotions – in parts very sad but also very funny. The progression of Alice's disease is made all the more poignant by the fact that we experience every moment from her point of view. A definite must-read'
Simon, Glasgow

'Having lost my father to Alzheimer's last year this gave me an insight into how he must have been feeling for the previous five years. Despite being a very emotional book I just didn't want it to end'
Jane, Gloucestershire

'The writing is so sensitive that you feel a window has been opened in Alice's brain and we, the reader, can watch as havoc is relentlessly let loose'
Sheila, Hertfordshire

'An amazing book, I absolutely loved it even though I was sitting on the train in tears for a couple of days running and my boyfriend refused to sit next to me'
Kirsty, Clapham

'I finished *Still Alice* on my way to my grandmother's house in South Woodford. I found it to be fantastically involving, and as the characters gained more flesh I found the book increasingly hard to put down. It made me so aware of human fragility, and that we cannot always see those catastrophes that are devastating the people around us. I spent the morning with my grandmother writing down tales from her childhood, fragments of poems she could remember, anything really, because of *Still Alice*; it just suddenly seemed to be something that needed to be done'
David, Essex

'Quite unexpectedly the best read – very poignant but also amusing. Wow'
Pippa, Gloucestershire

'An incredibly moving and humbling book. There were times when I had to turn away from the page to count my own blessings. Lisa Genova's cool, unsentimental style makes Alice's descent into oblivion all the more heartbreaking'
Louise, London

'There are few page-turners in this field of literature but this is one of them' *Alzheimer's Society*

'This remarkable first novel about a 50-year-old woman's descent into early onset Alzheimer's is frightening to read, especially for those who have experienced the odd "senior moment" ... With 700,000 people suffering from dementia in the UK, this illuminating view inside the mind of an Alzheimer's patient is highly relevant today' *Daily Mail*

'Reads like a gripping memoir of a woman in her prime watching the life she once knew fade away ... A poignant portrait of Alzheimer's, *Still Alice* is not a book you'll forget'
USA Today

'Genova reveals a story of extraordinary bravery, endurance and love. *Still Alice* is a tremendous affirmation of the powers of fiction'
Stefan Merrill Block, author of *The Story of Forgetting*

'After I read *Still Alice*, I wanted to stand up and tell a train full of strangers, "You have to get this book"'
Beverly Beckham, *Boston Globe*

'This is the clearest and most truthful piece of fiction I have read depicting living with Alzheimer's. You accurately describe the feelings and actions of both persons, together, entangled in this dance with Alzheimer's Disease. Thank you for writing this story'
Chuck Jackson, diagnosed with Alzheimer's age 50

'A wonderful, moving journey with relationships that inspire, sadden, charm, convince and terrify'
Rachel, Edinburgh

Also by Lisa Genova

Still Alice

Left
Neglected

LISA GENOVA

**SIMON &
SCHUSTER**

London · New York · Sydney · Toronto · New Delhi

A CBS COMPANY

First published in Great Britain by Simon & Schuster UK Ltd, 2011
This paperback edition published by Simon & Schuster UK Ltd, 2011
A CBS COMPANY

1 3 5 7 9 10 8 6 4 2

Simon & Schuster UK Ltd
222 Gray's Inn Road, First Floor
London, WC1X 8HB

www.simonandschuster.co.uk

Simon & Schuster Australia, Sydney
Simon & Schuster India, New Delhi

A CIP catalogue record for this book
is available from the British Library

ISBN 978-0-85720-340-3

Typeset by M Rules
Printed in the UK by CPI Cox & Wyman, Reading, Berkshire RG1 8EX

For Chris and Ethan

PROLOGUE

I think some small part of me knew I was living an unsustainable life. Every now and then, it would whisper, *Sarah, please slow down. You don't need all this. You can't continue like this.* But the rest of me, powerful, smart, and determined to achieve, achieve, achieve, wasn't hearing a word of it. If, once in a while these kinds of thoughts did manage to wiggle into my consciousness, I shushed them, scolded them, and sent them to their room. Quiet, little voice, can't you see I have a million things to do?

Even my dreams began tapping me on the shoulder, trying to grab my attention. *Do you even know what you're doing? Let me show you.* But each dream was elusive upon waking, and like a slimy fish captured in my bare hands, it slipped out and swam away before I could get a good look at it. Strange that

I can remember them all now. In the nights just before the accident, I think my dreams were trying to wake me up. With all that has happened, I honestly believe that they were guidance sent from a spiritual source. Messages from God. And I ignored them. I guess I needed something less fleeting and more concrete.

Like a traumatic smack to the head.

CHAPTER 1

"Survivors, ready?"

Jeff, the distractingly handsome host of the reality television game show, smiles, stretching out the wait, knowing he's making us crazy.

"Go!"

I am running through rain forest. Bugs are colliding with my face as I race. I'm a human windshield. The bugs are grossing me out.

Ignore them. Hurry.

Sharp branches are smacking and slicing my face, wrists, and ankles, cutting me. I'm bleeding. It stings.

Ignore it. Hurry.

A branch snags my favorite, most expensive silk blouse and rips it from shoulder to elbow.

Great, I can't wear this to my morning meeting. Fix it later. Hurry. Hurry.

1

I reach the beach and see the planks of driftwood. I'm supposed to make a raft. But I don't see any tools. I swat around in the sand with my hands. I can't find any tools. Then I remember the map that Jeff showed us for a second before lighting it on fire. He grinned as it burned. Easy for him to be so happy with his belly full of food and his April-fresh clothes. I haven't eaten or showered in days.

"Mom, I need help," Charlie whines at my waist. He's not supposed to be here.

"Not now, Charlie, I have to find a red flag and a set of tools."

"Mom, Mom, Mom!" he insists. He pulls down on my ripped sleeve and tears it clean through the cuff.

Great, now it's definitely ruined. And I don't think I'm going to have time to change before work.

I spot a red blur above the flat beach about a hundred yards away. I run toward it, and Charlie follows, begging desperately, "Mom, Mom, Mom!"

I look down and see shiny pieces of green and brown everywhere. Glass. Not sea glass. New glass, jagged and sharp. Shattered bottles cover the beach.

"Charlie, stop! Don't follow me!"

I'm doing a good job avoiding the glass while I run, but then I hear Charlie losing it and Jeff laughing, and I misstep. A piece of green glass carves deep into the arc of my left foot. It kills and is bleeding a lot.

Ignore it. Hurry.

I reach the red flag. Gnats are swarming in and out of my nostrils, mouth, and ears, making me spit and gag. Not the kind of protein I've been craving. I cover my face with the palms of my hands, hold my breath, and pace out twelve steps west of the red flag.

I dig with my hands amid a frenzy of gnats, find the box of tools, and hobble back to the planks of driftwood. Charlie is there, squatting, building a castle out of broken glass.

"Charlie, stop that. You'll cut yourself."

But he doesn't listen and continues.

Ignore him. Hurry.

I'm about halfway through assembling the raft when I hear the wolves howling.

Louder. Louder.

Hurry!

The half raft isn't strong enough to hold both of us. Charlie screams as I pick him up, ripping him from his glass castle. He kicks and punches me as I wrestle him onto the half raft.

"When you get to the other side, go get help."

"Mommy, don't leave me!"

"It's not safe here. You have to go!"

I push the half raft out onto the water, and the strong current grabs it. Just as Charlie floats out of sight, the wolves start tearing through my trousers and my favorite shirt, ripping my skin apart, eating me alive. Jeff is smiling as I'm dying, and I think, Why did I ever want to play this stupid game?

My human alarm clock, my nine-month-old son, Linus, wakes me with a bleating "Baaabaaa!" over the monitor before I die.

FRIDAY

The actual alarm clock reads 5:06, about an hour before the time I set it for. Resigned to getting up now, I click the alarm mode to Off. I honestly can't remember the last time I woke to the sound of *bomp, bomp, bomp*, instead of to the stirrings of one of my three kids. And the snooze feature is an even more distant memory. Mornings of bargaining for brief but luxurious extensions in bed. *Just nine more minutes, and I won't shave my legs. Nine more minutes, I'll skip breakfast. Nine more minutes, morning sex.* I haven't touched that button in a long, long time. Well, Charlie is seven, so it has to be about seven years. It seems like forever. I only bother to set the alarm clock every night now because I know, I just know, that the one time I don't, the one time I decide to rely on my little cherubs to wake me, it'll be the morning I have some critical deadline or a flight I can't miss, and they'll all sleep in for the very first time.

I stand and look down at Bob, his eyes shut, face slack, mouth open, splayed on his back.

"Possum," I say.

"I'm awake," he says, his eyes still shut. "He's asking for you."

"He's saying 'baba,' not 'Mama.'"

"You want me to get him?"

"I'm up."

I pad barefoot on the cold hardwood floor down the hallway to Linus's bedroom. I open the door to see him standing at the bars of his crib, sucking his nukie, ratty blanket in one hand, beloved and even rattier Bunny in the other. His whole face smiles when he sees me, which makes me smile, and he starts banging on the rail. He looks like an adorable baby prison inmate, all packed and ready on his last day in jail, awaiting his release.

I pick him up and carry him over to the changing table, where his good-mood collapses into a betrayed wail. He arches his back and twists onto his side, fighting with everything he's got against what happens five to six times a day, every day. I'll never understand why he so vehemently hates getting his diaper changed.

"Linus, stop it."

I have to use an unsettling amount of force to pin him down and muscle him into a new diaper and clothes. I try a few belly blasts and singing "Twinkle, Twinkle, Little Star" to snap him out of it, but he remains my uncooperative adversary throughout the entire process. The changing table sits next to the only window in his room, which is sometimes useful for distractions. *See the birdie!* But it is still dark out, and even the birds aren't up yet. It's still nighttime, for God's sake.

Linus doesn't sleep through the night. Last night, I rocked him back to sleep after he woke screaming at one, and Bob went in a little after three. At nine months, Linus isn't talking yet, only baba-mama-dada-ing. So we can't interview him to find out what the problem is, and we can't reason with him or bribe him. Every night it's a guessing game that Bob and I don't feel like playing, and we never win.

Do you think he's teething? Should we give him Tylenol? We can't just drug him every night. Maybe he has an ear infection. I saw him tugging at his ear earlier. He always tugs at his ear. Did he lose his nukie? Maybe he had a nightmare. Maybe it's separation. Should we bring him into bed with us? We don't really want to put that on the menu, do we? What did we do with the other two? I can't remember.

Every now and then, motivated by desperate exhaustion, we'll resolve to ignore him. *Tonight we're going to let him cry it out.* But little Linus has remarkable stamina and lungs that won't quit. Once he sets his mind to doing something, he commits 100 percent, which is a trait I think will serve him well in life, so I'm not fully convinced we should beat it out of him. Typically, he'll cry for more than an hour, during which time Bob and I will lie awake, not so much ignoring the crying as we are listening to it, focusing on it, searching for subtle changes in the pitch or rhythm that might indicate the end is near, finding no such thing.

One of the other two, usually Lucy, will eventually knock on the door and come in.

"Linus is crying."

"We know, sweetie."

"Can I have a drink of milk?"

Now I'm up with Lucy fetching milk, and Bob is up settling Linus. Plan aborted. Baby wins. Score: Harvard MBA-trained parents, both highly skilled in negotiation and leadership: 0. Nine-month-old child with no formal education or experience on the planet: too many times for my weary brain to count.

Once dressed and picked up off the dreaded changing

table, Linus is instantly righted. No hard feelings, no grudges, just living in the moment. I give my little Buddha a kiss and a squeeze and carry him downstairs. Charlie and Lucy are already up. I can hear Lucy moving around in her bedroom, and Charlie is lying in one of the beanbag chairs in the living room watching *SpongeBob*.

"Charlie, it's too early for TV. Shut it off."

But he's completely entranced and doesn't hear me. At least, I hope he doesn't hear me and isn't deliberately blowing me off.

Lucy comes out of her bedroom dressed like a lunatic.

"How do you like my fashion, Mom?"

She's wearing a pink and white polka-dot vest layered over an orange long-sleeve shirt, velvet leopard print leggings under a sheer pink ballerina tutu, Ugg boots, and six clips secured randomly in her hair, all different colors.

"You look fabulous, honey."

"I'm hungry."

"Come with me."

We walk into the kitchen, and Lucy climbs up onto one of the bar stools at the kitchen island counter. I pour two bowls of Lucky Charms, one for Lucy and one for Charlie, and a bottle of Similac for Linus.

Yes, my children are Peanuts characters. Charlie, seven, and Lucy, five, were given their names without thought or reference to the comic strip. Charlie was named after Bob's father, and we both just liked the name Lucy. Then, when I was unexpectedly expecting again, years after we'd donated or eBayed every piece of baby equipment, years after we'd celebrated the end of diapers and strollers and Barney, we had to come up with yet another name and were stumped.

"I'd go with Schroeder," a work colleague offered.

"No, definitely Linus. Or Woodstock," said another.

It was only then that I realized the pattern we'd started with our first two kids. And I liked the name Linus.

I feed Linus his bottle as I watch Lucy eat all of the colored marshmallows, "the charm," first.

"Charlie, come! Your cereal's getting soggy!"

Lucy eats two more spoonfuls of charm.

"Charlie!"

"Okay, okay."

Charlie drags himself onto the bar stool next to Lucy and looks down at his bowl as if it's the worst homework assignment ever.

"I'm tired," he says.

"Then why are you up? Go back to bed."

"Okay," he says and walks back upstairs to his bedroom.

Lucy drinks the milk from her bowl, wipes her mouth with her sleeve, hops down, and takes off without a word. In a hurry to be free like his sister, Linus drains his bottle and burps without any assistance. I release him onto the floor, which is cluttered with toys and crushed pieces of Goldfish crackers. I grab a ball and toss it into the living room.

"Go get it!"

Thrilled to be in on a game, he crawls after it like a playful puppy.

Alone for at least a moment, I eat Charlie's untouched, soggy cereal because someone should, then I clear all the dishes to the sink, wipe down the counter, put on a pot of coffee, pack lunch boxes and snacks for Charlie and Lucy, and pack the diaper bag for Linus. I sign a permission slip for Lucy to go to Plimoth Plantation. Next to the question, "Will you be able to chaperone?" I check "No." In Charlie's backpack, I find a note from his teacher:

Dear Mr. and Mrs. Nickerson,
   Report cards went out last week, and I'm hoping that you've had some time now to look it over. I'd like to schedule a time to talk with both of you in person about Charlie. Please give me a call at your earliest convenience.

Sincerely,
Ms. Gavin

Charlie's report card is not what every parent dreams of for her child, especially when that parent always, always received perfect report cards herself. Bob and I knew there would be issues, room for improvement with things like reading and paying attention. Last year prepared us a little. But in kindergarten, Charlie's below-average marks in a few categories were brushed off by both his teacher and Bob. *He's a boy! He'll be used to sitting still and to the long day by the time he's in first grade. I see it every year. Don't worry.*

Well, he's in first grade now, and I'm worried. He scored either an "N" for "Needs improvement" or a "3" for "Below expectations" in *most* of the categories. Even Bob's face blanched when he read down the column of 3's and N's. Whatever is going on with Charlie, a sweeping generalization about his gender isn't going to cover it this time. What's wrong with him?

The Lucky Charms are making me feel ill. I shouldn't have eaten all that sugar. I open my laptop on the counter next to the coffeemaker and check email while standing and waiting for the caffeine my addicted brain needs. I have sixty-four new emails. I was up until midnight last night clearing my inbox, so these all came in the last five hours. Several are from offices on the West Coast, sent late last night. At least two dozen are from offices in Asia and Europe, already well into today's workday. A couple of emails marked "urgent" are from a young and panicky analyst in the Boston office.

I become absorbed in reading and replying for too long without interruption. My ears tune in and hear nothing. Where are they?

"Lucy? Linus?"

Only the beanbags are watching *SpongeBob* in the living room. I bomb up the stairs and into Lucy's room. They're both there, which means that Lucy forgot to latch the gate at the bottom of the stairs, and Linus crawled all the way up by himself. Thank God he didn't try to climb back down because his preferred method right now is headfirst. But before I can thank God for keeping him in one piece, before I knock on the wood floor for even thinking of what could've happened, and before I can thoroughly chastise Lucy for not latching the gate, all of my senses heighten and narrow in on Linus. He's sitting on the floor, not investigating anything, with his mouth suspiciously shut. Lucy is a few feet away on the floor making bead jewelry. There are beads all over the floor.

"Linus!"

I grab the back of his head with my left hand and swipe inside his mouth with my right index finger. He resists, whipping his head side to side and clamping his mouth shut harder.

"Linus, open! What do you have in there?"

I feel it. I waggle my finger and scoop out a bubblegum-pink plastic bead, about the size of a cranberry. Violated and robbed and completely unaware that his life was in danger, Linus howls. Bob is now standing in the doorway, showered, dressed, and concerned.

"What happened?" he asks.

"He was just about to choke on this."

I display the murderous bead in the palm of my hand.

"Nah, too small. He's okay."

Still, there are plenty of bigger beads strewn on the floor around Lucy, plus some coins, hair elastics, a Super Ball. Lucy's room is a death trap. What if he'd decided to suck on a quarter? What if one of the larger orange beads had looked particularly tasty to him? What if I'd gotten here too late? What if Linus were lying on the floor, not breathing, lips blue?

If Bob could read my mind, which he probably could, he'd tell me not to go there. He'd tell me to stop imagining the worst and to relax. Everyone's fine. All kids put things in their mouths that they shouldn't. They eat paint chips and crayons and swallow dirt and pebbles and all kinds of things we don't even know about. They even climb stairs unattended. Kids are tough, he'd say. They survive.

But I know differently. I don't have to imagine the worst to go there. I can remember it. Sometimes kids survive. And sometimes they don't.

Being the highly superstitious, God-fearing, slightly obsessive-compulsive, type A perfectionist that I am, with the bead in my fist, I knock on the wooden bedpost, thank God for keeping him safe, and blame his sister.

"Lucy, this room is a disaster. You need to pick up all of these beads."

"But I'm making a necklace," she whines.

"Here, I'll help you, Goose," says Bob, now on his knees and gathering beads. "Why don't you pick out one of your already-made necklaces for today? Then you can come downstairs with me and Linus."

"Charlie hasn't dressed or eaten yet," I say, agreeing to the routine, passing the parenting baton over to Bob.

After a quick shower, I stand naked in front of the full-length mirror in the bedroom and assess myself as I slather Lubriderm over my arms and legs.

N, Needs improvement.

I'm still about fifteen pounds over my pre-Linus weight, which was, if I have to be honest, ten pounds over my pre-

Charlie weight. I grab a handful of the loose and puckered bread dough that used to be my taut belly and trace the rust-colored line that runs unfaded from a few inches above my belly button down to my pubic hair. I continue down to the pads of flesh cushioning my hip bones, which migrated sideways to make room for Linus, my biggest baby, leaving me with wider hips and a drawer full of pants that won't button.

The gym I belong to could more accurately be called my favorite charity. I never go. I really should cancel my membership instead of essentially donating a hundred dollars to them every month. There's also the gym equipment in the basement, positioned like statues, collecting dust: the elliptical machine, the Bowflex, and the rower Bob bought me for Christmas when I was eight months pregnant (was he insane?). I pass these hulking pieces of equipment every time I do the laundry, which with three kids, is often. I always walk by them at a quick clip, without looking at them, as if we've had some sort of emotionally charged fight, and I'm giving them the cold shoulder. It works. They never bother me.

I rub the remaining Lubriderm into my hands.

Don't be too hard on yourself, I think, knowing that is my tendency.

Linus is only nine months old. The phrase "nine months up, nine months down" from *The Girlfriends' Guide to Getting Your Groove Back* pops into my head. The author assumes I have time for things like manicures and shopping and trunk shows and that I have made my groove a priority. It's not that

I don't want my groove back. It's on my list. It's just unfortunately way at the bottom where I can barely see it.

Before I get dressed, I pause for one last appraisal. My fair skin is covered with freckles, courtesy of my Scottish mother. When I was a girl, I used to connect the dots with a pen to create constellations and tattoos. My favorite used to be the perfect five-point star my freckles outline on my left thigh. But that was back in the '80s, before I knew about sunscreen, back when I and all of my friends toted bottles of baby oil with us to the beach, quite literally sautéing ourselves in the sun. Now every doctor and the media are all saying that my freckles are age spots and signs of sun damage.

I hide most of the damage with a white camisole and my black Elie Tahari power suit. In all the right ways, I feel like a man in this suit. Perfect for the kind of day I'm facing. I towel dry my hair and work an emulsified gob of Shine-and-Hold into it. Auburn and thick and wavy to my shoulders, there is nothing masculine about my hair. I may be fat and freckled and dressed like a man, but I love my pretty hair.

After a perfunctory application of foundation, blush, eyeliner, and mascara, I head downstairs and reenter the fray. Lucy is now planted in one of the beanbag chairs singing along with Dora the Explorer, and Linus is penned in the Pack 'n Play next to her, sucking on the head of a plastic school bus driver. In the kitchen, Bob sits alone at the table, drinking coffee from his Harvard mug and reading the *Wall Street Journal*.

"Where's Charlie?" I ask.

"Getting dressed."

"Did he eat?"

"Cereal and juice."

How does he do it? Bob in Charge of All Three Kids is an entirely different show than Sarah in Charge of All Three Kids. With Bob, they're happily willing to be independent little taskmasters, content to leave him in peace until he comes to them with an offer of a new activity. With me, I have all the magnetism of a favorite rock star without the bodyguards. They're *on* me. A typical example: Linus is under my feet, whining, begging to be picked up, while Lucy hollers, "Mom, I need help!" from another room, while Charlie asks me forty-seven hundred relentless questions about what happens to trash.

I grab my coffee mug and sit opposite Bob for our morning meeting. I take a sip. It's cold. Whatever.

"Did you see the note from Charlie's teacher?" I ask.

"No, what?"

"His teacher wants to talk to us about his report card."

"Good, I want to know what's going on."

He reaches into his messenger bag and pulls out his iPhone.

"You think she can meet with us before school?" he asks.

I grab my laptop off the counter and sit back down.

"I could do early on Wednesday and Friday, possibly Thursday if I move something," I say.

"I can do Thursday. You have her email?"

"Yup."

I shoot an email to Ms. Gavin.

"You going to his game today?" he asks.

"No, are you?"

"I probably won't be back in time, remember?"

"Oh, yeah. I can't, my day's packed."

"Okay. I just wish one of us could be there to see him."

"Me, too, honey."

I believe he's being entirely sincere, but I can't help taking his words "I just wish one of us" and translating them in my brain into "I think you." And while the gears of my internal language interpreter are greased, it transforms "could" to "should." The majority of women in Welmont with children Charlie's age never miss a soccer game and don't earn special good mother status for being there. This is simply what good mothers do. These same mothers herald it an exceptional event if any of the dads leave the office early to catch a game. The fathers cheering on the sidelines are upheld as great dads. Fathers who miss the games are working. Mothers who miss the games, like me, are bad mothers.

A standard dose of maternal guilt sinks to the bottom of the cold coffee and Lucky Charms soup in my stomach. Not exactly the Breakfast of Champions.

"Abby can stay and watch him," I say, reassuring myself.

Abby is our nanny. She started working for us when Charlie was twelve weeks old, when my maternity leave ended. We were beyond lucky to get her when we did. Abby was twenty-two then, right out of college with a degree in psychology, and lived just ten minutes away in Newton.

She's smart, conscientious, has tons of energy, and loves our kids.

Before Charlie and Lucy were old enough for preschool, Abby watched them from 7:30 in the morning until 6:30 at night, Monday through Friday. She changed their diapers, rocked them to sleep, read them stories, wiped their tears, taught them games and songs, bathed and fed them. She grocery shopped and cleaned the house. She became an essential member of our family. I can't imagine our life without her. In fact, if I had to choose between keeping Bob and keeping Abby, there have been times when it would've been difficult to pick Bob.

This past spring, Abby told us the unthinkable. She would be leaving us to attend Boston College for her master's in childhood education. We were stunned and panicked. We couldn't lose her. So we negotiated a deal. With Charlie and Lucy already in school for seven hours a day, we were willing to put Linus in day care in September for the same hours. That would mean we'd need her only from 3:00 to 6:30, and we'd pay for part of her tuition.

Sure, we could've combed through Craigslist and found someone who would probably be good and would definitely be cheaper. Or we could've hired someone through a find-a-nanny agency. But Abby already knows our kids. She knows their routines, their moods, their favorite things. She knows how to handle Charlie's inquisitions, Lucy's tantrums, and she knows to never, never forget to bring Bunny wherever Linus goes. And she already loves them. How much is too much to pay for knowing without any doubt that your kids are well loved when you can't be there?

Charlie gallops into the kitchen, out of breath.

"Where are my Pokémon cards?"

"Charlie, you're still in your pajamas. Forget about Pokémon. Go get dressed," I say.

"But I need my Pokémon cards."

"Pants, shirt, shoes, and shut off your light," I say.

Charlie throws his head back in frustration but surrenders and barrels back upstairs to his room.

"Any house stuff?" Bob asks.

"Will you call the garage door guy this time?"

"Yup, he's on my list."

Our automatic door opener is one of the newer models, and it has a seeing-eye sensor that prevents it from closing if it observes something under the door, like a small child. It's a great safety feature in theory, but it only seems to drive us crazy. One of the kids, and we suspect Charlie, keeps knocking into the eye on the right side so it's not level with and can't see the left side. And when it gets cross-eyed, it won't work at all.

When we were kids, my brother Nate and I used to play Indiana Jones with our automatic garage door. One of us would hit the button on the remote, and then we would see who had the guts to wait the longest before running and rolling under the closing door. No safety features in those days. That garage door opener operated completely blind. It would've taken all the fun out of the game if the risk of getting crushed to death, or at least painfully squished, had been removed. Nate was great at it, diving and rolling at the last possible second. God, I still miss him.

Charlie tears into the kitchen wearing a tee-shirt, shorts, and no shoes.

"Mom, what if the earth runs out of gravity?"

"What did I tell you to put on?"

No answer.

"It's November, you need pants and a long-sleeve shirt and shoes," I say.

I check my watch. 7:15. He's still standing there, I think waiting for an answer about gravity.

"Go!"

"Come on, kiddo, let's find something better," says Bob, and they walk off together.

I wrangle the other two kids into hats and coats, send out a few more emails, buckle Linus into his bucket car seat, listen to my work voicemail, pack my own bag, leave a note for Abby about the soccer game, down the rest of the cold coffee, and finally meet Bob and a suitably dressed Charlie at the front door.

"Ready?" asks Bob, facing me.

We both cock our fists back into position.

"Ready."

Today is Friday. Bob drops the kids at school and day care on Tuesdays and Thursdays, and I take them on Mondays and Wednesdays. Fridays are up for grabs. Unless one of us makes an indisputable case for needing to get to work before school starts, we shoot for it. Scissors cut paper. Paper covers rock. Rock smashes scissors. We both take the shoot very seriously. Winning is huge. Driving straight to work with no kids in the car is heaven.

"One, two, threeeee, shoot!"

Bob hammers his closed fist on top of my peace sign and grins, victorious. He wins significantly more times than he loses.

"Lucky bastard."

"It's all skill, babe. Have a great day," he says.

"You, too."

We kiss good-bye. It's our typical morning good-bye kiss. A quick peck. A well-intentioned habit. I look down and notice Lucy's round, blue eyes paying close attention. I flash to studying my own parents kissing when I was little. They kissed each other hello and good-bye and good night like I would have kissed one of my aunts, and it terribly disappointed me. There was no drama to it at all. I promised myself that when I got married someday, I would have kisses that meant something. Kisses that would make me weak in the knees. Kisses that would embarrass the kids. Kisses like Han Solo kissing Princess Leia. I never saw my father kiss my mother like that. What was the point of it? I never got it.

Now I get it. We aren't living in some George Lucas blockbuster adventure. Our morning kiss good-bye isn't romantic, and it certainly isn't sexual. It's a routine kiss, but I'm glad we do it. It does mean something. It's enough. And it's all we have time for.

CHAPTER 2

"Mom, can I have a piece?" asks Lucy.

"Sure, honey, what piece do you want?"

"Can I have your eyes?"

"You can have one."

I pull my left eyeball out of the socket. It feels a little like a dev-iled egg, but warmer. Lucy snatches it from my hand and skips away, bouncing it on the ground like a Super Ball as she goes.

"Be careful with it; I need that back!"

I am sitting at the kitchen table, staring with my one eye at the hundreds of numbers on my Excel spreadsheet. I click the cursor onto an empty cell and input more data. As I'm typing, my eye is lured to something just above and beyond my focus on the laptop screen. My father, dressed in his full fireman's uniform, is sitting in the chair opposite me.

"Hi, Sarah."

"Jeez, Dad, you scared me to death."

"I need you to give me your appendix."

"No, it's mine."

"Sarah, don't talk back. I need it."

"No one needs their appendix, Dad. You didn't need a new one."

"Then why did it kill me?"

I look down at my computer. A PowerPoint presentation slide appears on the screen. I read it.

Reasons Why Your Father's Appendix Ruptured

- *He had a bad stomachache for two days and did nothing about it but drink a little Pepto-Bismol and some whiskey.*
- *He shrugged off the intense nausea and gave no consideration to his low fever.*
- *You were away at college, your mother was in her bedroom, and he didn't call the station or 911.*
- *It became inflamed and infected with poison.*
- *Like any living thing that is disregarded for too long, it eventually couldn't take it anymore and did whatever had to be done to get his attention.*

I look up at my father. He's still waiting for an answer.

"Because you ignored what you were feeling."

"I may be dead, but I'm still your father. Give me your appendix."

"It has no purpose. You're better off without it."

"Exactly."

He stares at me unflinching, transmitting his intention into my consciousness like a radio signal through my one eye.

"I'll be fine. Don't worry about me," I say.

"We're all worried about you, Sarah."

"I'm fine. I just have to finish this report."

I look down at the screen, and the numbers are gone.

"Shit!"

I look up, and my father is gone.

"Shit!"

Charlie runs into the kitchen.

"You said 'shit'!" he announces, delighted to be telling on me, even if he's only telling on me to me.

"I know, I'm sorry," I say, keeping my one eye glued to the computer screen, frantically searching for some way to retrieve all that data. I have to finish this report.

"That's a swear word."

"I know, I'm sorry," I say, clicking everything clickable.

I don't look up at him and wish he would take the hint. He never does.

"Mom, you know how I'm not good at listening?"

"Yes. You drive me crazy."

"Can I have your ears?"

"You can have one."

"I want both."

"One."

"Both, I want both!"

"Fine!"

I twist my ears off my head and throw them like a pair of dice across the table. Charlie fastens them over his own like earphones and cocks his head as if he's trying to listen for something off in the distance. He smiles, satisfied. I try to hear it, too, but then remember that I have no ears. He says something and runs away.

"Hey, my earrings!"

But he's already out of sight. I return to my computer screen. At least he's gone, and I can be sure to concentrate now in quiet.

The front door opens. Bob is standing on the other side of the table, a blend of sadness and disgust absorbing into his eyes as he looks at me. He says something.

"I can't hear you, honey. I gave Charlie my ears."

He says something again.

"I don't know what you're saying."

He drops his messenger bag and kneels down next to me. He flips my computer screen shut and grabs me by the shoulders, almost hurting me.

He yells at me. I still can't hear him, but I know he's yelling from the urgency in his eyes and the blue veins popping in his neck. He yells what he's trying to tell me in slow motion so I can read his lips.

"Way up?"

I look up at the ceiling.

"I don't get it."

He yells it again and again, shaking my shoulders.

"Wake up?"

"Yes!" *he yells and stops shaking me.*

"I am awake."

"No, you're not."

24

Left Neglected

Welmont is an affluent suburb of Boston complete with tree-lined streets, landscaped yards, a bike trail that winds throughout the town, a private country club and golf course, a center populated with boutique clothing shops, day spas, and a Gap, and schools that everyone brags about, the best in the state. Bob and I chose this town because of its proximity to Boston, where we both work, and because of the successful life it promises. If there is a house left in Welmont worth under half a million dollars, some savvy contractor is ready to buy it, tear it down, and build something three times its current size and value. Most everyone in town drives a luxury car, vacations in the Caribbean, belongs to the country club, and owns a second home on the Cape or in the mountains north of Boston. Ours is in Vermont.

Bob and I were fresh out of Harvard Business School and pregnant with Charlie when we moved here. Saddled with $200,000 in student loans and nothing saved, affording Welmont and all that goes with it was a daunting stretch. But we both landed ambitious jobs and had unshakable confidence in our earning potentials. Eight years later, we are in every way keeping up with the Welmont Joneses.

Welmont Elementary School is just about three miles and ten minutes from our house on Pilgrim Lane. Stopped at a traffic light, I glance up at the rearview mirror. Sitting in the middle, Charlie is playing something on his Nintendo DS.

Lucy is staring out the window as she mumbles along to some Hannah Montana song on her iPod. And facing backward in his bucket car seat, Linus is sucking on his nukie and watching *Elmo's World* through the mirror that Bob strapped to the car's backseat headrest; the video is playing behind him on the DVD player that came standard with my Acura SUV. No one is crying or complaining or asking me for anything. Ah, the miracle of modern technology!

I am still annoyed at Bob. I have a European staffing meeting at eight o'clock. It's for an important client, and I'm stressed about it, and on top of this, now I'm worried about getting there on time because it's Monday, my day to drive the kids to school and day care. When I told this to Bob, he looked at his watch and said, *Don't worry, you'll make it.* I wasn't looking for a Zen outlook.

Charlie and Lucy are enrolled in the school's Before the Bell program, which runs from 7:15 to 8:20 every day in the gym. This is where the kids with parents who need to get to work before 9:00 hang out under the supervision of a teacher until the school day officially begins at 8:30. At only five dollars a day per kid, Before the Bell is truly an economical godsend.

When Charlie first began kindergarten, I was surprised to see only a few of the kids in Charlie's class in Before the Bell. I had assumed that all the parents in town would need this service. I then guessed that most of the kids had live-in nannies. Some do, but it turns out that most of the kids in Welmont have mothers who have opted out of the workforce and are stay-at-home moms—all women with college, even graduate, degrees. Never in a million years would I have guessed this. I can't imagine opting out, wasting all that education and training. I love my children and know they're important, but so is my career and the life that career affords us.

Parked in the school lot, I grab their two backpacks, which I swear weigh more than they do, get out, and open the back door like a chauffeur. Who am I kidding? Not like a chauffeur. I am a chauffeur. No one moves.

"Come on, let's *go*!"

Still tethered to their electronic devices and without a molecule of urgency, Charlie and Lucy file out of the car and start heading like a couple of snails for the front of the school.

I press behind them, leaving Linus in the car with the engine and Elmo running.

I know someone from *60 Minutes* or *Dateline NBC* would have a bone to pick with me about doing this, and I half expect Chris Hansen to ambush me from behind a parked Volvo any day now. I've already rehearsed my side of the argument in my head. First of all, his bucket car seat, the car seat all babies are required to ride in under the age of one, weighs a ridiculous nineteen pounds. Add in Linus, who weighs almost as much as the car seat and the poor ergonomic design of the handle, and it's physically unmanageable to carry him anywhere. I would love to have a conversation with the exceptionally strong and obviously childless man who designed these things. Linus is content and watching Elmo. Why disturb him? Welmont is a safe town. I'll be only a few seconds.

It's an unseasonably warm morning for the first week of November. Just yesterday, Charlie and Lucy wore fleece hats and mittens outside, but today, it's already fifty, and they almost don't even need their coats. Undoubtedly because of the weather, the school playground is packed and wild with kids, which is not typical in the mornings. This catches Charlie's attention, and just before we reach the double doors, he bolts.

"Charlie! Get back here!"

My admonishment doesn't even break his stride. He's heading straight for the monkey bars and doesn't look back. I scoop up Lucy in my left arm and run after him.

"I don't have time for this," I tell Lucy, my cooperative little ally.

By the time I reach the monkey bars, the only sign of Charlie is his coat, which lies rumpled on a pile of woodchips. I grab it with the hand already holding two backpacks and scan the playground.

"Charlie!"

It doesn't take me long to spot him. He's sitting at the very top of the jungle gym.

"Charlie, down, right now!"

He doesn't appear to hear me, but the nearby mothers do. Dressed in designer sweats, tee-shirts and jeans, tennis shoes and clogs, these mothers appear to have all the time in the world to hang out at the school playground in the morning.

I feel the judgment in their stares and imagine the range of what they must be thinking.

He only wants to play outside on this gorgeous morning like the rest of the kids.

Would it kill her to let him play for a few minutes?

See how he never listens to her? She has no control over her kids.

"Charlie, please come down and come with me. I have to get to work."

He doesn't budge.

"Okay, that's one!"

He roars like a lion at a group of kids looking up at him from the bottom.

"Two!"

He's not moving.

"Three!"

Nothing. I want to kill him. I look down at my three-inch Cole Haan heels and wonder for an insane moment if I could climb in them. Then I look down at my Cartier watch. It's 7:30. Enough of this.

"Charlie, *now,* or no video games for a week!"

That does it. He stands, turns, and faces out, but instead of reaching down with his feet for the next bar level, he bends his knees and launches himself into the air. A few of the other mothers and I gasp. In that split second, I imagine broken legs and a severed spinal column. But he pops up from the ground, smiling. Thank God he's made of rubber. The boys who witnessed this death-defying stunt cheer with admiration. The girls playing nearby don't seem to notice him at all. The mothers continue watching to see how I'll handle the rest of this drama.

Knowing he's still a flight risk, I put Lucy down and grab Charlie by the hand.

"Ow, too tight!"

"Too bad."

He pulls on my arm as hard as he can, leaning away from me, trying to get away, like an excited Doberman on a leash. My hand is now sweaty, and he's beginning to slip out. I squeeze tighter. He pulls harder.

"Hold my hand, too," whines Lucy.

"I can't, honey, come on."

"I want to hold hands!" she shrieks, not moving, balancing on the edge of a tantrum. I think fast.

"Hold Charlie's."

Charlie licks the entire palm of his free hand and offers it to her.

"Gross!" Lucy squeals.

"Fine, here."

I slide the two backpacks and Charlie's coat to my elbow, and with a kid in each hand, I drag us into Welmont Elementary.

The gym is overheated and set with the usual cast of characters. The girls are sitting against the wall, reading, socializing, or just sitting and watching the boys, who are playing basketball and running all over the place. As soon as I let go of his hand, Charlie takes off. I don't have the will to holler after him for a proper good-bye.

"Have a good day, my Lucy Goose."

"Bye, Mommy."

I kiss her on her beautiful head and dump the backpacks onto the pile of book bags on the floor. There are no mothers or fathers lingering around in here. I don't know the other drop-off parents. I know some of the kids' names and might know which parent belongs to which kid. Like that woman is Hilary's mom. Most are flying in and flying out, no time for small talk. Without knowing much about any of them, I relate to these parents completely.

The only parent I know at Before the Bell by name is Heidi, Ben's mom, who is on her way out as well. Always in scrubs and purple Crocs, Heidi is some kind of nurse. I know her name because Ben and Charlie are friends, because she sometimes drops Charlie home after soccer, and because she has an approachable energy and a sincere smile that has many times in the last year communicated a world of empathy.

I have kids, too. I know.

I have a job, too. I know.

I'm running late, too. I know.

I know.

"How are you?" Heidi asks as we make our way down the hallway.

"Good, you?"

"Good. I haven't seen you with Linus in a while. He must be getting so big."

"Oh my God, Linus!"

Without offering any explanation, I sprint away from Heidi down the hall, out of the school, and down the front steps to my running car, which, thank God, is still there. I can hear poor Linus wailing before I even touch the door.

Bunny is on the floor, and the DVD is sitting idle on the menu screen, but my mother's ears and heart know his cry isn't about a stuffed lovie or a red Muppet. Once the video ended and Linus came out of its magical trance, he must've realized he was trapped and alone in the car. Abandoned. The number one primal fear for any baby his age is abandonment. His red face and hairline are soaked with tears.

"Linus, I'm sorry, I'm so sorry!"

I unbuckle him as fast as I can while he screams. I pick him up, hug him, and rub his back. He smears a gob of snot onto the collar of my shirt.

"Shhh, it's okay, you're okay."

It's not working. In fact, the intensity and volume of his sobs are escalating. He's not willing to forgive me so easily, and I don't blame him one bit. But if I can't console him, I might as well get him to day care. I pin his distraught body back into the car seat, place Bunny on his lap, hit Play on the DVD player, and drive while he screams murder to Sunny Horizons.

I hand a still-heaving Linus, Bunny, and diaper bag over to one of the day care assistant teachers, a kind young Brazilian woman new to Sunny Horizons.

"Linus, shhh, you're okay. Linus, please, honey, you're

okay," I say, trying one last time to convince him. I hate to leave him like this.

"He'll be fine, Mrs. Nickerson. It's better if you just go."

Back in the car, I exhale. Finally, I'm on my way to work. The clock on the dash reads 7:50. I'm going to be late. Again. Clenching my teeth and the steering wheel, I pull out of Sunny Horizons and start rummaging through my bag for my phone.

My bag is embarrassingly huge. Depending on where I am and whom I'm with, it functions as a briefcase, a pocketbook, a diaper bag, or a backpack. Wherever I am and whomever I'm with, I feel like a Sherpa carrying this thing. As I grope around for the phone, I touch my laptop, crayons, pens, my wallet, lipstick, keys, Goldfish crackers, a juice box, business cards, tampons, a diaper, receipts, Band-Aids, a Handi Wipes container, a calculator, and folders stuffed with papers. I do not touch my phone. I upend the bag, dumping the contents onto the passenger seat, and look for it.

Where the heck is it? I have about five minutes to find it. I'm aware that my eyes are spending significantly more time on my passenger seat and floor than on the road. The guy gunning past me on the right is flipping me off. And talking on his phone.

I suddenly see it, but it's in my mind's eye. On the kitchen table. Crap, crap, crap! I'm on the Mass Pike, about twenty minutes from work. I think for a second about where I could get off and find a pay phone. But then I think, *Do pay phones even exist anymore?* I can't remember the last time I saw one anywhere. Maybe I could stop in a CVS or a Starbucks. Some nice person there would probably lend me their phone. *For a minute. Sarah, your meeting is for the next hour. Just get there.*

As I race like a NASCAR driver on crack, I try crystallizing my notes for this meeting in my head, but I'm having trouble concentrating. I can't think. It isn't until I pull into the Prudential garage that I realize my thoughts are competing with Linus's video.

Elmo wants to learn more about families.

CHAPTER 3

I am sitting in the front row of the Wang Theatre, just to the right of center. I check my watch and look up again, stretching my neck, searching the faces of the densely crowded aisles for Bob. A small elderly woman walks toward me. At first I think the woman must want to tell me something important, but then I realize that she's eyeing the empty seat to my left.

"This seat's taken," I say, placing my hand on it.

"Is someone sitting here?" the woman asks, her brown eyes murky and confused.

"Someone will be."

"Huh?"

"SOMEONE WILL BE."

"I won't be able to see if I don't sit in front."

"Sorry, someone's sitting here."

The old woman's muddy eyes suddenly turn lucid and piercing.

"I wouldn't be so sure about that."

A man two rows back gets up from his seat and heads up the aisle, maybe to go to the men's room. The old woman notices this and leaves me alone.

I touch the collar of my snakeskin coat. I don't want to take it off. It's nippy in the theatre, and I feel beautiful in it. But I don't want someone to steal Bob's seat. I check my watch and my ticket. I'm exactly where I'm supposed to be. Where is Bob? I take off my coat and save Bob's seat with it. A chill slithers up the base of my back to my shoulders. I rub my bare arms.

I search for Bob again but soon get taken in by the magnificence of the theatre—the regal red velvet curtains, the towering columns, the Greek and Roman marble statues. I look up. The ceiling is open air, a breathtaking view of the night sky. While I am still enchanted with the stars above my head, I feel the subtle weight of a shadow fall upon my face. I expect to see Bob, but instead it's Richard, my boss. He tosses my coat to the floor and plops down next to me.

"I'm surprised to see you here," he says.

"Of course I'm here. I'm so excited to see the show."

"Sarah, the show is over. You missed it."

What? I look back at all the people standing in the aisles and see only the backs of their heads. Everyone is leaving.

TUESDAY

It's 3:30, and I have a half hour, the first gap of the day, before my next meeting. I begin eating the chicken Caesar salad my assistant ordered me for lunch as I return a call to the office in Seattle. While I'm chewing lettuce and the phone is ringing, I start skimming the emails that have accumulated in my inbox. The managing director picks up and asks me to brainstorm with him about who of our four thousand consultants would be available and best suited for an information technology project coming in next week. I talk to him while I alternately type responses to a number of emails from the UK about performance evaluations and eat.

I can't remember when I learned how to have two completely different professional conversations going at once. I've been doing it for a long time, and I know it's not an ordinary skill, even for a woman. I've also mastered the ability to type and click without making a sound, so the person on the other end of the conversation isn't distracted, or worse, offended. To be fair, I choose to answer only the emails that are no-brainers, the ones that just need my yay or nay, while on the phone. It feels a little like having a split personality. Sarah talks on the phone while her crazy alter ego types. At least the two of me are working as a team.

I'm the vice president of human resources at Berkley Consulting. Berkley has about five thousand employees in seventy offices located in forty countries. We offer strategic advice to companies all over the world in all industries—how to innovate, compete, restructure, lead, brand, merge, grow, sustain, and, above all, make money. Most of the consultants who work to deliver this advice have business degrees, but many are scientists, lawyers, engineers, and medical doctors. They are all extremely bright, know how to think analytically, and excel at finding creative solutions to complex problems.

They are also mostly young. Consultants at Berkley typically work where the client is. The consultants for any given project can be based anywhere in the world, but if the client is a pharmaceutical company in New Jersey, then that is where the consulting team will live for the duration of the project. So for twelve weeks, a consultant from our office in London, staffed on this case because of his medical background, will live Mondays through Thursdays in a hotel in Newark.

This lifestyle is workable for the young and single, and for a while, even the young and married, but add a few years and a couple of kids, and living out of a carry-on starts to get old fast. The burnout rate is high. That poor guy from London is going to miss his wife and kids. Berkley can throw more and more money at him to keep him, but at some point for most people, it's not enough to make it worth the toll this job takes on families. The few consultants who persevere beyond five years go on to become managing directors. Anyone still standing after ten years becomes a partner and, as a result, extremely wealthy. Almost all are men. And divorced.

I came to Berkley with a background in human resources and an MBA from Harvard, the perfect hybrid of experience and pedigree. My job requires a lot of hours—seventy to eighty a week—but I don't have to travel like the nomadic consultants. I go to Europe once every eight weeks, China once a quarter, and New York for one or two overnights a month, but this kind of travel is all predictable, finite, and manageable.

My assistant, Jessica, knocks and enters my office with a piece of paper that reads, "Coffee?"

I nod and hold up three fingers, meaning a triple shot of espresso and not three coffees. Jessica understands my sign language and leaves with my order.

I head up all recruiting, the assembly of high-priority case teams, performance evaluations, and career development at Berkley. Berkley Consulting sells ideas, so the people who think up those ideas are our most important assets and investments. An idea that any one of our teams comes up with today could easily be on the front page of the *New York Times* or the *Wall Street Journal* tomorrow. The teams at Berkley guide and even create some of the world's most successful companies. And I create the teams.

I have to know the strengths and weaknesses of each consultant and every client to fashion the best fit, to maximize the potential for success. The teams are asked to crack all kinds of cases (e-commerce, globalization, risk management, operations) in every kind of industry (automotive, health care, energy, retail), but not every consultant is best suited for every project. I juggle a lot of balls—expensive, fragile, heavy, irreplaceable balls. And just when I think I've got as many in the air as I could possibly handle, one of the partners will throw me another. Like some highly competitive Cirque du Soleil clown, I never admit to having too many. I'm one of the only women playing at this level, and I don't ever want to see that look in one of the partners' eyes. *There it is. She just banged her head on the ceiling. We've maxed her out. Go see if Carson or Joe can handle this one.* So they toss me more and more responsibilities, and I catch each one with a smile, practically killing myself at times to make it all look easy. My job is very far from easy. It is, in fact, very, very hard. Which is exactly why I love it.

But even with all my years of training and experience, my determined work ethic, and the ability to simultaneously eat, type, and talk, the hardness of it all does sometimes get overwhelming. There are days when there is no room for error, no time for lunch or to pee, no extra minutes to squeeze one more of anything out of me. On those days, I feel like a balloon blown to capacity, ready to burst. And then Richard will add another case to my pile with a Post-it stuck to the top page. *Your input is needed ASAP.* A big puff of air. Jessica will email me with a new meeting scheduled into the only unscheduled hour of the day. Puff. I feel transparent, uncomfortably taut. Abby will call. Linus has a rash and a fever, and she can't find the Tylenol. The final puff.

When I feel like I'm about to explode, I lock my office door, sit in my chair, spin to face the window overlooking

Boylston Street in case someone should look in, and let myself cry for five minutes. No more. Five minutes of silent crying to release the pressure, and then I'm back. That's usually all I need to reset. I remember the first time I let myself cry at work. It was in my third month here. I felt weak and ashamed and as soon as I dried my eyes, I swore to myself that I'd never do it again. So naïve. The stress at Berkley, like at all consulting firms of its caliber, is off the charts and gets to everyone. Some people drink martinis at Legal Sea Foods during lunch. Some smoke cigarettes outside the revolving doors on Huntington Avenue. I cry for five minutes at my desk. I try to limit my teary vice to twice a month.

It's now 3:50. I'm off the phone and drinking the coffee Jessica delivered. I needed it. The caffeine hurries my sluggish blood and splashes cold water on my sleepy brain. I have ten unclaimed minutes. How should I fill them? I look at my calendar.

4:00, phone conference, General Electric project.
4:15, Lucy piano lesson.
4:30, Charlie's soccer game. LAST ONE.

I always list the kids' activities in my calendar so, like an air traffic controller, I know where everyone is at any given time. I hadn't considered actually going to Charlie's game until just now. Bob said he didn't think he could make it again this week, and Abby won't be able to stay and watch after dropping Charlie off at the field because she'll have to loop back to the other side of town to pick up Lucy from her piano lesson. It's his last game of the season. I picture the end of the game and all the other kids running off the field and into the celebrating arms of their moms and dads. I picture Charlie's fallen face when he realizes his mom's and dad's arms aren't there to receive him. I can't stand the image.

Fueled by three shots of espresso and two additional shots of guilt and compassion, I check my watch one last time, then grab my cell phone, the GE folder, my bag and coat and leave the office.

"Jessica, tell the four o'clock meeting I'll be phoning in from my cell."

No reason why I can't do it all.

I'm talking on my cell phone, about forty minutes into the 4:00 meeting, when I arrive at the Welmont town fields. A baseball diamond is situated adjacent to the parking lot, and the soccer field is beyond that. From my car, I can see the kids in the distance already playing. I've been talking for a long stretch now about who our rising experts are in green technology. As I'm walking across the baseball field, I suddenly realize a lack of throat clearing, pen clicking, and general background conference room noise.

"Hello?"

No response. I look at my phone. No Service. Crap. How long have I been delivering that soliloquy?

I'm at the soccer field now but not at my meeting. I'm

supposed to be at both. I look down at my phone. Still no service. This is not good.

"Hey, you're here!" says Bob.

I'm thinking the exact same thing in my head but with an entirely different inflection.

"I thought you couldn't come," I say.

"I snuck out. I saw Abby when she dropped Charlie off and told her I'd take him home."

"We don't both need to be here."

I check my phone. No bars.

"Can I use your cell?"

"It's a dead zone here. Who you calling?"

"I need to be in a meeting. Crap, what am I doing here?"

He puts his arm around me and squeezes.

"You're watching your son play soccer."

But I'm supposed to be staffing the GE case right now. My shoulders start chasing the tops of my ears. Bob recognizes my telltale sign of building tension and tries rubbing them into submission, but I resist. I don't want to relax. This isn't relaxing.

"Can you stay?" he asks.

My brain races through the consequences of missing the last half of the GE meeting. The truth is, whatever I've missed, I've already missed it. I might as well stay.

"Let me just see if I can pick up a signal somewhere."

I wander the perimeter of the field, trying to find a coordinate that might catch a bar on my phone. I'm not having any luck. Meanwhile, first-grade soccer is hilarious. It shouldn't really even be called soccer. From what I see, there are no positions. Most of the kids are chasing and kicking at the ball all the time, as if the ball were a powerful magnet and the kids were helplessly pulled toward it wherever it goes. About a dozen kids are now gathered around it, kicking feet and shins and occasionally the ball. Then the ball is aimlessly knocked free of the mob, and they're all chasing it again.

A few of the kids can't be bothered. One girl is doing cartwheels. Another girl is simply sitting on the ground, ripping up the grass with her hands. Charlie is spinning. He spins in circles until he falls. Then he gets up, staggers, falls again, gets up, and spins.

"Charlie, get the ball!" encourages Bob from the sidelines. He spins.

The other parents are cheering their kids on, too.

"Go, Julia, go!"

"Come on, Cameron!"

"Kick it!"

I missed an important meeting for this madness. I make my way back over to Bob.

"Any luck?"

"No."

It has just started to snow, and now most of the kids have abandoned any thoughts of the ball or why they're here in favor of trying to catch snowflakes on their tongues. I can't help checking my watch more than once a minute. This game, or whatever it should be called, is going on forever.

"When is this over?" I ask Bob.

"I think they go forty-five minutes. You coming home after this?"

"I need to go see what I missed."

"You can't do that from home?"

"I shouldn't even be here."

"See you at bedtime?"

"If I'm lucky."

Bob and I don't often get home in time to have dinner with the kids. Their little bellies start growling at around 5:00, and Abby feeds them macaroni and cheese or chicken nuggets then. But we both try to be home to eat dessert together at around 6:30. The kids eat ice cream or cookies while Bob and I typically have cheese and crackers and wine, our dessert being more of an appetizer for the dinner we eat after the kids go to bed at 7:30.

The referee, a high school boy, finally blows the whistle, and the game is over. As Charlie walks off the field, he still hasn't noticed that we're here. He's so cute I can barely stand it. His mop of wavy brown hair always seems a little too long, no matter how often he gets it cut. He has blue eyes like Bob's and the longest black eyelashes I've ever seen on a boy. Girls are going to go crazy someday over those eyes. He's suddenly so old and yet so young all at once. Old enough to have homework and two adult teeth and be on a soccer team. Young enough to want to play outside every day, to still have baby teeth and missing teeth, and to care more about spinning and catching snowflakes than winning the game.

He sees us now, and his eyes light up. His whole face stretches wide with his goofy jack-o'-lantern grin, and he runs straight into our legs. I shove my phone into my pocket so I can hug him with both hands. This is why I came.

"Great job, buddy!" says Bob.

"Did we win?" asks Charlie.

They lost 10–3.

"I don't think so. Did you have fun?" I ask.

"Yup!"

"How about pizza tonight?" asks Bob.

"Yeah!"

We begin walking to the parking lot.

"Mom, are you coming for pizza?"

"No, honey, I have to go back to work."

"Okay, bud, race you to the car. Ready? Set? Go!" yells Bob.

They tear across the baseball infield kicking up clouds of dusty dirt. Bob lets Charlie beat him and hams it up. I can hear him saying, "I can't believe it! I almost had you! You're a speed demon!"

I smile. In my car, I check my phone. Three bars and seven new voice messages. I sigh, brace myself, and hit Play. As I wind and inch my way out of the parking lot, I end up right behind Bob and Charlie. I beep and wave and watch them turn left toward pizza and home. Then I turn right and head in the opposite direction.

CHAPTER 4

*I'm strolling through the Public Garden, past the statue of George
Washington on his horse, past the swan boats in the pond, beneath
the giant willow trees, past Lack, Mack, and the rest of the bronze
ducklings.*

*I'm wearing my favorite Christian Louboutin, black patent
leather, four-inch, peep-toe shoes. I love the sound they make as I
stroll.*

Clack . . . Clack . . . Clack . . . Clack . . . Clack . . . Clack.

*I cross the street to the Common. A tall man in a dark suit crosses
behind me. I walk through the Common, past the baseball fields and
the Frog Pond. The man is still behind me. I walk a little faster.*

Clack. Clack. Clack. Clack. Clack. Clack.

So does he.

I move quickly past the homeless man asleep on the park bench, past the Park Street T, past the business tycoon talking on his cell phone, past the drug dealer on the corner. The man follows me.

Who is he? What does he want? Don't look back.

Clack, Clack, Clack, Clack, Clack, Clack.

I pass the jewelry stores and the old Filene's Basement building. I weave and wind through the crowds of shoppers and turn left down the next side street. The cars and crowds are gone now. The street is empty except for the man pursuing me, even closer. I run.

CLACK! CLACK! CLACK! CLACK! CLACK! CLACK!

So does he. He's chasing me.

I can't shake him. On the side of the financial building ahead of me, I see a fire escape. Escape! I run to it and start to climb. I hear the man's footsteps echoing mine on the metal stairs, bearing down on me.

CLINK! CLOMP! CLINK! CLOMP! CLINK! CLOMP!

I crisscross up and up and up and up. My lungs are screaming. My legs are burning.

Don't look back. Don't look down. Keep going. He's right behind you.

I reach the top. The roof is flat and empty. I run to the far edge. There's nowhere else to go. My heart is hammering against the bones in my chest. I have no choice. I turn to face my attacker.

There's no one there. I wait. No one appears. I cautiously make my way back to the fire escape.

Clack. Clack. Clack. Clack. Clack. Clack.

It's not there. I walk the perimeter of the roof. The fire escape is gone. I'm trapped on the top of this building.

I sit down to catch my breath and think. I watch a plane take off into the sky out of Logan and try to imagine a way down other than jumping.

WEDNESDAY

I'm a Boston Driver. Traffic regulations like speed limits and DO NOT ENTER signs are more suggestion here than law. I navigate the city's one-way, helter-skelter streets, dodging potholes and nervy jaywalkers, anticipating the next construction detour, and gunning every yellow light with experienced bravado. All in the space of four blocks. The next traffic light turns green, and I'm on my horn in less than a blink of the eye when the Honda in front of me with New Hampshire plates doesn't move. Like any self-respecting Boston Driver would.

Driving home at the end of the day requires infinitely more patience than coming in, and having any patience at all has never been my virtue. There is always traffic both times of day, but the evening exodus is significantly worse. I don't know why this is. The whistle blows, the gates open, and we're all off, like a million picnic ants converging onto one of three trails of cookie crumbs—Route 93 for those who live on the North or South Shore and the Mass Pike for those, like me, who reside west of Boston. The civil engineers who planned and designed these roads probably never conceived of this many commuters. And if they did, I'll bet they live and work in Worcester.

I accordion along the Pike, wearing out my brake pads, swearing that one of these days I'll start taking the T. The only reason I subject myself to this daily erosion of my brakes and sanity is so I can see my kids before they go to bed. Most people at Berkley don't leave before 7:00, and many order dinner and stay well past 8:00. I try to leave at 6:00, right in the thick of the Going Home parade. My early departure doesn't go unnoticed, especially by the younger, single consultants, and as I walk out of the office each night, I have to resist the urge to remind all their judging eyes just how many hours a night I work from home. I have my faults, but I'm not, and never will be, a slacker.

I leave "early" because I hope to muddle through the traffic and get home in time for dessert, baths, stories, and tucking the kids into bed at 7:30. But every minute I now sit unmoving in my Acura is another minute that I won't get to see them today. At 6:20, it's already been dark out for over an hour, and it feels even later than it is. It's started to rain, which is slowing down progress even more. I'll probably miss dessert at this point, but we're creeping along, and I should get home in time for bath, book, and bed.

And then everything stops. It's 6:30. Red brake lights glow in an unbroken chain all the way to the horizon. Someone must've gotten in an accident. I'm not anywhere near an exit, so I can't even bail out early and take the back roads home. I turn off whoever's complaining on NPR and listen for sounds of an ambulance or police siren. I don't hear any. It's 6:37. No one is moving. I'm late, I'm trapped, and my barely contained anxiety breaks open. *CRAP! What is going ON?*

I look to the guy in the BMW next to me, like he might know. He sees me, shrugs his shoulders, and shakes his head in disgusted resignation. He's on his cell phone. Maybe that's what I should do. Use this time wisely. I pull out my laptop and start reading case team reviews. But I'm too aggravated to be productive. If I wanted to work, I would've stayed at work.

It's 6:53. The Pike remains paralyzed. I text Bob to let him know. 7:00. Bath time. I rub my face and breathe in and out into my hands. I want to scream the stress out of my body, but I worry that the guy in the BMW will think I'm crazy and gossip about me on his phone. So I hold it in. I just want to be home. I just want to click my Cole Haan heels and be home.

It's 7:18 when I arrive in front of 22 Pilgrim Lane. Fourteen miles in seventy-eight minutes. The winner of the Boston Marathon could've beaten me home on foot. And that's exactly how I feel. Beaten. I reach up to the visor and press the button on the garage door opener. I'm inches away from pulling in when I realize that the garage door didn't open, and I slam on the brakes. I made it through the gnarly streets of Boston and a gridlocked Pike without a scratch but almost totaled the car in my own driveway. I repeatedly click and curse at the stupid garage door button a few times before I get out of the car. As I run through puddles and freezing rain from my car to the front door, the saying "The straw that broke the camel's back" comes to mind.

I pray that I've at least made it home in time for bedtime stories and good-night kisses.

I'm lying in bed with Lucy, waiting for her to fall asleep. If I get up too soon, she'll beg for one more book. I already read *Tacky the Penguin* and *Blue's Best Rainy Day*. I'll tell her *no*, and she'll say *please*, stretching the *eez* out for several seconds to show me that she's being extra polite and that her request is extra important, and I'll say *no*, and in the course of this arousing tête-à-tête, she'll wake herself up. It's just easier if I stay until she's out.

I'm spooning her small body, and my nose is on her head. She smells like heaven—an elixir of Johnson's Baby Shampoo, Tom's of Maine Strawberry toothpaste, and Nilla Wafers. I think I'll cry the day all my kids stop using Johnson's Baby Shampoo. Who will they smell like then?

She's so warm, and her deepened breathing is hypnotic. I wish I could let myself drift off with her, but I have miles to go before I can sleep. This is the trick every night, to leave after she's surrendered the fight to be up, but before I give in to the desire to close my eyes. When I'm convinced she's fully unconscious, I slide out from under the covers, tiptoe around all the toys and crafts (land mines) strewn on the floor, and steal out of her darkened room like I'm James Bond.

Bob is eating a bowl of cereal on the couch.

"Sorry, babe, I couldn't wait."

No apologies necessary. I'm relieved. I love it when I don't have to think about what we're going to eat for dinner, and I love it even more when I don't have to cook anything. Well, I should admit, I don't exactly cook. I microwave. I heat up already prepared and cooked food. And the Takeout Taxi phone number is programmed into our speed dial. But cereal might just be my favorite dinner at home. It's not that I don't enjoy a sumptuous and elegant meal at Pisces or Mistral, but dinner at home on the couches with Bob isn't about ambiance and fine dining. It's about getting rid of the hunger pangs as quickly as possible and moving on.

We spend the next three hours in the living room on separate couches with our laptops on our laps. CNN is on the TV for background noise and the occasional interesting sound bite. I am mostly emailing our offices in China and India. Boston is twelve hours behind China and ten and a half hours behind India, so now is tomorrow morning for them. This still blows my mind. I'm a time traveler, doing business in real time on Thursday when it is still only Wednesday where I sit on my couch. Amazing.

Bob is clicking around the internet and networking for jobs. He's at a promising information technology start-up, and the payoff is potentially huge if they get acquired or go public, but as with most fledgling companies in this economy, things aren't looking so good. The recession is hitting them hard, and the skyrocketing growth trajectories Bob projected when he signed on three years ago feel like a distant, silly fantasy. At this point, they're simply trying not to bleed to death. He just survived a second round of layoffs, but he isn't planning on sticking around and holding his breath through a third. The problem is Bob is picky, and not many companies are hiring. I can tell by his pinched mouth and the vertical ravine between his furrowed brows that he isn't finding anything.

The uncertainty of his job, both current and future, has been really weighing on him. When he starts sliding down What-If's slippery slope to Doomsville—What if I lose my job tomorrow? What if I can't find another? What if we can't make the mortgage payments?—I try to brush them all off and make the load lighter for him. *Don't worry, honey, you'll be fine. The kids will be fine. We'll all be fine.*

But the What-Ifs take up residence in my head, and in my head, I'm captain of the champion luge team, barreling at record speed to Doomsville. What if he does get laid off and can't find another job? What if we have to sell the house in Vermont? But then what if we can't sell it in this depressed market? What if we can't pay the student loans, the car payments, the heating bill? What if we can't afford to stay in Welmont?

I close my eyes and see the word *DEBT* written in all caps and red ink. My chest tightens, and it feels like there's no air in the room, and my laptop is suddenly unbearably hot on my legs, and I'm sweating. Stop thinking about it. Take your own advice. *He'll be fine. The kids will be fine. We'll be fine.* Deluded mantra.

I decide to watch TV for a minute to take my mind off of Doomsville. Anderson Cooper is reporting about a San Diego mother who accidentally left her two-year-old toddler in the backseat of her locked car for eight hours while she worked at her job. When the mother returned to her car at the end of the day, her toddler was dead from heat exhaustion. Officials are deciding whether or not to press charges.

What was I thinking? CNN is the capital of Doomsville. My eyes fill with tears thinking about this woman and her dead child. I imagine the two-year-old, helpless to escape the car seat's five-point harness, terror and fevered desperation giving way to organ failure. How will that mother ever forgive herself? I think of my mother.

"Bob, can you change the channel?"

He flips to a local news station. One of the anchors is listing today's news from bad to worse—banks begging for bailouts, soaring unemployment rates, the stock market in free fall. Doomsville, U.S.A.

I get up and go to the kitchen to look for some chocolate and a big glass of wine.

We both surrender the day at eleven. Before the sun rises in Boston, consultants in the various European offices will be sipping their first espressos of the day, adding their emails to my inbox with their morning's questions, concerns, and reports. And, at about the same time, Linus will wake up. Groundhog Day all over again.

It used to take me a long time to fall asleep, anywhere from twenty minutes to a full hour. I used to have to read something totally unrelated to my day, like a novel, to distract and calm my racing thoughts. And Bob's snoring used to drive me crazy. It's truly nothing short of miraculous that he can sleep through all his own growling and whistling. He says he's protecting our cave from predators. While I appreciate his idea about the origin of the man snore, I believe that we as a species have evolved past the need for it. Like the dead-bolted front door, to begin with. But his Fred Flintstone snore will not be phased out by modern technology. There have been many nights when I wanted to suffocate him with my pillow and take my chances with the lions, tigers, and bears.

But no more. Since about the time that Lucy was born, I'm asleep within five minutes of my head hitting the pillow. If I try to read, I don't get past the page I start on. I can't remember the last time I finished a novel. And if I happen to surface into a light sleep during the night and notice Bob's snoring, I roll over and sink unperturbed back into slumber.

The negative side to this is its impact on our sex life. I'm embarrassed to admit this, but I can't remember the last time we had sex. I like sex with Bob, and I still want to have sex with Bob, but I don't seem to like and want it enough to stay awake long enough to make it happen. I know we're both busy and tired at the end of the day, but I'm not too busy and tired to read to Lucy, email China, and go through the piles of bills. Yet every night, I draw the line at sex. And so does Bob.

I remember when we used to have sex early in the evening, before we were too tired, sometimes even before going out (when we used to go out). Now, when we do manage to fit it in, it's always just before bed, always *in* bed, a pre-sleep activity like brushing teeth or flossing, although never with that kind of regularity.

When I was single, I remember reading in *Vogue* or *Cosmopolitan* or one of those magazines I only read at the hairdresser's that married couples with advanced degrees report having sex the least of all married couples. Only ten to twelve times a year. That's once a month. *That will NEVER be me*, I thought. Of course, I was twenty-something, single, without children, far less educated than I am now, and getting laid at least two to three times a week. I used to read the surveys in those magazines and think they were entertaining but pure fiction. Now I hang on every brilliant word.

I hope Bob doesn't doubt whether I'm still attracted to him. Ironically, if anything, I'm more attracted to him now than when we were dating and having sex all the time. Watching him feed Linus a bottle, kiss Lucy's boo-boo, teach Charlie over and over again how to tie his shoes, moments when I see him utterly unself-conscious and absorbed in loving them, I feel like I could burst with how much I adore him.

I regret the nights when I'm so tired that I fall asleep before telling him that I love him. And I'm irrationally angry with him on the nights that he falls asleep before he tells me. If we're too unmotivated to eat a grown-up dinner, too pre-occupied with emails and job hunting to snuggle on the couch and watch a movie, and too tuckered out to consider three minutes of sex, then we can at least say we love each other before we pass out.

I lie in bed alone and wait for Bob. I want to tell him that I love him, that even if he loses his job tomorrow, I'll still love him. That wherever What-If takes us, we'll be okay because we love each other. But he takes too long in the bathroom, and I fall asleep before I get a chance to tell him, worried for some reason that he doesn't know.

CHAPTER 5

On the way to the laundry room, I notice a door I've never seen before behind the exercise equipment. I stop and stare. How can this be?

"Bob, where'd this door come from?" I holler.

He doesn't answer.

I grab the knob that I swear never existed before now and pause. My mother's voice says, SARAH, MIND YOUR OWN BUSINESS.

I twist the knob to the right.

A menacing Alfred Hitchcock movie voice says, DON'T.

I have to know.

I push the door open. I'm standing in the threshold of a room I've never been in before, and in the far corner, a lion is drinking water from a stainless steel lobster pot. The room is bigger than our kitchen, but that's the only detail about it that I can take in because I'm transfixed by the lion—his muscular hind legs, his lively tail, his intolerable stench. I cover my nose and mouth with my shirt to keep from retching.

Moving was not a good idea. The lion looks over his shoulder, sees me, turns to face me square on, and roars. His stinky breath is hot and damp on my face. I don't dare to wipe it. Drool drips from his mouth, accumulating into a sizable puddle on the floor. Our eyes are locked. I'm trying not to blink. I'm trying not to breathe.

Bob strolls in carrying a bundle the size of Linus wrapped in white deli paper. He walks past me, untapes the package, and dumps a slab of bloody, raw, red meat onto the floor next to the lion. The lion forgets about me and pounces on it.

"Bob, WHAT is going on?"

"I'm feeding the lion dinner."

"Where did he come from?"

"What do you mean? He's ours. He came with the house."

I let out an uncertain laugh, thinking this must be the punch line to one of Bob's weird jokes, but stop when he doesn't join in.

Now that the lion is busy devouring something other than me, I look around the room. The walls are paneled, the concrete floor is covered in pine shavings, and the beamed ceiling is two stories high. A framed picture of me and Bob hangs on the wall. I notice another door in the wall opposite the lion. This one is small, about half the height of a regular door.

I have to know.

I tiptoe past the lion, open the door, and crawl inside. The door

slams shut behind me, leaving me in total darkness. I can see nothing
but assume that my eyes will adjust over time, like they do at the
movies. I sit cross-legged against the door, blink, and wait, excited
about what I'll see.

I'm not scared.

THURSDAY

Bob and I are standing in Charlie's empty classroom, on time,
hands in our coat pockets, waiting for Ms. Gavin. Every bone
in my body doesn't want to be here. However long this meeting lasts, I'll probably be late for work and can already
foresee chasing the rest of the day and never catching it. I
feel as if I'm coming down with a miserable cold, and I forgot
to down a shot of DayQuil before we rushed out the door.
And I really don't want to hear whatever it is Ms. Gavin is
going to tell us.

I don't trust this Ms. Gavin. Who is she, anyway? Maybe
she's a terrible teacher. I remember from Open House Night
that she's young, in her twenties. Inexperienced. Maybe
she's overwhelmed with her job and has been scheduling a
meeting like this with the parents of every kid in her class.
Maybe she has a thing against kids who challenge her. God
knows Charlie can be challenging. Maybe she doesn't like
boys. I had a teacher like that once. Mrs. Knight only called

on the girls, only gave the girls smiley faces on their papers, and was always sending one of the boys out into the hall or to the principal's office. Never one of the girls.

Maybe this Ms. Gavin is the problem.

I look around the room for evidence to support my well-reasoned suspicion. Instead of the individual desks with attached chairs that I remember from my elementary school days, this room has four low, round tables with five chairs arranged around each, like little dining tables. Ideal for socializing, I'd say, not for learning. But my nice long list of things that the inept and unqualified Ms. Gavin is doing wrong ends with that single, lame observation.

Art projects line the walls. At the front of the room, printed-out photos of kids are taped onto two giant poster boards titled "Stellar Spellers" and "Math Olympic Champions." Charlie's picture is on neither. Five vibrantly colored, stuffed, kid-sized armchairs sit in a corner labeled "The Book Nook" next to a shelving unit packed with books. At the back of the room, there are two tables: one with a hamster in a cage and the other with fish in a tank.

Everything looks organized, cheery, and fun. I'd say Ms. Gavin loves her job. And she's good at it. I really don't want to be here.

I'm just about to ask Bob if he wants to make a break for it, when she appears.

"Thanks for coming. Please have a seat."

Bob and I sit in the kiddie chairs, inches from the floor. Ms. Gavin sits high in her grown-up teacher's chair behind her desk. We are munchkins, and she is the great and powerful Wizard of Oz.

"So, Charlie's report card must be concerning to you both. Can I start by asking if you were surprised by his grades?"

"Shocked," says Bob.

"Well, they're about the same as last year," I say.

Wait, whose side am I on?

"Yeah, but last year was about the adjustment," says Bob.

Ms. Gavin nods, but not because she's agreeing with him.

"Have you noticed if he has a hard time completing the homework assignments?" asks Ms. Gavin.

Abby starts the process with him in the afternoon, and Bob and I continue with him often past his bedtime. It's supposed to take only twenty to thirty minutes. He struggles, agonizes, stalls, complains, cries, and hates. Worse than broccoli hates. We threaten, bribe, implore, explain, and sometimes just do it for him. Yup, I'd call it a hard time.

In his defense, I know I didn't have homework at his age. I don't think kids, with the exception of a few precocious girls, are ready for the responsibility of homework at the age of seven. I think the schools are putting too much academic pressure on our little kids. That said, we're talking one page of "greater than or less than," or spelling words like *man, can, ran*. It's not rocket science.

"He does," I say.

"It's brutal," says Bob.

"What are you seeing here?" I dare to ask.

"He's struggling. He can't complete any of the class

assignments on time, he interrupts me and the other children, and he daydreams a lot. I catch him staring out the window at least six times before lunch every day."

"Where is his seat?" I ask.

"There."

She points to the chair closest to her desk, which also happens to be right by the window. Well, who wouldn't get lost in thought when you've got a view? And maybe he's sitting next to someone who's distracting him. A troublemaker. A pretty girl. Maybe I gave Ms. Gavin too much credit.

"Can you try moving his seat to the other side of the room?" I ask, sure I've solved the whole problem.

"That's where he started the year. I need him right in front of me if I want any chance of holding his attention."

She waits to see if I have other bright ideas. I have none.

"He has a hard time following directions that have more than two steps. Like if I tell the class to go to their cubbies, get their math folders, get a ruler from the back table, and bring it back to their desks, Charlie will go to his cubby and bring back his snack, or he'll bring back nothing and just roam the room. Are you seeing anything like this at home?"

"No," says Bob.

"What? That's Charlie," I say.

He looks at me like he can't imagine what I could be talking about. Is *he* paying attention? I wonder what Bob would get on his report card.

"Charlie, go get dressed and put on shoes. Charlie, put on

your pajamas, put your clothes in the hamper, and brush your teeth. We might as well be speaking Greek."

"Yeah, but he just doesn't want to do those things. It's not that he can't. All kids try to get out of doing what they're told," says Bob.

I sneeze and excuse myself. My congested sinuses are killing me.

"He also doesn't participate well in activities that require taking turns. The other kids tend to shy away from playing games with him because he won't follow the rules. He's impulsive."

Now my heart is breaking.

"Is he the only one doing these kinds of things?" Bob asks, convinced that he's not.

"Yes."

Bob glances around at the eighteen empty little chairs and sighs into his hands.

"So what are you saying?" I ask.

"I'm saying Charlie is unable to focus on all aspects of the school day."

"What does that mean?" asks Bob.

"It means that Charlie is unable to focus on all aspects of the school day."

"Because?" challenges Bob.

"I can't say."

Ms. Gavin stares at us and says nothing. I get it. I envision the policy memos stamped and signed by the school lawyers. No one is saying the words I think we're all now thinking,

Ms. Gavin for legal reasons, Bob and I because we're talking about our little Charlie. My mother would be great at this conversation. Her next words would be about the nice weather we're having or Ms. Gavin's pretty pink shirt. But I can't stand the unspoken tension.

"Do you think he might have ADD or something?"

"I'm not a physician. I can't say that."

"But you think it."

"I can't say."

"Then what the hell can you say?" asks Bob.

I put my hand on Bob's arm. This is going nowhere. Bob is gritting his teeth and is probably seconds away from walking out. I'm seconds away from shaking her and screaming, "This is my boy! Tell me what you think is wrong with him!" But my business school training kicks in and saves us all. Reframe the problem.

"What can we do?" I ask.

"Look, Charlie's a sweet boy and he's actually very smart, but he's falling way behind, and the distance between him and the other kids will get worse if we do nothing. But nothing can happen fast enough here unless the parents initiate an evaluation. You have to ask for it in writing."

"Ask for what exactly?" asks Bob.

I half listen while Ms. Gavin describes the red-tape-lined mountain climb to an Individualized Education Program. Special education. I remember when Charlie was born, checking him for all ten fingers and toes, studying his delicate pink lips and the conch-shell curviness of his ears. *He's perfect*, I thought, amazed and grateful for his perfection. Now my perfect boy might have Attention Deficit Disorder. The two thoughts refuse to hold hands.

Kids are going to label him. His teachers are going to label him. What did Ms. Gavin call him? Impulsive. The kids are going to throw names that are sharper and uglier than that at him. And they're going to aim for his head.

"I want him to see his pediatrician before we start doing anything here," says Bob.

"I think that's a good idea," says Ms. Gavin.

Doctors give kids with ADD Ritalin. That's an amphetamine, isn't it? We're going to drug our seven-year-old son so he doesn't fall behind in school. The thought flushes the blood out of my brain, as if my circulation won't support the idea, and my head and fingers go numb. Ms. Gavin keeps talking, but she sounds muffled and far away. I don't want this problem or its solution.

I want to hate Ms. Gavin for telling us any of this. But I see the sincerity in her eyes, and I can't hate her. I know it's not her fault. And I can't hate Charlie. It's not his fault either. But I feel hate, and it's growing massive inside my chest and needs a place to go, or I'll hate and blame myself. I look around the room for something—the innocent faces of the kids on the "Stellar Spellers" board, the painted hearts and moons and rainbows, the hamster running on its wheel. The hate stays trapped inside my chest, crushing my lungs. I have to get out of here.

Bob thanks Ms. Gavin for informing us and promises that

we'll get Charlie whatever help he needs. I stand and shake her hand. I think I even smile at her, like I've enjoyed our conversation. How ridiculous. Then I notice her feet.

In the hallway, after Ms. Gavin has shut the door to her room, Bob hugs me and then asks me if I'm okay.

"I hate her shoes," I say.

Baffled by my answer, Bob decides not to ask any more questions of me at this point, and we walk to the gym in silence.

Before the Bell is just about over, and the kids are lining up to go to their classrooms. After saying hello and good-bye to Lucy, Bob and I find Charlie in line.

"Hey, bud, gimme five!" says Bob.

Charlie slaps his hand.

"Bye, honey, see you tonight. Do what Ms. Gavin says today, okay?" I ask.

"Okay, Mom."

"Love you," I say and hug him hard.

The kids ahead of Charlie begin to walk, following one another in a line, inching out of the gym like a single caterpillar. The line breaks at Charlie, who doesn't move.

"Okay, bud, get going!" says Bob.

Don't fall behind, my perfect boy.

CHAPTER 6

Ricky's mom, Mrs. Sullivan, tells us that the pool isn't ready yet. Mr. Sullivan still needs to vacuum and backwash it. The water is cloudy and littered with rotten brown leaves and looks more like pond water than pool water, but we don't care. It's the first day of summer vacation, and we can't wait for Mr. Sullivan.

I find an orange water wing and pull it onto my left arm up to my scrawny bicep. I rummage through the trunk of floats and water toys but can't find the other wing. I look up, and Nate is wearing it like it's an elbow pad.

"Give it," I say, and I strip it off his arm.

He usually throws a hissy fit whenever he doesn't get what he wants, so I'm surprised that he just lets me do this. Maybe I'm finally getting the respect an older sister deserves. I slide the orange wing onto my other arm, and Nate finds a mask and a kickboard.

I dip my big toe into the water and jump back.

"It's FREEZING!"

"Baby," says Ricky as he runs past me and cannonballs in.

I wish I could be just like him, but the water's too cold.

I go up onto the deck and sit on the stretchy plastic slat chair next to Mom. Mom and Mrs. Sullivan are lying on cushioned lounge chairs angled toward the sun. They're drinking cans of Tab and smoking Marlboro Lights, and they're talking to each other with their eyes closed. Mom's toenails are painted Hot Tamale Red. I wish I could be just like her.

I pull off my water wings and turn my chair to face the sun, too. Mrs. Sullivan is complaining about her asshole husband, and I'm embarrassed to hear her say "asshole" because I know it's a swear word, and I would get slapped across the face if I said it. I'm careful not to make any noise or fidget because I think Mom doesn't notice that I'm listening, and I feel embarrassed, but I want to hear more illegal words about Mr. Sullivan.

Ricky shows up on the deck, teeth chattering.

"I'm freezing."

"Told ya," I say, stupidly blowing my cover.

"Towels are in the bathroom. Go play Atari," says Mrs. Sullivan. "You want to go inside, too, Sarah?"

I shake my head.

"She wants to stay with the girls. Right, honey?" Mom asks.

I nod. She reaches over and pats my leg. I smile and feel special.

Ricky goes into the house, Mom and Mrs. Sullivan talk, and I close my eyes and listen. But Mrs. Sullivan doesn't say anything bad about Mr. Sullivan, and I get bored of listening, and I think maybe I will go inside and play Pac-Man, but Ricky's probably playing Space Invaders, and I want to be one of the girls, so I stay.

Then all of a sudden, Mom is screaming Nate's name. I open my eyes, and she is screaming Nate's name and running. I stand up to see what's happening. Nate is floating facedown in the pool. At first I think it's a trick, and I admire him for fooling us. Then Mom is in the pool with him, and he's still pretending, and I think he's mean for scaring her. Then Mom turns him over, and I see his closed eyes and blue lips, and I get scared for real, and my heart falls into my stomach.

Mom carries Nate onto the grass and is making wild sounds I've never heard come out of a grown-up and is blowing into Nate's mouth and begging Nate to wake up, but Nate is just lying there. I can't look at Nate lying on the grass and Mom blowing into Nate's mouth anymore, so I look down at my feet, and I see the orange water wings on the deck next to my chair.

"Wake up, Nate!" Mom wails.

I can't look. I stare at my selfish feet and the orange water wings.

"Wake up, Nate!"

"Wake up!"

"Sarah, wake up."

FRIDAY

"One, two, threeeee, shoot!"

My fingers are a pair of scissors. Bob's hand is a piece of paper.

"I win!" I yell.

I never win the shoot. I snip the air with my fingers and dance a ridiculous jig, a cross between the moves of Jonathan Papelbon and Elaine Benes. Bob laughs. But the thrill of my unexpected victory is short-lived, stolen by the sight of Charlie now standing in the kitchen without his backpack.

"The Wii won't save my level."

"Charlie, *what* did I tell you to do?" I ask.

He just looks at me. The strings of my vocal cords wind a little tighter.

"I *told* you to bring your backpack in here twenty minutes ago."

"I had to get to the next level."

I grind my teeth. I know if I open my mouth, I'm going to lose it. I'll yell and scare him, or cry and scare Bob, or rant and throw the damn Wii in the trash. Before yesterday, Charlie's inability to listen or follow the simplest instruction annoyed me but in the typical way that I think most kids annoy most parents. Now, a tidal wave of fear and frustration rises inside me, and I have to fight to contain it, to keep it from spilling out and drowning us all. In the few seconds that I struggle to stay silent, I watch Charlie's eyes become wide and glassy. The fear and frustration must be leaking out of my pores. Bob puts his hands on my shoulders.

"I'll take care of this. You go," says Bob.

I check my watch. If I leave now, I can get to work early, calm, and sane. I can even make a few phone calls on the way. I open my mouth and exhale.

"Thanks," I say and squeeze his piece of paper hand.

I grab my bag, kiss Bob and the kids good-bye, and leave the house alone. It's raw and raining hard outside. Without a hood or an umbrella, I run like hell to the car, but just before I throw myself into the driver's seat, I notice a penny on the ground. I can't resist it. I stop, pick it up, and then duck into the car. Chilly and drenched, I smile as I start the engine. I won the shoot and found a penny.

Today must be my lucky day.

Rain is coming down in sheets, splashing onto the fogged windshield almost faster than the wipers can keep pace. The headlights click on, its sensors tricked by the dark morning into thinking that it's nighttime. It feels like nighttime to my senses, too. It's the kind of stormy morning that would be perfect for crawling back into bed.

But I'm not about to let the gloomy weather dampen my good mood. I have no kids to shuttle, buckets of time, and traffic is moving despite the weather. I'm going to get to work early, organized, and ready to tackle the day, instead of late, frazzled, grape juice stained, and unable to kick some inane Wiggles song out of my head.

And I'm going to get some work done on the way. I fish in my bag for my phone. I want to make a call to Harvard

Business School. November is our biggest recruiting month, and we're competing with all the other top consulting firms, like McKinsey and Boston Consulting Group, to pluck the best and the brightest from this year's crop. We never lure in as many graduates as McKinsey does, but we usually beat out BCG. After our first round of a hundred and fifty interviews, there are ten particularly impressive candidates whom we plan to woo.

I find my phone and begin searching for the Harvard number in my contact list. I can't find it under H. That's odd. Maybe it's under B for Business School. I glance up at the road, and my heart seizes. Red brake lights glow everywhere, blurry through the wet and foggy windshield, unmoving, like a watercolor painting. Everything on the highway is still. Everything but me. I'm going 70 mph.

I slam on the brakes. They catch the road, and then they don't. I'm hydroplaning. I pump the brakes. I'm hydroplaning. I'm getting closer and closer to the red lights in the painting.

Oh my God.

I turn the wheel hard to the left. Too hard. I'm now outside the last lane of the eastbound highway, spinning between east and west. I'm sure the car's still moving very fast, but I'm experiencing the spinning like it's happening in slow motion. And someone turned off the sound—the rain, the wipers, my heartbeat. Everything is slow and soundless, like I'm underwater.

I hit the brakes and turn the wheel the other way, hoping to either correct the spinning or stop. The landscape bends into an unmanageable slant, and the car begins to tumble end over end. The tumbling is also slow and soundless, and my thoughts while I'm tumbling are detached and strangely calm.

The air bag explodes. I notice that it's white.

I see the loose contents of my bag and the penny I found suspended in air. I think of astronauts on the moon.

Something is choking my throat.

My car is going to be totaled.

Something hits my head.

I'm going to be late for work.

Then suddenly the tumbling stops, and the car is still.

I want to get out of the car, but I can't move. I feel a sudden crushing and unbearable pain on the top of my head. It occurs to me for the first time that I might've wrecked more than my car.

I'm sorry, Bob.

The dark morning gets darker and goes blank. I don't feel the pain in my head. There is no sight and no feeling. I wonder if I'm dead.

Please don't let me die.

I decide I'm not dead because I can hear the sound of the rain hitting the roof of the car. I'm alive because I'm listening to the rain, and the rain becomes the hand of God strumming his fingers on the roof, deciding what to do.

I strain to listen.

Keep listening.

Listen.

But the sound fades, and the rain is gone.

CHAPTER 7

The hazy bright whiteness above me focuses into a fluorescent light fixture on the ceiling. Someone is saying something over and over. As I study the brightness and shape of the light, I come to realize that someone is saying something over and over to me.

"Sarah, can you take a deep breath for me?"

I assume that I can, but as I do, my entire throat grips around something rigid, and I gag. I'm sure that I've stopped inhaling, but my lungs fill with air anyway. My throat feels bone dry. I want to lick my lips and swallow some saliva, but something inside my mouth won't let me. I want to ask, "What's happening?" but I can't gather the reins of my breathing, lips, or tongue. My eyes fill with panic.

"Don't try to talk. You have a tube in your mouth to help you breathe."

There is a fluorescent light on the ceiling above my head, a tube inside my mouth to help me breathe, and a woman's voice.

"Can you squeeze my hand?" asks the woman's voice.

I squeeze, but I don't feel a hand in my hand.

"Can you squeeze your other hand?"

I don't understand the question.

"Can you show me two fingers?"

I spread my index and middle finger.

Scissors.

I won the shoot. The shoot, the rain, the car. The crash. I remember. I hear electronic beeps and the whirring of mechanical equipment. The fluorescent light, the tube, the woman's voice. I'm in a hospital. Oh my God, what's happened to me? I try to think past the crash, but a searing pain slices through the top of my head, and I can't.

"Good, Sarah. Okay, that's enough for today. We're going to put you back to sleep so you can rest."

Wait! The shoot, the car, the rain, the crash, and then what? What happened? Am I okay?

The fluorescent light on the ceiling grows brighter. The edges of the light dissolve. Everything blurs white.

"Okay, Sarah, breathe out as hard as you can."

I blow as a nurse yanks the breathing tube out of me, and it feels like she's dragging a sandpaper-coated speculum up the tender lining of my throat. There's nothing delicate or hesitant about her approach to this procedure. The removal is ruthless, and the relief I feel when she's done borders on euphoria, a bit like giving birth. I'm good and ready to hate this woman, but then she tips a Dixie cup of melting ice chips to my lips, and she's my angel of mercy.

After a minute, she folds my hand around the cup.

"Okay, Sarah, keep sipping. I'll be right back," she says and leaves me alone.

I sip the cold water. My cracked and dusty lips, mouth, and throat are grateful sponges, like earth soaking in rain after a long drought. I just had a breathing tube removed. I needed a tube to breathe. That's not good. But I don't need one now. Why did I need a breathing tube? How long have I been here? Where is Bob?

My head feels strange, but I can't identify the sensation at first. Then it comes to me in full Technicolor, the volume turned all the way up. My head is scorching hot. I let go of the cup of ice and touch my head. I'm stunned and horrified by the mental image drawn by what my fingers feel. A large portion of my scalp, about the size and shape of a slice of bread, is shaved, and within that bald space, my fingers discover about a dozen metal staples. Somewhere just below the staples, my brain is the temperature of volcanic magma.

I grab the Dixie cup and pour the watery ice onto my stapled head. I actually expect to hear the water sizzle, but it doesn't. The ice doesn't lessen the fiery pain, and I've just used up all of my chips.

I wait and breathe in and out without the help of a tube. Don't panic. The nurse wouldn't have left you alone without a breathing tube and holding a disposable cup of ice if your brain were melting. But maybe it is melting. Check to see if it works.

Who are you? *I'm Sarah Nickerson*. Good. You know your name. *My husband is Bob. I have three kids—Charlie, Lucy, and Linus. I'm the VP of HR at Berkley. We live in Welmont. I'm thirty-seven years old*. Good. Sarah, you're fine. I touch the staples and trace the shape of the bald patch. *They don't shave your head and insert metal hardware into your scalp if you're fine*.

Where is Bob? Someone should tell Bob where I am and what's happened. Oh God, someone should tell work where I am and what's happened. How long have I been here? What happened?

Other than during and following childbirth, I've never needed any medical attention beyond a few Motrin and a couple of Band-Aids. I stare at the fluorescent light. I don't like this one bit. Where is the nurse? Please come back. Isn't there a button somewhere I can push to call her? I look for a button, a phone, a speaker to yell into. I see the fluorescent light on the ceiling and an ugly beige curtain hanging next to me. Nothing else. No window, no TV, no phone, nothing. This room sucks.

I wait. My head is too hot. I try to call out for the nurse, but my brutalized throat can manage only a raspy whisper.

"Hello?"

I wait.

"Bob?"

I wait. I wait forever as I picture my brain and everything I love melting away.

The fluorescent light again. I must've dozed off. My world is this fluorescent light. The light and the low, continuous, electronic whirring and beeping of whatever equipment might be monitoring me. Monitoring me and keeping me alive? God, I hope not. My world is meetings and deadlines, emails and airports, Bob and my kids. How did my world get reduced to this? How long have I been lying under this ugly light?

I move my hand beneath the bedsheet and down to my leg. Oh no. I'm feeling at least a week's worth of stubble. The hair on my legs is fair-colored, almost blond, but I have a ton of it, and I usually shave every day. I rub my hand up and down my thigh like I'm petting a goat at the zoo.

Oh God, my chin. I have a cluster of five hairs on the left side of my chin. They're coarse and wiry, like boar hair, and for the past couple of years, they've been my hideous secret and my sworn enemies. They sprout up every couple of days, and so I have to be vigilant. I keep my weapons—Revlon tweezers and a 10X magnifying mirror—at home, in my Sherpa bag, and in my desk drawer at work, so in theory, I can be anywhere, and if one of those evil little weeds pokes through the surface, I can yank it. I've been in meetings with CEOs, some of the most powerful men in the world, and could barely stay focused on what they were saying because I'd inadvertently touched my chin and become obsessed with the idea of destroying five microscopic hairs. I hate them, and I'm terrified of someone else noticing them before I do, but I have to admit, there is almost nothing more satisfying than pulling them out.

I stroke my chin, expecting to feel my Little Pig beard, but touch only smooth skin. My leg feels like a farm animal, which suggests I haven't shaved in at least a week, but my chin is bare, which would put me in this bed for less than two days. My body hair isn't making any sense.

I hear nurses' voices in conversation coming from what I imagine is the hallway outside my room. I hear something else. It's not the machine that may or may not be keeping me alive, not the nurses' chatter, not even the faint buzz of the fluorescent light. I hold my breath and listen. It's Bob's snore!

I turn my head, and there he is, asleep in a chair in front of the beige curtain.

"Bob?"

He opens his eyes. He sees me seeing him and pops upright.

"You're awake," he says.

"What happened?"

"You were in a car accident."

"Am I okay?"

He looks at the top of my head and then into my eyes and purposefully not at the top of my head.

"You're going to be fine."

His expression reminds me of what happens to his face

when he's watching the Red Sox. It's bottom of the ninth, two outs, the count is 3 and 2, there's nobody on, and they're four runs down. He wants to believe that they can still win, but he knows they've probably already lost. And it's breaking his heart.

I touch the staples on my head.

"They did surgery, to relieve the pressure. The doctor said you did really well."

His voice shakes as he says this. Not only are the Sox losing, they're playing the Yankees.

"How long have I been here?"

"Eight days. They had you sedated. You've been asleep for most of it."

Eight days. I've been unconscious for eight days. I touch my bald head again.

"I must look horrible."

"You're beautiful."

Oh please. I'm about to tease him for being so corny when he starts crying, and I'm stunned silent. In the ten years that I've known and loved him, I've never seen him cry. I've seen him tear up—when the Red Sox won the World Series in 2004 and when our babies were born—but I've never seen him cry. I'm an easy crier. I cry watching the news, whenever anyone sings the National Anthem, when someone's dog dies, when I get overwhelmed at work, when I get overwhelmed at home. And now when Bob cries.

"I'm sorry, I'm so sorry," I say, weeping with him.

"Don't be sorry."

"I'm sorry."

I reach over and touch his wet, contorted face. I can tell he's struggling to pull his emotions back in, but he's like a shaken bottle of champagne, and I just popped the cork. Only nobody's celebrating.

"Don't be sorry. Just don't leave me, Sarah."

"Look at me," I say, pointing to my head. "Do I look like I'm going anywhere?"

He laughs and wipes his nose with his sleeve.

"I'm going to be fine," I say with teary determination.

We nod and squeeze hands, agreeing to a certainty we both know nothing about.

"Do the kids know?" I ask.

"I told them you're away for work. They're good, business as usual."

Good. I'm glad he didn't tell them that I'm in the hospital. No need to scare them. I'm normally home with them for the hour or two before school and for the last hour of their day, but it's also normal for there to be times when I have to work late and miss seeing them before they go to bed. And they're also used to my frequent travel schedule and me being entirely away for many days at a time. Still, when I travel, I'm not usually gone for more than a week. I wonder how long I'd need to be here for them to really wonder where I am.

"Does work know?"

"Yes, they sent most of the cards. They said not to worry about anything and to get better."

"What cards?"

"Over there, taped to the wall."

I look over at the wall, but I don't see anything taped to it. They must be on the wall behind the curtain.

"How long do I need to stay here?"

"I don't know. How are you feeling?" he asks.

My head is no longer on fire, and it surprisingly doesn't hurt much. I'm sore all over, though, like how I imagine a boxer must feel after a fight. The boxer who lost. I also have intense cramping in my leg. I've noticed that sometimes there is some sort of device on my leg that massages the muscles, which helps. And I have no energy. Just talking to Bob these past few minutes has tuckered me out.

"Honestly?"

"Yeah," he says, and I can tell he's bracing himself for something gruesome.

"I'm starving."

He smiles, relieved.

"What do you feel like having? Anything you want."

"How about soup?" I suggest, thinking soup is probably safe. I'm not sure if I'm allowed to eat anything I want yet.

"You got it. I'll be right back."

He leans over and kisses my chapped lips. I wipe the tears off his cheek and chin and smile. Then he disappears behind the ugly beige curtain.

It's just me and the fluorescent light again. The fluorescent light, the beeping and whirring, and the beige curtain. And somewhere behind the curtain, wonderful get-well cards from work on the wall.

CHAPTER 8

"What's the matter, Sarah, you don't want your lunch?" asks the nurse.

I've been staring at yet another bowl of chicken noodle soup for a while wondering how to tackle it. It smells good. I'm sure it smells infinitely better than it will taste, and it looks a bit congealed now, but I'm starving. I want to eat it.

"I don't have a spoon."

The nurse looks at my tray and then back up at me.

"How about the brownie?" she asks.

I look at the tray I've been keeping company and then back up at her.

"What brownie?"

Seemingly out of nowhere, the nurse produces a spoon in

her hand and plunks a cellophane-wrapped brownie on the tray next to the bowl of soup. I stare at her as if she's about to pull a quarter out from behind my ear.

"You didn't see these on your tray?" she asks, handing me the spoon.

"They weren't on my tray."

"But you see them now," she says, more conclusive than curious.

"Uh-huh."

I slurp a spoonful of broth. I was right. The soup is dishwater. I move on to the brownie. Chocolate is always edible.

"I'll be back with Dr. Kwon in a few minutes," she says.

Okay. Can you abracadabra me a glass of milk when you do?

An Asian man in a white lab coat is standing at the foot of my bed holding a clipboard, clicking and unclicking his ballpoint pen as he peruses the pages of what I assume is my medical chart. His face is hairless, smooth, gorgeous. His face could be eighteen. But I'm guessing this is Dr. Kwon, my doctor, in which case he'd better have age-defying genetics and be at least thirty.

"Sarah, good to see you awake. How are you feeling?"

Anxious, tired, scared.

"Good."

He clicks his pen and writes something down. Oh, I'm being interviewed. I'd better concentrate. Whatever he's testing me on, I want to get an A. I want to go home. I want to get back to work.

"How would you say I'm doing?" I ask.

"Good. Things look pretty good considering. You came in pretty banged up. You had a depressed skull fracture and some bleeding on your brain. We had to go in and drain it. We got it all, but with the bleed and the inflammation, you sustained some damage. Your scan shows you've lost some real estate. But you're lucky the insult was on the right and not the left, or you probably wouldn't be talking to me right now."

I think his answer started with "good," but I'm having a hard time hearing any semblance of "good" in any of the words he uttered after that, even as I play it back. "Brain damage." That sounds like the opposite of "good" to me. I think he also said "lucky." I feel dizzy.

"Can you get my husband? I want him to hear this with me."

"I'm right here," says Bob.

I turn to see him, but he's not there. The only people in the room are me and the handsome Dr. Kwon.

"Why are you looking at the chair? I'm over here," says Bob.

"Bob? I can't find you."

"Stand on the other side of me," says Dr. Kwon.

"There you are!" I say, like we're playing a game of peek-a-boo.

Weird that I couldn't see him a second ago. Maybe my vision was affected by the accident. Maybe he was standing too far back. Dr. Kwon adjusts my bed so that I'm sitting upright.

"Sarah, focus on my nose and tell me when you see my finger."

He's holding his index finger up near my ear.

"I see it."

"How about now?"

"Yes."

"Now?"

"No."

"How about now?"

"No."

"Is she blind?" asks Bob.

Of course I'm not blind. What kind of crazy question is that? Dr. Kwon flashes a light into my eyes. I study his black coffee eyes as he studies something about mine.

"Follow my light. Good. No, the areas of her brain responsible for vision weren't damaged, and her eyes look fine."

He pulls out a sheet of paper from his clipboard, places it on my tray table, wheels the table in front of me, and hands me a pen. Uppercase and lowercase letters are scattered across the page.

"Sarah, can you circle all the A's for me?"

I do this.

"Are you sure you've found them all?" he asks.

I check my work.

"Yes."

He pulls out another sheet.

"Can you draw a vertical line through the middle of each of these horizontal lines?"

I divide the nine lines in half. I look up, ready to ace the next puzzle.

"All done? Okay, let's move this tray out of the way. Can you hold both arms straight out for me, palms up?"

I do this.

"Are you holding both arms out?"

"Yes."

"Is she paralyzed?" asks Bob.

Again, what kind of nonsensical question is that to ask? Did he not just see me move? Dr. Kwon taps my arm and leg with a small rubber hammer.

"No, she's got some weakness on the left, but that should come back with time and rehab. She has Left Neglect. It's a pretty common condition for patients who've suffered damage to the right-hemisphere, usually from a hemorrhage or stroke. Her brain isn't paying attention to anything on her left. 'Left' doesn't exist to her."

"What do you mean, 'it doesn't exist'?" asks Bob.

"Exactly that. It's not there to her. She won't notice you if you're standing to her left, she won't touch the food on the left side of her plate, and she might not even believe that her left arm and leg belong to her."

"Because 'left' doesn't exist to her?" asks Bob.

"Right," says Dr. Kwon. "I mean, yes."

"Will it come back?" asks Bob.

"It might, it might not. With some patients, we see symptoms resolve over the first few weeks as inflammation goes down, and the brain heals. But with others, it persists, and the best you can do is learn to live with it."

"With no left," says Bob.

"Yes."

"She doesn't seem to notice that it's missing," says Bob.

"Yes, that's true for most patients in the acute phase immediately following the injury. She's mostly unaware of her unawareness. She's not aware that the left side of everything is missing. To her, it's all there, and everything is normal."

I may be unaware of some unawareness, but Dr. Kwon and Bob seem unaware that I'm still here.

"Do you know you have a left hand?" Bob asks me.

"Of course I know I have a left hand," I say, embarrassed that he keeps asking these ridiculous questions.

But then I consider this ridiculous question. Where is my left hand? I have no idea. Oh my God, where is my left hand? How about my left foot? That's also missing. I wiggle my right toes. I try to send the same message to my left foot, but my brain returns it to sender. Sorry, no such address.

"Bob, I know I have a left hand, but I have no idea where it is."

CHAPTER 9

I've been in the hospital for twelve days now, and I've moved from the ICU to the hospital's neurology unit where I've been Dr. Kwon's pet guinea pig for the past couple of days. He wants to learn more about Left Neglect before they move me out of this wretched room and over to rehab. He says there's not a lot understood about this condition, which is news that I find more than a little depressing. But maybe he'll learn something from me that will advance the clinical understanding of Neglect. And maybe that will help me. I'm also happy to cooperate because learning more about my condition only involves questions, puzzles, pen, and paper and does not involve needles, blood draws, or brain scans. And it keeps me occupied for a good while, time that would otherwise be filled with nothing but obsessive worrying about work, missing Bob and the kids, and staring at the fluorescent light and peeled paint on the ceiling. So Dr. Kwon and I have been spending lots of quality time together.

As I answer questions and do word searches, I try to join Dr. Kwon and find it oddly fascinating instead of hopelessly terrifying that I never notice or include anything on the left. I'm not even aware that I've ignored anything until Dr. Kwon or one of my therapists or nurses tells me what I've missed. Then, when I realize the magnitude of what isn't there to me, instead of dissolving in a puddle of my own tears or wailing *This is bad, this is really, really bad,* I force the most positive thing I can think of. Usually something like, *Wow.* It feels like the mayor of Doomsville is offering me a key to the city, but I'm doing my best to stay out of town.

I do enjoy the drawing tests. It feels like a million years ago that I carried an artist's sketchpad everywhere I went. I majored in economics in college, but I took just as many courses in graphic design, art, and art history. I try imagining where in my cluttered attic those pads might be stored, but I can't find them. Maybe they're on the left. I hope I didn't throw them out.

Dr. Kwon asks me to draw a flower, a clock, a house, a face.

"You're good," he says.

"Thanks."

"Did you draw a whole face?"

"Yes."

I look at my picture with pride and love. I drew Lucy. As I admire her features, doubt creeps into my consciousness.

"Didn't I?" I ask.

"No. How many eyes do people have?"

"Two."

"Did you draw two?"

I look at my picture of Lucy.

"I think so."

He clicks his pen and writes. He's writing something negative about my drawing of Lucy Goose, and no one should do that. I push the paper toward him.

"You draw a face," I say.

He draws a simple smiley, done in two seconds.

"Did you draw a whole face?" I ask.

"Yes."

I click my pen as emphatically as I can, high in the air, and then pretend to write my evaluation on an invisible clipboard.

"What are you writing, Dr. Nickerson?" he asks, feigning deep concern.

"Well, don't faces have ears, eyebrows, hair? I'm afraid you have a very serious but fascinating condition, doctor."

He laughs and adds a tongue sticking out from the bottom of the line for the mouth.

"True, true. Our brains normally don't need every piece of information to assume a whole. Like our blind spot. We all have a blind spot where our optic nerve leaves the retina, but we don't normally notice this blank space in our field of vision because our brains fill in the picture," Dr. Kwon says. "That's probably what you're doing. You're relying on only the right half to assume a whole, and your brain is unconsciously filling in the blanks. Wonderful observation. Truly fascinating."

While I'm enjoying his attention and flattery, I know that what excites a nerdy doctor will probably be perceived as freakish and scary by the world outside this room. I want to draw both of Lucy's eyes. I want to hug Charlie with two hands, kiss both of Linus's feet, and see all of Bob. And I can't get away with reading only the right half of an Excel spreadsheet. I need my brain to see the left again, wherever it is, and stop making huge assumptions. Assumptions only get everyone into a lot of trouble.

Today's lunch is chicken, rice, and apple juice. The chicken needs salt, the rice needs soy sauce, and the apple juice could use a generous shot of vodka. But I apparently have high blood pressure, and I'm not allowed any salt or alcohol. I eat and drink every bland thing they bring me. I need to get my strength back. I'm moving to the rehab hospital tomorrow, and from what I hear, it's going to be a lot of work. I can't wait. As much as I like Dr. Kwon, this guinea pig wants out of her cage forever.

Dr. Kwon comes in to check on me before his rounds.

"How was your lunch?" he asks.

"Good."

"Did you use the knife to cut your chicken?"

"No, I used the side of the fork."

Click. He writes down this fascinating piece of data.

"Did you eat everything?"

"Uh-huh."

"Are you full?"

I shrug. I'm not, but I don't want seconds.

"What if I told you there was a chocolate bar on your plate?" he asks, smiling.

I've got to hand it to him for trying. Chocolate is definitely the right bait to use with me. But I don't need an incentive. I'm highly motivated. It's not that I'm not trying to see what he sees.

"I don't see it."

Maybe I can feel it. I wipe the clean, white plate with the palm of my hand. There's nothing there. Not one kernel of rice, not one morsel of chocolate.

"Try turning your head to the left."

I stare at the plate.

"I don't know how to do that. I don't know how to get to where you're asking me to go. It's not a place I can turn to or look at. It's like if you told me to turn and look at the middle of my back. I believe the middle of my back exists, but I have no idea how to see it."

He writes this down and nods while he writes.

"Intellectually, I understand that there's a left side of the plate, but it's not part of my reality. I can't look at the left side of the plate because it's not there. There is no left side. I feel like I'm looking at the whole plate. I don't know, it's frustrating, I can't describe it."

"I think you just did."

"But is there really chocolate there?"

"Yup, the kind Bob brought yesterday."

Lake Champlain. The best. Without understanding how this might work, I grab the top of the plate and rotate it to the bottom. Tada! Almond Butter Crunch. Bob's the best.

"That's cheating!" says Dr. Kwon.

"Totally fair," I say, chewing a sublime mouthful.

"Okay, but answer this. Where did that chocolate come from?"

I know he wants me to say "the left." But there is no left.

"Heaven."

"Sarah, think about it. It came from the left side of the plate, which is now on the right, and the right, which you just saw, so you know it exists, is now on the left."

He might as well have just said something about Pi times the square root of infinity. I don't care where the right side of the plate went. I'm eating my favorite chocolate, and I'm moving to rehab tomorrow.

It's been two weeks since the accident, and Bob's been taking a lot of time off from work to be here with me, which can't be good for his chances of surviving if there's another layoff. I told him he shouldn't be here so much. He told me to be quiet and not worry about him.

My favorite test aside from drawing pictures is called the Fluff Test. Rose, the physical therapist, tapes cotton balls all over me and then asks me to remove them. I love it because I imagine I must look like one of Charlie's or Lucy's art projects, like the snowmen they'll probably make in school in a few weeks. God, I miss my kids.

I pluck off the cotton "snow" and let Rose know when I'm done.

"Did I get them all?"

"Nope."

"Close?"

"Nope."

"Did I get any on the left?"

Wherever that is.

"Nope."

Weird. I truly believed I found them all. I don't feel any on me.

"Hold on a sec," says Bob, who has been sitting in the visitor's chair, observing.

Bob holds up his iPhone and says, "Say cheese."

He clicks a photo and shows me the LCD display. I'm stunned. In the picture of me on the screen, I'm covered head to foot in cotton balls. Crazy. That must be the left side of me. And there's my arm and leg. I'm beyond relieved to see that they're still there. I'd started to believe that they'd been amputated and no one had the courage to tell me.

I notice my head in the picture. It's not only covered in cotton balls, it's not shaved. My hair, aside from looking oily and matted, is exactly as I remember it. I reach up to touch it but feel only bald head and the Braille-like bumps created by my incision scars (a neurology resident removed the staples a couple of days ago). According to the picture, I have a full head of hair, but according to what my hand feels, I'm completely bald. This is too bizarre.

"I still have hair?"

"They only shaved the right side. The left still has all your hair," says Rose.

I stare at the picture while I run my fingers along my scalp. I love my hair, but this can't look pretty.

"You have to shave the rest," I say.

Rose looks over at Bob like she's checking for another vote.

"It's the best of the two looks, Bob, don't you think?"

He says nothing, but his lack of response tells me that he agrees. And I know it's like asking him, *Which do you like better, church or the mall?* He's not a fan of either.

"Can we do it now before I chicken out?"

"I'll go get the razor," says Rose.

As we wait for Rose to come back, Bob stands and checks email on his iPhone. I haven't checked my email since I've been here. They won't let me. My heart races when I think about it. My inbox must have a thousand emails waiting for me. Or maybe Jessica has been forwarding everything to Richard or Carson. That would make more sense. We're in the middle of recruiting, my most critical time of year. I need to get back to make sure we get the right people and place them where they'll best fit.

"Bob, where'd you go?"

"I'm over by the window."

"Okay, honey, you might as well be in France. Can you come over here where I can see you?"

"Sorry."

Rose comes back with the electric shaver.

"You sure?" she asks.

"Yes."

The shaver has been buzzing for a few seconds when I see my mother walk into the room. She takes one look at me and gasps as if she's beholding Frankenstein. She covers her mouth with her hands and starts hyperventilating. Here comes the hysteria.

"When did you tell her?" I ask Bob.

"Two days ago."

I'm impressed she made it here in two days. She doesn't like to leave her house much, and she panics if she has to leave the Cape. It's gotten worse as she's gotten older. I don't think she's been over the Sagamore Bridge since Lucy was born. She's never even seen Linus.

"Oh my God, oh my God, is she dying?"

"I'm not dying. I'm getting my hair cut."

She looks much older than I remember. She doesn't color her hair chestnut brown anymore; she's let it go silver. She wears glasses now. And her face is sagging, like her frown finally became too hefty and is pulling her entire face down.

"Oh my God, Sarah, your head. Oh my God, oh my God—"

"Helen, she's going to be okay," says Bob.

Now she's sobbing. I don't need this.

"Mom, please," I say. "Go stand over by the window."

CHAPTER 10

There are forty beds in the neuro unit at Baldwin Rehabilitation Center. I know this because only two of the forty beds are in private rooms, and insurance doesn't cover these. You have to pay out of pocket for privacy.

Bob made sure I got one of the "singles" with a window to the right of the bed. We both thought that a view of life outside the confines of my room would be good for my morale. We didn't realize that this simple request needed to be more specific.

On this sunny day, I'm staring out the window at a prison. My view is of nothing but brick and steel bars. The irony of this is not lost on me. Apparently, on the other side of the neuro unit, the patients have a view of the Leonard Zakim Bridge, a work of stunning architectural achievement by day and a breathtaking, illuminated masterpiece by night. Of course, all of those rooms are "doubles." Everything's a trade-off. Be careful what you ask for. I'm a brain-injured cliché.

Whatever I have to do here, I'm ready for it. Work hard, do my homework, get an A, get back home to Bob and the kids, and back to work. Back to normal. I'm determined to recover 100 percent. One hundred percent has always been my goal in everything, unless extra credit is involved, and then I shoot higher. Thank God I'm a competitive, type A perfectionist. I'm convinced I'm going to be the best traumatic brain injury patient Baldwin has ever seen. But they won't be seeing me for very long because I also plan to recover faster than anyone here would predict. I wonder what the record is.

But every time I try to get a concrete sense for how long it might take for someone with Left Neglect to fully recover, I get a vague and dissatisfying answer.

"It's highly variable," said Dr. Kwon.

"What's the average time?" I asked.

"We don't really know."

"Huh. Okay, well, what's the range?"

"Some recover spontaneously within a couple of weeks, some respond to strategies and retraining by six months, some longer."

"So what predicts who will get better in the two weeks versus longer?"

"Nothing we know of."

I continue to be astounded by how little the medical profession knows about my condition. I guess that's why they call it the *practice* of medicine.

It's now 9:15 a.m., and I'm watching Regis and some woman. It used to be Regis and some other woman. I can't remember her name. It's been a long time since I've watched morning television. Martha, my physical therapist, has just come in and introduced herself. She has streaky blond hair pulled into a tight ponytail and four diamond stud earrings crowded onto her earlobe. She's built like a rugby player. She looks no-nonsense, tough. Good. Bring it on.

"So when do you think I'll be able to go back to work?" I ask while she reads my chart.

"What do you do?"

"I'm the vice president of human resources at a strategy consulting firm."

She laughs with her mouth closed and shakes her head.

"Let's concentrate on getting you to walk and use the bathroom."

"Do you think two weeks?" I ask.

She laughs and shakes her head again. She looks long and hard at my bald head.

"I don't think you fully understand what's happened to you," she says.

I look long and hard at her ear.

"I do actually. I understand exactly what's *already* happened. What I don't understand is what is *going* to happen."

"Today, we're going to try sitting and walking."

For the love of God, can we please talk big picture? My goals are more expansive than watching Regis and going for a stroll to the bathroom.

"Okay, but when do you think I'll be back to normal?"

She grabs the remote, clicks off the TV, and fixes me with a stern look before she answers, like the kind I give Charlie when I really need him to hear me.

"Maybe never."

I do not like this woman.

My mother has figured out my little Stand to My Left trick and has perched herself on the visitor's chair to my right like a nervous hen on a nest of precious eggs. Even though I don't have a medical excuse now, I'm still trying to pretend she's not here. But she's sitting smack in the middle of my field of vision, so she's unavoidable. And every time I look at her, she's got this anxious expression carved onto her face that makes me want to scream. I suppose it's the sort of worried expression that would naturally form on anyone forced to sit next to me or the motorcycle accident guy next door with the mangled face and no legs or the young woman down the hall who had a postpartum stroke and can't say her new baby's name. It's the kind of concerned, mixed-with-a-spoonful-of-horror-and-a-dollop-of-dread look that anyone might have if forced to sit next to any patient in the neuro unit. It can't be that she's actually worried about me. She hasn't worried about me in thirty years. So, although it bugs me, I get her expression. What I don't get is who's forcing her to sit here.

Martha comes in and places a stainless steel basin on my tray.

"Helen, will you go sit on Sarah's other side?" she asks.

My mother pops up and disappears. Maybe I judged Martha too quickly.

"Okay, Sarah, lie back, here we go. Ready?" she asks.

But before I can give my consent to whatever it is we're about to do, she places her strong hand on the side of my face and turns my head. And there's my mother again. Damn this woman.

"Here's a washcloth. Go up and down her arm with it, rub her hand, all her fingers."

"Should I wash her other arm, too?"

"No, we're not giving her a bath. We're trying to remind her brain that she has a left arm through the texture of the cloth, the temperature of the water, and her looking at her arm while this is happening. Her head is going to want to drift back over here. Just turn it back to the left like I did. Good?"

My mother nods.

"Good," Martha says and leaves us in a hurry.

My mother wrings the cloth out over the basin and starts wiping my arm. I feel it. The cloth is coarse and the water is lukewarm. I see my forearm, my wrist, my hand as she touches each body part. And yet, although I feel it happening to me, it's almost as if I'm watching my mother wash someone else's arm. It's as if the cloth against my skin is telling my brain, *Feel that? That's your left shoulder. Feel that? That's your left elbow.* But another part of my brain, haughty and determined to get in the last word, keeps retorting, *Ignore this foolishness! You don't have a left anything! There is no left!*

"How does this feel?" asks my mother after several minutes.

"It's a bit cold."

"Sorry, okay, hold on, don't move."

She springs up and scurries into the bathroom. I stare at the prison and daydream. I wonder if she'd be fetching warm water for me if I were over there. Without warning, her hand is on my face, and she turns my head. She starts rubbing my arm again. The water's too hot.

"You know," I say, "Bob really needs to get to work on time. He shouldn't be driving you in here in the morning."

"I drove myself."

Baldwin sits in the eye of a colossal mass transit tornado, a difficult destination to reach for even the bravest and most seasoned Boston drivers. Add rush hour. And my mother.

"You did?"

"I typed the address into that map computer, and I did exactly what the lady told me to do."

"You drove Bob's car?"

"It has all the car seats."

I feel like I missed a meeting.

"You drove the kids to school?"

"So Bob could get to work on time. We've switched cars."

"Oh."

"I'm here to help you."

I'm still catching up to the fact that she drove my kids to school and day care and then into Boston by herself from Welmont during rush hour, and now I have to wrap my brain around this doozy. I try to remember the last time she helped me with anything. I think she poured me a glass of milk in 1984.

She's holding my left hand in hers, our fingers interlaced, and her hand feels familiar, even after all this time. I'm three, and my hand is in hers when she helps me climb stairs, when we sing "Ring Around the Rosy," when I have a splinter. Her hands are available, playful, and skilled. After Nate died, at first she held my hand a little tighter. I'm seven, and my hand is in hers when we cross the street, when she leads me through a crowded parking lot, when she paints my nails. Her hands are confident and safe. And then I'm eight, and my hand must be too awkward to hold along with all that grief, so she just lets go. Now I'm thirty-seven, and my hand is in hers.

"I need to go to the bathroom," I say.

"Let me get Martha."

"I'm fine. I can do it."

Now, since the accident, I have yet to get up and use the bathroom on my own, so I don't know why I suddenly feel like I'm perfectly capable of this. Maybe it's because I feel normal, and I have to pee. I don't feel like I'm paying attention to only half of me or half of my mother or half of the bathroom. I don't feel like anything's missing. Until I take that first left step.

I'm not sure where the bottom of my left foot is relative to the ground, and I can't tell if my knee is straight or bent, and then I think it might be hyperextended, and after a shocking and herky-jerky second, I step forward with my right foot. But my center of gravity is wildly off, and the next thing I know, I go crashing to the floor.

"Sarah!"

"I'm okay."

I taste blood. I must've cut my lip.

"Oh my God, don't move, I'll go get Martha!"

"Just help me up."

But she's already out the door.

I'm lying on the cold floor, trying to imagine how to get myself up, licking my wounded lip, and thinking that it might take longer than two weeks to get back to work. I wonder who's handling the Harvard recruiting for me. I hope it's not Carson. And I wonder who's overseeing annual evaluations. That's a huge project. I should be tackling that right now. My shoulder's throbbing. I wonder what's taking my mother so long.

Since giving birth to Linus, it's become embarrassingly difficult for me to contain a full bladder. Much to Bob's annoyance, I can no longer "hold it until we get there," and I have to beg him to pull over at least once whenever we're in the car for more than an hour. I drink twenty ounces of coffee at a time at work, which means I often spend the last ten minutes of any hour-long meeting tapping my feet under the table like I'm an Irish step dancer, consumed with a desperate plan to sprint to the nearest bathroom the second it ends.

I've abandoned any delusions I had of getting up on my own and am now devoting 100 percent of my energy and focus on not peeing right here on the floor. Thank God my bladder or whatever part of me I'm concentrating on is in the center of me and not somewhere on the left. I pray I don't sneeze.

My mother finally rushes in with Martha behind her. My mother looks frantic and pale. Martha sizes me up with her hands on her hips.

"Well, that was impulsive," she says.

I can think of a few choice things I could do or say right now that would be truly impulsive, but this woman is in charge of my care, and I need to get to the bathroom before I pee, and I need to get back to work before I lose my job, so I bite my bloody lip.

"I should've helped her," says my mother.

"No, that's not your job. That's my job. Next time, press the call button. Let me be the therapist, and you be the mother."

"Okay," says my mother, like she's just taken an oath.

Be the mother. Like she has any idea what that means. Be the mother. All at once, those three words irk me and amuse me and pinch a delicate part of me. But most of all, they distract me, and I pee all over the floor.

CHAPTER 11

It's early in the morning, before breakfast, before any of the therapists have started working on me, probably even before the kids have gotten dressed at home. And Bob is here.

"Can you see me now?" asks Bob.

I see the prison, the window, the visitor's chair, the TV.

"No," I say.

"Turn your head."

I turn my head. I see the prison.

"No, the other way."

"There is no other way."

"Yes, there is. Turn your head to the left. I'm standing over here."

I close my eyes and imagine Bob standing. In my mind's eye, he's wearing a black, long-sleeve, crewneck tee and jeans, even though he never wears jeans to work. He's got his arms folded, and he hasn't shaved. I open my eyes and turn my head. I see the prison.

"I can't."

"Yes, you can. It's simple."

"It's not."

"I don't understand why you can't just turn your head."

"I did."

"To the left."

"There is no left."

I hear him sigh in frustration.

"Honey, tell me everything you see in here," I say.

"You, the bed, the window, the chair, the table, the flowers, the cards, the pictures of me and the kids, the bathroom, the door, the television."

"Is that everything?"

"Pretty much."

"Okay, now what if I told you that everything you see is only half of everything that's really here? What if I told you to turn your head and look at the other half? Where would you look?"

He doesn't say anything. I wait. I imagine Bob standing in his tee-shirt and jeans, searching.

"I don't know," he says.

"Exactly."

*

Ellen is dancing to the Black Eyed Peas. She's hysterical. Much better than Regis and what's her name. I wish I could get up and boogie with her, but I've learned my lesson after yesterday's misadventure to the bathroom.

Bob left for work over an hour ago, and now my mother is here, hovering next to me in "her" chair. She's wearing a lavender fleece sweatsuit and white New Balance sneakers. She looks like she's ready for a jog or an aerobics class at a gym. I doubt she's ever done either. I catch her watching me instead of Ellen, and I feel like I just made eye contact with a cornered sparrow. She looks down and inspects her sneakers, shifts in her chair, turns to see what's going on outside the window, shifts in her chair, throws me a skittish glance, darts her focus to the TV, and fusses with her hair. She needs some sort of project.

"Mom, will you go get me a hat?"

"Which one?"

I have only one non-ski hat that I can think of, a huge straw sunhat, but I'm clearly not on a tropical vacation or sitting poolside. I own plenty of bandanas and scarves and could use one of those to cover my head, but I don't want to look like a cancer patient. I want to look normal, like someone who could theoretically go back to work in two weeks. And I don't want to scare the kids.

"Can you go buy me one?"

"Where?"

"The Prudential Mall."

She blinks a few times. I know she wants a way out of this

proposed field trip. *I don't know where that is, I don't know what kind you want, I don't want to lose my seat.*

"I need an address," she says.

"Eight hundred Boylston Street."

"Are you sure that's right?"

"Yes, I work there."

"I thought you worked at some business company."

She says this like she's busted me in a big lie, like I really work at the Gap, just as she's suspected all along.

"Berkley's in the mall."

"Oh."

I wish I could go myself. I'd pick out something hip and pretty at Neiman Marcus or Saks Fifth Avenue, and then I'd swing into work, check in with Jessica and Richard, find out what's going on with staff evaluations, correct any misguided decisions Carson is making about our next generation of consultants, and maybe sit in on a meeting or two before coming back.

"But you have therapy in a few minutes," she says.

"You can miss it."

"I need to see what they do so I can help you."

"I really need a hat before the kids get here. I don't want them to see me like this, and there might be traffic. You can sit in on therapy tomorrow."

Or the next day. Or the day after that.

"You sure?" she asks.

"Yes, really."

"Eight hundred Boylston Street," she says.

"You got it."

"And you'll tell me what happened in therapy when I get back."

"I'll fill you in on everything."

Or at least half of everything.

My mother writes the address down on a receipt she finds in her pocketbook, I reassure her that she has the exact address two more times, and she finally leaves. I relax and return to watching Ellen. She's smiling and chatting with someone named Jim. He sounds like Jim Carrey. After a couple of minutes, it occurs to me that I should be able to see Jim Carrey. But I can't. I try. But I still can't. I can only see Ellen. What if I can't ever see who Ellen's talking to? What if rehabilitation doesn't work? What if this never goes away? What if I can't ever go back to work? I can't live like this.

I don't want to watch Ellen anymore. I look out the window. It's a clear, sunny day, and in the glary reflection, I see my hideous bald head. I don't want to look at me anymore, but it's either Ellen, my hideous bald head, or the prison. Ellen's guest, whoever he is, says something that cracks her up, and Ellen laughs as I close my eyes and cry.

"Morning, Sarah."

The chair is empty. The TV is off. The voice sounds familiar, but I can't place it.

"Hello?" I ask.

"I'm over here."

I turn my head. I see the prison.

"Okay, we'll work on it," says the woman's voice.

The woman then materializes in my mother's chair, and it's Heidi, Ben's mom. That's a bit odd. I wouldn't expect her to take time out of her day to visit me. Maybe she has something to tell me about Charlie and school. God, I hope he's not in trouble.

"So, you don't get enough of me at Before the Bell?" she asks, smiling.

I return the smile, but I don't understand what we're happy about.

"Heidi, thanks so much for coming to see me."

"No need to thank me. I'm just doing what the board says. You're my eleven o'clock."

Huh?

"I'm your OT."

Again, huh?

"Your occupational therapist. This is what I do."

"Oh!"

The scrubs, the purple Crocs, the photo ID hung on the end of the lanyard around her neck. I always assumed she was some kind of nurse but never asked what she did or where she worked.

"How're you doing?" she asks.

"Good."

She stares at me, waiting, like I'm a troubled teen denying that the drugs are mine. I have a traumatic brain injury, my head is shaved, I can't walk because I have no idea where my left leg is, and she's here because she's my occupational therapist, and I'm her 11:00. "Good" isn't even close to a real answer.

"Actually, not so good. I don't want to be here. I don't want to have this condition. I just want to go home."

"Hey, I don't want you here either. As much as I like having the chance to finally get to know you better, I'd rather do that in my living room over a bottle of wine."

I smile, appreciating Heidi's kindness, but only for the slightest moment because now I'm too busy expanding on how "not so good" I am.

"I've missed so much work, so many important deadlines. I have to get back to work. And my kids. Charlie's struggling in school, and I miss tucking Lucy into bed, and Linus. I really have to get back home."

My voice starts to crack when I say Lucy's name, and it splits wide open when I get to Linus. Tears are rolling down my face, and I don't even try to stop them. Heidi hands me a tissue.

"I want my life back."

"We'll get you back. You gotta stay positive. I saw Charlie and Lucy yesterday before school, and they're doing fine. Have they seen you yet?"

"They're coming today for the first time."

It's been two and a half weeks since the accident, and Bob said that Charlie and Lucy have started asking, "When is Mommy coming home from work?" I wish I knew. I also wish they didn't have to see me here, like this, bald and disabled in a rehabilitation hospital, but I can't wait any longer to see them.

"Good. And I just met your mom. She's so sweet. She wanted to know where she could go buy you a hat."

Of course she did.

"Where did you tell her?"

"I sent her to the Pru."

"Did she ask for the address?"

"Yup, she's all set."

She's something.

"So, we're going to retrain you to pay attention to the left. Ready to get to work?"

"Yes."

I blow out a deep breath.

"Can you tell me what time it is?" she asks.

"Eleven o'clock."

"And how do you know that?"

"Because you told me I'm your eleven o'clock."

She laughs.

"I'm gonna have to be on my toes with you. I'm actually running a little behind today. Can you tell me how late I am?"

"I don't see a clock in here."

"Well, you're wearing a beautiful watch."

"Oh yeah."

My Cartier watch. Platinum, crown set with round-cut diamonds, and Roman numerals on the face.

"Can you tell me what it says?"

"I can't find it."

"Can you feel it on your wrist?"

"No."

"How did you put it on?"

"My mother did it for me."

"Okay, let's find your watch."

She gets up and appears to leave the room, but I don't hear the open-and-close of the door. I wait for her to say something. She doesn't.

"You smell like coffee," I say.

"Good, you knew I was still here."

"I'd kill for a coffee right now."

"There's a Dunkin' Donuts in the lobby. You tell me what time it is, and I'll go get you one."

I inhale her coffee smell again, and my heart pumps a little faster in anticipation as I imagine the weight of the extra-large Styrofoam cup, warm in my hand, filled to the top with heavenly vanilla latte. Where the heck is my watch?

"I'm sitting on your left. Can you see me?"

"No."

"Follow my voice. Keep going, past the TV."

"I can't."

There isn't anything past the TV.

"Mmm, that coffee was sooo good," she says, teasing me with her breath on my face.

I try to visualize the coffee aroma emanating out from Heidi as a visible vapor trail. I'm a cartoon mouse sniffing out a huge piece of Swiss.

"I can't."

"Yes, you can. Follow my voice. Come on, look to the left."

"I feel like I'm looking at everything that's in the room. But I know you're in the room, so I can't be, but that's what it feels like."

What I perceive and what I understand to be true are at war inside my head, fighting to the death, giving me a colossal headache. Or maybe I just need a colossal coffee.

"Okay, let's try some stimulation. Do you feel this?"

"Yes."

"What does it feel like?"

"Tapping."

"Good. What am I tapping?"

"The back of my hand."

"The back of which hand?"

I look down at my right hand.

"My left?"

"Good. Now try to look at where I'm tapping."

I look down. My stomach bulges embarrassingly far onto my lap. I was hoping that since I apparently eat only half of the food on my plate, I might at least shed some pounds while I'm here. Even on the weirdest diet ever, I don't seem to be losing any weight.

"Sarah, you still with me? Look at what I'm tapping."

"I don't feel it anymore."

"Okay, let's change it up. How about now?"

I see something moving at the edge of the room, but it's

too blurry and impermanent to make out what it is. Then suddenly, it snaps into focus.

"I see your hand!"

"Look again."

"I see your hand moving up and down."

"Notice any details about the hand?"

Details about the hand. Let's see. It was hard enough just locating and identifying it, and now she wants details. I strain as hard as I can to keep her moving hand within my field of vision, stretching my concentration so uncomfortably far into the periphery that it feels like I'm trying to describe something on the back of my own head. I'm just about to give up when I notice that the hand is wearing an emerald-cut diamond ring and Cartier watch.

"Oh my God, that's *my* hand!"

"Good job, Sarah."

"I see my left hand!"

I sound like Lucy announcing to everyone that she tied her shoes all by herself.

"Good. Now what time does your watch say?"

Oh yeah. The goal. I'm so close to getting that coffee now, I can taste it. Read the watch. But while I was busy congratulating myself for seeing my left hand and getting excited about my imminent reward, something awful happened. My left hand is gone. I try doing whatever it is I did before to see it again, but I hadn't followed some prescribed set of methodical steps to find it, and I can't seem to replicate the experience. It just sort of magically appeared. And then disappeared.

"I lost my hand."

"Oh no, that's okay. That happens. Your brain is gonna have a hard time sustaining attention on the left side. We'll help you to stretch it out."

"I guess I should start wearing my watch on my right wrist."

"Okay, and how will you put it on?"

I stare at my right wrist and realize the impossibility of accomplishing that.

"My mother?"

"I think you should keep it on your left. This'll be a good exercise for us to use. And I know your mom is here to help you, and that's okay for now, but having her do it for you isn't a good long-term solution."

I couldn't agree more.

"But it would be nice to know the time," I say.

"How about using your cell phone?" she suggests.

I would love to use my cell phone, but I haven't used my cell phone since the crash because Bob won't give it to me. I keep begging him to bring it in for me. My calendar and email are in my phone. And all of my contacts. The same information was stored in my laptop as well, but my laptop was totaled in the accident along with the Acura. So I really need my phone.

But Bob keeps dodging me whenever I bring it up. *Oh, I can't find it. Oh, I forgot it. Oh, I'll get it tomorrow.* Oh, he's so transparent. He doesn't want me to spend any time focusing on work while I'm here. He thinks I should put work out of my mind and devote 100 percent of my mental energy to getting better. He also thinks that if I dabble in a little bit of work, it'll only stress me out, and I don't need any added stress right now.

While I agree with him to some extent, and I do work as hard as I can on whatever task the nurses and therapists ask me to perform, there's quite a lot of downtime here at Baldwin. I have some kind of therapy for three hours each day. And meals can also count as opportunities for learning. For example, Martha always hides my dessert on the left side of my tray (and when I can't find it, my mother, the good little enabler, retrieves it for me). So if I include meals, there's maybe another two hours. But that's it. Five hours a day. I could easily fit in some emails and phone calls without overdoing anything. A few calls a day might even reduce my stress levels.

"Bob won't give me my phone," I say, tattling on him.

Heidi walks over to my mother's chair.

"This it?" she asks, holding my cell phone in her hand.

"Yes! Where did you get it?"

"It was on the table to your left."

For the love of God. I wonder how long it's been sitting in the black hole next to me. I imagine Bob placing it there, thinking, *She can use it if she can find it.*

"Here," she says, handing over my long lost friend. "You didn't find the time, but you found your hand and saw your watch for a few seconds. I'm gonna go down and get you a coffee."

"Really?"

"Yup. What kind?"

"Vanilla latte. Extra large. Thank you so much."

"You got it. I could use another, too. We'll start with coffee in rehab and work our way to wine in my living room. Deal?"

"Deal."

"Okay, back in a minute."

I hear the open-and-close of the door, and I'm alone in my room. My mother's at the mall, Heidi's getting coffee, I've got my cell phone, and for a few brief moments, I was aware of my left hand. I smile. I may not be good yet, but I'd say I'm already a little better than not so good.

Now, where should I begin? I think I'll call Jessica first and catch up on what's happened since the accident. Then Richard. We'll need to come up with a strategy for how I can best work from here. Then Carson. I can't wait to hear their voices. I push the power button, but nothing happens. I push it again and again. Nothing. The battery's dead.

And I have no idea where the charger is.

CHAPTER 12

My mother has been gone forever. I can't imagine what could be taking her so long. It's a strange thing, to be wishing for my mother to come back to me. I stopped throwing pennies down that well a long time ago. But here I am, sitting up in my hospital bed, saying hello to Jessica and Richard, trying to act normal, wishing my mother would hurry up and get here. I need that damn hat.

Jessica hands me a huge and heavy box of chocolate peanut butter fudge, sits down in my mother's chair, and asks how I'm doing.

In my very best everyday, no-big-deal but assured voice, I say, "Good. Much better," and thank her for the fudge.

I offer them a piece, but they both say, "No, thanks."

I dig into the box, pick out the thickest cube, and pop the

whole thing into my mouth. Big mistake. Now I'm unable to start up a conversation through all that chocolate and peanut butter, and Jessica and Richard aren't offering anything. They're just watching me chew. The silence feels thicker and more awkward than the giant wad of fudge in my mouth. I try to chew faster.

The image of me reflected in Jessica's facial expression isn't pretty. The incision scars, the bruising, the overall baldness. I'm a horror movie, and she desperately wants to bury her face in someone's shoulder. Her good manners keep her from looking away, but there's no hiding that my appearance scares her. This is not the confident image of health and competency I was hoping to project. Where the heck is my mother with that hat? I finally swallow.

"Thanks so much for coming. I would've been in touch, but my cell phone was missing, and my laptop didn't survive the accident. If you messenger one over, I can easily work from here."

"Don't worry about work, Sarah. We'll take care of everything until you come back," says Richard.

Jessica nods, disgust and terror bleeding through her queasy smile.

"But I really need to stay on top of recruiting. It's crunch time. My inbox must be insane."

"We've rerouted all your email to Jessica and Carson. Let them handle crunch time," says Richard.

"Yeah, don't worry," says Jessica, looking about as worried as a person can look.

Of course, they had to forward all my mail. That makes sense. They didn't know how long I'd be out of commission, and the decisions pending can't wait. Time may be a petrified forest here at Baldwin, but it's a raging river rapid at Berkley.

"I know I'm not physically back in the office yet, but there's no reason why I can't work from here," I say to Richard, looking at Jessica.

Wait. I'm talking to Richard, but I'm looking at Jessica. I've just realized that I'm not seeing Richard. He must be standing to her right. My left. Fantastic. In my mind's eye, I picture Richard. He's about six foot two, salt-and-pepper hair, brown eyes, slender, almost gaunt, blue suit, red tie, wingtips. The slender part is new. From a slightly more distant memory bank, I can also pull up Richard before his divorce—fifty pounds heavier, pink fleshy face, cantaloupe-sized, middle-aged paunch, bigger suit, same red tie. I imagine the contents of his refrigerator in his bachelor apartment at the Ritz—a six-pack of Corona, a few limes, an expired quart of milk. I try to picture his skinny face and wonder if he looks half as freaked out as Jessica does.

"It's all being taken care of, Sarah," says the voice of Richard.

"What about annual reviews?"

"Carson's handling it."

"Even Asia?"

"He's got it."

"And India?"

"Yes."

"Alright, well, if he has any questions, or if he needs me for anything, tell him to call me."

"I will."

"I can at least phone in to internal meetings. Jessica, can you send me my calendar and plan to conference call me in?"

A cell phone rings. God, I miss my ring tone.

"Hello? Yup," says Richard's voice. "Good, tell him I'll call him back in five minutes."

Following some cue from Richard I didn't see, Jessica picks up her bag from the floor and places it on her lap. The credits are rolling, the movie's over, and she's ready to get the hell out of here.

"Sorry to have to cut this visit short, but I've got to return that call," says Richard.

"Sure, that's okay, thanks for coming. And don't worry. I'll be out of here soon."

"Good."

"But while I'm here, Jessica, can you send me a laptop and keep me updated on meetings?"

"Sarah, we miss you," says Richard. "But we want you to take your time and come back when you're a hundred percent. The sooner you get better, the sooner we can throw you back into the fire. Focus on you, don't worry about work. Everything's under control."

"I'll send you more fudge," says Jessica, like she's a parent negotiating with a child, offering some lame alternative to what the child wants but can't have.

"Is there anything else we can get for you?" asks Richard.

A computer, a cell phone charger, my calendar, some lifeline to my job.

"No, thanks."

"Get better. We miss you," says Jessica as she backs away. Richard now steps into view.

"Good to see you, Sarah."

He bends down over me and leans in to give me a polite kiss on the cheek. At least, this is what I assume. I'm already committed to returning his innocent peck on the cheek when his lips are surprisingly right in front of mine, and without time to think about what I'm doing, I plant a full-mouth smooch right on his lips.

I'm sure the wide-eyed astonishment on his face matches mine. My embarrassment races for an explanation. He must've been going for my left cheek, the cheek whose existence I'm only aware of in theory. This neurological logic satisfies me, but Richard is looking at me as if I've forgotten the nature of our relationship. Like I've gone insane.

"Okay, then, um," he says, clearing his throat. "Get well soon."

And they're both out the door.

Great. I've just terrified my assistant and sexually assaulted my boss.

I flip open the box of fudge and pick out another big piece. They don't want me back at all unless I've recovered 100 percent. I chew on this piece of information as I chew the piece of fudge. *What if I don't recover 100 percent?*

I stuff another piece of fudge into my mouth. *What if I don't recover 100 percent?* I eat another cube. I keep eating until I feel sick, but I still can't manage to answer the question, and I can't stop asking it, so I finish the box. Only the box still feels heavy. I shake it and hear and feel fudge bump against the side of the box. The left side. The side I have no awareness of. I shake the box again, this time like I'm trying to murder it, and a few squares stumble into view. I eat them.

What if I don't recover 100 percent?

CHAPTER 13

Please tell me there are others," I say.

My mother has just modeled the three hats she purchased for me at the mall. She's still wearing the third one—an absurdly large Victorian tea hat covered with a heaping pile of red roses—along with a slightly deflated smile.

"What do you mean? What's wrong with this one?"

"You look like Minnie Pearl."

"I do not."

The price tag is even dangling over the side of the brim.

"Fine. You look crazy."

"I have one just like this I wear to my Red Hat events."

She takes the hat off her head and twists it around in her lap, admiring it from every angle. She then smells the fake flowers, returns it to her head, cocks it to the side, and smiles at me as if to say, *What about now?* Yup, it's a hat made for a crazy lady.

"You really didn't get anything else?"

She gives me an apologetic shrug instead of an answer and holds up the other two options—a brown leather cowboy hat and a neon-pink ski hat.

"I felt rushed. It's always chilly in here, so I thought the fleece hat would be good, and Bob has some country music CDs in the car, so I thought you might like that style."

I wonder what could possibly have been her reasoning behind the Minnie Pearl. Because she thought I might be just like her? I'm too afraid of that answer to ask.

"I'll take the pink one."

Minus the fluorescent highlighter color, I'll at least feel like me in a fleece ski hat. Bob and I both love to ski. Bob's family owned a condo in North Conway, New Hampshire, and they used to spend every weekend from December to April on the slopes of Attitash and Cranmore. His happiest childhood memories are of racing his older brothers down a mountain. I, on the other hand, grew up on Cape Cod where the biggest hills are sand dunes, and we never vacationed over the bridge. I didn't discover skiing until I went to Middlebury College in Vermont, where it's practically part of the core curriculum.

My first day on skis was a painful, frozen, and exhausting lesson in humiliation, and the only reason I mustered up the courage to endure another day of pure torture was because I'd purchased a weekend ticket and wanted to get my money's worth. I had no real expectation of improving, never mind enjoying it. But on that second day, a miracle happened. Somehow my clumsy limbs knew where to go and when to go there, and down I went—on my skis and not on my bottom. And I've loved skiing ever since.

Bob and I bought our house in Cortland, Vermont, the year after we bought our house in Welmont. The additional mortgage payment has kept us from being able to afford a bigger house with an additional bedroom in Welmont, which we need if we ever hope to hire a live-in nanny, but it's been well worth the sacrifice. During the winter months, when we go from house to car to office and back again, and the air inside all of those places is overheated, recycled, and contaminated with flu virus, skiing on the weekends means two full days of breathing fresh, healthy mountain air. And during those winter months, when we go from house to car to work and back again, we sit. We sit in traffic, sit at our desks, sit through meetings, and sit on the couches with our laptops on our laps. We sit every waking hour of the day until we're too mentally exhausted to sit for one more second.

When we go to Vermont, we slide our feet into boots, pop our boots into bindings, and ski. We slalom through moguls, carve through late-afternoon icy patches, and swoosh at exhilarating speeds down black diamond trails. We bend and flex and stretch until we're physically exhausted. But unlike the exhaustion we normally experience from sitting all day, this exhaustion is strangely energizing.

And there's something magical about the combination of

mountain air and physical exercise that interrupts that end-lessly looping and insistent voice inside my head that normally chatters on and on about all the things I need to do. Even though it's completely irrelevant now, I can still hear the nagging list that was playing in my head just before the accident.

You need to call Harvard before noon, you need to start year-end performance reviews, you need to finalize the B-school training pro-gram for science associates, you need to call the landscaper, you need to email the London office, you need to return the overdue library books, you need to return the pants that don't fit Charlie to the Gap, you need to pick up formula for Linus, you need to pick up the dry cleaning, you need to pick up dinner, you need to make a dentist appointment for Lucy about her tooth, you need to make a derma-tologist appointment for you about that mole, you need to go to the bank, you need to pay the bills, don't forget to call Harvard before noon, email the London office . . .

By my second or third run down the mountain, that con-stantly jabbering voice in my head would be rendered speechless, and a peaceful gratitude would fill the space where all that one-sided, bossy conversation had been. Even when the slopes are crowded with other skiers, and even if Bob and I talk while we ride the chairlift, skiing down to the base is a glorious experience in focused silence. No laundry list in my head, no TV, no radio, no phone, no email. Just the hush of the mountain. Hush. I wish I could bottle it, take it back with me to Welmont, and sip from it many, many times a day.

My mother hands me the hat. I try to put it on, but the opening keeps flopping shut, and I can't get it around my head.

"It doesn't fit."

"Here, let me help," says my mother.

She stretches the opening and slides the hat onto my head. It's soft and snug against my skin, and I have to admit, it feels good.

"There. You look great," she says, beaming, like she's just solved my biggest problem. "And Lucy will love that it's pink."

It's strange to hear my mother knowing my kids. She knows that Lucy is crazy for pink. Of course, discovering that Lucy loves the color pink takes about as much time and sensitivity as it does to notice that I'm bald. But still. My mother knows Lucy. My daughter. Her granddaughter.

"Yeah, she will. Thanks, it's perfect."

I touch the hat on my head and close my eyes. I imagine the end of a full day of skiing, sitting on the living room floor in front of a roaring fire with Bob, thawing under thick fleece blankets, eating hot chili and drinking frosty mugs of Harpoon. Sometimes we play backgammon or cribbage, and sometimes we go to bed early. Sometimes we make love right there on the fleece blankets in front of the fire. I smile as I remember the last time. But I stay in the glow of that warm and fuzzy memory for only a second because now I'm busy flipping back the pages, trying to remember how long ago that frolic took place.

God, I don't think we've seen that fireplace in three years. Can it really be that long ago? It seems like every time we consider making the trip, a million little excuses collude to keep us from packing up the car and heading north—work, travel, pregnancy, Charlie's karate lessons on Saturdays in the winter, T-ball games in the spring, various projects around the house, Lucy's ear infections, we're too busy, we're too tired. And now this.

I clench my teeth and resolve to eat, drink, and be merry with Bob in front of that fireplace after a long day of skiing this winter. No excuses. The chatter in my head begins reciting a new kind of laundry list. *You need to get better, you need to get out of here, you need to go home, you need to go back to work, you need to go to Vermont, you need to get better, you need to get out of here, you need to go home, you need to go back to work . . .*

As I become almost hypnotized by this inner mandate, I become increasingly aware of another voice in my head. The voice is a whisper, honest and scared. I recognize it. It is my voice repeating over and over the nagging question that I've been refusing to answer ever since I watched *Ellen*, ever since I saw Richard and Jessica.

What happens if I don't get better?

I ask my mother to tell me about her trip to the mall, hoping her prattle will drown out the voice. She happily launches into the story of her outing.

What happens if I don't get better?

For a whisper, it is remarkably difficult to ignore.

*

"Mommy!" yells Lucy, bounding in ahead of everyone else.

"Come over to this side," says my mother.

"Come on up," I say, patting the space of bed next to me.

Lucy climbs up over the rail and onto my lap. She's wearing her winter coat over her Little Mermaid nightgown, her sneakers with the heels that light up with the impact of each step, and her pink fleece hat. I give her a huge hug, and she squeezes me tight, her small hands wrapped around the back of my neck, her face pressed against my chest. I exhale a blissful "Mmm," the same sound I make when I smell bread baking or I've just eaten a sinful piece of chocolate. Her hug is that scrumptious. Then she sits back, just a few inches from my face, and studies me. Her eyes light up.

"We match, Mommy!" she says, delighted by my pink ski hat, just as my mother predicted.

"We're so fashionable," I say.

"Hey, babe," says Bob.

The rest of them file in. They're all wearing hats—a Red Sox cap on Bob, a navy blue bomber on Charlie, an ivory knitted skullcap on Linus, who is asleep in his bucket car seat, and of course, my mother, the Mad Hatter. Such a brilliant idea. Now the kids won't pay any special attention to my head. I toss Bob a grateful smile.

"Where's all your hair?" Lucy asks, concerned and puzzled.

So much for that theory.

"I had to get a really short haircut," I say.

"Why come?"

"Because it was too long."

"Oh. I liked it too long."

"Me, too. It'll grow back," I assure her.

I wonder when the left will "grow back" and wish that I had a similar level of confidence in its return.

"Is this where you live now?" she asks, still puzzled and concerned.

"No, sweetie, I live at home with you guys. I'm just staying here for a little while for a special program, to learn some new things. It's like school."

"Cuz you banged your head in the car?"

I look up at Bob. I don't know how much detail he's shared with them. He nods.

"Yes. Hey, who painted your pretty nails?"

"Abby," she says, now admiring her pink fingers. "She did my toes, too. Wanna see?"

"Sure."

I look to Charlie as Lucy starts undoing her laces, bracing myself for the more sophisticated cross-examination I assume is coming. He'd normally see straight through the gaping holes in my political candidate answers to Lucy's flimsy interview and sink his teeth into the interrogation. He'd tear apart my lame haircut story like a hungry pit bull with a juicy steak. But instead, he's standing in front of Bob and staring at the floor. He won't look at me.

"Hey, Charlie," I say.

"Hi, Mom," he says, arms folded, still looking down.

"How's school?"

"Good."

"What's new?"

"Nothin'."

"Come here," I say, extending my arm, inviting him in.

He shuffles forward a couple of measured steps and stops at a distance from me that can just barely be considered "here." I pull him into me and, because he's still looking down, I kiss the top of his blue hat.

"Charlie, look at me."

He does what he's told. His eyes are round and innocent, worried and defiant, framed by those thick, black lashes. It's so unfair that Lucy didn't get his eyelashes.

"Sweetie, Mommy's fine. Don't worry, okay?"

He blinks, but the worried defiance hanging in his gaze doesn't budge an inch. I'm selling a lie, and he's not buying it. Some child expert once said or I read somewhere that parents should never lie to their kids. I've never heard of anything so ridiculous. This so-called expert clearly doesn't have an inquisitive child like Charlie. Come to think of it, this "expert" probably doesn't have any children at all. There are days when I've had to dodge, fib, and outright lie a dozen times before breakfast. *What are weapons of mass destruction? What are you and Dad fighting about? Where do babies come from? What is this* [*holding a tampon*]*?* The truth is often too scary, too complicated, too ... adult for kids.

And lies are often the best parenting tool I've got. I have eyes on the back of my head. Your face will freeze like that.

This won't hurt. Spider-Man loves broccoli. Here, this [spray bottle full of water] will kill the monsters in your closet. In a minute.

Then there are those white lies that encourage and protect what is wondrous and magical for kids. Santa Claus, the Easter Bunny, the Tooth Fairy, Disney princesses, Harry Potter. I don't want to know the parent who tells a seven-year-old there are no such things.

The truth is, there is no Santa Claus, there are no wizards, parents pay cash for baby teeth, and pixie dust is store-bought glitter. There are people in this world who hate Americans and are this minute plotting ways to kill us all, and I insert that tampon into my vagina to absorb blood when I have my period. The cold, hard truth for kids needs to be wrapped in a warm and silky soft blanket of lies. Or in this case, in a hot-pink fleece ski hat.

"Honestly, Charlie, I'm fine."

"See?" says Lucy, pointing her toes in the air like a ballerina. Her toenails are painted a rebellious metallic blue.

"They're lovely," I say, lying. "Where's Linus?"

"He's on the floor next to me," says Bob.

"Can you lift him so I can see him?"

I wait and nothing happens.

"Bob, can you lift him up?"

"I did," he says quietly.

His face registers my Neglect.

"Lucy Goose, will you hop down for a sec?" I ask.

She crawls down to the foot of the bed, which is good

enough, and Bob places the bucket car seat on the bed next to me. Linus is sound asleep, breathing long, deep breaths, the nipple of his nukie propped against the roof of his open mouth such that it is kept dangling in position, ready for sucking. Thank God he's figured out how to do this.

I love how his cheeks, which are like plump, ripe, delicious peaches begging to be pinched during the day, sag well below his jawline when he sleeps. I love his clenched hands, the dimples he has instead of knuckles, the creases of his chubby wrists. I love the sound of his breathing. God, I could watch this show all night.

"I want to hold him," I say.

"You don't want to wake him," Bob warns.

"I know, you're right. I miss holding him," I say.

"Mommy, I want to sit with you," says Lucy.

"Okay," I say.

Bob removes Linus, and Lucy resumes her spot on my lap.

"Will you read to me?" she asks.

"Sure, sweetie. I miss reading to you at bedtime."

Bob came prepared with bedtime books and hands me a *Junie B. Jones*, Lucy's latest favorite series.

I open to the first page of the first chapter.

"'Chapter One, Confusing Stuff.'"

Huh. The title couldn't be more accurate. This page makes no sense whatsoever. *B stands for I just years old. When you get to go to last summer Mother took and rolled me grown-up word for signed made me go.* I keep going over the page like a rock climber stuck on a precipice, looking for the next foothold, not finding one.

"Come on, Mommy. 'My name is Junie B. Jones. The B stands for Beatrice, but I don't like Beatrice. I just like B and that's all.'"

The *Junie B. Jones* books all begin the same way. Lucy and I've both memorized it. I know the words that should be on this page, but I don't see them. I see *B stands for I just years old*. I try to think of what else I've read since my accident. The hospital meal menus and the CNN scroll. I haven't had a problem with either. Then again, the menus have seemed rather limited, and the scroll appears one word at a time, from the bottom right. I look up at Bob, and he sees me realizing for the first time that I can't really read.

"Charlie? Oh my God, where's Charlie?" I ask, transferring my panic, imagining that he's left the room and is wandering the hospital.

"Relax, he's right here," says Bob. "Charlie, come back over."

But Charlie doesn't come.

"Mommy, read!" says Lucy.

"You know what, Goose, I'm too tired to read tonight."

I hear water running in the bathroom.

"Bud, what are you doing? Come here," says Bob.

"I'll get him," says my mother, startling me. I forgot she was here.

Charlie runs full throttle into one of the chairs, climbs it, and starts banging on the window with his open hands.

"Hey, hey, that's enough," says Bob.

He stops for a few seconds, but then he either forgets that Bob told him to stop or he can't resist some overwhelming urge in his body to slap glass, and he starts banging the window again.

"Hey," says Bob, louder than a few seconds ago.

"Hey, Charlie, you know what that is out there? That's a jail," I say.

He stops.

"Really?"

"Uh-huh."

"It's a real jail?"

"It's a real jail."

"Are there real bad guys in it?"

"Oh yeah, it's full of 'em."

"Cooool," he says, and I swear I can hear the lid pop clear off the container to his imagination.

He presses his nose against the glass.

"What kind of bad guys?"

"I don't know."

"What did they do?"

"I'm not sure."

"How did they get caught? Who caught them?"

"I don't—"

"You live next to *bad* guys?" asks Lucy, nuzzling her face into my chest and clutching my shirt with her hands.

"I don't live here, Goose," I say.

"Do they try to escape? Who catches them?" asks Charlie. The volume of his voice has been dialing up with each question so that he's practically yelling now. Linus whimpers and sucks his nukie.

"Shhh," I say, scolding Charlie.

"Shhh," Bob says, soothing Linus.

"How about if I take Charlie and Lucy down to Dunkin' Donuts for a few minutes?" asks my mother.

That's exactly what Charlie needs at bedtime. Sugar.

"That'd be great," says Bob.

"Donuts!" yell Charlie and Lucy, and Linus whimpers again.

"Shhh," I say to everyone.

Charlie and Lucy scurry down off the chair and my bed and follow my mother out of the room like rats on the heels of the Pied Piper. Even after the door closes, I can still hear Charlie barraging my mother with excited questions about criminals as they make their way down the hallway to the elevators. And then it is quiet.

"How's work?" I ask, avoiding the terrifying topic of my apparent illiteracy.

"Still surviving."

"Good. And the kids seem okay?"

"Yup. Abby and your mother are keeping them in their routine."

"Good."

Bob's keeping afloat at his sinking company, the kids are managing without me, and I'm recovering from a traumatic brain injury. So we're all surviving. Good. But I want so much more. I need so much more. We all do.

You need to get better, you need to get out of here, you need to go home . . .

"I want to go skiing."

"Okay," Bob says, agreeing way too easily, as if I just said I wanted a glass of water or a tissue.

"This season," I say.

"Okay."

"But what if I can't?"

"You will."

"But what if I still have this Left Neglect?"

"You won't."

"I don't know. It doesn't feel like it's getting any better. What if this never goes away?" I ask, surprised that I've allowed this question a voice outside of my own fleece-covered head.

I don't know what I expect Bob to say to this, but I start crying, suddenly terrified that a plain and honest answer could forever change the course of our lives.

"Let me in," he says.

He wedges himself into the space between me and the bed rail and lies on his side, facing me. It feels good to feel him next to me.

"Is it possible that your brain will heal, and the Neglect will go away?" he asks.

"Yes, it's possible," I say, still crying. "But it's also possible that—"

"Then, you'll get better. If something's possible, Sarah, it doesn't matter what it is, I have complete faith that you can do it."

I should thank my lucky stars for Bob, and I should tell him that I love him for giving me this unconditional vote of confidence, but instead I choose to argue with him.

"Yeah, but I don't know how to do this. This isn't like getting all A's or getting the job I want or meeting a deadline. This isn't 'do these ten things and your brain will be back to normal.'"

The more therapy I have, the more I realize that this is not a math equation. No one will give me any guarantees. I might get better, and I might not. The therapy might help, and it might not. I can work as hard as I've always worked at everything I've ever done, and it might not be any more effective than just lying here and praying. I've been doing both.

"I know. I know a lot of this isn't in your control. But some of it is. Do the therapy. Be positive. Use that competitive spirit I love. Think about it. Some people recover from this. You're gonna let them beat you? No way."

Okay, now he's hitting me where I live. I wipe my eyes. The goal isn't to get better. The goal is to win! I know how to do that. Bob and I are cut from the same super-competitive cloth; I swear we each have a couple of threads from one of God's athletic jerseys sewn right into our DNA. In pretty much every facet of our lives, we love any opportunity to compete. Our first real flirtation involved a bet to see who could get the better grade in finance (he did, and then he asked me out). We vied for the title of Person with the Highest Paying Job out of B-school (I won that one). When

Charlie and Lucy were both in car seats, we used to race to see who could finish buckling first. When we play catch, we don't just throw the ball back and forth. We keep score. And the only thing better than skiing down to the base of Mount Cortland with Bob is racing him there.

And what does the winner get? The winner wins. This is exactly the pep talk I needed.

"I believe in you, Sarah. You're going to get better, and you're going to come home, and you're going back to work, and we'll go skiing this winter."

He sounds like the Laundry List announcer in my head, but much nicer.

"Thank you, Bob. I can do this. I'm going to beat this."

"There you go."

"Thanks. I needed this."

"Anytime," he says and kisses me.

"I need you," I say.

"I need you, too," he says, and kisses me again.

As we lie in my hospital bed together, waiting for the kids to come back with their bedtime donuts, I'm feeling wholeheartedly optimistic. I'm definitely going to conquer this. But when I try to visualize the "this" I'm competing against—the injured neurons, inflammation, the absence of left, the other people with Left Neglect vying for the same place in the winner's circle—the only image I see with any clarity is me.

CHAPTER 14

It's the first week of December, four weeks since the accident. I'm not back home. I haven't returned to work. I missed the most important part of recruiting season at Berkley and Thanksgiving. Well, Bob and my mother brought the kids and an entire Thanksgiving feast here to Baldwin, and we all ate dinner in the cafeteria, so technically, I didn't miss Thanksgiving. The home-cooked meal was delicious (certainly far more delicious than the grayish-looking turkey, mashed potatoes, and gravy I saw on the plastic trays in front of some of the other patients), and we were all together, but it didn't feel like Thanksgiving. It felt sad and weird.

I'm sitting in a room they call the gym. I chuckle a little to myself every time I come in here, thinking, *Look at what it takes to get me into a gym.* But it's not a gym in the traditional sense, not like the one I never go to in Welmont. There are no treadmills, free weights, or elliptical machines. There is one Nautilus-like machine, taller than Bob, with pulleys and a harness hanging from what looks like the machine's giant, extended steel arm. I want no part of whatever goes on in that thing.

In addition to this medieval contraption, there are two long tables pushed against one of the walls. A tidy stack of paper-and-pencil tests rests on one and a wild assortment of Rubik's Cube–type puzzles and games are piled on the other. There are some Reebok steps and blue PhysioBalls, which I guess can probably be found in a real gym, a set of parallel bars for practice with assisted walking, and a big mirror on one of the walls. And that's about it.

There's a poster on the wall above the puzzles table that I've become fascinated with. It's a black-and-white photograph of a fist positioned below the word *attitude* written in bold red letters. The message and the image don't seem quite right for each other, but the more I visit the poster and turn it over in my mind, the more the combination inspires me. The fist is power, strength, determination, fight. And attitude. A positive attitude. I will bring a positive attitude to my fight to get my life back. I clench my hand in solidarity with the fist in the picture. I am strong. I'm a fighter. I can do this.

I'm sitting directly in front of the wall with the big mirror. I spend a lot of time in front of this mirror, searching for the left side of me. I do manage to find pieces of me every now and then. My left eye for a second. The laces of my left sneaker. My left hand. It's a lengthy and grueling effort for such a temporary and tiny reward. I have found that my left hand is easier to locate than any other left part of me because I can look for my diamond ring. I used to think of my ring as a beautiful symbol of my commitment to Bob. Now it's a beautiful, two-carat, flashy target. I told Bob that my recovery would probably benefit from more jewelry—a diamond tennis bracelet for my left wrist, a cluster of diamonds dangling from my left ear, a diamond anklet, a diamond toe ring. Bob laughed. I was only half kidding.

Martha's late, and my mother's using the restroom, and there really isn't anything left to look at in here but me in the mirror, so I go ahead and check myself out. I'm not a pretty sight. It's always hot in this room, so I'm not wearing my fleece hat. My hair has started to grow back but just enough to stick straight out in every direction. I look like a Chia Pet. I'm wearing no makeup. Yet. That's part of what I'll probably do in here today. Martha will ask me to put on my makeup, and I will, and then my mother, who is usually hovering in the background, will either giggle or gasp depending on how the day is going, and Martha will tell me that I didn't apply anything on the left. The left half of my lips will have no lipstick, my left eye will have no mascara or liner or shadow, and my left cheek will have no blush.

And then I'll study my face in the mirror and really try to see what they see, and I'll see myself in full makeup, looking pretty good, minus the Chia Pet hairdo. It's a spooky and sometimes embarrassing moment, becoming aware of what they see, comparing it to what I see. And what I don't. I'm missing a whole continent of experience, and I'm not even aware of it. I'm not aware that I'm not noticing the left half of my face, the left half of Martha, the left half of that page of *Junie B. Jones*. To me, nothing is missing.

The first step in my recovery is to become aware of my unawareness, to constantly and repeatedly remind myself that my brain thinks it's paying attention to all of everything, but in fact, it's only paying attention to the right half of everything and nothing on the left. Every second of the day, it seems, I forget that this is so. While the part of my brain normally responsible for this awareness has taken a leave of absence, I have to recruit another part of my brain to be my own babysitter, to monitor my every move and to chime in whenever I need prompting.

Hey there, Sarah, you think you're seeing your whole face, but you're actually only paying attention to the right side. There's another half there. It's called the left. Honest to God.

Hey, Sarah, that page you're looking at? You're only reading the words on the right half of the page. And sometimes only the right half of the words. Really. There's a left half. That's why it doesn't make any sense to you. Trust me.

But so far, my inner babysitter has been less than reliable, not even showing up for the job most of the time. She's a flaky teenager obsessed with her boyfriend. I may have to fire her and start over with someone new.

The second step, once I become aware of my unaware-ness, is to expand this knowledge over to the left, to stretch my focus and imagination past what seems like the edge of the earth, and find the other half. What used to be auto-matic and entirely behind the scenes—seeing the world as whole and seamless—is now a painstaking and deliberate process of trying to reel a disconnected left into conscious-ness. Look left. Scan left. Go left. It sounds simple enough, but how do I look, scan, or go to a place that doesn't exist to my mind?

Bob keeps insisting that I can do anything I put my mind to. But he's referring to my old mind. My new mind is broken and doesn't give a whack about the left or my old mind's reputation for success.

Attitude. Fist. Fight. I can do this.

The strangest thing about sitting in front of this big mirror every day is seeing myself sitting in a wheelchair. Handicapped. I don't feel handicapped, and yet, there I am. But I'm not actually paralyzed, thank God. My left leg can move. The muscles, tendons, ligaments, and nerves in my leg are all connected, poised and ready, waiting for confident instruction, like one of Charlie's Wii avatars waiting for him to press the A button. *Come on, Sarah, press the A button.*

Martha enters the gym and stands behind me.

"Morning, Sarah," she says, talking to my reflection in the mirror.

"Morning."

"Did you make your way here on your own today?"

Here we go again. This is how Martha and I begin every morning together. I knew she was going to ask this, and I know she knows my answer, but I play along anyway. It's our shtick.

"I did not," I say like I'm a witness on the stand.

"Then how did you get here?"

I point to the guilty reflection of my mother, who is now standing behind Martha.

"Did you give it a try?"

"I don't see why I should waste any time learning to use a wheelchair. I'm walking out of here."

Attitude. Fist. Fight.

"How many times are we going to go through this? You should take any opportunity you get to use your left side."

Before I can get out my rebuttal, she grabs the back of my chair, spins me around, and wheels me out of the gym. I hear my mother's shoes tap-tapping at a quick clip behind us. We travel down the long hallway past my room to the elevators and stop. Martha spins me around.

"Okay, Sarah, let's see you get to the gym."

"I don't want to use this thing."

"Then you're spending your session today sitting in the hallway."

"Good, I like it here."

Martha stares down at me, her hands on her broad hips, her mouth pinched shut. I grind my molars to keep from sticking out my tongue at her. This woman does not bring out the most attractive side of me.

156

"Helen, let me know if she changes her mind," she says and starts walking away.

"Wait," I call after her. "Why can't I practice using my left side trying to walk in the gym?"

"You will. We're doing this first," she says, pausing to see if she should continue down the hallway.

Attitude. Fist. Fight. Fine.

"Fine."

Martha walks back toward me, a smug hop in each step of her navy blue Crocs. She places my left hand on the wheel and taps it.

"Feel your hand?" she asks.

"Yes."

"Feel the wheel?"

"Yes."

"Okay, let's go. Down the hallway. Follow the line."

A straight yellow line is painted on the floor and runs the length of the hallway, probably to guide handicapped patients like me. I roll the chair. I roll the chair. I roll the chair. I crash into the wall. And although this is what always happens, I'm startled by the collision. I didn't notice that I'd veered away from the yellow line, and I never saw the wall before I hit it.

"You have to use your left hand, or you won't go straight," says Martha.

"I know," I say in a tone dripping with adolescent annoyance.

Of course, I know this. I understand the fundamentals and

157

physics of how to use a wheelchair. That's not the problem. The problem is I can't sustain my attention on my left hand or the left wheel or the left wall that is looming closer and closer. I have it to begin with. Left hand on left wheel. Got it. But as soon as I start rolling my right hand over the right wheel, everything on the left vanishes. Poof. Gone. And with no special-effects smoke, good-byes, or fanfare of any kind. While I'm rolling the chair with my right hand, I'm not only unaware that I'm no longer using my left hand, but I actually become unaware that I have a left hand. It feels like an impossible problem to solve, and it's a homework assignment I don't want to begin with. I don't want to learn how to use a wheelchair.

Martha backs me up and straightens me out.

"Let's try it again," she says.

She places my left hand on the wheel and taps it.

"Feel your hand on the wheel?"

"Yes."

"Okay, keep feeling it, keep remembering your left hand, and follow the line."

I close my eyes and picture my left hand dressed in its sparkling diamond ring and resting on the rubber tire. Then I think of what I want to tell it. *Dear left hand, please roll the wheel of this chair forward.* But instead of simply telling my bejeweled hand to do this in words, I picture my mind turning this polite request into warm liquid energy and pouring it into the nerves that feed my left hand. I imagine feeling this deliciously warm liquid flowing from my head, down my neck, into my left shoulder, down my arm, and into each of my fingertips.

"Good, Sarah, keep going," says Martha.

My liquid mojo must be working. I whip up another batch and send it down my arm.

"You're doing it!" says my mother, sounding both surprised and thrilled.

I open my eyes. I'm not sitting next to the elevators anymore, and I haven't crashed into the wall. I've made real progress. My mother bounces her knees a couple of times and claps. If someone were to give her a set of pom-poms, I think she'd start cheering.

"That's it," says Martha. "Do it again."

I look down the length of the yellow line. I still have a long distance to cover. My mother's last clap ended with her hands together, so she looks like she's praying. *Okay, Sarah, do it again*. I pour another liquid cocktail into my hand.

But I must not have followed the same recipe as before because something goes wrong. I'm off the yellow line, and I feel pain, but I can't pinpoint what hurts. I look up at my mother, and the tight grimace on her face suggests that whatever it is should hurt. A lot. Then I realize it must be my left hand.

"Stop. Stop. Your hand's tangled in the wheel. Hold on," says Martha.

Martha squats down and edges my chair backward as she works my left hand out of the inner nucleus of the wheel.

"I'm going to go get an ice pack. Helen, will you take her

back into the gym, and I'll meet you there? We'll try some assisted walking next."

"Sure," says my mother.

My mother wheels me down the hallway and into the gym and parks me in front of the big mirror where I started. My fingers kill, but I'm smiling. I used my left hand, and I got out of using the chair. If I could walk, there'd be a smug hop in each of my steps.

CHAPTER 15

I'm sitting in a wheelchair (I refuse to call it *my* wheelchair) in front of a full-length mirror in my room trying to put my pants on. I've been at it for a while. I can't say exactly how long I've been at it because I'm not wearing my watch. That part of the daily Iron Man that is "Getting Dressed" will come after I wrestle myself into my shirt. If I have the strength for it.

For some reason, getting everything south of my waist dressed is infinitely easier than dressing everything up top, and even that is infinitely far from easy. I can now get socks onto both of my feet, all by myself. My left toenails are painted the brightest Hoochie Mama red my mother could find at CVS, and my right toenails are simply clear coated. I realize this looks weird, but it's not like I'll be wearing any open-toed shoes any time soon. The red nail polish acts like a big red flag, like my diamond ring, and it helps me notice my left foot. And when I find it, I can then pull and tug and wriggle my sock onto it with my right hand.

I also wear mismatched socks. Same logic as the Hoochie Mama nail polish. My therapists are trying to make the left side of everything, including the left side of me, as interesting and as noticeable as possible. So my right sock is usually a standard white ankle sock, and the left is rainbow-striped or polka-dotted or argyle. Today it is green and covered with reindeer. I wish they were all Rudolphs, and the noses lit up.

I've got my right foot already through the right pant leg, and I'm bent over, resting my chest on my bare thighs, clutching the open waist of my jeans with my right hand, ready to pounce on my left foot should I see it, like I'm stalking a rare butterfly with a net. The problem is I can't seem to do two things at once. I can see the reindeer sock, or I can use my right hand. If I see the sock, then as soon as I try to capture it using my right hand, it's gone.

I've got the reindeer sock in sight again and decide I'm going to go for it full-out. I hold my breath and try lassoing my pants onto my foot with every ounce of determination I've got. But I miss the sock, and all those ounces of determination tip my sense of balance, and I start to topple over, out of the wheelchair. As I'm pitching forward, and I realize that I can't stop myself, I also realize that there's no time to throw my hands out to break my fall. My right hand is still devoted to the left pant leg project, and who knows where my left hand is?

My mother screams and catches me before I bash my head on the dingy linoleum floor. Thank God. The last thing I need is another head injury. From putting on my pants.

My mother props me up against the back of the chair, grabs my left foot, and lifts it up like I'm her rag doll.

"Ow, I'm not that flexible," I say.

"Sorry. Try it sitting back."

"You're not supposed to help me."

"If I didn't help you, you'd be lying on the floor."

Good point.

"Fine, but not so high. Hold it there, I can see it there."

I finally thread my reindeer foot and the leg attached to it through my pant leg. I'm sweating and really want to take a break, but I see me in the mirror—jeans pulled up to my knees and naked from the waist up. I have to keep going.

My mother then helps me lift my bottom into the seat of the pants. This takes several minutes. Then she tugs at the front of my waist.

"These pants don't fit," she says.

"I know. Just zipper them."

She tries again and grunts to show me how hard she's trying.

"I can't," she says, looking at me like I'm an overpacked suitcase that won't close.

"Try now," I say.

I take a huge, deep breath in, trying to pin my belly button to my spine.

"You need bigger pants," says my mother, giving up.

"I don't need bigger pants. I need to lose weight."

"You want to add a diet to the list of things you need to do here? That's crazy. Let me buy you a bigger size."

I feel her checking for the tag, her cold fingers on the small of my back.

"Stop it."

"Sarah, you should accept yourself the way you are."

"This is the way I am. This is my size. I'm not going bigger."

"But you are bigger."

I suck my breath in again and pull on the zipper to no effect.

"You need to start accepting your situation."

"Huh. Are we talking about my jeans now or something else?"

She of all people can't possibly think she's going to lecture me about accepting the situation. When did she ever accept her situation? When did she ever accept me? I'm suddenly and surprisingly flooded with hot emotion, like every complicated feeling I'd ever had about my mother had been lying unexamined and undisturbed, a thick film of dust on a table in the attic, untouched for thirty years, and she just blew a puff of air across the surface, throwing every particle of hurt into turbulent motion.

"Just your pants," she says, sensing my agitation and backing down.

"I'm not wearing a bigger size," I say, shaking with fight or flight, flight not being a plausible option.

"Fine."

"Fine."

I stare at my mother's reflection in the mirror, an emotional tornado still gathering energy inside me, and I wonder how long we can sit in the same room and not talk about all the things we never talk about. She hands me my black Merrell mules, my only rubber-soled, flat shoes with no laces and no buckles, and with the help of the mirror and the holiday sock, I jam each mule onto each foot, without any help from her. There. Bottom half done. Reindeer socks, mules, and my unzipped, unbuttoned skinny jeans.

However competent I am at dressing the bottom half of me (for a preschooler), I completely fall apart on the top half. Barring a complete recovery, I can't fathom the day when I'll be able to figure out how to independently maneuver my way into my bra, like I used to, every day since I was thirteen. The left arm through the left loop, the left boob into the left cup. Never mind the clasp in the back. My poor injured brain gets all twisted up like some circus contortionist even trying to imagine how this procedure would work. I'm supposed to at least try every step of getting dressed on my own, but when it comes to the bra, I no longer bother. My mother just does it for me, and we don't tell the therapists.

She holds up one of my white Victoria's Secret Miracle Bras. I close my eyes, shutting out the humiliating image of my mother manhandling my boobs. But even with my eyes closed, I can feel her cold fingers against my bare skin, and as I can't help but picture what she's doing, humiliation saunters right in, takes a seat, and puts its feet up. Like it does every day now.

Once that's over with, next comes my shirt. Today it's my white, oversized, button-down boyfriend shirt. I get my right arm into the right sleeve with relative ease, but then I give myself over to my mother for the left sleeve. I can't describe with any level of justice the impossibility of finding my left shirtsleeve with my left hand. I end up flinging my left hand way up in the air, like I'm in a classroom and I have a question, completely overshooting the sleeve hole. Or I find and grab on to the left sleeve with my right hand, but when I try to wrangle the sleeve onto my left arm, I somehow end up pulling the whole shirt up and over my head. Even the suggestion of "left hand into left sleeve" sends my brain spiraling in circles, making me a little dizzy. It's pure madness.

So now I'm sitting in the wheelchair, dressed from the waist down, my shirt wide open, my bra and my pizza-dough belly exposed, dreading what is next.

Buttoning.

Buttoning the length of my shirt with Left Neglect and one right hand takes the same kind of singular, intricate, held-breath concentration that I imagine someone trying to dismantle a bomb would need to have. I've finished three of the five buttons I intend on buttoning, and I'm utterly exhausted. Before I start on the fourth, I notice Heidi in the mirror, and I exhale three buttons' worth of air and tension. Three's enough.

"Good job," says Heidi, sounding impressed.

"Thanks," I say, genuinely proud of myself.

"But why on earth would you wear that?" she asks.

"What do you mean?"

"Why would you wear a shirt with buttons?"

"Because I should use every opportunity I can to interact with the left?" I ask, quoting Martha, thinking the question is a test.

"Within reason. Let's be practical, too."

"So I shouldn't wear this?" I ask.

"I wouldn't. I'd pack my button-down shirts away and wear only pullovers."

I think of my wardrobe full of button-down shirts, the shirts I wear to work.

"For how long?"

"For now."

I take a mental inventory of the shirts hanging in my closet—Armani, Donna Karan, Grettacole, Ann Taylor— crisp, stylish, expensive, professional, all with buttons. And this doesn't even include what's presumably hanging in my closet on the left side. Heidi senses my reluctance to embrace her philosophy.

"It's like when Ben was born, and he had horrible reflux. For months, I had his spit-up on my shoulders, down my back, down my front. It was gross. I had to stop wearing all my dry-clean-only shirts and sweaters for almost a year. It would've cost me a fortune, not to mention all that time driving back and forth to the dry cleaners. I wore all machine-washable cotton instead. It wasn't forever. It was just for that phase of my life. This isn't a button-down shirt phase for you."

We both look at me in the mirror.

"In fact, it's not a zippered-pants phase either," she says.

It dawns on me that she's not only suggesting that I should say good-bye to all my beautiful work shirts and all of my jeans and trousers, but she's also suggesting that I should get redressed. I should take off my shirt and my jeans, which would also mean taking off my shoes, and start over entirely with some other outfit, and I can't handle even the possible suggestion. I start to cry.

"It's okay. Look, your day is hard enough, right?"

I nod and cry.

"Right. So let's make some simple adjustments where we can. Pullover shirts. Elastic-waistband pants."

Our eyes sidestep over to my mother, who is wearing black synthetic elastic-waist pants and a shapeless white pullover sweater. I cry a little harder.

"I know. I know you're used to looking very stylish and put together. But I think we should go for independence over fashion. *Vogue* is just going to have to wait to do their photo shoot with you."

Not funny.

"You think I like Crocs?" she says, kicking up one purple rubber foot. "Believe me, I'd much rather be in Jimmy Choos, but they're way too impractical for what I do here."

Heidi hands me a tissue.

"But if I'm trying to get back to one hundred percent, don't I have to practice doing what I was able to do before the accident?"

"Sarah, I hope that happens. I hope you get back to a hundred percent. But you might not. Instead of only focusing on getting better, you might want to also focus on getting better at living with this."

I've gotten used to hearing and ignoring this kind of defeated, negative attitude from Martha, but can't believe I'm now hearing this from Heidi, my ally, my friend.

"I know that's a really hard thing to accept, but it'll help your situation so much if you can."

There it is again. Accept the situation. Are she and my mother drinking the same Kool-Aid? Accept. Adjust. Those words don't sing to me at all. In fact, I have a hard time even considering those words without hearing *Give up. Lose. Fail.* Accept and Adjust. Give up. Lose. Fail.

What about the poster? Attitude. Fist. Fight. I clench my fist and sniffle.

"So are you saying I have to start over?" I ask, referring to what I'm now wearing.

"No, of course not. But for tomorrow, Helen, let's pick out something simpler, okay?"

"Okay," says my mother.

"Anything left to do with getting dressed?" asks Heidi.

"My watch."

My mother hands Heidi my Cartier watch, and Heidi passes it to me. But instead of beginning the long process of putting it on, I compare it to the watch on Heidi's wrist. Hers is a pink plastic sports watch, digital, with no buckle. It's shaped like the letter *C* and appears to simply hook around her wrist like a horseshoe rings around a post. And I have an idea.

"Wanna trade?" I ask, like we're in elementary school, and I'm offering her my tuna for her PB&J.

"No, Sarah, yours is—"

"Too complicated," I say.

"Expensive," she says.

"A daily source of aggravation. I need a degree from MIT to work the clasp."

"I couldn't," she says, but I can tell she's considering it. "This is like a thirty-dollar watch. Your mother or Bob could order one for you."

"Yeah, but I want to do this now. What about that speech you just made? Accept and adjust. I think this is a pink plastic watch phase for me."

A smile sneaks into her eyes.

"Okay, but when you want this back, you just tell me."

"Deal."

Heidi replaces my diamond-and-platinum Cartier with her pink plastic watch. I hold the edge of the opening in my right hand, find my diamond ring on my left, and in one lucky try, I slap her watch onto my left wrist. I even read the time. 11:12. My mother claps.

"Wow, Sarah, this is really gorgeous," Heidi says, admiring her upgrade. "You sure about this?"

I think about all the agonizing minutes I just saved.

Accept and Adjust.

You're giving up. You're going to lose. You're going to fail.

Attitude. Fist. Fight.

"I'm sure. But I don't care what you say or how hard I have to work, I'm never asking for your Crocs."

She laughs.

"Deal."

Don't worry, I'm not giving up, I tell my conflicted self. Sometimes I'm just too exhausted to fight.

CHAPTER 16

Meditation has been added to the list of rehabilitation techniques that may or may not help me return to my old life. So I meditate. Well, I try. I've never had any inclination to meditate, and even beyond that really, I can't imagine why anyone would want to. To me, meditation sounds a whole lot like doing nothing. I don't do nothing. I pack every second of every day with something that can get done. Have five minutes? Send an email. Read the school notices. Throw in a load of laundry. Play peek-a-boo with Linus. Got ten? Return a phone call. Outline the agenda for a meeting. Read a performance evaluation. Read a book to Lucy. Sit with my eyes closed and breathe without planning, organizing, or accomplishing anything? I don't think so.

So when I envision someone who meditates, it isn't anyone

like me. Most often, I picture an old, bald Buddhist monk sitting erect on a bamboo mat in an ancient temple somewhere in Tibet, his eyes closed, his expression wise and serene, like he holds the secret to inner peace. While I admire my imaginary monk's ability to achieve this apparent state of contentment, I'll bet my right side he doesn't have three kids, two mortgages, and four thousand consultants to manage.

But now I don't have any emails, phone calls, school notices, or laundry to deal with (no laundry being one of the few perks of living in a rehabilitation hospital), and the kids aren't here. Baldwin's no Buddhist temple, but I'm still sort of bald, and I've got buckets of time. Plus, I've started to worry that too much daytime television might be damaging the rest of my brain. So I'm giving meditation a try.

Heidi says it will help to increase my concentration, which I could definitely use more of. Before the accident, I could focus on at least five things at once. I was a multitasking genius with plenty of surplus brainpower to spread around. If concentrating on five things at once before the accident required five gallons of brain fuel, one gallon per thing, now I need four gallons of brain fuel to simply be aware of the left side, leaving only one gallon of fuel to concentrate on only one thing. And then I'm completely out of gas. So I could use some more focus. And meditation might also help to reduce my blood pressure and anxiety levels, both of which are unhealthily and unproductively high.

So here I go. I close my eyes.

Breathe in. Breathe out. Focus on my breath. Breathe.

Nothing else. Focus. Breathe. Oh, I have to remember to tell my mother to put a few blankets under one end of Linus's crib mattress to help him breathe. Bob says he's got a horrible head cold. I hate it when the kids are sick, and they don't know how to blow their noses. How old were the other two when they learned?

Poor Linus. He's probably going to be sick with something from now until May. I swear, once the winter coats come out of the closets, someone in our house is always sick. All those kids in school and day care sneezing and coughing all over one another, drooling on the toys, wiping their runny noses with their hands and touching each other, touching the water bubbler spigots with their mouths, sharing toys and snacks and germs. So gross.

Poor Linus. I should also tell my mother to run the shower as hot as it can get and let Linus breathe in the steam. That'll help. I miss our shower. The one here barely has any pressure and doesn't stay hot for long enough.

I miss our bath towels. Thick, soft, luxurious Turkish cotton. And they smell like heaven, especially when they're right out of the dryer. The ones here are thin and stiff and smell too strongly of industrial bleach. I should ask Bob to bring me a bath towel.

Wait. What am I doing? Stop thinking about bath towels. Stop thinking. Quiet. Breathe. Observe your breath. Meditate. I'm having a hard time with this. I'm having a hard time with everything. I don't think I've ever worked this hard at anything and not succeeded. I'm not succeeding. I'm failing.

I'm not accepting and adjusting. I'm just failing. I can't let Bob see me fail. Or work. How will either of them tolerate me if I don't get back to the way I was before this? I have to recover from this. Work won't take me back unless I recover from this. I don't blame them. I wouldn't take me back either.

What about Bob? Will he take me back? Of course he will. He'd look like a real jerk if he left his brain-injured wife. But he doesn't deserve a brain-injured wife. He married his partner, not someone he has to dress and provide for and take care of for the rest of his life. He didn't sign up for this. I'll be his cross to bear, and he'll resent me. He'll be stuck with a brain-injured wife to take care of, and he'll be miserable and exhausted and lonely, and he'll have an affair, and I won't blame him.

Wait, can I even have sex with this? I think I can. I should be able to. All the necessary parts are right down the middle. Thank God I don't have a left vagina to try to find. But will Bob even want to have sex with me like this? Sometimes I drool out of the left side of my mouth and don't know it. That's real attractive. And I can't shave either armpit or my left leg. I'm a drooling, hairy Chia Pet who can't walk. Bob and I were barely having sex before this happened. What's going to happen now? What if he stays with me out of obligation, and we never have sex again?

Sarah, stop. Stop all this negative thinking. This isn't helping. Be positive. Maybe the average person doesn't recover, or maybe even most people don't recover, but some people do. You can do this.

Remember Attitude. Fight. You can get better. It's still possible. Don't give up. Breathe. Focus. Clear your thoughts.

You're right. Breathe. Focus. Breathe. Who am I kidding? I'm so far from better. Better is a tiny village buried somewhere deep in the Amazon rain forest, not on any map. Good luck getting there. Good luck getting anywhere. I can't even walk yet. Linus is more capable than I am. Bob says he's already cruising around the coffee table. And I'm still dragging myself between the parallel bars as Martha commands my every labored move. Linus is going to walk before I do, and I'm not going to be home to see him take his first steps. Not that I was there to see Charlie or Lucy take their first steps. I was at work. But still. I want to go home.

Stop thinking! You're supposed to be meditating. You're not going home now. You have nowhere to go and nothing to do. Just be here. Breathe. Think of nothing. Blank wall. Picture a blank wall. Breathe. Didn't you always dream of having this kind of downtime to relax and catch your breath?

Yeah, but I didn't dream of having a brain injury in order to have the chance to sit and think about nothing in the middle of the day. That's kind of a high price to pay for a little R&R, don't you think? I could've just gone to a spa for a weekend.

Sarah, you're wandering again. You're all over the place.

Is this what it feels like to be Charlie? I bet it is. Bob took him to the doctor yesterday without me. That was hard, to not be there. I can't believe he's being evaluated for Attention Deficit Disorder. Please don't let him have it. But

I almost wish that he does have it. At least that would explain why he's having such a hard time. And if he has it, then there's something we can do for him other than yell at him all the time. Yeah, but that something is to medicate him. We're going to drug Charlie so he can pay attention. I don't even want to think about it.

Hello? Don't think about it! You're not supposed to be thinking about anything. Stop thinking.

Sorry.

Don't be sorry. Be quiet. Turn it off. Picture turning off the switch.

You're right. Stop thinking. Breathe. In. Out. Good. In. Out. Good, I'm doing it. Keep doing it.

Okay, stop cheering for yourself, though. You're not your mother.

Thank God. How long is she going to hang around? Why is she here? Doesn't she have a life to get back to on the Cape? Probably not. She checked out of her life when Nate was six and drowned in the neighbor's pool. So why does she suddenly want to be a part of mine? She can't just suddenly decide to be my mother and pay attention to me after all these years. Where was she when I needed her before? No, she had her chance to be my mother when I needed one. But I really do need her now. But I won't. As soon as I'm better, I won't need her, and then she can go back to the Cape where she belongs, and I can go back to my life where I belong, and we can both go back to not needing each other. And that will be better for everyone.

I open my eyes. I sigh. I grab the remote and click on the TV. I wonder who's on *Ellen* today.

CHAPTER 17

It's just after 10:00 a.m., and I'm already having a really bad day. I tried calling Bob a few minutes ago, but he didn't answer. I wonder if he knows.

I'm in the gym, sitting at the puzzles and games table, tasked with transferring the red plastic beads from the white cereal bowl on my right to the invisible cereal bowl on my left with the spoon I'm holding in my left hand. My right arm is bent at the elbow and wrapped in a sling, immobilized against my chest. Constraint-induced therapy is supposed to help me resist the urge to use my right hand, and because we've eliminated the competition, this is supposed to help me feel more comfortable choosing to use my left hand. But mostly, it just makes me feel like a woman with no arms.

Even before I had to face straitjacket therapy, I was feeling upset and utterly demoralized. After some meeting my medical team had without me earlier this morning, it was decided that I will be going home in three days. It actually wasn't so much decided by them as it was ceremoniously rubber-stamped. My insurance carrier figured out long before my accident through some cost-benefit outcome analysis, not unlike the kinds of analyses many of the Berkley consultants are likely running on Excel spreadsheets for various companies right now, that I'd be going home in three days. It was predetermined by the intersection of some billing code and the code for my medical condition, with only marginal consideration given to my progress or lack thereof. Or maybe it was determined all along by the intersection of Venus retrograde in Scorpio. Whatever the faceless bureaucratic or mystical reason, this is my fate. I'm going home in three days.

While my medical team delivered the good news to me in super-cheery voices and faces dressed in community theatre smiles, I sat silent, stunned, expressionless. Here I am, sitting in a rehabilitation bed in a rehabilitation hospital, working hard every day in my rehabilitation sessions, all the while thinking I would be here until I was rehabilitated. As it turns out, this was never the case. And the joke's on me.

Here's what I learned this morning. In the world of rehabilitation hospitals, if a patient's condition is slipping downhill, the patient stays. Everyone believes, *We must save her.* Alternatively, if the patient is making significant strides toward wellness, the patient stays. Everyone hopes, *We can still save her.* Acceleration either up- or downhill means more rehab. But standing still with nothing but miles of flat terrain on the horizon means the patient is going home. Everyone agrees, *Don't waste your time. She can't be saved.* If the road to recovery plateaus, insurance will no longer pay the bill, which, by the way, is about as steep as the hill I've been trying to climb.

I should be thrilled. I'm going home in three days. In time for my wedding anniversary and Christmas. I'm going home. I've been praying for this day. I should feel triumphant. But instead, knots of terrified uncertainty are pulling tight inside my stomach, and I feel like throwing up. They're done with me here. My insurance company has deemed that my rehabilitation effort here is no longer a wise investment. *She can't be saved.*

This can't be it. There has to be more for me. I can walk on my own, but barely and only if I use the cane they gave me. The cane they gave me is one of those hospital-grade, stainless steel granny canes, the kind with the four rubber-capped feet. My cane is wearing Crocs, for God's sake. Not cool. There's nothing subtle about my quad cane. It's a cane that screams, *Look out, I have a serious brain injury!* I hate it, and I want to learn to walk without it.

I still can't read the left side of a page without lots of correcting and prompting and reminding to use my L-shaped red bookmark. *Scan left, find the left margin, keep going until you find the red bookmark.* I'm still not getting dressed without assistance. I need help with brushing my teeth and showering.

How am I going to take care of my kids and my house? How am I going to do my job? I can't even release the spoon I'm holding in my left hand without professional coaching. I want the insurance analyst who determined my length of stay to come over here right now and look me in the eye while I point my spoon at his head and threaten, "Do I look rehabilitated to you?"

Martha explained to me that I'll continue working at home on the techniques I've learned here. Heidi assured me that I'll meet with other therapists doing the same kind of work on an outpatient basis. Dr. Nelson, the doctor here who oversees my care, said, *The brain's a funny thing. You never know.* And he went to medical school for these words of wisdom.

None of what they're telling me sounds like good news. It all sounds a bit vague and dismissive, less intensive, less committed to my progress, less committed to a belief in my progress. It sounds like I'm no longer on the road to recovery. It sounds instead like I've been detoured onto some slow, crappy dead-end road that leads to an abandoned, boarded-up building where everyone has given up on me.

The knots inside my stomach twist and squeeze. I lose my concentration and spill a spoonful of red beads. The beads spin and bounce and roll off the table. As I listen to them scatter across the linoleum floor and consider the thought of scooping out another spoonful, the twisting and squeezing dissolves into an acidic hot anger, scorching a hole through my stomach, seeping into every inch of me. I can even feel it burning into my left hand. I want to throw the spoon, but

I can't undo my own kung fu grip, so instead I squeeze the spoon as hard as I can, and I feel my fingernails dig into the tender palm of my hand. It hurts, and I think I might even be bleeding, but I can't unfold my hand to see.

"I'm not doing this anymore. I want to go back to my room."

"It's okay. Just load another spoonful. You're doing great," says Martha.

What's the point? How is this ridiculous task going to change anything? Why don't I just go home today? What is three more days in this prison going to do for me? Nothing. It's been determined. *She can't be saved.*

My face is flushed and sweaty, and hot tears fill and sting my eyes. I want to wipe the tears away, but my right hand is unavailable and the best I could hope for from my left hand would be a poke in the eye with a spoon.

"I want to go back to my room," I say, my voice cracking.

"Come on, let's finish this first. You can do it."

"I don't want to. I don't feel good."

"She doesn't look well," says my mother.

"What doesn't feel good?" asks Martha.

"My stomach."

Martha checks her watch.

"It's almost lunchtime. You think food will help?"

No, I do not think a crappy cafeteria lunch will help.

I shrug.

She checks her watch again.

"Okay, with the time we have left, how about you walk

back to your room with your cane and your mom, and I'll go get you an early lunch and meet you there."

That sounds great. I'll spend the next twenty minutes walking a length of corridor that should take me thirty seconds.

"Helen, will you help her out of the sling and guide her back to her room?"

"Sure," says my mother.

Martha eyes my hand still clutching the spoon.

"I'll get you some soup."

My mother works my right arm out of bondage, hands me my granny cane, and we begin the journey back to my room. I have no more positive attitude. No more fist. No more fight. I have no interest in accepting or accommodating. I have a brain injury that has not healed and no promise that it ever will. I used to have a full and successful life. Now what do I have?

I have a granny cane in one hand and a spoon in the other.

And three more days.

"I don't understand what's wrong, Sarah," says my mother.

We're now back in my room, my mother in her chair, me in my bed.

"I'm fine," I say.

"This is great news. It means you're not in medical danger."

"I know."

"And you'll see, you'll do much better in your own home."

"Uh-huh."

I am looking forward to saying good-bye to this place. In three days, I will have been here for five weeks, and I never wanted to stay one second longer than I had to. I won't miss this uncomfortable bed, the weak shower, the coarse towels, the bland food, the pervasive smell of hand sanitizer and disinfectant, the gym, the miserable view of the prison, Martha. I especially won't miss the creepy nocturnal hospital sounds that shake me awake and hold me wide-eyed and unsettled every night—the moans of unbearable pain, the panicked and wild shrieking of someone waking from a nightmare, probably reliving whatever gruesome accident precipitated admission here, the coyote wails of the young mother deprived of language and her newborn, the code blue announcements delivered over the intercom carrying their unspoken, chilling message that someone—maybe someone in the next room, maybe someone with a brain injury like mine—has just died. No, I will not miss this place at all.

But I imagined leaving on much different terms. According to the scene that I've been directing in my head for weeks, my exodus always went something like this: With joyful tears in everyone's eyes, I would hug and thank each member of my medical team for their role in my full recovery and promise to keep in touch. Then, accompanied by the theme song to *Chariots of Fire* and while waving farewell with my left hand, I would walk with confidence and without a cane through the lobby, which would be packed with applauding therapists, physicians, and patients. The staff would be overwhelmed with pride, the patients would be filled with hope, and I'd be an inspiration to everyone. At the end of the lobby, the automatic doors would peel open, and I'd step through into a clear, sunny day. Into freedom and my old life.

And, conveniently forgetting that my car is in a junkyard, I even pictured driving myself home in my Acura. Sitting in my room now with three days left, involuntarily gripping a spoon in my left hand as I wait for Martha to come back with soup, exhausted from the embarrassingly short and granny cane–dependent trek down the hallway, I feel beyond ridiculous for ever constructing and then believing in such a far-fetched fantasy.

"And I'll keep helping you with the therapy," says my mother.

This is not an offer or a question. It's an assumption, a foregone conclusion. I stare at her, trying to figure her out. She's wearing black elastic-waist pants tucked into black imitation Uggs, a white cable-knit sweater, black-rimmed glasses, dangling red Christmas ornament earrings and lipstick to match. I can still see the young woman that she was beneath the makeup and old age on her face, but I have no actual sense of what she looked like in between.

I remember the shade of peachy pink rouge she used to wear on her freckled cheekbones, her favorite powder green eye shadow, the wisps of fine hair by her ears that never stayed in her long ponytail, how her nostrils bounced in and out when she laughed, the sparkle in her pale blue eyes, the smell of her lipstick (plus or minus Marlboro Lights and

Juicy Fruit gum) that lingered on my mouth after she kissed me.

I'm pretty sure she stopped wearing any makeup or doing anything to her hair after Nate drowned. I know there were no more nostril-bouncing laughs and no more smelly kisses. But I have no specific memory of what she looked like or how she changed after 1982. When did she start getting crow's-feet? And how does someone get crow's-feet if she never laughs or leaves the house? When did her hair begin turning gray, and when did she cut it chin length? When did she start wearing glasses? When did she quit smoking? When did she start wearing lipstick again?

And I can't imagine that she has any specific memories of me and what I looked like or how I changed after 1982. She didn't spend even one of the thousands of tedious minutes of the last month sharing nostalgic stories of my childhood. Because, for the most part, after 1982, she didn't witness my childhood.

After burying their only son, my mother then buried herself in her bedroom, and my father buried himself in construction work whenever he wasn't at the firehouse. While my mother did nothing but feel the loss of Nate, my father felt nothing at all. Stoic and emotionally distant before Nate died, now he was emotionally gone for good. But physically at least, my father eventually came back to his job as my parent. He mowed the lawn and took out the trash, he did the laundry and the grocery shopping, he paid the bills and fees for my after-school activities. I always had food on my plate and a roof over my head. But no part of my mother ever returned. And it was always my mother whom I needed most.

She didn't notice if I went to school wearing dirty clothes or clothes that were two sizes too small. She didn't attend my soccer games or parent–teacher conferences. She didn't guide or comfort me through the year and a half that I obsessed and lost myself over Richie Hoffman. She didn't tell me about safe sex or good sex. She forgot my birthday. She didn't praise my perfect report cards or celebrate my admission into Middlebury or Harvard. She preferred to be alone after my father died when I was twenty, and she didn't welcome Bob into what was left of our pitiful little family when I was twenty-eight.

I suppose I resembled Nate enough to be a constantly throbbing reminder of inconsolable grief. I suppose I can understand, especially now having kids of my own, the paralyzing horror of losing a child. But she didn't have one child. She had two. And I didn't die.

My childhood after Nate died wasn't easy, but it made me who I am today: strong, fiercely independent, driven to succeed, determined to matter. I'd managed to put my past behind me, but now my past is sitting in the chair across from me, telling me she's going to be sticking around. She feels me studying her. A nervous smile tiptoes onto her red lips, and I want to slap it off.

"No, this is it. I'm going home, so you're going home. Everybody's going home."

"No, I'm staying. I'm staying to help you."

"I don't need your help. I don't need anyone's help."

Martha is now standing in front of me holding a lunch tray, eyebrows raised.

"If I need anything, I'll ask Bob."

"Bob asked me to stay and help take care of you," says my mother.

I stare at her, voiceless, an unleashed tantrum pounding its fists inside my chest. Martha and Heidi met without me this morning and decided that I'm leaving in three days, and Bob and my mother met without me who knows when and decided that I need taking care of and that my mother will be my caretaker. Betrayal and helplessness kick and scream as they sink into the deep, dark layers of my gut, where, even having lived there once for years, they don't feel at all at home and can't remember the way out.

"Since when do you care about me? You haven't cared about me since Nate died."

Her face loses all color but for her red lips. Sitting in her chair, her posture assumes a heightened stillness, like a rabbit sensing danger, readying to run for its life.

"That's not true," she says.

I would normally back off. We don't talk about Nate or my childhood. We don't talk about me and her. I would normally choose to say nothing and eat my soup like a good girl. And then she would continue to be the good mother and wipe the broth that will undoubtedly dribble down the left side of my chin. And I would be the good daughter and smile and thank her. But I'm done with this charade. So done.

"You never helped me with my homework or boyfriends or going to college or planning my wedding. You never helped me with anything."

I pause, armed with a thousand more examples, poised to slay her if she tries to come at me with a reinvented history.

"I'm here now," she says.

"Well, I don't want you here now."

"But Sarah, you—"

"You're not staying."

"You need help."

"Then I'll get it from someone else, just like I've always done. I don't need you."

I glare at her, daring her to contradict me, but I've already ended it. She's crying. Martha hands her a box of tissues. My mother blows her nose and dabs her eyes as she continues weeping. I sit and watch her, encouraging her in my unapologetic silence. Good. I'm glad she's crying. I don't feel bad for her. I'm not sorry. She should feel like crying. She should feel sorry.

But as much as a part of me wants to see her tarred and feathered in the center of town, I can sustain this tough and heartless stance for only a minute or two, and then I do feel bad for her. She has helped me through the last five weeks. She's been here every day. She's helped me to walk and eat, to get showered and dressed, to go to the bathroom. I have needed her. And she is here now.

But I can't skip over thirty years of abandonment and just pretend that she chose not to be my mother for most of my life. I can't stand watching her cry anymore, but I'll be damned if I'm apologizing or acquiescing to her plan to stay. We're all done here. I'm going home and back to my life, so she's going back to hers. I grab my granny cane with my right hand, lean on it, and swing my legs over the side of the bed.

"Where are you going?" asks Martha.

"I'm going to the bathroom," I say, planting both feet on the floor.

Martha moves to stand next to me in the spotter's position.

"Don't help me. I don't need anyone's help."

She pauses, raises her eyebrows at me again, and then backs off and moves out of my way. I realize Martha must be thinking that I'm a spoiled brat and a horrible daughter, but I'm beyond caring what anyone here thinks of me. Well, I care what Heidi thinks of me, but she's not here right now. And right now, I'm a spoiled brat horrible daughter who is hell-bent on getting to the bathroom without anyone's help.

But walking with a left leg that fades in and out of existence is enormously frustrating and complicated. Even stepping forward with my right foot requires a conscious and continued faith in the existence of my left side, because when that right foot is in the space between here and there, I'm standing only on my left leg. My left leg and foot have to be appropriately activated, compromising between flexion and extension, responsible for balancing me and holding all of my weight upright—a tall order for an appendage that feels no loyalty toward me whatsoever.

I sometimes think it would be easiest to hop on my right

foot to get from place to place, but I haven't yet had the courage to try it. Logically, hopping should work, but somehow I just know I'll end up sprawled out on the floor. Anticipating this outcome really shouldn't deter me from giving it a shot, as I end up sprawled out on the floor most of the time anyway. I have big, colorful bruises all over me. I can't believe I haven't fractured a hip or dislocated my knee. Thank God I have strong bones and loose joints. I guess I realize that hopping isn't a practical long-term solution for mobility.

This is where the granny cane helps. Before I take a step with either foot, I take a step with my right hand on the cane, gaining some stability and assurance. Then I shift my weight into my right hand as much as possible to lessen the burden on my untrustworthy left leg, and I step my right foot forward to meet the cane.

Now my left leg is somewhere behind me, and the trick is to first remember that I have a left leg and to believe that it is somewhere behind me. Then I have to find it and get it next to me. The natural way to do this, of course, would be to pick it up and take a stride forward. But, much to the dismay of my pride, I don't do this. I lift my left leg up and try to walk like a normal person (well, a normal person with a granny cane) only if I'm on the mat in the gym and someone's spotting me. If I lift my left leg up off the ground, I can and do lose track of where it is in the blink of an eye, and then I can't anticipate when it's going to make contact with the floor, and I always guess too soon or too late, and I end up doing something weird and painful to myself that concludes with me sprawled out on the floor.

So I drag my left leg. It's much safer, and my chances of forward progress go up considerably if my left foot never loses connection with the floor. I know this looks pathetic, but I'm wearing black elastic-waist pants just like my mother's, a hot-pink fleece hat, mismatched socks, and no makeup. I think it's safe to say that vanity is no longer my biggest concern. Plus now's not the time to be daring. If I fall, Martha and my mother will scurry over to help me off the floor. And I don't want anyone's help.

Cane. Step. Drag. Breathe.

Cane. Step. Drag. Breathe.

I can feel them watching me. *Don't think about them, Sarah. You can't afford to get distracted. You are walking to the bathroom. You are walking to the bathroom.*

Cane. Step. Drag. Breathe.

My mother blows her nose. She's not coming home with me. She thinks she can just show up and be my mother. It's not happening. It's too little, too late. *Stop it. Don't think about her. You are walking to the bathroom.*

Cane. Step. Drag. Breathe.

I can't believe Bob talked about this with her without talking to me first. I can't believe he *decided* this with her instead of deciding the exact opposite thing with me. What was he thinking? *Don't think about it now. Talk to him later. You are walking to the bathroom.*

Cane. Step. Drag. Breathe.

Breathe.

I've made it to the toilet, and I want to yell out, *I did it!* and *See, I don't need either of you!* but it would be premature to celebrate and probably unwise to gloat. I haven't done what I came in here to do, and I have miles to go before I pee.

I take a deep breath, preparing to let go of the granny cane, aiming to grab the stainless steel safety rail next to the toilet. In the terrifying moment between cane and rail, I feel like a flying trapeze artist swinging from one bar, reaching for the next, high above the ground, showstopping catastrophe only the slightest miscalculation away. But I make it.

Breathe.

Next step. *Dear left hand, I need you to find the waistband of my pants and underwear and pull them down. I know this is a lot to ask, and I hate to bother you with this, but my right hand is busy keeping us off the floor. And I don't want to ask anyone else for help. So I really need you to do this. Please.*

Nothing happens. Where the heck is my left hand? It has to be in here somewhere. I find my diamond ring and then my hand. Oh no. I'm still holding that damn spoon. *Dear left hand, please let go of the spoon. You have to let go of the spoon so you can find the waistband of my pants and underwear and pull them down before I pee. Please let go of the spoon.*

Nothing happens. *Let go. Release. Open. Unfold. Relax. Please!*

Nothing. I'm about to lose it. I feel like I'm trying to persuade an overtired, disobedient, willful toddler to see reason and cooperate. I want to scream, *Listen to me, hand, do what I say right now or you're spending the rest of the day in time-out!*

I really have to pee, and I'm not at all good at holding it, but I refuse to ask for help. I can do this. I went to Harvard Business School. I know how to problem solve. Solve this problem.

Okay. Keep the spoon. That's fine. We'll use it. *Dear left hand, find the waistband of my pants and underwear and spoon them down.*

To my amazement, this works. It takes me several tries and calm coaxing, and I'm glad no one is in here to witness this process, but I manage to pry my pants and underwear down to my thighs with a spoon. Almost there. Holding on to the safety rail for dear life with my right hand, I lower myself onto the toilet seat.

Sweet relief.

The rest is relatively easy. I wipe with my right hand, wriggle my underwear and pants back on while seated with my right hand, grab on to the safety rail, hoist myself up, and lurch from the rail to my granny cane. Then I turn and take a few small steps over to the sink. I lean my pelvis against it and let go of the cane.

Like I've been working on in therapy every day, I scan left of the spigot to find the hot water handle with my right hand. I turn the hot water on and wash my right hand. I don't bother trying to wash my left hand. I dry my hand on my pants, get a firm hold of my cane, and walk out of the bathroom.

Cane. Step. Drag. Breathe.

I'm almost there. *See? You don't need Martha. You don't need any more rehabilitation at Baldwin. And you definitely don't need your mother.*

I hear Martha laughing. Against my better judgment, I look up from my cane and foot. I look up and see that Martha is laughing at me. And my mother is trying not to.

"What's so funny?" I ask.

"You might want to reconsider your mother's offer to help you," says Martha.

That tipped the scale for my mother, and now they're both cracking up.

"What?" I ask.

My mother puts her hand over her mouth like she's trying to stop herself, but she makes eye contact with Martha and gives in, laughing even harder.

"Where is your left hand?" asks Martha, wiping her eyes with the heel of her hand.

I don't know. A tingling prelude to unrecoverable embarrassment rushes through me as I search for my left hand. Where is my left hand? I have no idea. I ignore their laughter and the fact that I'm not concentrating nearly enough on standing upright in the middle of the room and try to find my diamond ring. But I don't see it anywhere.

Whatever. Ignore them. I'm about to carry on with getting back to my bed when I suddenly notice the feel of smooth metal against my thigh. My bare thigh. The spoon. I look down and scan left.

My left arm is tucked into my pants.

CHAPTER 18

I'm in the gym, sitting at one of the long tables, copying a picture of a cat. I finish and put my pencil down, satisfied. Heidi looks it over.

"You really are good," she says.

"Did I get the whole cat?"

"No, but what you drew is far better than what I could do."

"What did I miss?"

"The left ear, the left whiskers, and the left paws."

I inspect the two sketches, going back and forth between the original cat and my cat. They look exactly the same to me.

"Oh," I say, my voice dropping.

"But you got both eyes and the left sides of the nose and

197

mouth, and most of the body on the left. This is really good, Sarah. You're including so much more than you did when you first got here," she says, shuffling through the pages of drawings I've copied so far this morning.

I have improved. But *really good* is a really big stretch. Charlie and Lucy could copy the whole cat. And I still can't. And today is my last day.

Heidi places the next sheet on the table, an elaborately detailed picture of a city square populated with buildings, cars, people, a fountain, pigeons, far more complex than any picture I've been asked to replicate during my stay here. I take my pencil in hand, but I freeze up, unsure of where to place the tip down. I have to find the left side of the entire scene. Then I have to draw everything in that maddeningly impermanent space, including the maddeningly imperma- nent left side of each thing I find there. Then I also have to find the left side of each thing on the right side of the scene—the left side of each car, each pigeon, every person, the left half of the fountain. I notice a dog walker to the right of the fountain, but then I become hopelessly drawn to a man holding a bouquet of red balloons to the right of him, and the dog walker disappears. How on earth am I supposed to tackle this? This is probably the picture I was supposed to be able to copy on my last day had I fully recovered, taken from the final pages of some rehabilitation textbook, hun- dreds of pages ahead of the chapter I've been hopelessly mired in.

"What's wrong?" asks Heidi.

"I can't do this," I say, panic swelling at the back of my mouth.

"Sure you can. Try starting with the buildings."

"No. No, I can't do this. I can't even copy a cat."

"You did great with the cat. Take it one thing at a time."

"I can't. I can't go home like this, Heidi. How am I going to do everything I'm supposed to do?"

"Calm down. You're going to be fine."

"I'm not fine. I'm not. I can't even copy a cat."

"You got most of the cat—"

"I went to Harvard, and now I'm an idiot who can't copy a cat," I say, choking back tears.

Before the accident, I could make quick sense of any sheet of paper—complicated cost analyses, org charts, decision trees. Now, a page from Charlie's *Where's Waldo?* would probably bring me to my knees. I look back down at the picture, hunting for the guy with the red balloons. Waldo's gone.

"Hold on a sec," says Heidi.

She swipes the city square picture off the table, probably to keep me from melting down any further, and runs out of the gym. I try to hold it together until she returns, feeling like my freak-out needs an audience to be most effective. Where did she go? Maybe she's looking for an easier task, something I can readily master and feel good about, so we can end my last session neat and tidy on a positive note. Or maybe she's gone running to Dr. Nelson and is pleading with him to reverse the decision to send me home. *She can't even copy a cat!*

"Okay," she says, carrying a canvas bag and returning to her seat next to me. "Take a look at this picture."

She centers a white sheet of paper on the table in front of me. I see two simple houses, one on the top half of the paper and the other on the bottom. They each have two windows and a front door. They're identical in every way.

"Which one would you rather live in?" asks Heidi.

I wouldn't want to live in either of these dinky little houses.

"They're the same," I say.

"Okay, but if you had to pick one, which one would you live in?"

"It doesn't matter."

"Then just pick one for me."

I study the twin houses one last time, searching for something subtle in one of them that I might've missed, an extra pane in one of the windows or a missing shingle on one of the roofs. Nope, they're the same.

"Fine," I say, pointing to the top one.

Heidi smiles, delighted for some unknown reason by my choice of hypothetical residence. She pulls out my red, L-shaped bookmark and places it on the paper.

"Okay, scan left. Find the red edge."

My eyes crawl west along the white page until I see red. Then I roll my gaze to the right of the red margin, and I'm stunned by what I find drawn on the page, so unmistakable, so obvious. I see two simple houses, identical in every way, except that the left half of the bottom one is consumed in fire.

"Oh my God," I say.

"Do you see it?" asks Heidi.

"The bottom one is on fire."

"Yes! And you chose the top house!"

"So? I had a fifty-fifty chance."

"It's not chance. Your brain saw the whole picture. You're just not always conscious of what it's seeing on the left. But your intuition told you to pick the top house. You need to listen to that intuition. You're not an idiot, Sarah. Your intelligence is intact."

I guess. But so what if my brain sees the whole picture? If it doesn't share what it knows with me in a way that I can be conscious of, then what good does that do me?

"You're so lucky. There are so many people here who can't think anymore or remember anyone or talk or move. Imagine if you couldn't talk to Bob or your kids or if you couldn't remember them or hold them."

Many times over the last month, I glimpsed the unfathomable devastation that the human body and mind can survive. In the cafeteria, in the hallways, in the elevator, in the lobby, I would suddenly bear witness to missing arms and legs, missing pieces of skull, deformed faces, memories erased, language strangled, tubes and machinery supporting nutrition and breath. I always forced myself to look away and told myself I was being polite by not staring. But in truth, I didn't want to see anyone worse off than me because I didn't want to explore one inch of the perspective that Heidi just posed—that I was lucky.

"And you could've easily died, Sarah. You could've died in

that accident or in surgery or after surgery. You could've crashed into another car and killed someone else. What if your kids had been in the car with you? You're so lucky."

I look her in the eye. She's right. I've been so focused on what's horrible and unfair and terrifying about my condition that I hadn't acknowledged what is positive about my condition, as if the positive had been sitting quietly by itself on the far edge of the left side of my condition, there but completely ignored. I can't copy a whole cat. But I can recognize it, name it, know what one sounds and feels like, and I can copy most of it, enough for anyone who looks at it to know what I've drawn. I am lucky.

"Thank you, Heidi. Thank you for reminding me."

"You're welcome. You're gonna be fine. I know it. And . . ."

She leans down, reaches into her canvas bag, and presents me with a bottle of white wine wearing a festive red ribbon around its neck.

"Tada! For the next time I see you, my living room or yours."

"Thank you," I say, smiling. "I can't wait."

She places the bottle of wine on top of the burning house on the table and hugs me.

"Trust your intuition. It'll guide you," she says, holding me in her hug.

"Thank you, Heidi. Thank you for everything," I say and squeeze her a little harder with my right arm.

Her cell phone vibrates. She lets go of me and reads a text message.

"I have to make a call. I'll be back in a minute, and we'll get you ready to go home."

"Okay."

Alone in the gym for the last time, I let my gaze wander around the room. Good-bye, parallel bars. Good-bye, mirror. Good-bye, poster. Good-bye, puzzles and games table. Good-bye, bowls and beads. Good-bye—wait.

I go back to the poster. Something's different. I'm aware only that something about the poster is different without being able to pinpoint precisely what is different for a few seconds, and then I see it, so unmistakable, so obvious, like the burning house.

The picture on the poster is of two hands, not one. And the hands aren't clenched into individual fists, ready for battle. The hands are clasped together. Holding hands. And the word above the hands in red letters isn't *Attitude*. The word above the holding hands is *Gratitude*.

I start to cry, loving this poster that I'd been looking at all wrong. I think about Heidi and Bob and my kids and even Martha and my mother and all the help and love I've been given and all that I have. I think my brain saw this whole poster the whole time and kept drawing my attention to it, trying to show me. A part of me, unspoken and unconscious and intact, always knew what this poster was about. *Thank you for sharing this with me.*

I'm going home today, unable to copy a whole cat but able to see this whole poster, filled with gratitude.

CHAPTER 19

Bob is driving us home. Home! Even riding in my mother's two-door Volkswagen Bug, which I've never been in before, feels like home. I'm in a car again! There's the Museum of Science! I'm on Route 93! I'm on the Mass Pike! There's the Charles River! I greet the passing of each familiar landmark like I've just bumped into a dear old friend, and I feel that escalating excitement I get whenever I'm driving home from Logan after a long business trip. But today, multiply that excitement by ten. I'm almost there. I'm almost *home*!

Everything feels heightened. Even the afternoon light of the outdoor world feels exceptionally bright and gorgeous to my eyes, and I see now why photographers prefer natural light. Everything looks more vibrant, more three-dimensional, more alive than anything I've seen for a month under the flat, fluorescent indoor lighting of Baldwin. And it's not just the bold beauty of the outside light that I'm taken with. The sunlight shining through the windshield feels deliciously warm on my face. Mmm. Fluorescent lighting doesn't do that. There's no comparison.

And the air at Baldwin was always stale and stagnant. I want to feel real air again, its fresh crispness (even if somewhat polluted with exhaust) and the movement of it. I "roll" the window down a crack. The chilly air whistles into the car through the slit and dances through my short hair. I draw it in through my nose, fill my lungs, and sigh pure bliss.

"Hey, it's cold," says Bob, zipping my window back up with the driver's master control switch.

I stare out my closed window, but within seconds I can't resist the urge to feel a wild breeze again. I press the button, but my window doesn't budge. I press and press and press.

"Hey, my window's stuck," I say, whining and blaming, realizing that Bob must've clicked the lock button, deciding for everyone in the car that the windows will remain up. Now I know how the kids feel when I do it to them.

"Listen, before we get home, I want to talk about your mother," says Bob, ignoring my complaint. "She's going to stay with us for a while longer."

"I know, she told me," I say.

"Oh. Good," he says.

"Nooo, not good. I do not want her to stay. We don't need her. I'll be fine," I say.

He doesn't say anything. Maybe he's mulling this over. Or maybe he's glad to finally have my very strong opinion on the matter (which he should've asked for long before now), and he agrees with me 100 percent. Maybe he's smiling and nodding. But I have no idea what he's doing or thinking. I'm too mesmerized by the scenery outside my window to redirect my attention to my left, so I don't know what his silence means. He's in the driver's seat. He's a voice in the car when he talks, and he's an invisible chauffeur when he's silent.

"Sarah, you can't be home alone yet. It's not safe."

"I'm fine. I can handle it."

"What do we need—some sort of twelve-step program for you? You're not ready to be home alone yet. All the doctors and therapists said so."

"Then we can hire someone."

"We really can't. You've used up all your sick and vacation time, and your disability insurance isn't even half what you were making before. I'm hanging on to my job by my fingernails. Hiring someone is expensive, and your mother's here, and she's free."

Well, my mother may not charge an hourly wage, but I guarantee if she stays, I'll pay a high price for it. There's got to be another solution. I do understand how terrifying our financial situation is becoming. I make more money than Bob does, and now my income is slashed, and I can't pinpoint with any accuracy when exactly in the future I might get it all back. The possibility that I might never get it all back waltzes across the floor of my worried thoughts at least once a day now, flaunting showstopping leaps and pirouettes, taking center stage for too long before exiting into the wings. I need to get my salary back. This has to happen. Even if Bob manages to cling to his job, and the economy manages to turn around, we won't be able to afford our life without my full contribution.

I have to confess that I've been praying for Bob to lose his job. Even more specifically, I've been praying for him to lose his job *and* for him to not find another one for four months. I know this is playing with fire, and it doesn't sound like the kind of prayer that God would pay any attention to anyway, but I find myself getting desperately lost in this wish many times a day. If Bob gets laid off now, he'll get four months' severance pay, and if he doesn't have another job lined up straightaway, he can stay home with me. And if he's home with me, we won't need my mother's help, and then she can hop in her Volkswagen Bug and drive back to the Cape. And at the end of four months, when Bob starts his new, stable, even-better-paying job, I'll not only be ready to stay home alone, I'll also be ready to go back to Berkley. But so far, none of this is happening. If God is listening, He has a different plan.

"What about Abby? Maybe Abby can be around a little more," I say.

Silence again. I stare out the window. The thick snow on the trees and fields is glowing in the late-day sun. I didn't notice any snow back in the city, but now that we've ventured west into the suburbs, there are trees and golf courses and open spaces where snow can settle peacefully without being pushed aside or removed.

"Abby's leaving us right after Christmas for a teaching internship in New York."

"What?"

"I know. It's awful timing."

"It's the worst timing imaginable!"

"I know, and she was all torn up about the decision, but I told her to go. I told her that you'd want her to go."

"Why would you tell her a crazy thing like that?"

"Sarah—"

"Why didn't you tell me about this?"

"I knew it would stress you out."

"Crap!" I say, completely stressed out.

"Right. So with no Abby and no time to find a replacement and your mother always hinting around that she's in no rush to leave, I asked her to stay. We need her, Sarah."

I continue to look out the window, the landscape whizzing by, as we fast approach home. Almost home. Almost home with my mother and soon no Abby. The sun is now directly at eye level in the western sky, hanging just below where the visor would block it out, blinding me. Its rays through the windshield, which felt gloriously warm on my face at the beginning of the ride, are now uncomfortably hot, and I feel like an ant under a magnifying glass about to be incinerated.

"Can I please have control over my own window?"

I press the button and hold it there, "rolling" my window all the way down. Cold air whips into the car. It feels great for a few seconds, but then it's way too cold and way too windy, but I leave the window where it is, determined to have my way about something.

Bob turns onto our exit, and then we turn right onto Main Street in Welmont. The center of town is all dolled up for Christmas. Wreaths are hung on the streetlamps, garlands and white lights line the windows of the storefronts, and, although not lit up at this hour, the magnificent two-hundred-year-old spruce tree in front of the town hall is strung to the top with colored lights. The sun is low now, no longer blinding. It'll be dark any minute, and Main Street will be aglow with postcard-perfect holiday cheer. Nearing the shortest day of the year, it changes from day to night in the blink of an eye, reminding me of how everything can change in an unnoticed moment.

Bob turns onto Sycamore Street. We drive up the hill, around the bend, and onto Pilgrim Lane. He pulls into our driveway, and there it is.

Home.

CHAPTER 20

I remember coming home after Charlie was born, stepping through the front door into the mudroom, looking into the kitchen and the living room beyond that and thinking that everything had changed. Of course, I was seeing the same kitchen table and chairs, the same brown couch and matching love seat, the same Yankee candle centered on the same coffee table, our shoes on the floor, our pictures on the walls, the stack of newspapers by the fireplace, all exactly as we had left them two days before. Even the bananas in the bowl on the kitchen counter were still yellow. The only thing that had really changed was me. I'd left the house forty-eight hours ago an enormous pregnant woman and returned (only slightly less enormous) a mother. Yet somehow, the home I'd lived in for almost a year felt strange, like we were acquaintances being formally introduced for the first time.

I have that same feeling today. Only this time, it's not just me who's changed. As I inch my way through the mudroom, granny cane in my right hand, Bob guiding me on the left, an overwhelming but nonspecific sense that something is different washes over me. Then, one by one, each something reveals itself.

The first change that registers is orange. Streaks of bright orange are splattered all over the kitchen. The walls, the doorframes, the table, the cabinets, the floors are all covered with bright orange graffiti, like the ghost of Jackson Pollock paid us an inspired visit. Or, more likely, someone gave Charlie a tub of orange paint and ignored him for the afternoon. But before I scream for someone to fetch paper towels and a bottle of Clorox, it dawns on me. The streaks aren't paint, and they're not haphazard. Bright orange tape lines the left side of the doorframe. It runs the left edge of the cabinets, the left side of the refrigerator. It covers the doorknob on the door leading to the backyard. And who knows how many more orange strips of tape are stuck to surfaces I'm not even noticing? Probably many, many more.

Then I notice the handrail drilled into the stairwell wall, which is stainless steel like the grab bars at Baldwin and not at all like the handsome oak banister on its other side. I guess that was necessary. The handsome oak banister is on the right when going up the stairs, but then it's on the left, and therefore not really there at all, when going down. There's also a new, more industrial-grade baby gate installed at the bottom of the stairs and another one at the top, which I first assume are for our now toddling Linus, but then I think they might also be for me. We're not allowed up or down without adult supervision. My house has been baby-proofed and Sarah-proofed.

My granny cane and right foot take their first steps into the living room and land on a floor that feels completely foreign.

"Where are the rugs?" I ask.

"In the attic," says Bob.

"Oh yeah," I say, remembering Heidi telling us that we'd need to get rid of them.

Three handmade, expensive Oriental carpets. Tripping hazards. Rolled up and gone. At least the hardwood floors are in good shape. In fact, they're gleaming, pristine. I scan the length of the room. Unless they're all clustered somewhere to my left, there are no Matchbox cars, tiaras, puzzle pieces, balls, Legos, crayons, Cheerios, Goldfish crackers, sippy cups, and nukies strewn all over the floor.

"Do the kids still live here?" I ask.

"Huh?"

"Where's all their stuff?"

"Oh, your mother keeps the place really neat. All their things are in their rooms or down in the playroom. We can't have you tripping over toys."

"Oh."

"Let's sit you down on the couch."

Bob replaces my granny cane with his forearm, tucks his

other hand under my armpit, and performs what the therapists at Baldwin would call a moderate upper-body assist. I sink deep into the plush cushion and exhale. It took us probably fifteen minutes to walk from the driveway to the living room, and I'm wiped out. I try not to think of how easily, how unconsciously, I used to whip into the house and how much I used to get done in the span of fifteen minutes. I'd normally already have booted up my laptop, I'd have listened to the phone messages on the machine, gone through the mail, I'd have the TV on, coffee brewing, and at least one of the kids at my feet or on my hip.

"Where is everyone?" I ask.

"Abby's picking up Charlie from basketball, and Linus and Lucy should be here somewhere with your mother. I asked your mother to keep them out of the living room until I got you settled. Let me go find them."

Now that I'm facing the way I came in, the other side of the living room and the sunroom beyond that, which were hiding in the shadows of my Neglect during the journey in, show themselves. Our Christmas tree is up and decorated, colored lights strung and aglow, angel spinning on the top. It's a big tree this year, even bigger than our usual big, well over ten feet. Our living room ceiling is vaulted and at least twenty feet high, and we always buy the biggest tree on the lot. But every year, just before we do, I always hesitate. *Do you think it's a little too big?* And Bob always says, *Bigger is better, babe.*

I'm more than a little unnerved by the fact that I didn't

notice the tree as I entered the living room. It's one thing to ignore a piece of chicken on the left side of my plate or words printed on the left side of a page, but I just missed a ten-foot-tall evergreen covered in blinking colored lights and shiny ornaments. Even the fresh pine smell, which I love and did notice, didn't tip me off. Whenever I think my deficit might actually be subtle and not that big of a deal, I experience something like this, indisputable evidence to the contrary. The extent of my Neglect is always bigger than I think. *Sorry, Bob, sometimes bigger isn't better.*

The French doors to the sunroom are closed, which is unusual if no one is in there. Bob or I will go in and close the doors if we take a work call and need to muffle out the madness of the rest of the house, but otherwise, we keep them open. I love spending time alone in there on Sunday mornings in my pajamas, drinking coffee out of my deepest Harvard mug, reading the *New York Times* in my favorite chair, soaking in the warmth of the coffee through the palms of my hands and the warmth of the sun on my face. In my fantasy life, I spend an entire Sunday morning in this sanctuary undisturbed until I finish both my coffee and the paper, and then, in my ultimate dream world, I close my eyes and take a luxurious catnap.

This never happens. I probably get only about fifteen minutes at a time before Linus cries or Lucy screams or Charlie asks a question, before someone needs something to eat or something to do, before my cell phone vibrates or my laptop announces an incoming email, before I hear something break or something spill or the most attention-grabbing of all—the eerie sound of everything gone suddenly too quiet. But still, even fifteen minutes can be bliss.

It occurs to me that I should now be able to fulfill this fantasy quite easily. Monday through Friday, the kids will be at school and day care, and I won't be at work. I'll have six whole hours each day of uninterrupted time. And it just might take me six hours a day for five days to read every word of the entire Sunday paper, but I don't care. I'm excited about the challenge. Today's Thursday. I'll try my first day in my sunroom retreat tomorrow.

I peek through the windowpanes of the French doors from where I sit on the couch and notice that the sunroom appears to have been redecorated. My favorite reading chair has been turned and pushed up against the wall, and I don't see the coffee table at all. I see some sort of green-leaved potted floor plant that looks like it requires watering, in which case, if I'm at all responsible for this, it will be dead within the week. I wonder where that came from. And is that a dresser?

"Mommy!" yells Lucy, running to the top of the stairs.

"Slow down," says my mother, walking behind her and holding Linus.

My breath catches for a second, and I swear my heart stalls. Hearing my mother mother Lucy, watching my baby boy at home on her hip, seeing my mother here, living in my house. Living in my life. I don't think I can handle this.

Lucy works both gates open, barely breaking stride, bounds through the living room, and dives onto my lap.

"Easy, Goose," says Bob.

"She's okay," I say.

She's barefoot and smiling and giddy in her eyes as she bounces up and down on my lap. She's more than okay.

"Mommy, you're *home*!" she says.

"I am! Is this new?" I ask, referring to the Disney princess dress she's wearing.

"Yeah, Grandma got it for me. I'm Belle. Aren't I beautiful?"

"The most."

"Linus is the Beast."

"Oh, Linus is too cute to be the Beast. I think he's the handsome Prince," I say.

"No, he's the Beast."

"Welcome home," says my mother.

My inner teenager rears its hot head and begs me in her awkward and whiny voice to pretend that I didn't hear her.

"Thanks," I say in a barely audible tone, my inner adult compromise.

"What do you think of the tree?" asks Bob, beaming.

"It's huge, I love it. I'm surprised you didn't put it in the sunroom this year to keep Linus away from it," I say, imagining that they've been constantly defending the irresistible glass and ceramic ornaments.

"There isn't any room in there with the bed," says Bob.

"What bed?"

"The futon bed. That's where your mother is sleeping."

"Oh."

I guess that makes sense. She needs to sleep somewhere, and we don't have an extra bedroom (if we had that extra bedroom, then we'd have a live-in nanny, and then my mother wouldn't need to be here). For some reason, though, I'd been picturing her on the pull-out couch in the basement, probably because with the door to the basement shut, I could pretend that she's not here. Even with the sunroom doors closed, I'll still be able to see her through the windowpanes. She's here. Maybe we could buy some shades.

But where am I going to read the paper and drink my coffee and take my restorative nap now? What about my retreat? My inner teenager is outraged. *She stole your sacred space!* I seriously don't know if I can handle this.

"Mommy, watch me dance!" says Lucy.

She hops down and begins spinning with her arms overhead. My mother lowers Linus onto my lap. He feels heavier than I remember. He turns his head, looks up into my eyes, touches my face, smiles, and says, "Mama."

"Hi, honey," I say and wrap my arm tighter around him.

"Mama," he says again, patting my cheek over and over.

"Hi, sweet boy. Mama's home."

He snuggles into my lap, and we both watch Lucy perform. She kicks her bare feet and wiggles her hips and twirls, delighted to show off her billowing red and gold skirt, and we all clap and beg for more. Always a ham, she happily obliges with an encore.

My gaze travels over Lucy's head through the kitchen to the windows overlooking the backyard. The outdoor lights are on. I see the swing set and playhouse draped in snow. I see a snowman wearing one of Bob's winter hats, a carrot nose, and at least five stick arms. I see a red saucer sled at the top of our modest hill and a wild tangle of footprints and sled trails.

And no prison anywhere.

In some ways, everything about my life has overwhelmingly changed. But in other ways, my life is exactly the same. Backyard winter joy, Lucy dancing, Linus's fingers on my face, Bob laughing, the smell of Christmas pine. This, I can handle. And I soak it all in.

CHAPTER 21

The biggest change around here turns out not to be the orange tape on the walls or my mother sleeping in the sunroom. Charlie has ADHD. Attention Deficit Hyperactivity Disorder. Bob broke the news to me in bed on my first night home, said that the doctor was sure and that Charlie's symptoms are classic but not severe, and I cried quietly in his arms while he assured me until I fell asleep that Charlie would be okay.

Charlie's taking Concerta, which is like Ritalin but releases medication steadily over time for twelve hours. He takes one each morning with breakfast. We call them vitamins instead of medicine so he doesn't think of himself as sick or disabled or broken. So far, he hasn't complained of any headaches or loss of appetite, and Ms. Gavin says she's noticing a positive difference in his behavior at school.

We've also started making lots of "lifestyle" adjustments that are supposed to help him succeed. We've modified his diet—no more sugar cereal, no more gummy sharks and Popsicles loaded with Red No. 40 and Blue No. 2, no more soda, no more fast food. He's less than thrilled about this particular change, and I don't blame him. Even I miss the gummy sharks. He has a morning and evening To Do list neatly printed out in a grid on a poster board taped to his bedroom wall, so he can clearly see and check off what he needs to accomplish before school and before bed each day. And Charlie's Rules are written on a piece of paper magnetized to the refrigerator.

No hitting.

No yelling.

No interrupting.

Listen and do what you are told.

Do your homework without complaining.

With Ms. Gavin's guidance, Bob and I also designed an incentive program—Marble Minutes. Charlie starts each day with six marbles in a coffee mug. Each marble is worth ten minutes of TV plus or minus video games. If Charlie follows all of the rules without infraction all day, by five o'clock, he can have one hour of television. But for each crime he commits, he loses a marble.

Today, he's having a typical day. It's 4:00, and he's already lost half his marbles. He ripped Lucy's iPod out of her hands and smacked her on the head with it when she tried to grab it back. My mother had to ask him three times to pick his coat up off of the floor and hang it on a hook in the mudroom. And I was talking on the phone with my outpatient occupational therapist when he peppered me with a machine-gun volley of *Mom, Mom, Mom, Mom, Mom, Mom*. I should've taken away one marble for each *Mom*, but he's desperate to play Super Mario, and I already know better than to run out of marbles before we tackle homework.

We're sitting at the kitchen table, his homework in front of him, my outpatient homework in front of me, both of us wishing that we could be doing something else. I know he's praying that he doesn't lose the rest of his marbles. I hope I don't lose mine along with him. Bob is at work, and my mother and Linus are at Lucy's dance lesson. The TV is off, the house is quiet, and the table is cleared.

"Okay, Charlie, let's get this done. Who should go first?"

"You," he says.

I size up the cafeteria tray centered in front of me. A vertical line of orange tape divides the tray in half. The tray is empty.

"Okay, go," I say.

Charlie's job is to drop up to five red rubber balls, each about the size of a clementine, onto the left side of my tray. My first job is to identify how many balls are there.

"Did it," he says.

I begin my homework by tracing the bottom edge of the tray with my right hand, moving left until I feel the right angle of the bottom left corner. An uneasiness invades me whenever I cross my own midline with my right hand and leave it somewhere in the unknown Land of the Left. The feeling reminds me of a trust exercise that I once participated in at a Berkley employee workshop. Standing, eyes closed, I was asked to fall backward and trust that my colleagues would catch me. I remember that split second before allowing myself to fall, not being able to see or control how and where I'd land, not wanting to crack my head on the hard floor over a silly exercise, when common sense and primitive instinct chimed in, *Do not do this*. But somewhere inside, I was able to hit the override button. And of course, my colleagues caught me. I go through a similar experience when my right hand crosses the orange line. Instinctive fear, inner courage, blind faith.

Now I scan to the right of my right hand, which feels natural and easy, and which happens to be across what is the left side of the tray.

"Four," I say.

"Yes! Good job, Mom!" says Charlie. "Gimme five!"

Finding the balls is the easiest part of my homework and doesn't deserve a celebration, but I don't want to discourage his encouragement. I smile and give him a quick slap of the hand.

"High-five me with your *left* hand," says Charlie.

He loves working me. I have to find my left hand for the next part of this exercise anyway, so I humor him and begin the search. I find it dangling down by my side and manage to lift it up, but I can't say for sure exactly where it is now. Charlie is waiting, his high-five hand held up as my target. But he's using his right hand, which is on my left, which makes it less than easy to keep track of. Charlie might just be the toughest occupational therapist I've had yet. Without a shred of confidence that I'll succeed, I swing my arm from the shoulder. I miss his hand and smack him square in the chest.

"Mom!" he says, laughing.

"Sorry, honey."

He bends my arm at the elbow like I'm one of his action figures, spreads my fingers open, winds up, and slaps my hand with his, connecting with a loud and satisfying clap.

"Thanks. Okay, next step," I say, eager to finish.

Now I have to pick up one of the red balls with my left hand and squeeze it. The palm of my left hand is still tingling from Charlie's high five, which is a nice stroke of good luck because that keeps my hand from disappearing, and I'm able to move it onto the tray with relative ease. I feel around and grab the nearest ball. Then I give it a feeble squeeze.

"Yay, Mom! Now put it back."

Here's where I get stuck. I can't release the ball. I'll carry that ball to bed with me, not even conscious of the extra passenger I'm toting, and wake up the next morning with it still nestled in my obstinate hand unless someone comes along and mercifully peels it out of my grip.

"I can't. I can't let go."

I try shaking it loose, but my grasp is too tight. I try to relax my hand. Nothing happens. My brain has always preferred holding on to letting go.

"Charlie, will you help me?"

He pries the ball out of my rigid hand, drops it onto the tray, and pushes the tray to the other side of the table. It's his turn now.

"I wish I had your homework. Your homework's easy," says Charlie.

"Not to me, it isn't," I say.

He aligns my red page marker on the left edge of his homework sheet so I can follow along, and we both start reading. But within seconds, the most noticeable thing he's doing isn't reading or writing. He's moving. He's wiggling all over the seat of his chair, rocking back and forth, up on his knees, back onto his bottom, swinging his legs. Before my accident, I always entered Charlie's homework process several hours in, after he'd already been beaten by it. By then, his body was a listless lump and resembled nothing of this chaotic, undulating bundle of energy I'm witnessing now.

"You're going to fall out of your chair. Sit still."

"Sorry."

His inner perpetual motion machine is quieted for a minute, but then something twitches, and all gears are up and running again in full force.

"Charlie, you're moving."

"Sorry," he says again and looks up at me, his gorgeous eyes wondering if he's about to lose another marble.

But I can see that he isn't consciously acting out or

disobeying. I'm not going to punish him for fidgeting. But it's clear that he can't devote his mental energy to the words on the page when so much of it is ricocheting through his body.

"How about we get rid of your chair? Can you do your homework standing up?" I ask.

He pushes the chair back and stands, and I notice the difference immediately. He's tapping one of his feet on the floor, as if he's keeping time with a stopwatch, but the rest of his squirming is gone. And he's answering the questions.

"Done!" he says, tossing his pencil down. "Can I go play Mario now?"

"Hold on, hold on," I say, still reading the third question. *Jane scored 2 goals in the first game and 4 goals in the second game. How many goals did she score in all?* I check his answers.

"Charlie, the first three answers are all wrong. Go back."

He groans and stomps his feet.

"See, I'm stupid."

"You're not stupid. Don't say that. Do you think I'm stupid?"

"No."

"Right. Neither of us is stupid. Our brains work in a different way than most people's do, and we have to figure out how to make ours work. But we're not stupid, okay?"

"Okay," he says, not really believing me at all.

"Okay. Now why did you go so fast?"

"I dunno."

"You have plenty of time to play Mario. You don't have to

rush. Let's slow down and do one problem at a time together. Read the first problem again."

I read it again, too. *Billy has 2 pennies in his left pocket and 5 pennies in his right pocket. How many pennies does Billy have in all?* I look over at Charlie, expecting him to be looking back at me, poised and ready for my next instruction, but instead he's still reading. And his eyes appear to be focused three-quarters of the way down the page.

"Charlie, is it hard to concentrate on one question at a time when there are so many on the page?"

"Yes."

"Okay, I have an idea. Go get the scissors."

I draw a horizontal line under each question with Charlie's pencil. He returns to the table with scissors, the very thing I asked him for, which is a significant victory all on its own.

"Cut each question out along the lines I drew."

He does.

"Now pile them like a deck of cards and hand them to me."

I hand him question number seven first. He taps his foot and reads.

"Eight?" he asks.

"You got it!"

His face lights up. I'd give him a high five to congratulate him, but I don't want to distract him or lose momentum. I turn over another card. He reads it and counts in a whisper as he presses his fingers one at a time on the table.

"Six?"

"Yes!"

With no other words tempting his attention, he sees only the one question, and it doesn't get jumbled up with any other information. I hand him all ten "question cards," and he gets all ten right. We're done in about fifteen minutes. A 22 Pilgrim Lane record.

"That's it, Charlie, no more cards. You did them all."

"I'm done?"

"Yup. Awesome job."

Jubilant pride skips along every inch of his face. It strikes me that he looks like me.

"Can I go play Mario?"

"You can. But you know what? That was so awesome, I think you earned three marbles back."

"I did?!"

"Yup. You can play for a whole hour if you want."

"Woohoo! Thanks, Mom!"

He barrels out of the kitchen and then barrels back in.

"Hey, Mom? Can you tell Ms. Gavin about the question cards and standing up? I want to do all my work that way."

"Sure, honey."

"Thanks!"

He's gone again as fast as he reappeared, and I hear his feet speed down the basement stairs like a drumroll.

I look down at Ms. Gavin's homework assignment, shredded into strips, and hope she'll understand. We could always tape them back together if she cares. Our brains are wired differently, and we have to figure out how to make them work.

I hear the familiar bleeping sounds of Super Mario and picture the unfamiliar look of self-satisfaction on Charlie's face. I stay seated at the kitchen table, waiting for my mother and the other two kids to come home, also feeling satisfied. Like a Super Mom.

CHAPTER 22

It's the night of our anniversary, and Bob and I are going out to Pisces, our favorite restaurant in Welmont. I'm so excited. There will be no food served on plastic trays or out of Styrofoam containers; there will be no macaroni and cheese or chicken nuggets on the menu; there will be no children crying or whining or parents begging them to eat their macaroni and cheese and chicken nuggets; and there will be salt and a wine list on every table. It's been a long time since I've enjoyed a civilized meal in civilized company. My mouth is watering already.

"Everyone's out tonight," says Bob as we inch along Main Street, desperate to find a parking space, stalking pedestrians who look like they might be leaving, annoying every driver behind us.

We pass by a handicapped parking space, which is empty and so very tempting. But we don't have a handicapped parking permit, and I don't want one. For the same reason that we call Charlie's Concerta pills vitamins, I don't want to own license plates or a sticker or any sort of paper sign stamped with that picture of a stick figure in a wheelchair. I am not a stick figure in a wheelchair. Bob supports this philosophy and applauds my healthy self-image, but right now, I'm wishing we had that space. Bob slows down to a crawl as we approach Pisces and then stops, double-parked, right in front.

"Why don't I let you off here, and I'll keep circling?" asks Bob.

"Sure, I'll just hop out and run in," I say, not budging.

"Oh yeah," says Bob, realizing that I don't hop and run anywhere anymore. "They really should have a valet."

We eventually find a spot in front of The Cheese Shop, four blocks away. Four long blocks.

"What time is it?" I ask.

"Six forty-five."

Our reservation is at seven. Fifteen minutes to walk four blocks. It's going to be close. I look down at my feet. I wanted to wear heels, but both Bob and my mother insisted that I wear my Merrell mules. They look ridiculous with my dress, but thank God I didn't get my way. I'd never make it four blocks in three-inch heels.

Bob opens my door, unfastens my seat belt (we'd definitely lose our table if I had to unbuckle myself), hoists me up by my armpits, lifts me out of the car, and plants me onto the sidewalk, where my granny cane is standing at attention, waiting for me. I grab onto my cane, and Bob grabs onto my left arm.

"Ready, m'lady?" he asks.

"Let's go."

And we're off, a couple of turtles racing to dinner. I've never before been a slow walker. I don't amble or stroll. I throw it into fifth gear, and I go. And I'm not unusual in this respect around here. I think most Bostonians walk quickly and with purpose. We've got things to do, important things, and lots of them, and we're running late. We don't have time to dillydally, chitchat, or smell the roses. This may sound self-important, rude, or even unenlightened, but it's not. We're most likely being practical and responsible and just trying to keep pace with everything that is demanded of us. And besides, from November to May, those roses aren't in bloom anyway. It's freezing cold outside, and we're walking as fast as we can to get back inside where the heat is.

Like tonight. Tonight the temperature has dropped into the low twenties, and the wind whipping down Main Street is soul stiffening. It doesn't help matters that I buttoned only the top two buttons of my wool coat before I gave up, rationalizing that *we'll barely be outside for a second*. If I didn't have Neglect, I'd be game for running. But I do have Neglect, and so we plod along. Cane, step, drag, breathe.

The sidewalks are brick and unpredictably uneven, and they slope down and then up again with every cross street, making this terrain far more challenging than the yellow-lined hallways of Baldwin or our rugless living room floor. With every step and drag, I thank God for my cane and Bob. Without either one of them, I know I'd be sprawled out on the cold, hard ground, humiliated and late for dinner.

More so than usual because it's the week before Christmas, the sidewalks look like high-speed consumer conveyor belts. Oncoming shoppers whizz by us at an enviable clip, while the foot traffic behind us clogs, impatient at our heels, until a slight break in the oncoming lane allows them to weave past us. It's the typical demographic—women with newly manicured nails and newly done hair, boutique clothing store bags slung over one elbow, garish yet expensive purse slung over the other, and teenagers, always in packs of three or more, always carrying iPods and iPhones and sipping mocha Frappuccinos, everyone spending lots of money.

In the few moments here and there that I dare to steal a look up at the approaching crowd, I notice that no one looks directly at me. Everyone walking by us either has tunnel vision narrowly focused straight ahead at some pinpoint in the distance or is looking down at the ground. Embarrassed insecurity swells in my stomach and then scrambles to hide itself. Let's face it. I may not have a picture of a stick figure in a wheelchair tattooed onto my forehead, but I'm handicapped. These people aren't looking at me because I'm too awkward to look at. I almost tell Bob that I want to go home, but then I remind myself that most people walking in downtown Welmont (myself included) don't typically make eye contact with anyone, especially if those people are fighting through a crowded sidewalk on a cold night, which everyone clearly is. It's not personal. The embarrassed insecurity in my stomach apologizes and excuses itself, leaving only an intense chill and a building hunger. Pisces is one tantalizing block away.

Bob removes my coat, gets me safely situated in my chair, and takes a seat opposite me. We both exhale and smile, grateful to be in one piece, finally warm, and about to eat. I take off my pink fleece hat, hang it on the handle of my granny cane, and tousle my hair with my fingers as if I were scratching a dog's belly. Although by no means long, my hair is now just long enough that it looks like it has an intentional style, rather than looking like it's growing back after being shaved because I needed emergency neurosurgery. Catching my reflection in the mirrors at home looking like Annie Lennox still jolts me with the split-second flash, *Who the heck is that?* But there's a little less gawking and dissociation each time. Like with all the changes that have been thrust upon me in the last month, I'm getting used to it, redefining normal. I do love that my hair looks great without needing to blow it dry, straighten it, spray it, or fuss with it in any way. I simply shower, towel dry, dog belly scratch, and I'm done. I should've shaved my head ages ago.

As is typical for a Saturday night, Pisces is full, seemingly recession-proof. From where I sit, I can see a young couple on a date, a table of serious-postured men and women in suits, and a large table of boisterous women—ladies' night out. And then there's me and Bob.

"Happy anniversary, babe," says Bob, handing me a small white box.

"Oh, honey, I didn't get you anything."

"You came home. That's all I wanted."

That's sweet. But I also didn't get him anything yet for Christmas, and since I've now just given him "coming home," I'd better get cracking. I study the white box for a second before lifting the lid, grateful that he either had the compassionate foresight or not enough time and left it unwrapped for me. Inside is a sterling silver bracelet with three dime-sized discs attached. Three charms engraved: Charlie, Lucy, Linus.

"Thank you, honey. I love it. Will you put it on for me?"

Bob leans across our small table and holds up my left wrist.

"No, I want it on my right wrist where I can see it."

"But it's for your left. The jingle of the charms will be good for helping you find your left hand."

"Oh. Okay."

So it's not just a thoughtful anniversary gift, a sentimental piece of jewelry. It's a therapeutic tool for my Neglect. A cigar is never just a cigar. He fits the clasp and smiles. I waggle my right shoulder, which in turn automatically moves my left shoulder, and sure enough, I hear my wrist jingle. I'm a sheep with a bell around its neck.

"You know, if you're trying to help me recognize my left hand, diamonds are more noticeable than silver," I say, offering a not-so-subtle hint for future rehabilitative trinkets.

"Yeah, but they don't make noise. And we can add more charms on the different links."

I've seen these clinking clunkers crammed with ornaments on the wrists of other women—hearts, dogs, horseshoes, angels, butterflies, representations of each child. I'm not a collector. I don't own Hummels, Lladrós, bobbleheads, Elvis memorabilia, coins, stamps, none of it. I look at the pleased smile on Bob's face and see that I'll now be collecting silver bracelet charms. I wonder if Annie Lennox wears one of these things.

"Thank you."

Bob's iPhone buzzes against the surface of the table, and he picks it up.

"Work," he says, reading a text message, his expression journeying through increasing stages of concern.

"No. Oh, no. Oh, jeez," he says.

He pecks out a response with his index finger, pressing much harder than is necessary, his face clenched into an intense grimace. He stops typing, but now he's tapping and scrolling, probably reading email, his face still holding on to whatever bad news came in on that text message. Now he's typing again.

His hair, which is normally stick straight and military short, is well overdue for a cut, cowlicked at his forehead and wavy along his ears and by the nape of his neck. He's also grown a beard, which I'm never a fan of because it hides his handsome face and scratches up the kids' delicate skin when he kisses them. He looks tired, but not tired from lack of sleep, although I'm sure he's not getting enough. He looks weary. Poor Bob.

I'm done studying Bob's face, but he's not done with whatever he's gotten sucked into, so I decide to people watch. The young couple next to us is sharing a bottle of champagne. I wonder what they're celebrating. The young woman laughs a flirtatious and contagious cackle. The young man leans over the table and kisses her. She touches his face and then explodes into laughter again.

I smile, infected by their romantic energy. I return to Bob, wanting to share the young couple with him, and recognize the hypnotic, impenetrable intensity of his focus. He's really gone now. His body may be sitting across from me, but this Bob's a pod, a hologram, an avatar of the real Bob. My smile fades. I wait and wait. The intrusion of work into our personal lives isn't an unusual phenomenon, and it's never bothered me in the past. Heck, a month ago, we'd both be sitting here with our heads down, bewitched by our phones, two avatars having dinner. But I don't have anything to text or any emails to read or anyone to call, and I'm feeling increasingly lonely, self-conscious, and bored. The young couple next to us lets out another raucous burst of laughter, and I almost shush them.

Our waitress appears, snapping Bob out of his trance, saving me from myself. She introduces herself and the specials and asks if we'd like anything to drink.

"I'll have the house Shiraz," I say.

"Really?" Bob asks.

I shrug and smile, wondering if he's going to try to coerce me into a ginger ale. I'm not not allowed to drink alcohol, but I'm sure Martha wouldn't approve. I know I still have to manage four blocks back to the car after dinner, and I probably shouldn't drink and granny cane, but it's just one glass. I want to have a normal dinner with my husband, and normally I would order a glass of wine. Actually, we'd normally split a whole bottle, and I'm only going to have one glass, so I'm not completely throwing caution out with the dishwater, or whatever the saying is. I want to celebrate, and it'll relax me. I deserve to relax for a minute. Everything I do now is about looking left, scanning left, finding left. I want to hold a glass of delicious red wine in my right hand and toast to my anniversary with my lovely, if slightly hairy and rude, husband. I want to eat, drink, and be merry like the young couple next to us.

"I'll have the same," says Bob. "We can probably get our order in now, too."

We know the menu by heart, which is especially handy tonight because that means I don't have to struggle to read the left page or the left side of the right page or ask Bob to read it for me. We order our usuals.

"You back?" I ask, nodding at his phone.

"Yeah, sorry. Looks like there's going to be another layoff. Man, I hope my head's not on the chopping block."

"Would that really be the worst thing?" I ask. "You'd get severance, right?"

"Not necessarily."

"But everyone else has been getting three to four months."

"Yeah, but that well is going dry, if it isn't already."

"But say you did get four months, that wouldn't be so bad."

"It wouldn't be so good, Sarah. I've invested too much of myself to have it all be for nothing. I've got to hang on. The economy's going to turn around at some point. It has to. I've got to hang on and see this through."

It seems that while I've been praying for Bob to lose his job, he's been praying to keep it. I don't know if God is much of a mathematician, but my guess is we've been canceling each other out, like when I vote Democrat and Bob votes Republican. I do understand and admire his drive to succeed and never give up. I've got that same natural will to win, but while I've got it in my blood where levels fluctuate from time to time, Bob's is rooted in the marrow of his bones.

"What did we do for our anniversary last year?" I ask, hoping to move our conversation away from Bob's job.

"I don't remember," he says. "Did we come here?"

"I can't remember. We might've."

We got married in Cortland, Vermont, nine years ago. We picked the week before Christmas because it's such a festive and magical time of year there. Lights, bonfires, Christmas carols, and good cheer all seemed to be celebrating our union in addition to the coming holiday. And we spent our honeymoon skiing on freshly packed, wide-open trails for an entire week, knowing that everyone else and their kids would be coming after Christmas.

The downside to having married this time of year is that our anniversary now tends to get lost in all the hoopla that surrounds preparing for Christmas with young children. It's also year-end performance evaluations time for me, which means I'm even more slammed and preoccupied than usual. So our anniversaries have been less than monumental events.

We give up on our doddering memories and talk about the kids. I talk a little about my outpatient therapy and carefully avoid talking about Berkley or my mother. Meanwhile, every few seconds, Bob glances down at his phone, which is sitting there in plain sight on the table in front of him, silent but begging to be touched. He looks tortured, like a recovering alcoholic staring down his favorite martini. I'm about to suggest that he either check it again or put it away when our meals arrive.

I ordered the grilled beef tenderloin with horseradish whipped potatoes and roasted asparagus, and Bob got the Nantucket sea scallops with butternut squash risotto. Everything looks and smells amazing. I'm starving and ready to dig in, but then I'm stumped and embarrassed, realizing that I didn't think my dinner choice through.

"Honey, I can't eat this," I say.

"What, is there something wrong with it?"

"No, there's something wrong with me."

He looks up and down between me and my untouched meal, trying to figure out what I'm talking about, using the same analytical thinking he brings to any high-priority work problem, not seeing it. And then he does.

"Ah. Here, let's switch for a minute," he says.

He swaps my plate for his, and I eat a few of his scallops and some of his risotto while he cuts my meat. I feel foolish as I watch him cut my entire tenderloin into neat, bite-sized pieces, like I'm an incapable child. The young couple next to us burst into more laughter. I look over my shoulder, discreetly eyeing them, my insecure ego assuming that they must be laughing at me, the thirty-seven-year-old woman who can't cut her own meat. The young woman is still laughing, wiping tears from her eyes, and the young man is grinning as he lifts his glass of champagne. I can't figure out what was so funny, but it clearly wasn't me. They're so into each other, they probably haven't even noticed that Bob and I are here. I need to get a grip.

"Here you go," says Bob, re-swapping our plates.

"Thank you," I say, still feeling a bit sheepish.

I stab a piece of my precut beef tenderloin and pop it into my mouth. Bob does the same with a scallop.

"How is it?" asks Bob.

"Perfect."

We finish dinner, too full for dessert, and wait for the check. My glass of wine turns out not to have been the best idea, not because I feel buzzed (although I do just a little), but because I now have to go to the bathroom, and there's no way that I can hold it until we get home. But I really don't want to use a public restroom. I try to put it out of my mind and think about something else. *I really want to go to Vermont soon. I really want to go back to work. I really want to go home and go to the bathroom.* It's no use. I won't be able to hold it four long blocks plus the car ride. If I thought a thirty-seven-year-old woman needing her husband to cut her meat looked embarrassing, imagine the sight of a thirty-seven-year-old woman wetting herself in the middle of Pisces. The young couple next to us would definitely roar over that one.

"Bob? I need to go to the ladies' room."

"Uh, okay. Let's get you there."

We maneuver past the young couple, who I swear still don't notice us, through the labyrinth of tables, past a tight spot where we block a waitress with a tray full of food and a barely disguised look of impatient irritation, and amble into an empty corridor. Cane. Step. Drag. Breathe. Hold.

We stop in front of the door to the ladies' room.

"You okay from here?" Bob asks.

"You're not coming with me?"

"Into the ladies' room? I can't go in there."

"Sure you can. No one will care."

"Fine, then let's go into the men's room."

"No, okay. But what if I need you in there?"

"Then call for me."

"And you'll come in if I call you?"

"I'll come in if you call me."

"And you'll wait right here at the door?"

"I'll be right here."

"Okay. Here I go."

Bob holds the door open, and I carefully make my way inside. The sinks are in front of me and to the right, which means that the stalls must be somewhere to my left. Of course. Scan left, look left, go left. I find them. There are three regular stalls and one handicapped. The handicapped stall is large with plenty of room for walking in and turning around and would be the stall that any of my therapists would tell me to use. But it's also the farthest away, and I really, really have to pee. And I'm not handicapped.

I make it to the first stall and push the door open with the forward step of my granny cane. It swings open and then swings back, banging into my cane. I inch forward until I can't move anymore and am now standing over the toilet. For the first time in my life, I wish I were a man.

But I'm not a man, so I begin the painstaking process of trying to turn around and sit down. This is where the grab bars at Baldwin and the ones installed in our bathrooms at home always seem to magically appear in just the right spot, exactly where I need to cling on for dear life. There are no such generously placed handholds in a public restroom. The door has no doorknob, only a flimsy metal latch, and the toilet paper dispenser is now somewhere to my left and so completely useless to me.

After a lot of banging around, grunting, and muttering to myself, I manage to turn around and slide my underwear and pantyhose down. I hear the toilet paper spin in the stall next to me. Great. I'm sure whoever it is can't imagine what I'm doing. *Forget about her. You're almost there.* I decide my best route to the toilet seat is to slide my hand, slowly and carefully, down my granny cane, like a fireman down the pole, until I land. Miraculously, I make it squarely onto the seat.

When I finish, I realize, to my complete horror, that I'm stuck here. I must've knocked my cane forward during the landing because it's now leaning against the stall door, out of reach. I try to visualize standing up without it, without a grab bar, without a moderate upper-body assist from a highly trained therapist, without Bob, but when I do I see myself either falling headfirst into the metal stall door or falling backward into the bowl.

"Bob?" I yell.

"Uh, no, it's Paula?" says the woman in the stall next to me.

Paula flushes.

"Bawwwb?!"

I hear Paula's stall door fly open and her feet walk toward the sink.

"Hi, how are ya? Nice dress," says Bob.

"Uh, I uh," says Paula.

"Sorry, it's our anniversary, and we can't stand to be apart," he says.

I laugh and hear Paula's shoes scurry out of the room. The stall door gently swings open, knocking my cane back toward me. I grab it. And there's Bob, grinning at me.

"You called?"

"Can you please help me out of here?"

"Ready?"

He lifts me by my armpits and drags me out of the stall.

"You should've seen the look on that woman's face," he says.

We both burst into laughter.

"She couldn't get out of here fast enough," I say.

We both laugh harder.

The ladies' room door opens. The young woman from the table next to us enters. She takes one look at Bob holding me up by my armpits, glances down at my feet, gasps, spins on her heels, and rushes back out.

Bob and I look down. My underwear and hose are lying limp around my ankles. We both lose it. I haven't laughed with such abandon in Bob's arms in a long time.

"Well, babe, I don't think we'll ever forget this anniversary," says Bob.

No, I don't believe we ever will.

CHAPTER 23

"Come on," says Bob.

He's wearing his blue North Face ski jacket, ski pants, his reflective sunglasses hanging from a black cord around his neck, and his very best cheery optimism. He's holding my new skis. K2 Burnin' Luvs. They're sleek and shiny, sporting a rusty orange swirl design on never-used white, my big Christmas gift from Bob. They're gorgeous, and normally I'd feel giddy at the sight of brand-new skis, imagining how great they'll respond, anxious to get onto the slopes as early in the morning as possible. But all I feel is pressure.

"I'm not ready," I say.

It's three days after Christmas, and we're in Vermont. Linus is napping, and Charlie and Lucy are in the mudroom getting dressed for a day of ski lessons. I'm sitting at our dining table still in my pajamas with last Sunday's *New York Times* spread out in front of me. Bob's here through the weekend, and my mother, the kids, and I are staying for the week of school vacation. Bob's not too keen about leaving me up here for a whole week without him and in a house that hasn't been professionally Sarah-proofed, but I convinced him that a week in Vermont would be good for me. A week in Vermont is always good for me.

"This was your idea," says Bob.

"I never said I wanted to ski," I say.

"Then why are we up here if you don't want to ski?" he asks.

"I like it here."

"Come on, I think you should give it a try," says Bob.

"How am I going to ski? I can't even walk."

"Maybe it'll be easier than walking."

"How would that be possible?"

"I don't know, maybe the thing that reconnects you to the left isn't picking balls up off a tray. Maybe it's getting back to doing the things you love to do."

Maybe. Maybe skiing would awaken that dormant part of my brain that doesn't seem to be jazzed one bit about picking up red balls. Maybe I could simply point myself down Mount Cortland in my new K2s, and my left and right appendages would naturally work in concert, carrying me safely to the bottom. Or maybe, and more likely, I'd fall and break my leg or tear the ligaments in my knee, or I'd veer off the trail and crash into a tree. My red ball therapy may not be my recovery's magic bullet, but at least it doesn't carry the risk that I could end up in a wheelchair and even more dependent on my mother than I am now.

"What's the worst that can happen?" asks Bob.

Two broken legs. Another brain injury. Death. Bob should know better than to ask me, of all people, an extreme question loaded with doom. I tilt my head and raise my eyebrows. Bob sees that he's chosen the wrong tactic.

"The only way to know if you can ride the horse again is to get back in the saddle," says Bob.

A lame cowboy cliché. I shake my head and sigh.

"Come on. Give it a try. We can take it nice and slow. We'll stay on the bunny slope with the kids. I'll hold on to you and be with you the whole time."

"Bob, she's not ready to ski. She could break a leg," says my mother.

She's standing behind me in the kitchen, cleaning up the dishes from breakfast. She made buttermilk pancakes and sausage. It feels strange to have my mother here, making breakfast for my family. And it also feels strange to hear her come to my defense, to be of the same opinion. But I have to admit, her pancakes are delicious, and her voiced concern gives me the best possible excuse to stay home in my pajamas. *Sorry, my mother says I can't go.*

"You're not going to break anything. I promise, I'll stay with you," says Bob.

"It's too soon. You're pushing me," I say.

"You need a little push here. Come on, I think it'll be good for you."

Skiing would be good for me. But even if I subtract out the possibility of death or serious injury, I still can only envision myself in a constant tangled knot of legs and skis, my skis popping off with each embarrassing fall, the impossibility of balancing on my left foot on a slippery hill while trying to fit my right boot back into the binding, and the equally impossible thought of balancing on my right foot while trying to coax a less than responsive left foot, toe first, into the binding of my left ski. Not one second of this sounds fun to me. And it can hardly be called skiing.

"I don't want to."

"You know, you're the one who said you wanted to ski this year," says Bob.

"This *season*," I say, correcting him. "I do. I will. But not today."

He stares at me with his hands on his hips, thinking.

"Okay, but you can't stay squirreled inside forever," he says and looks over at my mother for a pointed second. "You have to get back to all the things you used to do—your job, skiing. We're getting you on that mountain this season, Sarah."

"Okay," I say, knowing he means well but feeling a bit more threatened than inspired.

Bob leans my new skis against the kitchen table across from where I'm sitting, probably so that I can see them and think about what I'm missing, the consequences of my decision. I kiss Bob and the kids good-bye, wish them a fun and safe day, and listen to them swish in their nylon shell pants and clomp in their heavy boots out the door.

After I hear the car pull out of the driveway, I sigh and prepare to settle into a nice, quiet morning of reading. I look for where I left off in the paper. I read a couple of words and look across the table at my shiny new skis. *Quit staring at me. We're not going today.* I read a couple of words. My mother is clanging dishes and pans in the sink. I can't concentrate. I need a coffee.

I bought Bob a new coffeemaker for Christmas, the Impressa S9 One Touch, the best of the very best, top-of-the-line cappuccino, café mocha latte, latte macchiato machine. It's insanely expensive, so it wasn't a smart purchase given our current financial situation, but I couldn't resist it. With the touch of a single button on its polished stainless steel panel, it grinds beans, froths milk, and brews coffee to the precise temperature, volume, and strength desired. It cleans itself automatically, boasts being the quietest coffeemaker available today, and looks oh-so-pretty sitting on our kitchen countertop. It's like the perfect child— well groomed and educated, it does exactly what we want, does its chores without even being asked, and brings us nothing but joy.

Bob and I both drank ourselves silly yesterday. I must've peed at least a dozen times, including the three times that necessitated pit stops on the way up to Cortland (Bob was ready to diaper me), and I lay in bed wide-eyed, caffeine still grooving in my veins, unable to put the brakes on my buzzing thoughts for hours after I should've been sound asleep. But it was worth it.

Since both of us couldn't bear to spend the weekend apart from our new baby, we brought the Impressa up to Vermont with us. But unfortunately, we somehow forgot to bring any coffee beans, and the closest grocery store up here that sells coffee worthy of touching the Impressa is in St. Johnsbury, which is about twenty miles to the south. As much as I crave another perfect latte macchiato and to breathe in that rich and comforting aroma throughout the house, the quickest way this morning to a cup of coffee (and relief from the caffeine-withdrawal headache twisting its screws into my temples) is to go to B&C's Café.

"Mom?" I call over my right shoulder into the kitchen behind me where she's washing the dishes. "Will you go to B&C's and get me a large nonfat latte?"

She followed us up last night in her Volkswagen so we'd have a car to get around in while Bob is gone for the week.

"Is that in the village?"

"Yes."

Everything is in the village. There's only one traffic light in Cortland, and the handful of country roads all lead either to the town village, to the mountain, or to the highway. And the village itself is nothing more than a short section of Main Street dotted with mostly quaint mom-and-pop shops selling quilts, cheddar cheese, fudge, and maple syrup. The village also has a sporting goods store, the only gas station, a church, a library, the town hall, a couple of restaurants, an art gallery, and B&C's. My mother has been here for less than twenty-four hours, and she already seems comfortable with the lay of the land, even without Bob's GPS. A five-year-old could figure it out. Heck, even a thirty-seven-year-old with Left Neglect could probably navigate without incident to the village and back.

"You'll be okay here without me?" she asks.

"I'll be fine. It's just a few minutes."

She's not convinced.

"I'm reading the paper. Linus is asleep. I'll be fine."

"Okay," she says. "I'll be right back."

I hear the door close behind her and then her car pulling out of the driveway. I smile, knowing that I'll have a steaming hot cup of coffee in a few minutes. And in those same few minutes, Charlie and Lucy will probably start their full-day lesson, and Bob will be riding the quad lift to the summit. I'm surprised I don't feel left out or the slightest twinge of jealousy. The view from the top of Mount Cortland of the snow-frosted treetops, the majestic Green Mountains, the glacial lakes, and the rolling valley below is breathtaking. Bathed in soft early morning light, the whole world from the summit feels quiet and peaceful and still. Glorious. I'll get there. I will.

In the meantime, with Linus asleep and everyone else gone, it's quiet and peaceful and still here. I gaze out through the sliding glass doors overlooking the yard—three acres of sprawling meadow abutting wooded conservation land. A zigzag of animal tracks, probably deer, break up the otherwise untouched smooth blanket of snow. There is no picket fence to keep the wildlife out or to cage our kids in or to obstruct the panoramic view. The nearest neighbor's house can only be seen from the front and only once the leaves have fallen off all the maple trees. Life here is private, tranquil, expansive. Glorious.

I've been reading this same newspaper for the last six days. I'm now on the Sunday Business section. The last section. Hallelujah. To be fair and honest, I didn't read every word of every other section. I read most of the front-page articles. This took all of last Sunday and most of Monday. Those columns are dense and labor intensive, and are generally national and international scale stories of misery, corruption, ruin, and political finger pointing. I feel informed after completing these pages but not necessarily better off for the effort.

I skipped the Sports section entirely. I'm not at all interested in the NFL, NHL, NBA, N-whatever, whatever. I never have been. I've never read the Sports pages, and I'm not about to start now for the sake of some type A need to prove that I can read *the whole* Sunday paper. I also skipped the Book Reviews (since the newspaper is challenging enough) and Style (since I'm relegated to elastic-waist pants and mules). Pre-accident me is shaking her head in disapproval, wagging her index finger, and calling me a slacker. But post-accident me tells her, in a firm and not-open-for-discussion voice, to lighten up and shush. Life may not be too short to read the entire Sunday *New York Times*, but the week certainly is. At least it is for me. Skip, skip, and skip!

The Business section is by far my favorite and not just because it's the last one. Because Berkley consultants service every industry in pretty much every developed nation, most columns in this section are relevant in some way to a past, present, or future Berkley case. Almost every article is a delicious taste of the juicy, salty, bittersweet corporate world I used to inhabit and love. Wall Street, trade with China, the auto industry, big pharma, fuel cell technology, market shares, mergers and acquisitions, profits, losses, IPOs. The Business section feels like home.

And probably because I love the content, I find it the easiest section to read. Huh. I look up at my shiny, new skis. Maybe there is something to Bob's Ski Therapy theory—that healing and normal functioning might come more readily from immersing myself in doing something that I love to do rather than dutifully going through the motions of some meaningless, emotionally void task.

"I know you're dying to go, but I need some time," I say to my skis. I swear they look disappointed.

I have noticed that I can now read every word on the page, and this exciting development isn't limited to the Business section. In addition to the red, vertical left-margin bookmark that I brought home with me from Baldwin, I now use a second bookmark, a regular white cardboard one from Welmont Books, held horizontally beneath the line of text that I'm reading. When I reach the end of the line, I scan left across the words I just read until I hit red, then I slide the white bookmark down, and begin reading the next line. I feel like I'm the carriage return on a typewriter when I do this, and I even play that *ding* in my head each time I return to the left and move down.

Without the horizontal bookmark, I often got hopelessly lost on the page as I worked to return to the left margin. I would get to the red bookmark, but like a weak swimmer aiming to cut a straight line across a strong ocean current, my focus drifted up or down along the way, sometimes whole paragraphs from the words I'd just read. And I always knew when I was somewhere north or south of my intended destination because the sentence I was reading would suddenly become a nonsensical Mad Lib. The additional bookmark keeps me in line. Interestingly, the idea to use this second bookmark didn't come from Martha or Heidi or Bob or any of my outpatient therapists. It came from Charlie. This is how he reads. And now it's how we read.

Using this technique, I'd consider my reading accuracy and therefore comprehension back to normal. Which is incredibly fantastic news. It's so incredibly fantastic, in fact, that I should be jumping up and down (metaphorically of course) and calling Richard to let him know that I've recovered and am ready to return to work. But I haven't told anyone about my incredibly fantastic news yet, not even Bob.

I don't understand the reason for my own uncharacteristic secrecy. I think it's because I know I'm still not ready. My reading pace is still much, much slower than it was. And where I used to skim, I don't dare to now. I read every word, which is great for accuracy but lethal for efficiency. Read, scan, *ding*, down, read. It works, but it's a tedious process, and I'd never be able to keep up with Berkley's daily volume of email and paperwork at that rate. My job is already seventy to eighty hours a week, flat out. There isn't room for slower. So it would be premature to announce my return. Wise to keep quiet.

But the real reason I'm hesitant to reveal my reading recovery to the world doesn't feel like it stems from responsible caution or a fear that I'll never pick up the pace. And it's certainly not because I'm modest or have a need for privacy. In fact, I usually brag quite shamelessly about my successes, to a level bordering intolerable, especially to Bob, who is always proud to hear them. But I don't want to tell anyone, and until I do, I'm respecting my instincts and keeping my incredibly fantastic news to myself.

I finish the Business section and turn the last page of the newspaper. Done! *Well, except for the Sports and Style and the Book Review*. Shush. *Hardly something to celebrate*. Shush. *It took you seven days! You should be able to read it in a single morning*. Shush, shush, shush! I banish pre-accident me from my mind and insist instead on basking in the glory of this moment. I'm in Vermont, the sun is shining, the house is quiet, and I finished the Sunday *New York Times*. I smile at my skis, looking to share my accomplishment with someone. I swear they smile back. The only thing missing from this moment is a hot coffee. Where is my mother? She should be back by now.

Feeling unable to wait one more minute for some form of caffeine and boosted with confidence from my reading prowess, I decide to walk over to the refrigerator for a Diet Coke. If Bob thinks I'm ready to ski down two thousand vertical feet of trails, then I should be able to walk a few horizontal feet into the kitchen, right? I take hold of granny, and the two of us hobble the few steps over from the dining table to the fridge. I find the door handle, which is on the left and not even bandaged with brightly colored tape. So far, so good. I let go of granny and lunge for the handle. Got it. I pull the door open, but I'm standing square in front of the refrigerator, so I only succeed at banging the door into myself. I push the door shut. I've got to step out of the way first. To the left. Using the door handle as a grab bar, I shuffle myself sideways enough to give the door clearance, and I pull again.

But here's the important difference between hospital grab bars and refrigerator handles. Grab bars don't move. I can lean, teeter, push, and pull with all my weight, and that grab bar (like Bob in most arguments) won't budge an inch. Not so for a refrigerator door handle once the door is open. I realize this is an obvious fact, but it's one I never physically relied upon before, and so I didn't consider the significance of this before I pulled.

As the door swings open, my arm and body go with it, and I'm unexpectedly flung over at the waist, feet still planted, every muscle in my outstretched arm quivering from the burden of posing in this awkward position. Staring down at the floor and clinging on to the handle for dear life, I gather my strength and wits and try to rock myself upright, but I over-estimate the reverse force needed, and I end up leaning too far backward, and I slam the door shut. I try again and do the exact same thing. I try again and again. I weeble out and wobble back. And each time I weeble out, I catch a teasing glimpse of the silver Diet Coke cans sitting on the top shelf. Then I wobble back, the door suctions shut, and they're gone.

Sweating and panting, I decide to give myself a minute to catch my breath. Despite the seriousness with which I'm taking this quest, a tickled laugh bubbles out. For God's sake, I've become Laverne De Fazio. Okay, Sarah, come on. There's got to be a way in.

This time as I pull, I sneak a quick step and drag forward. This keeps me from weebling out, but now I'm pinned between the door I'm still holding on to and the shelves inside the refrigerator. Not ideal, but it's progress. I'm face-to-face with five cans of Diet Coke.

Because of the way I'm standing, I'm not sure that I can let go of the door handle with my right hand and not go crashing to the ground. With no one else home, I don't want to risk it. So it's my left hand or bust. The refrigerator shelf edges are chilly and pressing into my left shoulder, elbow, and wrist, which is uncomfortable but also fortunate, because the sensory stimulation makes me aware of the existence of my left arm and hand. But when I send my cold left hand the message, *Dear Left Hand, please reach up and grab a Diet Coke*, it won't budge. It's wedged against the shelf. I try to free it by easing up a touch on the tension of my pull on the door handle, but as I do, I start to weeble out. I tense up and snap back. I think and come up with nothing. I'm stuck in the fridge. *Good going, Laverne. You're really in a pickle now.*

I stare at the Diet Coke cans, inches from my nose. So close and yet so far away. As I try to come up with a plan to either get a Coke or get out of the fridge (or both really), I happen to notice a bag behind the cans. It's the bag of coffee beans! We did remember to bring it! How on earth did Bob not see it in here?

This drives me absolutely crazy. Bob's never been good at finding what he's looking for in the fridge. A typical example (and I'm always in another room of the house when he does this):

Sarah, do we have any ketchup?

On the top shelf!

I don't see it!

Next to the mayonnaise!

I don't see any mayonnaise!

Check the door!

It's not in the door!

Touch everything!

I'll eventually hear the refrigerator alarm beeping, announcing that the door has been left open for too long, and decide it's time to rescue him. I'll walk over to the fridge where he's still searching, look at the top shelf for one second, reach in, grab the ketchup (which was next to the mayonnaise), and hand it to him. It's like he has Refrigerator Neglect. With what he's put me through this morning, he should have to go to some kind of rehabilitation program.

After I'm done imagining the lecture and taunting I'll subject Bob to when he gets home, I grin, thrilled and proud of myself. I found the bag of coffee beans! I get to use the Impressa! *Yeah, but you're a thirty-seven-year-old woman stuck in a refrigerator.* Shush.

I have a renewed sense of determination. This mission now isn't for some crummy, cold can of Diet Coke. It's for the Holy Grail of caffeine—a hot, fresh-brewed latte. Time to step it up, Sarah. Come on. You went to Harvard Business School. Solve the problem.

I lean my head forward and aim to knock over the cans I no longer care about, like my head is a bowling ball and the cans are pins. I knock them all down in two tries, a respectable spare. Then I stick my neck out as far as it will stretch, and I bite the rolled top of the coffee bag with my teeth. Gotcha!

Now to get out. I decide that I've got to walk backward. This sounds simple, but I have no confidence that it will be. I haven't walked backward since before my accident. I guess backward walking isn't something the occupational and physical therapists at Baldwin foresee as a necessary skill. Clearly, they didn't foresee one of their patients stuck in a refrigerator biting onto a bag of coffee beans. I'll have to tell Heidi that they should add it to their regimen.

Here I go. I take a step backward with my right foot, but

before I can even think about what to do next, my backward momentum sends me into an outward weeble. The door swings open too fast, and the force rips my hand off the handle. I fall backward and bang the back of my head on the tile floor.

I've wiped out so many times now, falling doesn't even really faze me. The pain, the bumps, the bruises, the indignity—I've learned to take them all on the chin (literally and figuratively). It's all part of the delightful everyday experience that is having Left Neglect. So it's not the fall itself that makes me cry.

I'm crying because I opened my mouth on the way down and dropped the bag, and it opened when it hit the ground, spilling my precious coffee beans all over the floor. I'm crying because I can't walk a few horizontal feet to the refrigerator and get a Diet Coke. I'm crying because I can't drive to B&C's myself. I'm crying because I wish I were skiing with Bob. I'm crying because I'm now sprawled out on the floor until someone rescues me.

While I indulge in my pity party on the floor, I've forgotten that Linus is napping, and my pathetic wailing wakes him up. He wails along with me.

"I'm sorry, baby!" I yell up to the second floor. "Don't cry! Everything's okay! Grandma will be home soon!"

But the sound of his mother's voice faking reassurance from another floor isn't what Linus wants. He wants his mother. He wants his mother to walk upstairs and pick him up. And I can't. I cry.

"Oh my God, what happened?" says my mother's voice.

"I'm okay," I sob.

"Are you hurt?"

She's standing over me now, a Styrofoam cup in her hand.

"No. Go get Linus, I'm fine."

"He can wait a minute. What happened?"

"I tried to get coffee."

"I got your coffee. Why didn't you wait for me?"

"You took too long."

"Oh, Sarah, you're always so impatient," she says. "Let's get you up."

She pulls me by my arms to a sitting position, wipes a spot on the floor next to me clear of beans, and sits down. She hands me the cup of coffee.

"This isn't from B&C's," I say, noticing no label on the cup.

"B&C's is closed."

"On a Saturday?"

"For good. The place is empty, and there's a 'for lease' sign in the window."

"Where is this from?" I ask.

"The gas station."

I take a sip. It's terrible. I resume crying.

"I want to be able to get my own cup of coffee," I whimper.

"I know. I know you do."

"I don't want to be helpless," I say, my crying intensifying as soon as I hear myself say the word *helpless*.

"You're not helpless. You need some help. They're not the same. Here, let me help you all the way up."

"Why? Why are you helping me?"

"Because you need it."

"Why you? Why now? Why would you want to help me now?"

She takes the coffee cup from my hand and replaces it with her hand. She squeezes and looks me in the eye with a steady resolve I've never seen in her before.

"Because I want to be in your life again. I want to be your mother. I'm sorry I wasn't there for you when you were growing up. I know I wasn't a mother to you then. I want you to forgive me and let me help you now."

Absolutely no way! She had her chance, and she abandoned you. What about all those years you needed her? Where was she then? She's too selfish, too self-absorbed. She's too late. You can't trust her. She had her chance.

Shush.

CHAPTER 24

"Come on," I say through a mouthful of toothpaste. "Stay."

Bob and I are in our master bathroom. I'm leaning against the sink, getting ready for bed. Bob is standing behind me, getting ready to drive back to Welmont. He's also watching over my brushing, just like he did a few minutes ago with Charlie and Lucy.

The kids can't be trusted to brush their teeth without parental supervision. Charlie will go into the bathroom and forget why he's in there. He'll draw on the walls with the bath crayons or spin the entire toilet paper roll into an irreversible heap on the floor or start World War III with his sister. Lucy never forgets why she's been sent in there, but she's sneaky. She'll wet her toothbrush with water, place it back in the holder, and then spend the next twenty minutes practicing different facial expressions and talking to herself in the mirror. So we can't send them into the bathroom alone and expect any kind of dental hygiene to happen.

We keep them on task with verbal reminders. *Brush the top. Get all the way back. That was too fast, you're not done.* We sometimes sing "Twinkle, Twinkle, Little Star," and they brush for the duration of the song. And Bob flosses for them.

Now it's my turn. I can't be trusted to brush my teeth properly without supervision either. It's early in the evening for me to be getting ready for bed, but Bob wants to get me settled before he leaves.

"I can't," he says. "You're not brushing the left side."

Staring at my face in the mirror, I poke my toothbrush wildly around in my mouth, hoping to make incidental contact with the left side. God knows I can't get there on purpose. Unless I concentrate really hard, I'm not at all aware that the left side of my face exists. And at the end of the day, it's really hard to concentrate really hard on anything.

No matter what time of day it is, the nonexistence of the left side of my face creates less than desirable consequences. I sometimes drool out of the left side of my mouth and don't know it until someone (my mother) dabs me with a napkin or one of Linus's bibs. While a little slobber sliding down the chin is arguably cute on Linus, I'm quite sure it does nothing good for me.

I now also have a reputation for unknowingly hoarding partially chewed wads of food in the pocket between my left teeth and gums, like I'm a chipmunk collecting nuts for the winter. This is not only gross, it's a choking hazard, so my mother does a "chipmunk check" several times a day. When I've been found guilty of hoarding, she either clears the food out with her finger or hands me a glass of water and asks me to swish and spit. Either way, the solution is just as gross as the problem.

And I have an expensive collection of cosmetics that no longer sees the light of day. Mascara, liner, and shadow on one eye, blush on one cheek, and lips colored in ruby red only on the right side made everyone noticeably scared of me. I asked Bob to apply my makeup for me only once—I looked like I should be walking the red-light district. Since my options seemed to be limited to deranged lunatic or prostitute, I decided that we'd all be better off if I kept my makeup in the drawer.

So, needless to say, brushing my teeth on the left side isn't my gold medal event. Bob always makes me give it a Girl Scout try, and then he does it for me. I poke around, accidentally jab the back of my throat, and gag. I retch over the sink, spit, and hand the brush over to Bob.

"Is anyone else going in?" I ask.

"I doubt it. Maybe Steve and Barry."

Senior management at Bob's company told everyone on Christmas Eve that they'd be shutting down for the week between Christmas and New Year's—a forced, unpaid vacation for the entire staff, an effort to save costs during an annually slow week for many businesses, even in the absence of a recession. From what Bob has told me, Steve and Barry are insane workaholics, even by our standards. Steve loathes his wife and has no kids, and Barry is divorced. Of course they're going in. They have nothing better to do.

"That's crazy. Stay. Take the week off. Ski with the kids, watch movies by the fire with me. Sleep. Relax."

"I can't. I have a ton to do, and this is the perfect chance to catch up. Now stop talking so I can brush your teeth."

Because of all the layoffs, Bob is short-staffed and has been doing the work of three other employees plus his own job. I'm amazed that he's able to do this but also concerned about the toll it's taking on him. Aside from the time he spends helping me and the kids in the mornings before school and in the evenings before bed and the handful of hours he sleeps each night, he does nothing but work, easily logging eighteen-hour days. He's burning the candle at both ends, and I'm worried that at some point there'll be nothing left of him but a puddle of wax.

I raise my right hand, signaling that I need to spit.

"So you're going to work for no pay instead of spending the week with us," I say.

"I'd love to stay, Sarah, but I've got to do everything I can to keep this company and my job alive. You know I have to do this."

Each time my mother brings in the mail at home, and I see the white envelopes stacked on the kitchen counter, the scary dark pit in my stomach deepens, becoming darker and scarier. Even if Bob keeps his job and his salary, if I don't go back to work, we're living beyond our means. The bills keep coming in like a relentless winter storm, and we're starting to get snowed in. And if Bob loses his job without another position lined up before I'm able to return to Berkley, then we're going to have to start making some dark and scary choices. My heart races, acknowledging what my mind is too chicken to imagine.

"I know. I understand. I just wish you could stay. When's the last time we both had a week off at the same time?" I ask.

"I don't know."

We haven't been on a weeklong family vacation or a vacation away together without the kids since Lucy was a baby. Whenever I could take a week, Bob couldn't. And vice versa. We most often ended up taking vacation days in dribs and drabs and for reasons that can hardly be considered a holiday, usually when Abby was away or called in sick. With the exception of this year, when I used up all of my days sitting bedside at the lovely Baldwin Resort Hotel, I've never taken all of my allotted vacation time in a given year. Bob never uses all of his either. And this time doesn't roll over to the following year; if we don't use it, it's gone forever.

For the first time, this behavior strikes me as absurdly sinful. Our employers offer to pay us to spend five weeks a year together, away from our desks and meetings and deadlines, and every year we basically say, *Thanks, but we'd rather work*. What's wrong with us?

"You sure? The company can't sink or be saved this week,

or they wouldn't have shut the doors. You're exhausted. Stay. Ski. Rest. A week off would be so good for you."

"Open," he says, floss wound around his fingers and seeming a little too pleased with having the power to shut me up.

I cooperate, and he begins flossing my teeth. There's no way I could do this myself. I'd probably have better luck training my right big toe to hold one end of the string while flossing with my right hand than trying to get my left hand to participate in this task. But I'm not willing to look like a chimpanzee for the sake of my dental health. So thank God that Bob flosses for me, or I'd probably be toothless by the time I'm forty.

I watch his eyes concentrating on the inside of my mouth. Before I left Baldwin, I cried every time I pictured Bob taking care of me like this. I grieved the imagined loss of our equal partnership, for the lamentable burden forced upon him as my caregiver, embarrassed for our pitiful fate. But now, when I actually see him taking care of me, I feel none of what I imagined. I watch his calm and tender concentration, and my heart swells with warm and grateful love.

"I can't, babe. I'm sorry. I'll be back end of the week."

Pre-accident me nods, understanding the life-and-death stakes completely. He's doing exactly what I would've done. But I'm worried more about him than his job right now and can see what pre-accident me is blind to—that he and his job are, in fact, two separate things. Finished with my teeth, we walk together over to the bed. Bob retrieves my pajamas from the dresser.

"Arms up," he says in the same playful tone we both use with the kids.

"How'd I do?" I ask, not knowing if my left arm obeyed the command.

"You tell me."

He taps my charm bracelet, and I hear the jingle coming from somewhere near my thighs, not up above my head. I'm not surprised. Whenever I ask both arms, both hands, or both feet to do something at the same time, it's as if the sides compete to see who gets to do it, and the right side always wins. When my brain hears *arms up*, the gun goes off, and my right arm sprints to the finish while my left arm, knowing it's way out of its league, doesn't even bother inching one fingernail over the start line, paralyzed in place, awed by the magnificent abilities of my right arm.

Come on, left arm, lift UP!

I imagine my left arm answering in a voice similar to Eeyore's. *Why bother, the right arm's already there.* I wish my left side would realize that this isn't a competition.

Bob pulls my buttonless wool sweater up over my head, down my left arm, and off. Next he reaches behind my back to unclasp my bra. He never had a second's hesitation undoing my bras while we were dating, but now they befuddle him. I guess motivation matters. The side of his face is next to mine as he pinches at the hooks. I kiss his cheek. He stops working at my bra and looks straight at me. I kiss him on the lips. It's not a sweet kiss or a thank-you-for-brushing-and-flossing-my-teeth kiss. And it's not one of our hurried, courteous good-bye kisses. All my wanting—wanting to recover, wanting my job back, wanting to ski, wanting Bob to stay, wanting him to know how much I love him—is in that kiss. He goes there with me, and I swear I can feel his kiss in my left toes.

"You're not going to seduce me into staying," he says.

"You're not staying," I say and kiss him again.

He pulls my bra off without any further struggle, helps me onto the bed, and slides my pants and underwear off. He takes off his clothes and lies on top of me.

"We haven't done this in a long time," he says.

"I know."

"I'm worried I could hurt you," he says, stroking my hair with his hand.

"Just don't pound my head against the headboard, and I'll be fine," I say and smile.

He laughs, revealing how nervous he is. I reach behind his neck and pull him toward me for another kiss. His bare chest, broad and strong and smooth, feels so good against mine. And the weight of him on top of me. I'd forgotten how much I love the feel of his weight on top of me.

I didn't think this through before I kissed him, but even in this most passive of positions, I need to actively use my left side. My right leg is wrapped around him, but my left leg just lies there on the bed, a lifeless lump of flesh, not aroused one bit, and my asymmetry is making it difficult for Bob to get into the groove of things, so to speak. And although I'm game for trying all kinds of wacky rehabilitative tools and techniques for reading and walking and eating, I refuse to allow any kind of red ruler, orange tape, granny cane, therapeutic sex prop into our bedroom. I want to have normal sex with my husband, please.

"I'm sorry, I can't find my left leg," I say, feeling suddenly overcome with the wish that it were a prosthetic, and I could simply detach the useless thing and chuck it to the floor.

"That's okay," he says.

We manage to get going, and I notice that Bob is holding my left leg, pushing up on it from under my knee, balancing me out, reminding me of how he held my leg when it came time to push during the births of our babies. My mind wanders into memories of labor—contractions, epidurals, stirrups, episiotomies. I catch myself and snap out of it, realizing that this kind of imagery is completely inappropriate and counterproductive for what I'm doing.

"Sorry my leg is so hairy," I say.

"Shhh."

"Sorry."

He kisses me, probably to shut me up, and it works. All intrusive and self-conscious thoughts dissolve away, and I melt into his kiss, under the weight of him, from how good he feels. This might not be perfectly normal sex, but it's normal enough. And kind of perfect, actually.

Afterward, Bob dresses, helps me into my pajamas, and we lie back down next to each other.

"I miss doing that with you," he says.

"Me, too."

"How about a date in front of a roaring fire when I get back?"

I smile and nod. He checks his watch.

"I'd better get going. Have a great week. I'll see you on Saturday," he says and kisses me.

"Come Friday."

"I'll be here first thing Saturday morning."

"Take Friday off. Come Friday morning."

"I can't. I really have to work."

But he paused ever so slightly before he spoke, so I know there's a chink in the armor.

"Let's shoot for it," I say.

We stare at each other for a suspended second, both realizing what happened after the last shoot.

"Okay," he says and pulls me into a seated position facing him.

We both cock our fists back.

"One, two, threeeee, shoot!" I say.

Bob's paper covers my rock. I lose. But Bob doesn't celebrate his win.

"I'll take half a day on Friday. I'll come up early Friday evening," he says.

I reach for his hand, pull him toward me, and give him a huge one-armed hug.

"Thank you."

He tucks me in under a thick fleece blanket and down comforter.

"You good?" he asks.

It's not my bedtime, but I don't mind going to bed early. I've been getting tons of sleep since coming home from Baldwin, at least nine hours each night and another hour or two in a nap each afternoon, and I'm loving it. For the first time since I can remember, I don't feel exhausted when I wake up in the morning.

"Yes. Please drive safe."

"I will."

"I love you."

"I love you, too. Sweet dreams."

I listen to the sounds of him leaving and then watch the beams from his headlights slide across the bedroom walls as he pulls out and drives away. It's after eight o'clock, but I can see the branches and trunks of the maple and pine trees out the window, jet-black silhouettes against a creamy blue sky. There must be a bright moon out tonight. I don't think there are any streetlamps in all of Cortland.

Bob left the bedroom door open a crack, probably so that my mother can hear me if I need to call for help. Light from the fire still burning in the fireplace dances in through the opening. I listen to the popping and crackling of the wood as I drift to sleep in shades of gray.

CHAPTER 25

It's Monday morning, and my mother is clearing the dishes from breakfast. I had steel-cut oatmeal with maple syrup and strawberries and a latte, and the kids and my mother ate scrambled eggs, bacon, English muffins, and orange juice. My mother is a firm believer in a hot and hearty breakfast, which is news to me. I grew up on Cocoa Pebbles, Pop-Tarts, and Hawaiian Punch.

I've been learning a lot about my mother since coming home from Baldwin. She also believes in saying grace before dinner, in wearing slippers or socks and never shoes or bare feet in the house, that all laundry needs to be ironed (including towels and underwear), that everyone should get at least fifteen minutes of fresh air every day regardless of the weather, that the kids have too much "stuff" and watch too much TV, that Bob is a "good man" but he's "working himself into an early grave," and that God has a plan. With the exception of the obsessive ironing, I agree with her opinions and ways of living (even if I haven't been living by them myself) and am surprised by how alike we are.

But in all that I'm discovering about her, I have little sense for what she believes about me, except that she believes that I need her help. I find myself wanting to know more, studying her for clues, unable to ask, like I'm back in junior high school, gaping at the back of Sean Kelly's head in homeroom, wondering in my unbearably awkward silence if he likes me. Does my mother believe that I'm a good woman? A good mother? Is she proud of me? Does she believe that I'll fully recover? I wonder.

And the more I learn, the more questions this seems to unearth, especially about the past. Where was this woman during my childhood? Where were my rules and hot meals and ironed clothes? I wonder if she knows how many hours of *The Brady Bunch* I logged, how many bologna and mayonnaise sandwich dinners I ate alone in front of the TV and without saying grace while she stayed sequestered in her bedroom and my father worked the night shift at the station. Why wasn't I enough for her? I wonder.

Mount Cortland weather this morning is reporting high winds and all summit lifts closed. Even though this wouldn't affect Charlie and Lucy on the beginners' slopes, we've decided to lie low and stay home today. I assumed they'd be dying to watch a movie or play a video game, since they haven't done either since the car ride up on Friday, but they both want to go outside to play in the yard.

"Snowsuits, hats, mittens, boots," I say as they race each other into the mudroom.

"Where's the beach stuff?" hollers Charlie, referring to the bin of shovels, pails, and castle molds as suitable for playing in snow as they are for sand.

"Everything's already outside," calls my mother. "Charlie, hold up! Your vitamin!"

He swishes and clomps in his suit and boots back into the kitchen and dutifully swallows his Concerta.

"Good boy. Off you go," says my mother.

We watch them out the picture window. Lucy, wearing one of her many sets of fairy wings over her coat like a backpack, is collecting sticks into a red pail. Charlie runs out closer to the woods and starts rolling in the snow. Meanwhile, Linus is cruising around the coffee table in the living room, still wearing his feety pajamas, clicking magnetic trains together.

"I'll take Linus out for some fresh air in a few minutes," says my mother.

"Thanks."

She sits down in the chair next to me, to my right, her favorite place to position herself so I can be sure to see her. She holds her mug of herbal tea in her hand and flips open *People* magazine. I have yesterday's *New York Times* in front of me. I'm searching for page C5, a continuation of the article I started yesterday from the front page about the cost of the Afghan war. I can't find it.

"I know you have this thing about the Sunday *Times*, but there are easier ways to get the news and practice your reading."

"Tell me you're not saying *People* magazine is news."

"I'm just saying. You could be done reading this today," she says, turning the page for emphasis.

She doesn't get it. It's not about reading simply anything or taking the easy way out. It's about reading what I normally read. Reading the Sunday *Times* is about getting my life back.

"You won't know anything about Angelina Jolie after reading all that," says my mother, smirking.

"Somehow, I'll survive," I say.

Still smiling from her little joke, my mother opens a clear plastic pillbox, pours a handful of white and yellow pills into her palm, and swallows each one with a separate sip of tea.

"What are those for?" I ask.

"These?" she asks, shaking her pillbox. "These are *my* vitamins."

I wait for further explanation.

"They're my happy pills. My antidepressant medication."

"Oh."

"I'm not me without them."

In all this time, it never occurred to me that she could be clinically depressed. My father and I would tell each other and anyone who asked about her that she was still grieving or having a hard time or not feeling well today, but we never used the word *depressed*. I thought her lack of interest in what was left of her family, in me, was her choice. For the first time, I consider the possibility of a different story.

"When did you start taking them?"

"About three years ago."

"Why didn't you go to a doctor sooner?" I ask, assuming that she needed them long before then.

"Your dad and I never thought of it. Our generation didn't go to the doctor for feelings. You went for broken bones or surgery or to have babies. We didn't believe in depression. We both thought I just needed some time to mourn, and then I'd be able to put a smile on my face and carry on."

"That didn't happen."

"No, it didn't."

In all my limited experience with my mother, our conversations have always skimmed the surface and gone nowhere. It's such a small thing, to hear my mother admit what has never been in dispute, that she wasn't happy and never carried on, but her candid confession encourages me to continue the conversation, to dive into our big and murky water. I take a deep breath, not knowing how far down the bottom might be, or what I might bump into along the way.

"Did you notice a difference when you started taking the pills?"

"Oh, right away. Well, within about a month or so. It was like I'd been existing inside a dark, polluted cloud, and it finally lifted and floated away. I wanted to do things again. I started to garden again. And read. I joined a book club and the Red Hat ladies and started going for walks on the beach every morning. I wanted to wake up every morning and do something."

Three years ago. Charlie was four, and Lucy was two. Bob was still passionate and dreamy about his start-up, and I was still working at Berkley—writing reports, flying to China, ensuring the success and longevity of a multimillion-dollar company. And my mother was gardening again. I remember her vegetable garden. And she was reading and beachcombing. But she wasn't trying to reconnect with her only daughter.

"Before I started taking the medication, I didn't want to wake up in the morning. I was paralyzed with What-Ifs. What if I'd paid closer attention to Nate in the pool? He'd still be here. I was his mother, and I didn't protect him. What if something happened to you? I didn't deserve to be your mother. I didn't deserve to live. I'd been asking God to let me die in my sleep every night for almost thirty years."

"It was an accident. It wasn't your fault," I say.

"Sometimes I think your accident was my fault, too," she says.

I stare at her, not comprehending what she could possibly mean by this.

"I used to pray to God for a reason to be in your life, for a way to know you again."

"Mom, please, God didn't conk me on the head and take away the left side of everything so you could be in my life."

"But I am in your life because you got conked on the head and lost the left side of everything."

God has a plan.

"You know, you could've simply called me."

And not involved God and a debilitating brain injury.

"I wanted to. I tried, but every time I picked up the phone, I froze before I could finish dialing. I couldn't imagine what I'd say that would be enough. I was afraid you must hate me, that it was too late."

"I don't hate you."

These words slip from my mouth without conscious consideration, as if I were responding with a pat reply, like saying *Good* after someone asks *How are you?* But in the next quiet moments, I realize that these words are true and not simply polite lip service. In my complex web of not-so-admirable feelings about my mother, not one strand is woven from hatred. I study my mother and notice a palpable change in her energy, as if her baseline level of nervous vibration dials down. Not off, but considerably down.

"I'm so sorry I failed you, Sarah. I live with so much regret. Not watching Nate more closely, not getting to him before it was too late, losing all those years with you, not getting on antidepressants sooner. I wish these pharmaceutical companies would make an anti-regret pill."

I take in this sincere wish and study my mother's face—the worry lines, which are really more like worry trenches, dug between her eyebrows and along her forehead, the sorrow in her eyes, regret etched into every feature. Some future FDA-approved, prescription medication isn't the cure for her pain. My mother doesn't need another pill in her pillbox. She needs forgiveness. She needs my forgiveness. And although *I don't hate you* and *It wasn't your fault* came as ready, honest offerings, I know they're only palliative at best. "She's not ugly" isn't the same as "she's beautiful," and "he's not stupid" isn't the same as "he's smart." My mother's cure for a lifetime of regret lies within the words *I forgive you,* spoken only by me. I intuitively know this, but some part of me, old and wounded and needing a miracle cure of its own, resists this generosity and won't allow the words to leave my head. And even then, before they can be spoken, they'd have to make the long journey from my head to my heart if they're to earn the sincerity they'd need to be effective.

"I feel regret, too," I say instead, knowing that the weight of a young sister's remorse must feel infinitesimal compared to a mother's, a speck of dust resting on my shoulders compared to an entire planet on hers. "I still miss him."

"I do, too. Every day. And I'm still sad. But the sadness doesn't swallow me whole like it used to. And there's joy now. I see a little of Nate from when he was a toddler in Linus, and I see lots of him in you and Charlie. It heals my soul to witness pieces of him still alive."

I watch Linus pulling a dozen trains linked together around the edge of the coffee table. I was only three when Nate was Linus's age, and I don't remember enough about him, either physically or in personality, to see a resemblance in this moment. I wonder what it is that my mother sees. I look out the window and see Charlie playing off in the distance, building a mountain out of snow. I remember Nate's sense of grand adventure, his determination, his imagination. Charlie has all of those traits. And so do I.

"What about Lucy? Do you see any of Nate in her?"

Lucy is still playing close to the house. Her mittens are on the ground, and she's sprinkling glitter onto several nests assembled out of twigs and rocks and pinecones, presumably homes for the woodland fairies she believes in.

"Nope. That adorable little nut is a one-of-a-kind."

We both laugh. I like the sound of my mother's laugh. I wish she'd found these pills when I was a kid, that I wasn't learning the sound of my mother's laughter at the age of thirty-seven and at the price of a traumatic brain injury. I look over at her pillbox. It suddenly occurs to me that she took many more pills than should be prescribed solely for depression. What else could she be taking medication for? I wonder.

CHAPTER 26

It's Thursday, and everyone's been having a great vacation week. I did spend the first couple of days granny caning on eggshells after realizing that we forgot to bring the Wii up with us from Welmont, assuming this oversight was going to precipitate a monumental disaster involving tears and tantrums and a possible overnight FedEx shipment from Bob, but the kids haven't even asked for it. Charlie and Lucy have either been outside or content to play "olden day" games inside with my mother and me, games that don't require a left side, like I'm-Going-on-a-Picnic, I'm-Thinking-of-an-Animal, and Rock-Paper-Scissors (even the kids always beat me). My mother also bought a twelve-pack of Play-Doh, and we've all enjoyed hours of rolling, sculpting, and pretending (and Linus has enjoyed some unauthorized tasting).

I did remember to bring the mug of marbles, but we haven't needed that either. With all the time they're spending outdoors, the kids are exhausted at the end of the day, and I've been happy to give them an hour of Nick Jr. before bed, free of charge. And Charlie's attention has seemed normal all week. This could be attributed to his Concerta, but my mother and I think he noticeably benefits from so much unstructured time outside, from not being confined by walls or fences or a seat in a classroom, from so much physical activity, and from days that aren't spent rushing from one thing to the next.

And to be honest, I think I've been benefiting from being unplugged and unscheduled as well. The only TV I've seen all week is *Ellen*. I haven't checked the CNN crawl or watched any news, and I don't miss it. Of course, I miss work, but I don't miss that jumpy feeling that comes with having to react all day at any given second to the next urgent phone call, to the thirty unexpected emails that come in while I'm in a meeting, or to whatever unforeseen crisis is undoubtedly heading my way before 6:00. Sure, it's exciting, but so is watching the family of deer who stop to notice us while they're crossing the field in the backyard.

My mother took Charlie and Lucy to the mountain this morning for their lessons and brought Linus along for the ride. After a lot of sincere begging, I granted Charlie his wish to switch from skis to a snowboard. He had his first lesson yesterday and absolutely loved it. Snowboarding is the coolest, and I was pronounced the coolest mom ever for letting him become a wicked cool snowboarder.

Left Neglected

This morning over breakfast, he argued, quite skillfully, for permission to skip the lesson today and go off on his own, but I told him no. Bob and I don't know how to snowboard, so we won't be able to offer him any help on the slopes (assuming I get back on the slopes). He needs to learn the basic skills properly, and I have to believe that takes more than a day. He claims he's got it down, and that today's lesson will be *BORING*, but Charlie always possesses more confidence than skill, and even more impatience, and I don't want him breaking his neck. He then tried sulking, but I didn't budge. Then he tried roping Lucy into his cause, hoping to gang up on me and wear me down, but Lucy likes her lessons. She's cautious and social and prefers to be under the watchful eyes and enthusiastic encouragement of the instructors. When he finally realized it was the lesson or nothing, he gave up, but he took away my "coolest mom ever" status. At least I had it for a day.

I'm sitting at the kitchen table painting a picture of the backyard, using the oils from the beautiful artist's kit that my mother gave to me for Christmas. The kit is a smooth, plain wooden briefcase on the outside, but inside it contains rows of oil paints, pastels, acrylics, charcoal pencils, and brushes— a feast of color and creative possibility. I've squeezed gooey puddles of lamp black, titanium white, cadmium yellow, ultramarine blue, burnt sienna, raw umber, alizarin crimson, and phthalo green onto my glass palette, and I've mixed as many combinations together with my stainless steel palette knife. Some of my mixtures turned to mud, but some swirled as if by divine magic into new colors that sing and pop and live.

Our backyard landscape already looks like an oil painting, so it's easy inspiration—the snow-covered field guarded in the distance by maple and pine trees, the rolling hills behind them, the cloudy blue sky above, our shed painted bright barn red, the aged copper green rooster weathervane nested on its roof. It's been years since I've held a paintbrush, but it comes effortlessly back to me, like riding a bike (although I'm sure riding a bike probably isn't the best example of this for me now). Painting is all about seeing. It's about focusing past the quick and dirty assumptions normally made by the eyes and mind and seeing what is actually there. It's about spending leisure time in every detail. I see the sky, which isn't simply blue but many blues and whites and grays, whitest where it touches the hills and bluest where it kisses the heavens. I see the three different tones of red on the shed produced by sunlight and shade, and the shadows of clouds dancing like sooty black ghosts along the hills.

I study my canvas and smile, satisfied with what I've created. I drop my brush into the glass pickle jar holding the other brushes I've already used and push the canvas to the side to let it dry. I sip my coffee, which is now stone cold, and rest my eyes on the view. After a few minutes, I grow tired of the yard and want something else to do. My mother should be home soon. She told me not to go wandering around the house while she's out, and even though I'd really like to go lie down on the couch, I've learned my lesson from the time I "wandered" over to the refrigerator. I decide to limit my next activity to something that can be done from where I'm sitting.

My Sunday *New York Times* is on the table and within easy reach. I drag it over to me and begin removing sections, looking for the Week in Review. Mixed in with the folded pages, I find my mother's *People* magazine. I pick it up and study the cover. Pre-accident me can't even believe that I'm considering this. Oh what the heck. Let's see what Angelina Jolie is up to.

I push the newspaper aside and flip open the magazine, casually taking in photographs of stars and the small snippets describing who's seen with whom. I'm a few pages in when my mother bursts into the living room, huffing and puffing, toting Linus on her hip.

"You okay?" I ask.

"He's getting so heavy," says my mother.

He is heavy, similar in size and shape to a Thanksgiving turkey, but he's actually slimmed down some since learning to walk. My mother places Linus on the floor, pulls off his boots, and unzips his coat. She then lets out a loud, cleansing exhale and looks over at me. Her face lights up.

"Aha!" she says, catching me red-handed.

"I know, I know."

"Isn't it great?"

"Great is a little much."

"Oh come on, it's fun. Call it a guilty pleasure. There's nothing wrong with a little reading for pleasure."

"The Sunday *Times* gives me pleasure."

"Oh please! The look on your face while you're reading that thing is more pained than Charlie's on his worst homework day."

"Really?"

"Yes, you look like you're getting dental work done."

Huh.

"But I can't replace the *New York Times* with *People*. I still need to get the news."

"That's fine, but this can be good practice for you, too. Like, okay, name all the people on this page," she says, standing over my shoulder.

"Renée Zellweger, Ben Affleck, I don't know who that woman is, and Brad Pitt."

"Katie Holmes, married to Tom Cruise. Anyone else?"

I look the page over again.

"No."

"Anyone next to Brad Pitt?" she asks in a flirty voice, so I know it's not a yes or a no, but a who answer.

Without trying to find out who is there, I go with the odds and take a guess.

"Angelina."

"Nope," she says, urging me in her tone to try again.

Huh. I don't see anyone. Okay. Look left, scan left, go left. I imagine searching for my red bookmark even though I don't have it here. Oh my God. Look at that. There he is.

"George Clooney."

I wouldn't think that even a traumatic brain injury could keep me from noticing him.

"Yeah, this will be good practice for me," I say, enjoying George's mischievous, smiling eyes.

"Good, I'm proud of you," says my mother.

She's never said that she was proud of me before. Not for graduating from college, not for going to Harvard Business School, not for my impressive job or my not-nearly-as-impressive-but-still-adequate parenting skills. The first time she ever tells me that she's proud of me, it's for reading *People* magazine. That might be the strangest thing a parent has ever been proud of.

"Sarah, this is beautiful," says my mother, her attention shifting to my painting.

"Thanks."

"Truly, you're talented. Where did you learn to do this?"

"I took a couple of classes in college."

"You're really good."

"Thanks," I say again, watching her face enjoy what I've painted.

"I even like how the left sides of things are missing or fade off."

"Where?"

"Everywhere."

Look left, scan left, go left. I find the left edge of the canvas with my right hand and then move my attention across the picture from left to right. The first thing I notice is the sky—completely untouched white canvas at the left border, gradually turning a cloudy gray, becoming almost clear day blue by the time I hit the right edge. It looks almost as if a foggy morning were burning off from right to left across the horizon. The maple trees have no branches on the left, the pine trees only half their green needles. And although the conservation land extends many acres beyond what the eye can see in either direction, the forest in my painting grows only on the right. The left side of each rolling hill rolls flat, and the left side of the shed sort of dissolves into nothingness. I forgot to paint the entire rooster weathervane. It stands on the left half of the shed's roof.

I sigh and pluck a soaking brush from my glass pickle jar.

"Well, this will be good practice, too," I say, wondering where to begin filling in the blanks.

"No, don't. You should leave it. It's good the way it is."

"It is?"

"It's interesting to look at, sort of haunting or mysterious, but not creepy mysterious. It's good. You should leave it the way it is."

I look at my painting again and try to see it as my mother does. I try, but now instead of noticing only the right side of everything, I notice everything that is missing. Everything that is wrong.

Omissions. Flaws. Neglect. Brain damage.

"You want to watch the end of the kids' lessons later and have lunch at the lodge?" asks my mother.

"Sure," I say.

I continue to stare at my painting, at the brushstrokes, the shading, the composition, trying to see what my mother sees.

Trying to see what is good.

CHAPTER 27

I'm sitting at a booth inside the base lodge at Mount Cortland, my right shoulder pressed up against the window overlooking the south side of the mountain. My mother is sitting across from me knitting an impractical but adorable ivory wool sweater for Linus, who is asleep in his umbrella stroller. I'm amazed that he can sleep through all the activity and noise in here. It's nearing lunchtime, and the room is starting to become crowded with chatty, hungry skiers, all stomping in their heavy boots on the hardwood floor. There are no rugs or curtains or decorative fabric of any kind in the lodge, nothing to absorb sound, and so every boot step and every voice bounces all over the room, creating an unmusical reverberation that will eventually give me a headache.

My mother noticed a workbook of word search puzzles in

the checkout line at the supermarket yesterday, and remembering that Heidi used to give word searches to me at Baldwin, she bought it. She loves any chance she gets to be my therapist. I'm working on one of the pages now, and I've found eleven of the twenty words. I assume the remaining nine are hidden somewhere on the left side, but I don't feel like hunting them down. I decide to daydream out the window instead.

It's turned into a bright and sunny day made even brighter by the reflection of the sun off so much white, and it takes a minute for my squinting eyes to adjust. I look around for the kids at their lessons on Rabbit Lane over by the Magic Carpet lift and spot Charlie in the middle of the hill on his snowboard. He falls backward onto his bottom or forward onto his knees every few seconds, but for the few seconds in between while he's actually up, he appears to be moving really well, and it does look fun. Good thing he has young bones and is only about four feet tall, not very far from the ground he keeps crashing down onto. I can't imagine how sore and bruised and worn out I'd be if I were to fall that many times. I think about these last couple of months. Well, maybe I can imagine it.

Then I find Lucy waiting at the top of the lift, probably for instruction. Unlike her fearless brother, she won't move one ski on her own without express permission. She's still doing nothing, and I've lost sight of Charlie, so my attention drifts to the right, as it's prone to do, to the bottom of Fox Run and Wild Goose Chase, my two favorite trails. I watch the skiers, indistinct blobs of red, blue, and black, sailing on a sea of white to the bottom, then snaking into the line for the quad lift in front of me.

I wish I were out there. I watch one couple, I assume a husband and wife, come to a stop side by side just outside my window. Their cheeks and noses are pink, and they're smiling and talking. I can't make out what they're saying. For some reason, I want them to look up and notice me, but they don't. They turn back toward the mountain and get into the lift line, sliding forward a few feet at a time, getting ready to go again. They remind me of Bob and me. Everything around me is bombarding my senses, triggering an almost overwhelming urge to get my shiny, new skis and get on that mountain—the sounds of the lodge, the smell of French fries, the intense brilliance of the outdoor light, imagining the feel of the cold mountain air inside my lungs and pressed against my cheeks and nose, watching the young couple's shared exhilaration after finishing a great run. I want to be out there.

You will be. But I'm not so sure of myself. I'm having a hard enough time walking on flat, nonskid floors with the assistance of my granny cane. *You WILL be,* insists pre-accident me, her tone leaving zero room for any other acceptable possibility. Pre-accident me is so black-and-white, and it occurs to me that, like Charlie, she has more confidence than the goods to back it up. *You will be.* This time it's Bob's voice in my head, assured and encouraging. Reluctantly, I believe him.

"What's that?" asks my mother.

"What?" I ask, wondering if I said any of what I was just thinking about aloud.

"Out there. That person coming down the mountain sitting down."

I scan the blobs on the hill and don't see what she's talking about.

"Where?"

"There." She points. "And there's a skier standing behind it."

I finally locate what she's looking at. Closer now, it looks like the front person is sitting on a sled attached to a ski, and the person behind is skiing and holding on to some kind of handle attached to the sled, most likely steering it.

"Probably someone who's handicapped," I say.

"Maybe you could do that," she says, her excited voice bouncing across the table at me like a ping-pong ball.

"I don't want to do that."

"Why not?"

"Because I don't want to ski sitting down."

"Well, maybe there's a way for you to do it standing up."

"Yeah, it's called skiing."

"No, I mean a special way."

"You mean a handicapped way."

"I mean, maybe there's a way for you to ski now."

"I don't want to ski now unless I can do it the normal way, and I'm not ready. I don't want to be a handicapped skier."

"You're the only one using that word, Sarah."

"It doesn't matter. We don't own any 'special' equipment, and I'm not investing thousands of dollars in some kind of ski sled that I don't want to use in the first place."

"Maybe they have them here. Excuse me, miss?"

My mother flags the attention of a young woman walking by our table. She's wearing the signature red and black Mount Cortland staff ski jacket.

"See that person out there skiing sitting down? Did that person rent that equipment here?"

"Yes, it's from NEHSA, New England Handicapped Sports," she says. She glances over at my granny cane. "It's in the building next door. I can take you over if you want."

"No thanks," I say before my mother has a chance to start packing up our things. "Just curious, thanks."

"Can I bring you some information about it?"

"No, we're good, thanks," I say.

"Okay, well, NEHSA's right next door if you change your mind," she says and walks away.

"I think we should check it out," says my mother.

"I don't want to."

"But you've been dying to ski."

"That's not skiing, it's sitting."

"It's more like skiing than sitting in this booth. It's outside. It's a way down the mountain."

"No thanks."

"Why not just give it a try?"

"I don't want to."

I wish Bob were here. He'd have choked the life out of

this conversation in its first couple of breaths. The "skier" and the dogsled musher behind him come to a stop in front of our window. The musher is wearing the same red and black jacket worn by the woman we just spoke with. An instructor. The "skier's" legs are strapped together and onto the sled. The "skier" is probably paralyzed from the waist down. I'm not paralyzed. Or maybe the "skier" is an amputee, and one or both of his legs are prosthetics. I have both of my legs. The "skier" and the instructor talk for a minute. The "skier" has a huge smile on his face. The instructor then guides the "skier" directly to the front of the line, where they both board the quad lift with far more ease than I expected.

I watch them ride up the mountain and follow their ascent until their chair gets too small to distinguish. I spend the next half hour before lunch watching skiers and snowboarders zigzagging down Fox Run and Wild Goose Chase. But if I have to be honest, I'm not simply watching the activity on the mountain with passive eyes. I'm searching for the sitting "skier" and his musher. But I don't see them again.

I continue to steal glances out the window all through lunch but still catch no sight of them. They must've moved over to a different set of trails. I check one more time as we're packing up our things to leave for home. I still don't see them.

But if I close my eyes, I can see the "skier's" smiling face.

CHAPTER 28

It's nearing the end of January and Bob and I are back in Ms. Gavin's first-grade classroom, but this time she's provided us with adult-sized chairs, and my shoes are arguably as ugly as hers. The school year at Welmont Elementary is divided into thirds, and we're about halfway through the second third. Ms. Gavin asked to meet with us to discuss Charlie's progress before the next report cards go home.

We sit down, and Bob reaches over and takes hold of my left hand. Ms. Gavin acknowledges us before she begins with a kind smile, probably interpreting our hand-holding to mean that we're nervous and bracing for the impact of discouraging news, a sweet offering of emotional support. While I detect an element of anxious solidarity in Bob's touch, I think the primary reason he's holding my hand is to keep it still.

Most of the time, my left arm dangles straight down from my shoulder, useless but not calling attention to itself either. But recently, my left hand has started showing an interest in conversation, and unbeknownst to me, it gestures.

My outpatient therapists, Heidi, my mother, and Bob all think this is a good development, a positive sign of life returning to my left side, and I agree, but to me it's also a freaky new symptom because it feels like someone other than me is the puppeteer. Sometimes the gestures are small expressions that add appropriate emphasis to whatever I'm saying, but other times, the movements are completely disconnected from any decipherable content, and my arm just seems to aimlessly, even spastically, roam around. Yesterday, during a shamefully passionate discussion about *Kate Plus Eight* with my mother, my left hand wandered onto my left boob and stayed there. And I only know this now because, after Bob and my mother shared a long, eye-watering laugh at my expense, my mother let me in on the big joke and removed my hand from my boob for me (since I couldn't let go of my own volition). So Bob might be holding my hand in loving support, but he's probably more concerned with keeping me from feeling myself up in front of Ms. Gavin. For either reason, I'm grateful.

"We're all so glad you're back home, Mrs. Nickerson," says Ms. Gavin.

"Thank you."

"How are you doing?" she asks.

"Good."

"Good. I was so worried when I heard what happened.

And with you not being home for so long, I was also concerned that Charlie would start acting out and slip even further behind."

I nod and wait for her to elaborate on the itemized details of his acting out and the significant extent of his slippage. Bob squeezes my hand. He's waiting, too.

"But he's been doing really well. I'd say he does better in the mornings than the afternoons, and this could be because the medication spikes just after he takes it in the mornings and tapers off as the day goes on, or it could be that he's more tired by the afternoon, but overall I can definitely see an improvement."

Wow. I was hoping all along to hear this kind of news about Charlie but hadn't dared to hope it aloud. He's been doing so much better at home—finishing his homework in less than an hour and without major negotiations or drama, remembering to put his shoes on if I ask him to put his shoes on, not losing more than half his marbles in a day—but we didn't know if any of these behavioral improvements at home were translating to the classroom. Bob gives my hand a happy shake, and we wait for Ms. Gavin to elaborate on the details and extent of Charlie's improvement.

"He's doing better at following instructions, and he's more often than not able to finish the worksheets I give to the class."

She hands Bob a stack of white papers. Still holding on to my left hand, Bob passes me one sheet at a time. Each paper has Charlie's name at the top, printed in his penciled handwriting. On most of the sheets, Charlie has answered all of the questions, which in and of itself is a noteworthy achievement, and so far I see only one or two or three wrong out of ten or so questions on each page. *Great job! Well done! Good work!* are written in red marker at the top of almost every sheet, extra exclamation points and smiley faces added to many. I don't think I've ever seen celebration on Charlie's work before.

"Here's the last one," says Bob.

It's a sheet of simple math problems. *100%! ! !* is written and circled at the top. A perfect score for my beautifully imperfect boy.

"Can we take these home?" I ask, beaming.

"Of course," says Ms. Gavin, beaming back.

I can't wait to gush over this particular page of addition and subtraction with my mother, who will be equally thrilled, and to magnetize it to the center of the fridge. Or maybe we should frame it and hang it on the dining room wall.

"It's a huge improvement, don't you think?" asks Ms. Gavin.

"Night and day," says Bob.

"I let him use an extra-large, yellow index card to block out the questions below the one he's focusing on. Cutting the questions into individual strips was too time-consuming, and the other kids got interested in his 'craft project' and suddenly everyone wanted to cut up their papers, too. So I don't mind if you do that at home, but we use the yellow index card here, and it seems to work well."

"Okay, that would be easier for us, too. Does he sit or stand?" I ask.

"I've told him he can do whatever he prefers, and he used to mostly stand, but now he's back to sitting. I do think standing helps him stay still and focused on what he's doing, but some of the other kids were giving him a hard time about it. Some of the boys have been teasing him."

Who? Who is giving him a hard time? Give me names, I want names.

"Like how?" Bob asks.

"Well, when he was standing, someone was sliding his chair back so that when he went to sit back down, he'd fall on the floor. One day, one of them put a chocolate cupcake from snack on Charlie's chair, and after he finished his work, he sat on it. They teased him, saying the chocolate was poop. They call him Poopy Pants."

I feel like Ms. Gavin just kicked me in the chest with her ugly shoe. My poor Charlie. I look past Ms. Gavin and notice the poster board of "Stellar Spellers." Charlie's picture has been added to the cast of characters. His eyes are squeezed shut from an exaggerated smile. There are four other photos of boys on the board. They're also smiling. A minute ago, I would've said they were all cute little boys, but now I see a gang of rotten little monsters. Bad seeds. Why hasn't Charlie said anything about this to us?

"What have you done about it?" asks Bob.

"I reprimand the kids who are teasing him when I'm aware of it, but I'm sure a good deal of it goes on underneath my radar. And unfortunately, the punishments do seem to spur the boys on even more."

I can imagine it. Verbal warnings, no recess, or being sent to the principal's office are only going to stoke the fire. But surely, there's got to be something we can do. Implausible revenge fantasies start playing out in my mind. An eye for an eye, poop for poop. I squeeze my impotent anger into the handle of my granny cane. Caning. Caning would work for me.

"So, what then, Charlie just has to suffer through it?" Bob asks. "What about moving the kids who are bothering him to a different part of the room?"

"I did that. So he should be able to stand now if he wants to without anyone disturbing him, but he's been choosing to stay in his seat while he works. I think he just wants to be like everyone else."

I know how he feels.

"I know you're not supposed to use this word in today's politically correct world, but do you think he'll ever be 'normal'?" I ask.

My heart winces. I know I'm asking about Charlie, but I feel my own question as if I were asking it about me. Will I ever be normal? Will I ever see "100%" at the top of my sheet? Ms. Gavin pauses, and I can see her choosing her words carefully before she opens her mouth. I know her answer is simply going to be one young teacher's opinion about one young student based on a very limited amount of experience with him. But my heart, impermeable to this logic, feels that somehow the truth of both Charlie's and my fates will rest in what she's about to say, like she's about to deliver my prophecy. I clutch my cane.

"I think between the medication and the behavioral and dietary adjustments like the ones you've been making and all the positive reinforcement and support he's getting, Charlie's ADHD won't get in the way of him reaching his full academic potential. I really do applaud you both for taking such quick action. A lot of parents would've ignored me or blamed me and the school system for ages before doing what you did to help him."

"Thank you. That's such a big relief to hear," says Bob. "But what about the other normal kid stuff, like fitting in?"

She hesitates.

"Off the record?" she asks, still hesitating. "I have one student who obsessively bites her nails to the nub, another who can't stop picking his nose, another who hums while she works, and another who stutters. Every year, the kids with pronounced overbites get called 'Bugs Bunny,' and the kids with glasses get called 'four eyes.' I know every parent wants their child to fit in, and no one deserves to be teased, but Charlie's experience for a first-grader feels pretty normal to me."

I laugh, releasing all fear and vengeful emotion from my heart, replacing it with an open-armed acceptance and empathy that extends first to Charlie with his yellow index card and his mug of marbles and his less-than-one-hundred-percents and his chocolate-stained bottom. And then it expands to include his entire first-grade motley crew class with all their crazy tics and idiosyncrasies and deficiencies. And then it reaches Ms. Gavin in her ugly shoes for possessing the patience and courage to teach and deal with them every day. And, because I have a bit more, it stretches to include me. A thirty-seven-year-old woman whose husband is holding her left hand so she won't unconsciously grab on to her own boob.

"And normal's overrated if you ask me," Ms. Gavin says.

"I agree," I say.

Ms. Gavin smiles. I do wonder about Charlie's future, though. When the other students stop picking their noses, and the kids with bad teeth start seeing an orthodontist, and the kids with glasses get contact lenses, will Charlie's ADHD continue to make him an outsider? Sports are a great way to belong, but Charlie has a hard time waiting his turn, staying in position, playing within the rules—all necessary qualities for being successful at soccer, basketball, T-ball. He already doesn't love playing any of these sports, but he's too young to realize that they're optional. We sign him up for whatever is offered for his age, and he shows up for practices and games like he shows up for school, because we tell him to and take him there. But at some age, likely not too far off from now, if he doesn't improve, he'll probably opt out. And he'll lose all those opportunities for fitting in and forming lasting friendships that being part of a team affords. It's too bad we don't live near a mountain. He'd probably thrive on a snowboarding team.

"So keep up with what you're doing at home. I just

wanted you to know that he's doing much better here. I think you'll all be so proud of his report card this time," says Ms. Gavin.

"Thank you. We will," says Bob.

The kids from Charlie's grade have been playing outside at recess during our meeting. With a few minutes still left before they have to return to their classrooms, Bob and I decide to walk over and say hello to Charlie before Bob drives me home and he returns to work. We make it to the edge of the long cobblestone walkway when we both stop to notice a big commotion erupting near the swings. It looks like two kids are fighting, and one teacher is having a heck of a time trying to break it up. All other activity on the playground has ceased in mid-motion; everyone's watching to see what will happen. I can't make out the faces of the two kids from where Bob and I are standing, but in the next instant, I recognize one of the two coats. Charlie's orange North Face ski coat.

"Charlie!" I yell.

Bob releases my left hand and takes off toward Charlie. Every muscle in my body wants to run to Charlie, too, but my broken brain won't let me. My child is in danger or in trouble or both and within sight, and I can't get to him to either save or scold him. Bob is on the ground with Charlie now, and the teacher is dragging the other child away by the hand. I cane, step, drag, and breathe, frustrated with each cane and impatient with every drag, mad at myself for not already being over there.

"What happened?" I ask when I finally reach them.

Charlie kicks at the dirty snow with his boots and says nothing. His nose is running, and he's breathing hard through his mouth. His face and fingernails are filthy, but I don't see any blood.

"Go ahead, answer your mother," says Bob.

"He said a bad thing," says Charlie.

I look at Bob. This must be one of the boys who've been teasing him. I try to scan to the left to see which boy the teacher has taken into custody, but I can't find them.

"Did that boy call you a name?" I ask.

Charlie stops kicking at the ground and casts his eyes up at me.

"No," he says. "He called you one. He called you a dumb cripple."

I pause, stunned, unable to launch into the prepackaged, clichéd speech every mother has filed in her apron pocket about sticks and stones and the high road. I try scanning to the left again, wondering if the boy might be the Nose Picker or the Stutterer, but I still can't find him. I return to Charlie.

"Thank you for sticking up for me," I say, loving him. "But you shouldn't fight."

"But—" says Charlie.

"No buts. No fighting. Plus, that kid doesn't even know what he's talking about," I say. "I'm the smartest cripple he's ever seen."

CHAPTER 29

My mother and I have been watching Bob and Lucy ski together on Rabbit Lane from our booth in the base lodge for the past hour. After a lot of badgering, whining, pleading, and negotiating—and ultimately because he truly did master the basics last week over February school vacation—Charlie finally won his wish to leave the lesson hill. We catch sight of him every so often bombing around on Fox Run. I can never see his face, but I imagine he's grinning ear to ear.

"I think I'm going to go back to the house," says my mother, her eyebrows knotted, coping with some kind of pain.

"What's wrong?" I ask.

"Nothing really. I think the sun is giving me a little

311

headache. And I didn't sleep well. I think I'm going to go take a nap with Linus. You want to come?"

"No, I'll stay."

"You sure?"

"Yeah. You sure you're okay?" I ask.

"I just need to lie down. Call me if you need me."

She collects the cans of Play-Doh, board books, and trucks Linus was playing with and tosses everything into his diaper bag. Then she slides out of the booth, buckles Linus into his stroller, and leaves.

It's early in the morning, and the lodge is quiet. I look out the window, but I don't see Bob and Lucy or Charlie. My mother left me with a sketchpad and pencils, the word search workbook, and the latest *People* magazine. But I've already combed through this issue of *People*, and I don't feel like drawing. I should do a word search. My outpatient therapist thinks that doing word searches might help me get faster at finding the leftmost letters on my computer keyboard, and I need to speed up my typing if I want to go back to work, and I definitely want to go back to work, so I should do every word search in this book. But I don't feel like it.

Without a particular destination in mind, I decide to go for a walk. There's nowhere to really go on foot except for the parking lot, and that's probably not the safest place to go wandering around for someone who doesn't easily notice information coming from the left and who can't readily get out of the way. But I'm tired of sitting in this booth and reason that the fresh air will be good for me.

My granny cane and I step outside, and I'm instantly perked up by the cold air and the hot sun. Without planning to aim there, and continuing to aim there even after I fully realize where I'm going, I walk over to the building next door. I pause only to read the sign over the door. NEW ENGLAND HANDICAPPED SPORTS ASSOCIATION. Then I continue up the handicapped ramp and walk inside.

I'm surprised to see that it looks like a typical ski lodge—pine floors, wooden benches, clear glass bowls displayed on a counter filled with hand warmers, ChapStick, and sunscreen, a wire rack loaded with polarized sunglasses. I think I was expecting it to look more like a rehabilitation hospital. There's only one person in the room besides me, a young man in a wheelchair, I'd say in his twenties. From his crew cut and age, I guess that he's an Iraq war veteran. He looks confident and relaxed, like he's been here dozens of times before. He's busy adjusting the straps around his legs and doesn't seem to notice me.

"Can I help you?" asks a man wearing a red and black staff jacket and an enthusiastic smile.

"Just having a look around," I say, trying not to make eye contact.

"You a skier?" he asks.

"I used to be."

We both acknowledge my granny cane with a solemn nod.

"I'm Mike Green," he says.

He holds on to his smile, posed in gracious cheerfulness,

expecting to greet my name in return, but I'm more than a little reluctant to give up my anonymity. His big white teeth, made whiter by the contrast of his skier's tan—golden brown all over his face except for the pale, sunglasses-shaped mask around his eyes, a sort of reverse raccoon—show no sign of backing down.

"I'm Sarah Nickerson," I say, giving in.

"Sarah! We've been expecting you! Glad you finally came in."

Now he's grinning at me like we're old friends, making me feel uneasy and like it's time to excuse myself and take my chances dodging cars in the parking lot.

"You have?"

"Yup. We met your lovely mother a few weeks ago. She already filled out most of your paperwork."

Oh, now I get it. And of course she did.

"I'm sorry, she didn't need to do that."

"Don't be sorry. We're ready to get you on the mountain whenever you are. But you're right. You're not a skier any-more. At least not for now."

Here we go. Here comes the inspiring and persuasive sales pitch about the wonderful and miraculous ski sled. I start brainstorming effective ways to interrupt him and politely communicate *Not in a million years, mister,* without insulting him and before he wastes too much of his breath and my time.

"You're a snowboarder," he says, dead serious.

Not what I was expecting to hear at all. Not in a million years.

"I'm what?"

"You're a snowboarder. We can get you on a snowboard today if you're game."

"But I don't know how to snowboard."

"We'll teach you."

"Is it a normal snowboard?" I ask, seeing the way out.

"It's got a couple of extra bells and whistles, but, yeah, it's a regular snowboard," he says.

I throw him the same look that Charlie and Lucy give me when I tell them that broccoli is delicious.

"What's normal anyway? Everyone needs equipment to get down the mountain. Normal's overrated if you ask me," he says.

Normal's overrated. The exact words Ms. Gavin used when talking about Charlie. And I agreed with her. My face softens, like I'm considering how delicious broccoli might be with a little Parmesan cheese sprinkled on it, and Mike sees his opening.

"Come on, let me show it to you."

My intuition tells me to trust him, that this man knows a lot more about me than my name and whatever my mother might've told him.

"Okay."

He claps his hands together.

"Great. Follow me."

He walks past the veteran in the wheelchair and over to the doorway of an adjacent room, too quickly for me to keep up with him. He waits in the threshold, watching me walk. Assessing me. Cane, step, drag. Probably reconsidering this whole snowboarding idea. Cane, step, drag. Probably thinking that the ski sled would be a better fit for me. Cane, step, drag. I can feel the veteran watching me, too, and he probably agrees. I look up at the wall in front of me and notice a poster of someone on the mountain sitting in a ski sled, his musher skiing behind him. Panic starts racing willy-nilly through my head, begging any part of me that might listen to reason to tell Mike that I can't follow him, that I have to go, that I'm supposed to meet my husband in the lodge, that I have to get back to my word search puzzles, that I have somewhere else I need to be right now, but I say nothing and follow him into the adjacent room.

The room looks like a storage warehouse crammed with modified ski and snowboard equipment. I see lots of ski poles of varying heights affixed with miniature skis on the bottoms, wooden dowels with tennis balls stuck to the ends, all kinds of boots and metal hardware. When I come face-to-face with a long row of ski sleds lined up against the wall in front of me, my panic can't take it anymore and whips into a full-blown tantrum.

"This is the one I'd like to start you on."

As I scan to the left, trying to locate Mike, his white teeth, and the ski sled he wants to start me on, I feel increasingly light-headed. I should've stayed in the lodge with my *People* magazine and my word searches. I should've gone home with my mother and taken a nap. But when I find him, he's not standing next to any of the ski sleds. He's in front of a snow-board. My panic sits down and quiets itself, but it remains skeptical and on alert and isn't one bit embarrassed or apologetic for the false alarm.

From what little I know about snowboards, this one looks mostly normal. A metal hand railing is screwed into the board in front of the boot bindings, extending up to about waist height, reminding me of a grab bar. But otherwise, it looks like a regular snowboard.

"What do you think?" he asks.

"It's not horrible. But I don't understand why you think I'm a snowboarder."

"You can't keep track of your left leg, right? So let's essentially get rid of it. We'll lock it in place next to your right leg on the board, and there you go, you don't have to drag it or lift it or steer it anywhere."

That does sound appealing.

"But how would I turn?"

"Ah, this is also why you're a snowboarder. Skiing is about shifting balance left to right, but snowboarding is shifting your balance back and forth."

He demonstrates, pushing his hips forward and then sticking his bottom out, bending his knees in both positions.

"Here, give me your hands, give it a try."

He faces me, grabs my hands, and holds my arms out in front of me. I try to copy what he did, but even without a mirror in front of me to see myself, I can tell that whatever

I'm doing looks more like Martin Short imitating something sexual than like someone snowboarding.

"Sort of," he says, trying not to laugh. "Imagine you're squatting over a public toilet seat that you don't want to sit on. That's back. Then imagine you're a guy peeing for distance in the woods. That's front. Try it again."

Still holding on to his hands, I'm about to rock forward, but I freeze up, feeling funny about pretending to pee on Mike.

"Sorry, my description's a little graphic, but it works. Forward and up on your toes, back and sitting on your heels."

I give it another go. I send my right hip forward and then back, forward and then back. And, unlike when I move my right leg or my right hand, when I move my right hip, my left hip goes with it. Always. If this is how to steer a snowboard, then it seems as though I could do it.

"But what about stopping? How would I control my speed?"

"This rider bar here is for your balance, like how you're holding on to my hands now. But to begin with, it's also for one of us instructors to hold on to. If we go up today, I'll snowboard facing you, and I'll control how fast you go. When you've got your balance down, we'll transition you to one of these."

He shows me another snowboard. This one doesn't have a grab bar, and at first I don't notice anything special about it. Then Mike loops a black cord through a metal loop attached to one end of the board.

"Instead of me pushing against you from the front, I'll

hold on to this tether from behind you to help regulate your speed."

I imagine a dog on a leash.

"And then, from there, you'll do it on your own."

He whips the tether out of the loop as if to say *Tada! A normal snowboard!*

"But how would I keep from crashing into other people on the trail? If I'm concentrating on anything, I can't see things on my left."

He smiles, recognizing that he's got me imagining myself on the mountain.

"That's my job until you can do it on your own. And when you try it without the rider bar, you can transition to using an outrigger if you want," he says, now holding up a ski pole with a small ski attached to the bottom. "This would give you an additional point of contact with the ground, like your cane does, offering you some extra stability."

"I don't know," I say.

I search around for another *but,* but I can't find any.

"Come on, let's give it a try. It's a beautiful day, and I'd love to get out there," he says.

"You said that my mother filled out *most* of my paper-work?" I say, turning over my last stone of possible resistance.

"Ah, yes. There are a couple of standard questions we always ask that only you can answer."

"Okay."

"What are your short-term winter sport goals?"

I think. As of a few minutes ago, my only goal for today was to go for a walk.

"Um, to snowboard down the hill without killing myself or anyone else."

"Great. We can accomplish that. And how about long-term goals?"

"I guess to snowboard without needing any help. And eventually, I want to ski again."

"Perfect. Now how about life goals? What are your short-term life goals?"

I don't quite see how this information would in any way affect my ability to snowboard, but I have a ready answer, so I offer it to him.

"To go back to work."

"What do you do?"

"I was the vice president of human resources for a strategy consulting firm in Boston."

"Wow. Sounds impressive. And what are your long-term goals?"

Before the accident, I'd been hoping to be promoted to president of human resources in the next two years. Bob and I were saving to buy a bigger house in Welmont with at least five bedrooms. We planned to hire a live-in nanny. But now, since the accident, those goals seem a little irrelevant, if not ridiculous.

"To get my life back."

"Alright, Sarah, I'm so glad you came in. You ready to go snowboarding with me?"

Spent from all the unnecessary distress, my panic is now snuggled in a soft blanket and sleeping peacefully. Pre-accident me isn't jumping up and down about this idea, but she isn't arguing against it either. And Bob isn't here to weigh in. So it's up to me.

"Okay, let's do it."

Mike pulls me by the rider bar onto the Magic Carpet lift, and we move, both standing on our snowboards, up the slight but steady incline of Rabbit Lane. The Magic Carpet is like a conveyor belt, and the people on it—mostly young children, a few parents, a couple of instructors, Mike and me—remind me of pieces of luggage at the airport or groceries at the supermarket riding along a ribbon of black rubber, waiting to be scanned.

I look around for Bob and Lucy, both wanting them to see me and praying that they don't. What is Bob going to think when he sees me on a handicapped snowboard? Will he think I've given in to my Neglect and given up? Have I given up? Is this accommodating or failing? Should I have waited until I'm recovered enough to ski like I used to? What if that never happens? Are my only two acceptable choices sitting in the booth in the lodge or skiing like I did before the accident, with nothing in between? What if someone from work is here for the weekend and sees me? What if Richard is here and sees me clutching on to a grab bar, guided by an instructor from the New England Handicapped Sports Association? I don't want anyone to see me like this.

What am I doing? This might've been a really impulsive, really bad decision. As we approach the top—which isn't the top of anything but simply the arbitrary end of the Magic Carpet, visible from the booth I was safely sitting in back in the lodge before I had to go nosing around—the anxious chatter in my head grows louder and stronger, blooming into a full-fledged panic.

I've changed my mind. I don't want to do this. I don't want to snowboard. I want to go back to my booth and work on my word search puzzles. I want to be at the bottom of the hill. But we're at the top of the lift now, and there is no Magic Carpet ride to the bottom. And unlike the kids who freeze up and freak out for their own legitimate or irrational reasons, I can't decide to abandon my board and walk the moderate distance to the bottom. My granny cane is back inside the NEHSA building, and I can't imagine that Mike would agree to assist me down the hill on foot without at least my giving the snowboard an honest try.

Mike yanks me to the side so I don't cause a pileup at the end of the conveyor belt. He then turns and faces me and places his hands outside of mine on the rider bar.

"Ready?" he asks, his teeth all excited.

"No," I say, clenching mine, trying not to cry.

"Sure you are. Let's start by sliding forward a little."

He leans downhill, and we begin to move. Whether I like it or not (and it's decidedly *not*), I'm about to snowboard.

"Great, Sarah! How does it feel?"

How does it feel? It feels like excitement and terror are tumbling around inside my chest like clothes in a dryer. Each second I'm overwhelmed with one and then the other.

"I don't know."

"Let's try turning. Remember, peeing in the woods to go left, squatting over the toilet to go right. Forward and up on your toes, back and on your heels. Let's try forward first."

I rock my hips forward, and we begin to turn left. And that feels horribly wrong. I lock up my knees, stack my hips over my thighs, and stand upright. I lose all control over my balance, but then I feel Mike correcting for me, and he keeps me from falling down.

"What happened?" he asks.

"I don't like turning left. I can't see where I'm going before we're already there, and it scares me."

"Don't worry. I'll keep an eye out for where we're going. I promise we won't hit anyone or anything, okay?"

"I don't want to go left."

"Okay. Let's slide a little, and when you're ready, go back on your heels and turn right."

He nudges backward on the rider bar, and we begin sliding down the hill together. After a few seconds, I go back onto my heels, squatting over the imaginary toilet, and we turn to the right. I return my hips to neutral, and we slide forward. I decide to do it again. *Squat, heels, neutral, forward. Squat, heels, neutral, forward.*

"Great, Sarah! You're snowboarding!"

I am? I release my concentration from the death grip it's got on the separate steps of what I'm doing and begin to realize the whole of what I'm doing. *Slide, turn, slide. Slide, turn, slide.*

"I'm snowboarding!"

"How do you feel?" he asks.

How do I feel? Even though Mike is maintaining my balance and checking my speed, I decide when we turn and when we go downhill. I feel free and independent. And even though I'm holding on to a handicapped bar and normal snowboards don't have handicapped bars, I don't feel abnormal or handicapped. Walking with Neglect is so belabored and choppy, requiring miles of effort to drag myself a few miserable feet. As we glide down the hill on our snowboards, I feel fluid and graceful and natural. I feel the sun and breeze on my face. I feel joy.

We come to a stop at the bottom, still facing each other. I look at Mike's smiling face and see my reflection in his polarized sunglasses. My teeth look as huge and excited as his do. How do I feel? I feel like Mike hurled a huge rock through the glass wall of my preconceptions, hitting it dead center, shattering my fear into a million glittery pieces on the snow around me. I feel unburdened and beyond grateful.

"I feel like I want to do that again."

"Awesome! Let's go!"

Now on flat terrain, Mike pops one of his boots out of the binding and tows me by the rider bar over to the Magic

Carpet. Because he's with NEHSA, we're heading to the front, cutting the entire line.

"Mommy! Mommy!"

It's Lucy, standing next to Bob in line ahead of us. And Charlie is with them. Mike pulls me alongside them, and I introduce him to my family.

"Look at you!" says Bob, surprised to see me, but beaming, not a trace of disappointment or judgment in his words or in his eyes, where I can always see his truth.

"Look at me!" I say, bursting with childlike pride. "I'm a snowboarder, just like Charlie!"

Charlie looks me up and down, inspecting the validity of this statement, lingering on Mike's gloved hand, which is resting on my rider bar, deciding if my declaration needs qualifying, if my enthusiasm needs a reality check.

"Cool!" he says.

"She just had her first run and did awesome. She's a natural," says Mike.

"We were about to do one more run before lunch," says Bob. "Can you join us?"

"Can we jump in here?" I ask.

"Sure," says Mike, and he pulls me into line behind Lucy.

We ride the Magic Carpet and gather together at the top.

"Ready?" Mike asks.

I nod. He leans back, and we begin to slide. *Slide, turn, slide.* I smile as we're snowboarding, knowing that Bob and the kids are hanging back to watch me, knowing that Bob is probably smiling, too. I'm at the top of Rabbit Lane instead of the summit, and I'm on a handicapped snowboard instead of skis, but nothing about this experience feels less than 100 percent, less than perfect. I'm on the mountain with my family. I'm here.

Slide, turn, slide. Smile.

CHAPTER 30

It's Monday morning. I know it's Monday morning because we drove back to Welmont from Cortland last night, and so last night was Sunday night. It's the beginning of March, and I've been out of work for four months now, which also means that I've been existing for four whole months outside of the rigorous daily schedule that used to map out my Who, What, When, Where, and Why for every single waking hour of the day. I know it's a weekend when we're in Vermont, and I know Mondays and Fridays because we've either just returned or we're packing to leave again, but the days in between have started to blur together. By Wednesday, I won't know if it's Tuesday or Thursday. And it doesn't much matter.

I also know it's Monday because Linus didn't go to day

care today. He still goes there Tuesdays through Fridays, but he doesn't go at all now on Mondays—one of the many efforts we're making to save money. Charlie and Lucy are at school, Bob is at work, and Linus and my mother went to the grocery store. I'm home alone, still in my pajamas, sitting in my favorite chair in the sunroom. My sacred space.

I'm reading *The Week* magazine instead of the Sunday *New York Times*. I'm so done with the Sunday *New York Times*. I discovered *The Week* in the waiting room at the pediatric dentist's office, and I love it. It debriefs me on the week's main stories in three quick pages and includes opinions from the editorials and columnists of major newspapers like the *New York Times*. It even devotes a page to us closet *People* fans on the latest Hollywood "news." All the articles begin and end on the same page, and the whole magazine is a pleasurably manageable forty pages.

It possesses the same qualities I appreciate most in my favorite Berkley consultants—efficient yet thorough, cutting straight to the chase. As I flip the page and dwell on this comparison, I suddenly remember the 80–20 rule.

Considered to be a universal truth and one of the Ten Commandments for Berkley consultants, the 80–20 rule is an economic principle that states that 20 percent effort yields 80 percent value. Essentially, it means that for anything anyone does, only 20 percent really matters. For our consultants who need to deliver an answer to the client in a few weeks and therefore don't have the luxury of studying a particular business problem for the next year, the 80–20 rule reminds them to focus on the 20 percent of information that is vital and to ignore the 80 percent that is likely to be irrelevant (our superstar consultants are the ones who have an intuitive sense for what to focus on and what to ignore).

The editors of *The Week* have basically culled the 20 percent of news that matters to me and published it in a tidy little magazine. I'll finish this whole issue by tomorrow if not today, which means I'll be sufficiently informed of the week's world events by Tuesday, which leaves the rest of my week free and clear to do something else. The 80–20 rule is pure genius.

I look out the windows into our suburban yard and then through the French door windows into the living room and sigh, unable to think of what that something else might be. There are only so many word search puzzles I can work on, only so many red balls I can find and pick up off a tray. My outpatient therapy, which was two times a week, is now over. It's not over because I've fully recovered (I haven't) or because I quit (I didn't), but because our insurance only pays for ten weeks, and my time was up. How any human being with a molecule of reason, a shred of compassion, and a pulse could establish and stand behind this preposterously premature cutoff is beyond me.

After waiting on hold on the phone for what felt like ten weeks to speak with an actual human being at our insurance company, I expressed my unedited outrage to some poor customer service representative named Betty, who I'm confident had no part in creating the policy and who surely has no influence over changing it. But it felt good to vent. And so that's it. If I'm to recover 100 percent, it's going to be 100 percent up to me from here on out to make it happen.

I finish reading *The Week*. Now what? I'm surprised that my mother and Linus aren't back yet. Linus is really on the move now, running whenever he gets the chance simply because he can. He hates to sit still, and he's exceptionally single-minded, a trait my mother claims descended directly from my DNA. *He doesn't get it from the wind*, she says. I hope he isn't giving her a hard time. She's been amazing with all three kids, juggling their schedules, preparing their meals, laundering all their clothes, and she's enjoying the time she spends with them, but I can see by four o'clock on most days that she's worn out. I feel bad that she's working so hard, but I can't imagine how we'd be managing without her.

I snuggle into the deep chair, close my eyes, and absorb the relaxing greenhouse-like warmth of the sunroom. But I'm not tired and don't feel like napping. I wish it were Saturday. If it were Saturday, we'd be in Vermont, and I could go snowboarding. I can't wait to go back.

The phone rings. My mother handed me the phone like she always does before leaving me alone in the house, but I don't see it tucked into the cushion next to me where I normally keep it. It rings again. I follow the direction of the sound and locate it on the small occasional table opposite me, remembering now that Linus had been playing with it and must've discarded it there. Three feet and miles away.

I could get up and granny cane over to the table, but probably not in four rings. I should let the machine answer the call, but I was just wishing for something to do. I'm going to try to beat the machine. The phone rings again. I only have three more.

I grab Granny by the shaft and shimmy down until I'm holding one of the rubber feet. Then I reach out and lob the handle end onto the table. I wiggle the cane until the phone sits inside the U of the handle. Ring number four. I yank on the cane, and the phone flies off the table and smacks me square on the knee. Ow. The phone rings at my feet. I reach down, pick it up, press Talk, and almost yell *I win!* instead of *Hello?*

"Hi, Sarah, it's Richard Levine. How are you?"

"I'm good," I say, trying not to sound out of breath or in pain.

"Good. I'm calling to see how you're doing, and if you'd be ready to discuss the possibility of your coming back to work."

How am I doing? It's almost noon, I'm in my pajamas, and the proudest moment of my day will be that I retrieved the phone with my granny cane before the sixth ring.

"I'm doing great, much better."

Am I ready to consider going back? My mother would probably point out that if I can't coordinate the steps it takes to change a diaper, how would I possibly coordinate human resources? But Bob would say that I'm ready. He'd tell me to go for it. And customer service Betty from our health insurance company would tell me that I'm ready. Pre-accident me is popping corks of champagne, patting me on the back, practically pushing me out the door.

"And I'd love to discuss coming back."

"Great. When can you come in?"

Let's see. I was planning on going for a walk around the block this afternoon before taking my nap, my mother's coming home from the grocery store, which means I probably own a new word search puzzle book, and there's a new episode of *Ellen* on the DVR.

"Any time."

"How about tomorrow at ten o'clock?"

"Perfect."

"Great, we'll see you then."

"See you tomorrow."

I hang up the phone, tuck it into the seat cushion, and absorb the impending consequences of that unexpected conversation along with the heat from the sun. Both are making me sweat. I'm ready to discuss returning to work. But am I ready to go back? I ripped into poor customer service Betty, denouncing her criminal policy for discontinuing my therapy before I was 100 percent recovered. Before I was 100 percent ready. So how recovered and ready am I? I can read and type, but it's slow. Walking is even slower. I worry about being late for meetings and deadlines, about not noticing some critical document placed on the left side of my desk, about forgetting to open files stored on the left side of my computer desktop. I think of the 80–20 rule. Am I even at 20 percent?

I've always prided myself in being a perfectionist, for dotting 100 percent of my *i*'s, for doing it all. But what if less than 100 percent were enough? What if I'm 20 percent recovered, and that's enough to return to my job? It could be. My work is in human resources, a desk job. It's not performing surgery (requiring two hands) or the fox-trot (requiring two feet). I can be less than 100 percent better and still be brilliant at my job. Can't I?

I sit in my favorite chair in my sacred space, my heart pounding, each beat fueled by equal parts exhilaration and fear, wondering if my proclaimed readiness is reasonable optimism or a laughable lie. I look out the windows into our yard and sigh, unable to lean far enough either way into an answer. I guess we'll all find out tomorrow.

CHAPTER 31

I glance over at my alarm clock again. It's four minutes later than the last time I checked. And we're still working on my pants. I keep sucking in, and my mother keeps tugging, but my black wool suit pants won't zipper all the way up.

"I think you should wear these," says my mother, holding one of my many identical, black synthetic, elastic-waistband pants.

"I think you should try one more time," I say.

"That's as high as it's going to go."

"It's fine then. Once my suit jacket is buttoned, it'll cover everything."

We move on to my blouse. In the time it used to take me to get fully dressed without memorable effort, I manage to fasten two of my blouse buttons by myself. I fasten one

335

more, not breathing and grinding my teeth, before I give up and turn the entire project over to my mother. I look at the clock. I can't afford to be late.

My mother finishes with the buttons of my blouse and then the suit jacket. She clasps my turquoise bead necklace around my neck and my jingle charm bracelet around my left wrist. I pick out diamond stud earrings. She fits them into my pierced ears and secures the backings. She brushes my entire face with foundation and bronzing powder, sweeps a light pink eye shadow over my lids, plucks a few rogue hairs from between my eyebrows and my chin, and colors my lips with a subtle gloss. I look in the mirror and approve of her job.

We reach a gridlock, though, when it comes to my footwear. I refuse to wear my Merrell mules (or her other suggestion—white sneakers!), and my mother refuses to drive me into work if I choose to wear heels.

"I have to look completely put together. I need to portray power and sophistication."

"How powerful and sophisticated are you going to look when you trip and fall flat on your face?"

Sadly, it's not an implausible prediction. I decide not to risk that particular humiliation with a compromise. Bruno Magli ballet flats. My mother prefers the sticky rubber soles of the Merrells to the "slippery" bottoms of the flats, but she acquiesces and fetches them for me. There. Aside from my Annie Lennox hairdo, which I happen to love, I look pretty much like I did four months ago. Appropriately corporate, sophisticated, powerful, and most important, not disabled.

Until I grab hold of my granny cane. There's nothing powerful or sophisticated about this accessory, but unfortunately, I'm stuck with it. I wish I'd progressed to a regular cane by now. A handsome wooden shaft and a fancy brass handle conjure far more attractive associations than harsh stainless steel and gray rubber—a distinguished gentleman with a slight, inconsequential gimp as opposed to a frail grandmother recovering from a recent hip replacement. My mother offers to dress Granny up for the occasion with a pretty silk scarf tied around the handle, but I don't want to call any unnecessary attention to it. Better to just ignore it and hope that everyone can follow my lead.

The kitchen is oddly quiet with the kids already gone. Bob brought them to school and day care early today, giving me and my mother uninterrupted space and time to get ready. I down a cup of coffee. My stomach is too full of butterflies for food. I check the time.

"Let's go."

I've been tense since I woke up, and I think my mother's feeling it, too, but getting dressed, even when I was only offering direction, provided us both with an activity to channel all our nervous energy into. Now we're driving into Boston, and I'm a passenger strapped into my seat, and my anxiety is trapped inside the car with nothing to do and nowhere to go, claustrophobic and expanding exponentially by the second.

My shoulders crowd my ears, my right foot bears down on the imaginary gas pedal on the floor, and my nerves are screaming *Go, hurry up, let's get there so I'm not late!* Meanwhile, my mother has gone to a calm place in the opposite direction, driving slower than usual, proceeding with extra caution on this critically important day, crawling safely in the first lane of the highway while everyone in Massachusetts seems to be whizzing by us. She is the tortoise, and I am the hare. Under the best of circumstances, we were never meant to share a morning commute.

I'm about to lose it when I notice where we are, and every preoccupied, panicky thought inside me goes eerily still. Goosebumps scuttle up my spine and down my arm. There's nothing significant about this stretch of the Mass Pike, no meaningful landmark, exit, or sign on either side east or west, nothing anyone else would take note of. This is where it happened. This is where I lost control of the car. This is where my whole life changed.

I want to point out the spot to my mother, but before I can coordinate my thoughts with my voice, we're already past it, and then it doesn't feel worth sharing. I decide to keep quiet, both about the location of my accident and about my mother's driving. We'll get there. We're going fast enough.

We park in the Prudential garage and take the elevator to the mall level.

"Okay, Mom, I can take it from here. Where do you want to meet?"

"I'm not going in with you?"

I'm trying to present myself as independent, confident,

and ready. Not exactly the three words that jump to mind if I walk back into work for the first time with my mommy.

"No, you can go do some shopping. Let's meet in the food court when I'm done. I'll call you."

"But I wanted to see where you work."

"Another time. Please."

I can tell I've hurt her feelings, but there's too much at stake. I don't even want anyone suspecting that my mother drove me into work. Let them assume that I drove myself here.

"You sure?" asks my mother.

"Yes. I'm a big girl. I'll call you."

"Okay. I'll get Linus some bigger onesies at the Gap."

"Perfect."

"Good luck," she says and hugs me, surprising me.

"Thanks."

I make my way beyond the retail stores, following the route I've walked thousands of times, to Berkley's lobby, nestled in a private, exclusive-feeling corner of the mall. The reception area is exactly as it was—sleek, modern, creamy leather chairs and a glass coffee table arranged like a mini living room in a waiting area, today's *New York Times* and *Wall Street Journal* available on the table, an expensive arrangement of fresh flowers set on the imposingly tall reception desk, BERKLEY CONSULTING embossed in gold lettering on the wall behind it. Heather, our receptionist, sits behind the desk on a platform so that she's well above the floor, looking down, adding to the authoritative impression Berkley stamps on its guests.

"Good morning, Heather."

"Sarah, welcome back!"

"Thank you. It's good to be back. I'm here to see Richard."

"Yes, they have you in the Concord Room."

"Great. Thank you."

I walk past Heather's desk, doing my best to minimize the obvious drag of my left foot.

"Oh, Sarah? The Concord Room is this way," she says, pointing in the opposite direction and like she's talking to a sweet but obviously confused elderly woman. Damn this cane.

"I know. I want to say hello to someone first."

"Oh, sorry."

I walk down the long hallway, slower than I ever have, and feel like I've come home. The predictable order of offices as I pass by, the framed aerial photographs of major world cities on the walls, the lighting, the carpeting, all feel inviting and comfortable in their familiarity. I thought I might bump into Jessica along the way, but I wasn't truly planning on saying hello to anyone on this side trip. I stop in front of my office.

I open the door and flick on the lights. My computer screen is off, and my desk is clear of papers. The pictures of Bob and the kids are angled exactly as I left them. Even my black wool sweater is still hanging over my desk chair, ready for days when I feel chilly and need an extra layer, usually in the over-air-conditioned summer months.

I thought I'd want to go in, sit in my chair, fire up the

computer, enjoy a few minutes of people watching out the window on Boylston Street, but I don't step one ballet flat inside. The reception area and hallway felt like home to me, but my office, which I've probably logged more hours in over the last eight years than in my actual home, feels somehow too strange, like it's now a crime scene under investigation, and although there's no police tape, I'd better not go in and disturb anything. I flick off the lights and quietly close the door.

When I acted on the impulse to visit my office, I imagined that it would be a quick detour. I should've known better. Berkley's Boston office is the company's world headquarters, a massive, sprawling corporate space, and my office is located about as far away as it could be from the Concord Room. I jingle my bracelet and find Heidi's watch on my left wrist. Crap.

By the time I cane, step, drag, and breathe to the Concord Room, everyone is already there, seated, drinking coffee, waiting for me, and now watching my grand, granny-caned entrance. I should've gotten here early. What was I thinking?

"Sarah, come in," says Richard.

Richard and Carson are seated at the immediate right end of the ten-seat-long conference table. I scan to the left. Gerry and Paul, two of the managing directors, are seated opposite Richard and Carson, and Jim Whiting, one of the partners, is sitting next to Paul. From the caliber of the crowd, I draw two quick conclusions. One, this decision is critically important. And two, this decision will take all of ten minutes. I might be done here before my mother even finds the babyGap.

I can also tell from the polite silence and hesitant smiles that everyone is concerned if not surprised and unnerved by my walk and my granny cane. I draw in a deep breath and all the courage I can muster and shake hands with everyone before I sit down at the head of the table. I've got a great handshake—firm but not crushing, confident and engaging—and I pray that it cancels out the damage done by this first impression of me.

I decline Richard's offer of coffee or water, not wanting to risk dribbling anything down the left side of my mouth, but wishing I could say yes to both. I'm tuckered out and my throat is dry from the long walk across Berkley, and I could use a drink. I'm also feeling sticky under my arms and beneath my bra, and so I'd also love to remove my wool suit jacket, but I don't dare throw that sideshow into the act. Plus, it's hiding my unzipped pants. I find my left hand with my right and pin it between my knees. A touch late, sweaty, thirsty, and praying that my left hand doesn't come loose and do anything inappropriate or disabled-looking, I smile at Richard, as if everything is business as usual, ready to begin.

"Well, Sarah, we have a number of big projects coming in next quarter, and we've experienced some unexpected turnover. Carson's been doing a great job filling in for you for the last few months, but we absolutely can't afford to limp along going forward."

I smile, flattered. I imagine human resources dragging

itself around with its own granny cane for the last four months, handicapped, unable to function at 100 percent without me.

"So we wanted to check in with you and see if you're feeling ready to jump back in."

I want to dive back in. I miss my life here—the fast pace, the high intensity, contributing to something important, feeling powerful and sophisticated, being effective. I look from person to person, trying to read how much they believe in my readiness to return, to see if anyone's expression or body language mirrors the enthusiasm I can feel popping all over me, but I'm not getting the positive reinforcement I want. Gerry and Paul have their arms crossed, and everyone is poker-faced. Everyone but Jim. I shook hands with Jim a moment ago, but I don't see him anywhere now. It's possible that he snuck out, that he was paged and had somewhere more important he needed to be. But it's more likely that he pushed his chair back ever so slightly, or Carson's pen tapping is drawing too much of my focus to the right side of the room, or who knows why, and he's still here, sitting in the black hole of my Neglect.

Who am I kidding? I'm dealing with more than a pronounced limp. My mother had to dress me and drive me in, my left hand is pinned between my knees, I'm afraid to drink a cup of coffee in front of anyone, I'm exhausted by the trek from my office to this conference room, and I have no idea where the managing partner is. Whatever percentage ready I am, it's not enough. I think of the volume of work I used to process each day, the volume of work expected of me. Given my current level of recovery and ability, there simply aren't enough hours in the day. And however much I want to dive back in, I'm not willing to compromise the quality of work that the company needs or my reputation for delivering it.

"I really want to come back, but in total fairness to everyone here, I'm not ready to be back full-time. I'm capable of doing everything, but it all still takes me a bit longer."

"How about part-time?" asks Richard.

"Is that really an option?" I ask.

Berkley doesn't have any part-time employees. You work here, they own you. Not part of you. All of you.

"Yes. We understand that you might need some more time before you're fully up to speed, but it'd be more efficient and effective to pull you back in, even part-time, than for us to find, recruit, and train someone new."

I imagine the cost-benefit analysis run by one of our analysts. Somehow, my numbers, even at part-time, must've come out more attractive than the numbers for a new VP of HR, at least for next quarter. I wonder what discount factor they used to account for Left Neglect.

"Just to be clear, part-time means how many hours a week?"

"Forty," says Richard.

I knew this would be the answer before I asked the question. At most companies, forty hours is full-time, and twenty would be part-time. I know I could handle twenty. But this is Berkley. It would probably take full-time hours for me to produce what's expected of part-time productivity, but I could probably do it. Eighty hours of time and effort for forty hours' worth of work and pay. Bob and I really need my income, even part of it.

"And when would you want me to start?"

"Ideally, right away."

I was hoping he'd say next month, giving me more time to recover, but I suspected from the urgency of this meeting and the number of bigwigs in the room that they need someone up and running in this position today. I think of all the balls I used to juggle every day—expensive, fragile, heavy, irreplaceable balls—barely able to keep them all in the air, loving every adrenaline-packed minute of it. And now here I am, back at Berkley, and Richard's got an armful for me. My right hand is ready to catch them, but my left hand is pinned between my knees.

"Well, what do you say?" asks Richard.

Here I am, back at Berkley, and Richard has spoken the welcoming words I've been praying to hear every day for four months. I'm standing in the threshold of the door to my old life. All I have to do to reclaim it is walk through.

CHAPTER 32

I'm going to turn it down."

Bob's elated face unravels into fathomless wonder, like I told him in one breath that we won the lottery and in the next that I gave the winning ticket to the homeless woman who begs for change on the corner of Fairfield and Boylston.

"Have you lost your mind?"

"No," I say, insulted. Well, I actually have lost some of my right mind, but now's probably not the best time to be literal.

"Then why on earth would you do that?"

"I'm not ready."

He rakes his fingers up and down repeatedly over his eyebrows and forehead, like he does whenever the kids have pushed him to the edge, and he's trying to buy a calm second. Only the kids aren't even home. We're alone in the house, sitting opposite each other at the kitchen table.

"They think you are," he says.

"They don't know what we know."

They don't know how hard it is for me to read every word on every page, especially the words on the left side of the left page. They don't know how long it takes me to find the letters on the left side of the computer keyboard. They don't know that my office would need to be decorated in orange tape and signs reminding me to *LOOK LEFT*. They don't know how long it took me to walk from my office to the Concord Room and that I crashed into several doorframes and one potted plant along the way, and they don't know that Jim vanished mid-meeting because he was seated too far to my left. They haven't seen me fall or drool or try to take off my coat.

"I really think you're ready," says Bob.

"I'm not."

Bob's encouragement since the accident has been unwavering, confidently walking the fine line between optimism and denial, determination and desperation. Some days, it's exactly the morale boost I need to keep going, but others, like today, it seems more disconnected from reality than I am from the left side of the room.

Even part-time work at Berkley would be too much volume under too much time pressure, like having to read the Sunday *Times* in a day. I can only too well imagine the costly mistakes, the omissions, the embarrassment, the apologies.

My ego and I could suffer through it all, but in the wake of my suffering, the consultants would suffer, the clients would suffer, and Berkley would suffer. No one would win.

"This is exactly what you said about skiing, and now you're on the mountain every weekend," says Bob.

"But I'm not skiing, I'm snowboarding."

"The point is you got back out there. And it's been the best therapy for you. I think going back to work will be so good for you. What's the worst that could happen?"

"I'd fail miserably."

"You won't. You've got to at least give it a try."

"Would you?"

"Definitely."

"No, you wouldn't. You wouldn't go back unless you could be at your best."

"I would. And you'll get there. You won't know unless you try."

"I know I can't ski, and I haven't tried."

"This is different than skiing."

"I know."

"This is really important."

"I know."

He starts raking at his eyebrows and forehead again. And now he's got that pulsing twitch in his temples that he gets when he's trying to reason Lucy out of one of her tantrums, an impossibly futile goal, like trying to convince a hurricane to change its course or downgrade to a mild tropical storm. I can ignore her, but Bob can't resist trying to do something.

He talks and twitches. She wails and thrashes. Her tantrums can sometimes be tricked by distraction, but mostly they have to run their course before she's calm enough to reach with words.

"I'm freaking out here, Sarah. I can't do this alone. We can't afford this lifestyle without you—the kids' private lessons, day care, our school loans, the mortgages. And I don't know how long your mother's going to put her life on hold for us. We should probably start to look into selling the house in Vermont."

"Or maybe we should sell this one," I offer.

"And then where would we live?" asks Bob, humoring me but in a condescending tone.

"Vermont."

He looks at me like I suggested we should sell one of our kidneys, but this seems like a reasonable idea to me, one that's been fuzzy and fragmented but gradually coalescing in my mind for some time. Our Welmont mortgage and the cost of living here are our biggest expenses. It could take over a year to find a buyer for our house in Vermont, but even in this economy, Welmont real estate values have been holding steady. Our house here is a modest four-bedroom, and most people looking in Welmont want more space, but it's well maintained and would show well. It would probably sell right away.

"We can't live in Vermont," says Bob.

"Why not? The cost of living there is practically nothing compared to here."

"That's because there's nothing there."

"It has plenty there."

"It doesn't have our jobs."

"We'd get jobs."

"Doing what?"

"I don't know, I haven't thought about it yet."

But I want to. There's not a lot going on in the Northeast Kingdom of Vermont. It's not Corporate America. It's rural New England, only sparsely populated, mainly by artists, skiers, mountain bicycling enthusiasts, ex-hippies, farmers, and retirees.

"I could open a coffee shop," I say, brainstorming.

"What?"

"A coffee shop. B&C's is closed, and Cortland needs a good coffee shop."

"Maybe B&C's closed because Cortland can't support a good coffee shop."

"Maybe it just didn't have good management."

"It's a ridiculous business idea."

"What's so ridiculous about it? Is Starbucks a ridiculous business?"

"So you want to open a Starbucks?"

"No, I—"

"You want to compete with Starbucks?"

"No."

"You want to be the Juan Valdez of Cortland County?"

"Not funny."

"None of this is funny, Sarah. I love Vermont, too, but

we're too young and ambitious to live there full-time. It's a place to vacation. Our life is here. Our jobs are here."

I don't see why they have to be.

"You know, we might both be out of a job here soon. I don't see why we can't at least look up in Vermont."

"Again, doing what? You want to run human resources at Mary's Maple Syrup Company?"

"No."

"You want me to sell lift tickets at the mountain?"

"No. I don't know what's there."

"There's nothing there."

"You don't know that. We haven't looked."

"So you want to turn down your job at Berkley and look for a job in Vermont?"

"Yes."

"This is a completely crazy conversation."

"Maybe."

"No, it is."

"Okay, so we're having a crazy conversation."

Bob, a natural risk taker with a brilliant business mind and entrepreneurial spirit, should be open to this kind of discussion. He should also know that some of the world's best ideas, biggest innovations, and most successful businesses were first resisted and perceived as crazy. He's stopped raking his face, and his temples are no longer twitching. He's looking at me like he doesn't know who I am. His eyes are lonely and scared.

"I'm sorry, Sarah. I don't want to have this conversation.

And I don't want to pressure you. I know you're still going through a lot, but I don't think you should pass up this opportunity. If you wait, they'll have to find someone else, and they might not offer this to you again. This is your way back. We need you to go back to Berkley."

His last sentence feels more like an order than an appeal. But just like he couldn't order me back onto skis, he can't order me back to work. My stubborn independence has always been a brick wall that Bob's wanted to kick down. All these years later, it amuses me that he still tries. As much as he'd like to be at times, like now, he's never been the boss of me. For better or worse, we've enjoyed a marriage of equal partnership. It's usually a positive asset, something we're both proud of, but sometimes it's admittedly difficult having two captains of the same ship, with two sets of hands on the wheel. When Bob wants to steer left, and I want to go right, one of us has to compromise else we risk hitting the rocks dead ahead of us and sinking.

"I know you're afraid. I'd be afraid, too. But you're brave. Look at what you're capable of facing and conquering. I'm so proud of you. If you can call up the strength and courage to do battle with your Neglect every day, then I know you have the strength and courage to go back to work. I know it's scary, but I believe in you. They believe in you. You can do this. You're ready."

The thought of going back to Berkley now is scary. But it's not scary like snowboarding for the first time, trying to walk without a cane, or Martha in a miserable mood. And it's not the reason I don't want to go back. Ever since business school, I've had my head down, barreling a thousand miles an hour, wearing the flesh of each day down to the bone, pointed down one road toward a single goal. A successful life. And not just run-of-the-mill success. The kind of success that my fellow elite classmates would envy, the kind that my professors would cart out to future students as a shining example of achievement, the kind that even the exceptionally prosperous citizens of Welmont would aspire to, the kind that Bob would be proud of. The kind of visibly successful life that would in every way be the exact opposite of the broken, shameful life of my childhood.

And then I crashed my car. For the first time in almost a decade, I stopped barreling a thousand miles an hour down that road. Everything stopped. And although much of the stillness of the past four months has been a painful and terrifying experience, it has given me a chance to lift my head up and have a look around.

And I'm starting to wonder. What else is there? Maybe success can be something else, and maybe there's another way to get there. Maybe there's a different road for me with a more reasonable speed limit. Whether it's because I can't, I'm too afraid, something inside me has changed and wants something different, or a complex blend of all three, I can't say, but I don't want to go back to Berkley. I don't want to go back to that life. The same intuition that led me to Mike Green and snowboarding is leading me somewhere else. And I trust it.

"I'm not going back to Berkley."

CHAPTER 33

I t's early Saturday morning, before the black-backed woodpeckers have started playing percussion on the maples and pines and before the lifts open at the mountain. Linus has just hopped down off my lap and is now lying on the floor with a truck in one hand, Bunny in the other, sucking on his nukie, still in pajamas, watching a *Sesame Street* video with the volume barely on. Charlie and Lucy are, for the moment, playing quietly in their rooms. My mother and I are sitting on the couch in front of a gently crackling fire, enjoying this peaceful entry into the day. Bob stayed in Welmont, said he had too much work to do this weekend, but I suspect he's still mad at me and doesn't want to contribute one feel-good moment to my "cocka-mamie idea" of living here. I breathe in the smell of my latte before taking another hot sip. Mmm. I'd say he's missing one right now.

I'm ostensibly doing a word search puzzle, but I'm mostly savoring my coffee, relaxing in front of the fire, and observing my mother. She's knitting a bright red shawl, completely focused on her needles, every so often naming the order of the stitches under her breath. She stops to massage her shoulder.

"You okay?" I ask.

"I think my arm's sore from holding Linus so much."

She's squeezing her upper left arm. I'm pretty sure she usually holds Linus with her right.

"Maybe you're tensing your shoulders while you're knitting," I suggest, even though her posture doesn't look tensed.

"I think it's Linus."

She rubs her arm, shoulder to elbow, a few more times and then resumes knitting. The shawl cascades down from her needles across her lap and onto the couch like a blanket. It appears to be almost done, and I imagine that it'll look pretty on her, complementing her silver hair, her black-rimmed glasses, and the red lipstick she loves to wear.

"You must miss your Red Hat friends," I say.

"I do," she says without looking up or interrupting her clicking needles. "But I talk to them all the time."

"You do?"

I never see her on the phone.

"We Skype."

"You *Skype*?"

"Uh-huh."

This is the woman who missed the advent of the microwave, the VCR, and the television remote control, all of which still befuddle her. She doesn't own her own cell phone or a laptop, and she doesn't have a GPS navigation system for her car. But she Skypes?

"How do you even know what Skype is?" I ask.

"I saw it on *Oprah*."

I should've known. My mother's three sources of all information come from Oprah, Ellen, and *People* magazine. The academic snob in me wants to belittle her, but I have to give her credit. She's come a long way in four months. She uses Bob's GPS like a pro and drove into Boston during rush hour every day while I was at Baldwin. She eventually manages to find the correct remote control (we have five) and press the right combination of buttons to switch inputs from cable to VCR to Wii (even Abby found this to be confusing). She answers the cell phone Bob gave her to use while she's with us whenever we call her. And apparently, she Skypes on our home computer.

"What about your home? You must miss being in your own house," I say.

"I miss parts of it. I sometimes miss the quiet and my privacy. But if I were there, I'd miss the kids' voices and their laughter and all the activity here."

"But what about all your things? And your routine."

"I have a routine here and plenty of things. Home is where you live. For now, I live with you, so this is home to me."

Home is where you live. I think of that sign at the end of Storrow Drive in Boston: IF YOU LIVED HERE, YOU'D BE HOME NOW. I look out the windows at the natural beauty of our open land, the gray morning filling with color as the sun rises over the hills. I would love living here. And I think the kids would love it. But Bob's right. We can't simply move here and uproot everyone without a concrete plan for our livelihood. I envision a sign at the Vermont border: IF YOU'RE GOING TO LIVE HERE, YOU'RE GOING TO HAVE TO FIND JOBS. *Real jobs*, I hear Bob's voice add in my head.

"I would like to be back for summer, though. I'd miss my garden and the beaches. I love summer on the Cape," says my mother.

"Do you think I'll be better by summer?"

"Oh, I think you'll be a lot better by then."

"No, I mean, do you think I'll be back to the way I was before this happened?"

"I don't know, honey."

"All the doctors seem to think that if I haven't fully recovered by the summer, I probably won't."

"They don't know everything."

"They know more than I do."

She checks her row.

"I bet they don't know how to snowboard," she says.

I smile, picturing a scared and unsteady Martha strapped to a board on Fox Run, falling hard onto her bottom every few inches.

"Nothing's impossible," she says.

The doctors and therapists would've probably also told me that I couldn't snowboard yet, that it wouldn't be possible. And yet, I'm doing it. *Nothing's impossible.* I sit still and absorb my mother's words until I feel like they've penetrated the deepest part of me where they can't be shaken loose. My mother clicks her needles, keeping focused on the construction of her shawl, so she doesn't notice me watching her, loving her simple yet beautiful words of wisdom, proud of her for doing whatever has been asked of her to be here, grateful that she came at all and then stayed to help me even when I told her not so nicely to go home. Thank God she ignored me.

I reach over and squeeze her socked foot.

"What?" she asks, looking up from her stitch.

"Nothing," I say.

She returns to her shawl. I sip my coffee and watch the fire, enjoying another feel-good moment. I'm home with my mother.

CHAPTER 34

A classic winter nor'easter socked all of New England on St. Patrick's Day, and while the foot of snow in Welmont for everyone over the age of eighteen was mostly an endured nuisance—school cancelations, flight delays, slow and sloppy roads, traffic accidents—the twenty-plus inches of snow here in Cortland was welcomed by everyone as a fluffy white blessing from heaven. The conditions on the mountain on this sunny, windless Saturday couldn't be better.

I've been making all kinds of exciting progress on my snowboard. Last weekend, Mike removed my rider bar, and in its place I now use only a single pole in my right hand. The pole has a small, barely noticeable ski attached to the bottom, which gives me the security of additional stability and contact with the hill, much like an outrigger does for a canoe or my granny cane does for walking. But my outrigger pole is significantly cooler than my granny cane. There's nothing grandmotherly about it.

I'm also tethered to Mike, who now snowboards behind me, by a cord that runs through a loop at the toe of my board to Mike's hands. He must look like Santa Claus holding the reins to his reindeer, which would make me Dasher or Dancer or Rudolph, but I don't really care what we look like to anyone else. From where I'm standing, I see a normal snowboard and a gorgeous trail of fresh packed powder. From his position behind me, he keeps my speed in check with the reins and calls out encouragement, reminders about technique, and warnings about anything happening on our left. He says that I might want to keep the pole, but by the end of the season, I should be able to snowboard alone, which is both thrilling and almost unbelievable to imagine. But for now, I still don't notice icy patches, turns in the trail, or other skiers and snowboarders to my left unless Mike points them out (and sometimes even then I don't), so I know I'm not ready to give up believing in this Santa just yet.

We've advanced past Rabbit Lane to my favorite intermediate trails, and I'm beyond happy to be off the Magic Carpet lift and the beginner hill and onto the real mountain. Right now, we're in the middle of Fox Run. I've got my eyes and ears open for Charlie. Every so often I see him on his board, delighted to see me, then even more delighted to shred on by. He makes snowboarding look effortless. I don't know what I look like doing this, but I'm guessing that the extraordinary effort and concentration I'm exerting shows. But again, I don't care what I look like. I may not look like a cool snowboarder, but I feel like one.

Even though the conditions are pristine, I'm enjoying Charlie's flybys, I have complete faith in Mike to keep me safe, and I feel like Shaun White, I'm not experiencing the pure visceral joy and tranquil hush I typically experience when I'm on the mountain. I'm concentrating on my technique and the feel of the board on the hill with extreme focus, but a small part of my focus is listening to a dramatic monologue running in my head, thoroughly captivated by the performance.

What if Bob is right? What if Berkley was the only way back? What if I'm giving up on my only chance at returning to a real life? Maybe living in Vermont is a crazy idea.

I sit back onto my heels and turn right. But I'm a little too far back on my heels when my edge catches, and I wash out, slamming down hard onto my bottom. Mike stops beside me and helps me up.

"You okay?" he asks.

"Yeah," I say, even though I know both my tailbone and ego are bruised.

I point the toe end of my board down the mountain, and we're sliding again.

What would Bob and I do up here? I don't want to open a coffee shop, sell lift tickets, or open an art gallery (my mother's idea). Maybe there isn't anything here for us. Would living here mean abandoning our expensive and hard-earned educations, everything we've wanted to achieve and contribute in the world, everything we've dreamed about?

"Hey, Goofy!"

It's Charlie. He calls me Goofy because I lead with my right foot on the board, which is called Goofy-footed. He thinks this is a riot. I think the nickname fits me perfectly. He doesn't slow down this time, and I see only the back of his orange coat as he bombs past us. I smile.

"Show-off!"

Maybe I'm just disabled and scared and trying to drag Bob down with me. Maybe I'm trying to run away and hide. Maybe I'm crazy.

Am I crazy?

My board is aimed directly downhill, and I'm already going as fast as I feel comfortable going when the slope abruptly dips, and I accelerate. My heart jumps, and every muscle in my body tightens. Mike senses my panic and pulls back hard on the tether, and instead of tumbling into a painful fall, I ease into a gentle stop.

"Everything okay?" Mike calls from behind me.

"Yup. Thank you."

I wish he could similarly pull back on the reins of my out-of-control thoughts. We continue down the hill again.

I don't want to go back to Berkley. There has to be another choice. Another dream for my life. I know it like I know snow is white. But what? Where? Can we have a full and successful life here? It feels impossible.

I shift my weight up onto my toes. To my own amazement, I don't freeze up, and I don't fall. I realign my weight over my hips and continue downhill. I just made a clean left turn.

Nothing's impossible.

Maybe, but do I trust my intuition or Bob? Do I return to my old life or start a new one? Am I crazy to think that I could even go back to my old life? Am I crazy to want something else? I don't know what to do. I need some sort of sign.

God, please give me a sign.

We finish our last run of the afternoon, my mind still unspooling doubt and worry without offering any answers, leaving the whole tangled, messy, heaping pile on the floor somewhere just behind my eyes, giving me a headache. For the first time since I began snowboarding, I'm glad to be done for the day. Mike and I make our way back to the NEHSA building where I can return my equipment and retrieve my granny cane.

I sit on the wooden bench and remove my helmet. I find my boots and my cane.

"You felt a little tentative today," says Mike.

"Yeah."

"That's okay. Some days you'll feel braver than others. Just like anyone, right?"

"Right."

"And some days you'll see big improvements, and others you won't."

I nod.

"Don't get discouraged, okay? You coming tomorrow?"

"First thing in the morning."

"Good girl! Oh, I have that packet of literature for your friend. It's on my desk. Can you wait here a minute?" asks Mike.

"Sure."

I offered to pass along information about NEHSA to Heidi so she can let her patients know about it. I don't have any scientific or clinical data to back this up, but I think snowboarding is the most effective rehabilitative tool I've experienced. It forces me to focus on my abilities and not my disability, to overcome huge obstacles, both physical and psychological, to stay up on that board and get down the mountain in one piece. And each time I get down the mountain in one piece, I gain a real confidence and sense of independence I haven't felt anywhere else since the accident, a sense of true well-being that stays with me well beyond the weekend. And whether snowboarding with NEHSA has a measurable and lasting therapeutic effect for people like me or not, it's a lot more fun than drawing cats and picking red balls up off a tray.

Mike returns with a stack of folders in hand.

"Sorry to take so long. I got caught on the phone. Our director of development is moving to Colorado, and we're having an impossible time finding someone to fill his position. Too bad you don't live here year-round. You'd be perfect for it."

I've been wishing on stars, knocking on wood, picking up

pennies, and praying to God about one thing or another my whole life, but never have I received a more obvious, direct, and spine-tingling response before now. Maybe it's just serendipity. Maybe Mike Green is an angel on earth. Maybe God is throwing poor Goofy a bone. But this is it. This is the sign.

"Mike, you of all people should know," I say. "Nothing's impossible."

CHAPTER 35

There's no Mangia in Vermont," says Bob.

I say nothing. We're all piled into Bob's car, going to dinner at Mangia, my favorite family restaurant in Welmont. But I'm not conceding any points to Welmont for Mangia. There are plenty of decent restaurants in Vermont. Normally, I can't see Bob when he drives, but for some reason my field of vision is expanded to include part of his profile, enough to see his right thumb poking around on the screen of his phone.

"Stop!" I yell.

He hits the brakes. My seat belt locks and presses into my chest as I lurch forward. Sandwiched in a long line of 35 mph traffic, we're lucky we weren't rear-ended.

"No, not the car. Put the phone away," I say.

"Jeez, Sarah, you scared me. I thought something was wrong. I have to make a quick call."

"Have you learned nothing from what happened to me?"

"Sarah," he says in his singsong, please-don't-be-over-dramatic-and-ridiculous voice.

"Do you want to end up like me?"

"There's no right way for me to answer that question," he says.

"I'll answer it for you then. No. No, you do not want to end up like me. And you don't want to kill someone either, do you?"

"Stop, you're going to scare the kids."

"Put the phone away. No more phones in the car, Bob. I mean it. No phones."

"It's a quick call, and I need to catch Steve before the morning."

"No phones! No phones!" chant Charlie and Lucy from the backseat, loving the chance to tell their father what to do.

"It's a two-second call. I could've already been done with it."

"We're ten minutes from Mangia. Can your call wait ten minutes? Can Steve and the big important world wait ten minutes to hear from you?"

"Yes," he says, drawing out the word in an exaggerated calmness, an attempt to mask his annoyance towering behind it. "But we'll be at the restaurant then, and I'm not doing anything now."

"You're *DRIVING*!"

I used to fill my morning and evening commutes with calls (and even texts and emails in stop-and-go traffic). Now I'll never use my phone in the car again (assuming I'm someday able to drive again). Of all the lessons I've learned and adjustments I've made so far following this experience, No Phones in the Car is probably the most elementary.

"How about this?" I ask. "You could talk to me now. Let's have a nice ten-minute conversation, and then when we get to the restaurant, and you park the car, you can make your call, and we'll all wait for you."

"Fine."

"Thank you."

Bob drives and says nothing. The kids have stopped chanting. The six of us sit in the car through an entire red light with the radio off and no DVD playing, and the silence feels oppressive. He doesn't get it, which worries me at first, but through the catalyst of his silence, I quickly convert from being worried to being mad. When we wait through the next red light, and he still doesn't say anything, I go from being mad that he doesn't get why I don't want him using his phone in the car to being mad that he doesn't get why I don't want to go back to Berkley or why I want to live in Vermont. We slow down behind the car in front of us, which is turning right, and I can't believe that he doesn't get me.

"What do you want to talk about?" Bob finally asks, Mangia now only a couple of blocks away.

"Nothing."

CHAPTER 36

My mother and I are killing time with Linus in Welmont Toy Shop while Lucy is at her dance class down the street and Charlie is at basketball practice at the community center across town. Freed from his umbrella stroller, Linus is in heaven playing at the Thomas train table, linking and unlinking trains, pushing them along the tracks, through tunnels, and over bridges. He could do this all day, but we have only about twenty more minutes before the end of Lucy's class, and my mother and I are already resigned to how Leaving the Toy Store is going to play out.

I'll tell him in a happy, this-will-be-buckets-of-fun voice that it's time for us to go. Not fooled for a second, he'll instantly lose his mind and try to shoplift as many trains as his pudgy little hands can cling to. My mother and I will then dumbly explain to a completely distraught one-year-old who lacks the capacity for rational thought that the trains belong to the store and have to stay here. He'll then throw himself onto the floor, trying to resist our plan to leave through civil disobedience, and we'll have to pry the trains loose and carry him, utterly uncooperative, stiff as a board, and screaming, out the door. It'll be ugly. But for now, he's a delightful toddler in a state of pure bliss.

"Look at this," says my mother, holding up an elaborately gemmed and frilly princess gown.

"She'd love it, but she doesn't need it."

Lucy has an entire steamer trunk stuffed with dress-up costumes.

"I know, but she'd look so cute in it."

I'm standing in front of the display of Wii games, looking for We Ski & Snowboard, but I don't see it anywhere. I could order it online, but I actually want this game for myself and was hoping to play it with the kids today.

"Mom, can you help me look for the snowboarding video game?"

Before I give up, I want to make sure it isn't hiding somewhere on the left. She walks over and stands next to me, places her hands on her hips, squints, and looks up and down the display.

"What am I looking for?" she asks.

"We Ski and Snowboard."

"I don't see it," she says. "We should get going. I need to pick up my prescription at CVS."

CVS is three blocks down the street.

"You go, we'll wait for you here," I say, both wanting to give Linus more time with the trains he loves and to save myself the walk.

"You sure?" she asks.

"Yeah, we'll be fine."

"Okay, I'll be right back."

Not seeing any video games that the kids want or that we don't already have and acknowledging that we certainly don't *need* any of them, I continue browsing near the train table. They have every classic board game I remember from my childhood—Candy Land, Chutes and Ladders, Yahtzee, Clue, Sorry—plus many shelves more that I haven't heard of. I roam past the games and stop to admire the Alex display— paints, modeling clay, glues, yarns, puppets, beads, origami—I would've gone crazy for all of this stuff when I was a kid. Lucy likes anything crafty, but if she were here, she'd be exactly where my mother was shopping, probably coveting the very dress my mother showed me.

I look back over at the train table. Linus isn't there. He's probably standing somewhere to my left. Look left, scan left, go left. No Linus.

"Linus?"

I do a full lap around the table. He's not there.

"Linus, where are you? Linus?"

I hear my own voice sounding scared, and that scares me further. I cane, step, and drag myself within sight of the teenage girl behind the register.

"Have you seen a one-year-old little boy?" I ask.

"Yeah, he's at the train table."

"He's not there now. I can't find him. Can you help me?"

I don't wait for her to answer. I turn around and start walking through the store.

"Linus!"

Where could he be? The shop is modest, quaint, and open, with most of the toys displayed on shelves against the walls. There aren't any long aisles with toys stacked to the ceiling. It's not Toys R Us. Even if he's hiding, I should be able to see him. I search under the dress-up costumes, behind the puppets, over by the cars and trucks, his second favorite area of the store. Look left, scan left, go left. He's not anywhere.

"Ma'am, he's not in the store," says the teenager.

Oh my God.

I head for the door as fast as I can. As I push it open, a bicycle bell dings. The door is heavy, too heavy for Linus to open on his own. There were some teenagers in the store earlier. He must've wandered out with them. I remember hearing the bell ding. A while ago. Oh my God.

I look down the length of the sidewalk. There are clumps of pedestrians scattered all over it. I look through all the legs. I don't see him.

"Linus!"

I turn my body around and look the other way. I don't see him. Oh my God. I start walking down the sidewalk, praying that I've chosen the right direction, hating myself for not being able to run.

"Linus!"

Assuming he wasn't kidnapped (please God), where would he go? His favorite things in the world are trains, cars, and trucks, especially loud ones. Ones that are moving. Time and sound and life itself seems to blur and warp around me as I stop and look out into the street. Main Street. Busy in late afternoon with tired drivers, drivers on their cell phones, drivers not expecting to see a jaywalking toddler. I stand on the edge of the sidewalk, scanning the road for the horror my mind is imagining, my legs frozen in place. In fact, every inch of me feels frozen in place—my left side, my right side, my heart, my lungs, even my blood—like every moving, living part of me has paused to witness what is about to unfold, as if their very existence hangs in the balance. I don't see him anywhere. He's gone. I can't breathe.

"Sarah!"

I look and look. I don't see him. My vision narrows. Details and color dissolve. My lungs turn to stone. I'm suffocating.

"Sarah!"

My mind registers my mother's voice. I look across the fading street and down the sidewalk, but I don't see her.

"Sarah!"

Her voice is louder now and coming from my left. I turn and see her running down the sidewalk toward me, holding Linus on her hip. Air and life rush back into my body.

"Linus!"

She reaches me before I can move.

"I came out of CVS and just happened to look the other way. He was about to wander into the road," she says, her voice short of breath and shaking.

"Oh my God."

"What happened?"

"I don't know. One minute he was at the trains, and the next . . ."

My throat goes dry. I can't say it. I can't relive it, even if it's only what could've happened and fortunately didn't. I burst into tears.

"Come here, sit down," she says, leading me to the bench outside The Cheese Shop.

We sit, and my mother passes Linus to me. I hold him tight in my lap and kiss his face over and over while I cry. My mother is panting, her eyes wide and facing the street, but they don't look like they're actually seeing anything except for whatever scene is playing out in her mind. A landscaping truck rumbles by us.

"Truck! Truck!" says Linus, delighted.

I hold him tighter. My mother snaps out of her trance and checks her watch.

"We have to go get Lucy," she says.

"Okay," I say, wiping my eyes. "His stroller is still at the toy store."

I look over my beautiful baby boy before I pass him back to my mother to be carried. He's completely unharmed and oblivious to what could've happened. I kiss his neck and squeeze him one more time. Then I notice his hands.

"And we have to return these trains."

Later that night, feeling restless, I get out of bed, creep into Linus's room, and watch him sleeping in his crib. He's lying on his back, wearing blue feety pajamas, one arm up over his head. I listen to his deep-sleep exhales. Even years past those fragile newborn months, it still gives my maternal ears relief and peace to hear the sounds of my children breathing when they're asleep. His orange nukie is in his mouth, the silky edge of his favorite blanket is touching his cheek, and Bunny is lying limp across his chest. He's surrounded by every kind of baby security paraphernalia imaginable, and yet none of it protected him from what could have happened today.

Thank you, God, for keeping him safe. I imagine what could've happened today, and then I imagine standing here now, but instead looking into an empty crib. The image knocks the wind out of me, and I can barely stand here and think it. *Thank you, God, for keeping him safe.* And while I believe it's always proper manners and good policy to thank God for life's blessings and miracles, I know this time I should also be thanking someone else.

I leave Linus's room as quietly as possible and make my way downstairs, through the living room, to the sunroom. I'm about to knock when I think I hear one of the kids. Oh no, I probably woke up Linus. But after a second listen, I realize the sound is coming from behind the French doors.

"Mom?" I ask and enter without permission.

She's lying on her bed, curled up under her quilt, surrounded by a pile of crumpled white tissues. She's crying.

"What's wrong?" I ask.

She rolls over to face me, pulls a clean tissue from the box, and presses it against her eyes.

"Oh, I'm feeling emotional about today."

"Me, too," I say.

I walk over to her and sit on the edge of her bed.

"I don't think my heart could've taken it if anything happened to him," she says.

"Me either."

"You don't know, Sarah. I hope you never know what it's like."

I realize now that today wasn't just about Linus for my mother.

"I shouldn't have left you alone in the toy store," she says.

"No, I should've been watching him."

"I should've been there."

"You were there when it counted. You found him. He's okay."

"What if I hadn't seen him? I keep thinking about what could've happened."

"Me, too."

"I should've stayed with you."

She starts sobbing.

"It's okay, Mom. He's okay. I just checked on him. He's asleep and dreaming about trains. We're all okay."

"I'm sorry I wasn't there for you."

"You were."

"No, for you. All those years. I'm so sorry."

She pulls the last tissue out of the box and blows her nose while she cries. There aren't enough tissues for the sorrow she's been living with. I reach around her neck with my right hand and hug her into me.

"It's okay, Mom. I forgive you. You're here now. Thank you for being here now."

Her crying body softens while I hold her in my hug. When she's finally quiet, I lie down next to her and fall asleep.

CHAPTER 37

Heidi opens the bottle of wine she gave to me on my last day at Baldwin and pours us each a glass. She then carries both glasses while I "carry" my granny cane. I can feel her watching me as we move from the kitchen to the living room.

"Your walk is much better," she says. "Much smoother and a lot less drag."

"Thanks," I say, surprised by the compliment.

A lot of things are a lot smoother and less of a drag now than they were four and a half months ago—finding the food on the left side of my plate, threading my left arm into my left shirtsleeve, typing, reading. But the improvements don't happen overnight. They're slow, small, sneaky, and shy, and only accumulate into something remarkable after weeks and months, not days. So I hadn't noticed that my walk has improved since Baldwin. It's nice to hear.

We sit down on the couch, and Heidi passes me my wine.

"To your continued recovery," she says, raising her glass.

"I'll definitely drink to that," I say, holding my glass out in front of me but waiting for Heidi to do the clinking (I'd probably miss and spill my wine all over her).

She taps my glass with hers, and we drink to my continued recovery. She's probably the only health care professional at this point who openly believes that this is possible. Everyone else either says nothing, avoids giving any kind of concrete prediction, or they say *maybe*, but then they drown the *maybe* in a list of *but*s, caveats, and *I don't want to give you any false hope* speeches. And denial is a big problem. No one wants me to live in denial, to go on believing that I might get better if the odds are overwhelmingly against it. God forbid. But then, maybe Heidi doesn't hold out hope for my full recovery as an occupational therapist. Maybe she believes in the possibility because she's my friend. When it comes to Neglect, I'll take the hope of a friend over the cautious prognosis of a physiatrist any day.

"How are things at Baldwin?" I ask.

"Pretty much the same. We have a new woman with Neglect. She's sixty-two, had a stroke. Hers is a lot worse than yours, and she has some other deficits. She's been with us three weeks and is still completely unaware that she has it, thinks she's perfectly healthy. She's going to be a real challenge to rehabilitate."

I think back to those early days at Baldwin, when I was the new woman with Neglect. It feels like a million years ago and just yesterday. Without knowing anything else about this new woman with Neglect, I feel a connection to her, like when I hear of someone who went to Middlebury or HBS or when I meet someone from Welmont. However different we are, we share a similar life experience.

There are times now when I forget that I have Left Neglect, but it's not because of an unconscious unawareness like it was in the beginning. I know I have this. So I don't try to walk without my cane, thinking that my left leg works. I know I need help getting dressed, so I don't do it by myself and then leave the house with my shirt half on and my left pant leg dragging behind me. And I don't use the stove because I know it's dangerous (not that I used it much before). I know that I need to constantly remind myself that there is a left side, that I have a left side, to look left, scan left, and go left, and even if I do, there's a good chance that I'm still registering only what's on the right.

But when I'm not walking or reading or searching for the carrots on my dinner plate, when I'm relaxing in the sunroom or talking with the kids or having a glass of wine on the couch with a friend, I feel perfectly healthy. I don't feel like there's anything wrong with me. I'm not a woman with Neglect. I'm Sarah Nickerson.

"How's Martha?" I ask.

"Oh, she misses you terribly," she says, smiling.

"I'm sure."

"I'm glad we finally found the time to do this," she says. "Me, too."

Heidi has called to check on me at least once a week since I came home from Baldwin. She's also stopped by many times, usually when dropping off Charlie after basketball. But between her work schedule and me being in Vermont every weekend and school vacation days, we hadn't found time to get together for our wine date until now, almost the end of March.

"I love your house," she says, having a look around the living room.

"Thank you."

"I can't believe you might move from here."

"I know. It'll be a big change if it happens."

"Tell me about the job."

"It's the director of development for NEHSA. I'd be responsible for developing and growing their strategies for raising funds. So finding corporate sponsors, donors, leveraging relationships to help market the program, writing grants. It's twenty hours a week, and I could work at least half of those hours from home."

"It sounds like the perfect job for you."

"It really does. All the business skills I've accumulated at HBS and Berkley give me the ability to do the job well. And my disability gives me the empathy and experience as someone who has benefited from NEHSA to do the job with passion. I'd be contributing in a necessary way to an important organization that I believe in. And the hours are perfect."

"What about Bob? Would he be able to work at NEHSA, too?" she asks.

"No, no. The organization is mostly volunteer. And he'd want something else anyway."

Heidi checks her watch. My old watch. It looks good on her.

"Where is Bob?" she asks, realizing the late time.

The kids and my mother are already in bed.

"Still at work."

"Wow, late night."

"Yeah."

I don't elaborate. While it's not atypical for Bob to have stretches where he needs to work late every night for a month, this particular stretch began right about when I turned down the job at Berkley, and the timing feels too exact to be coincidental. He could be working extra hours to ensure that he, as our sole breadwinner, doesn't get laid off, or he could be under even more extreme pressure to help his weak company survive to fight another day, but I think he's simply avoiding me and my job offer in Vermont.

"When would you go?"

"Well, NEHSA needs an answer from me ASAP, but I wouldn't need to start until the fall. So we have some time."

"So, what are you going to tell them?"

"I want to tell them yes, but I can't unless Bob feels confident that he can find something up there, too. We'll see. If it doesn't work out, I'm sure I can find something around here," I say, not sure of this at all.

"What about your mom? Would she go with you?"

"She's going back to the Cape for the summer, but she's coming back to live with us after Labor Day."

"And what does she think about living in Vermont?"

"Oh, she loves it up there. Better than here."

"And what will you do for help in the summer?"

"If we're in Vermont, Mike Green's niece is home from college for the summer and needs a part-time job. She's nannied for years, she's in school for nursing, and Mike thinks she'd be great with me and the kids. And if we're here, Abby will be back from New York in May and said she could nanny for the summer."

"Sounds like you've got everything lined up but Bob."

"Yup."

Everything but Bob.

CHAPTER 38

It's the last weekend in March, and while most parts of the country are enjoying the beginning of spring, Cortland is celebrating its annual Forever Winter Festival. Bob, Charlie, Lucy, and I just finished eating lunch in the main lodge after a full morning on the slopes. My mother and Linus spent the morning at the festival, and now Bob and the kids want to go, but I'm feeling too tired. We decide that Bob will drop me off at home for a nap, and he and the kids will go without me.

The festival is a weeklong affair, quintessential small-town Vermont and great family fun. There are snowman contests, bonfires and s'mores, hot cocoa and snow cones, ice-skating on the lake, cross-country ski races, and live music. And all the local businesses sell their goods at the festival market— maple syrup, fudge, jams, cheese, quilts, paintings, sculpture.

We're in the car, and I'm reading aloud from the festival brochure to get the kids excited.

"Ooo, they're having the dogsled races today!"

"Maybe I could be a professional dogsled musher," Bob says.

"Yeah!" yell out Charlie and Lucy.

"And ice fishing," I say, trying to stay on the subject of the festival.

"I could be a frozen lake fisherman," Bob says.

"Yeah!" cheer Charlie and Lucy.

"Bob," I say.

"Or I could raise cows in the yard and make ice cream!"

"Yeah!" they yell, giggling.

I laugh, too, but only because I can't help picturing Bob with his shirtsleeves rolled up, trying to milk a cow.

"And I could have my own ice cream truck, and I'd be the ice cream man!"

"Yeah!" they shout.

"Do that one, Daddy," says Lucy.

"Yeah, be an ice cream man!" says Charlie.

"The votes are in, babe. I'm Vermont's newest ice cream man. I'm going to need a white truck and a hat."

Again, I crack up, picturing Bob in the hat. I've also added red suspenders.

It feels good to joke around about this topic. Our conversations about Bob's job and Welmont versus Cortland have been charged and stressful with no resolution as of yet. He's at least open to the idea now, and he's actively looking for a job in Vermont. But he's picky. If he wasn't finding anything suitable enough for him in Boston, I have less and less faith with each passing day that he's going to find anything acceptable to him here.

We pull into our driveway, and Bob helps me out with the car still running.

"You got it from here?" he asks, handing me my cane.

"Yeah, I'm fine. Will you bring me home some fudge?"

"You got it. I'll watch to make sure you get in."

I walk down the gravel pathway to the front door. I let go of the cane, turn the knob, and push the door open. Then I turn and wave good-bye as Bob pulls out of the driveway. I'm getting better and more confident at standing without relying on the cane or holding on to anything, and it feels thrilling to experience even a few successful seconds of standing on my own two feet.

As I walk through the mudroom, I hear a high-pitched whistling sound. It sounds like the whistle from one of Linus's battery-operated trains, but he should be smack in the middle of his three-hour nap. He'd better not be up playing with trains.

"Mom?" I call out, but not too loudly in case he's napping as he should be.

I walk into the living room. My mother's asleep on the couch. Linus must be up in his crib. Good. But the whistling sound is louder in here. And constant. Maybe the button to one of his electronic trains is stuck pressed in. I look around the living room for the train, but I don't see one anywhere.

The room is clean, and all of Linus's toys are put away. I check the TV. It's off.

I granny cane over to Linus's toy box and listen. The whistle doesn't appear to be coming from Linus's toys. I listen again, trying to localize the sound. I can't figure it out. I'm more curious about what the heck it is than annoyed or worried by it. It's not so loud that it's disturbing Linus or my mother, and I'm sure I wouldn't hear it at all from my bedroom. But what is it?

I cane, step, and drag myself into the kitchen and listen. The sound is definitely coming from in here. I open and close the refrigerator. Nope, it's not that. I look across the floor, the table, and the counter for one of Linus's trains. Everything is clean. No trains. No electronic toys. No cell phones. No iPods.

I look at the stove top. Nothing there. Then I remember to *look left*, and I see the teakettle sitting on a bright red burner, steam billowing out from its spout. I look across the counter again, this time remembering to *scan left*, and I notice my mother's empty mug, the string and paper square from her tea bag hanging over the side.

My heart drops into my stomach, and my skin goes clammy. I turn the knob to Off and move the kettle to the right. The whistling stops.

I granny cane back into the living room. I listen. Everything is quiet. I sit on the edge of the couch next to my mother and know, even before I hold her hand, that she's not sleeping.

CHAPTER 39

We sold our house in Welmont and moved to Cortland in June, after Charlie and Lucy finished the school year. Bob took the summer off, Charlie and Lucy spent mornings at the YMCA camp, all three kids played in the yard or swam in Lake Willoughby most afternoons, and I learned to kayak in the same lake through NEHSA's summer recreation program. Even though my mother had always planned to spend the summer back at her own house on Cape Cod, it still felt strange to be here without her. I kept expecting to see her walk through the front door, for her to bring me the latest *People*, to hear the sound of her laugh. I still do. I had imagined making at least a couple of road trips with Bob and the kids to visit her over the summer. I'd imagined spending time with her on the beach, eating fresh tomatoes from her garden, meeting her Red Hat friends. And when we weren't together with her on the Cape, I'd imagined that we'd Skype.

It's now the first week of November, past peak foliage and mountain biking season and at least a month before there's enough snow on the mountain. It's a sleepy month in a town that's drowsy all year, but I don't mind. Bob and I are seated at our favorite table by the fireplace at Cesca's. We didn't need reservations, we didn't have any trouble finding a parking space right in front of the restaurant, and we didn't have to wait for our favorite table. We're the only two people here, partly because it's so early in the evening, but the place won't fill up at any point tonight.

Bob slides a small white box across the table.

"What's this?" I ask, not expecting a gift for this occasion.

"Open it," he says.

We're here to celebrate the anniversary of the day I survived my car crash. We've consciously chosen to make this a day of celebration and not a day of regretful What-Ifs—What if I hadn't won the shoot? What if it hadn't been raining? What if I hadn't tried to use my phone? What if I'd looked up sooner? What if I hadn't banged my head? We're here to celebrate the life we have and not bemoan the life we've lost. But before I open Bob's gift, I can't help but reflect on both.

I miss my old job at Berkley. I miss Richard and Jessica, the brilliant consultants, the feeling of conquering a seemingly impossible day, staffing interesting projects, recruiting season, managing career development, and being really good at it all. But I don't miss my old commute, the travel, the hours, and the stress that accompanied all of those.

I love my new job at NEHSA. I love Mike and the volunteer staff, a diverse group of people with the most generous hearts on the planet. I love the hours. I'm typically there from eight to noon, Monday through Friday, and usually put in five additional hours a week from home, but some days I work entirely from my living room couch. I love the work itself. It feels challenging and important. And I'm really good at it. I've been working there for two months now, and I haven't had to cry yet. I don't suspect that I will.

I don't miss my dry-clean-only, button-down shirts and suits. NEHSA is strictly casual dress. I do miss my high heel shoes.

I miss my old paycheck and the sense of pride, power, and worth that it gave me. I make a lot less money now. A lot less. But what I've lost in dollars, I've gained in time. I have time in the afternoons now to help Charlie and Lucy with their homework, to play Wii with them, to watch Charlie's soccer games, to take a nap with Linus. I can't wait to spend afternoons snowboarding. I have time to paint a portrait of Lucy (my only child who will sit still long enough) or the apples we picked at the local orchard. I have time to read novels, to meditate, to watch the deer walk across the backyard, to have dinner every night with my family. Less money, more time. So far, the trade-off has been worth every penny.

Neither of us misses Bob's old job. He found a position at Verde Inc. working to help an international list of clients develop economically favorable plans for converting to renewable energy sources. The company is young, smart, growing, and passionate about what they do, and Bob loves it. It's located in Montpelier, about fifty miles from our house in Cortland, but it's all highway, and there's never any traffic, so it only takes him forty-five minutes, which is the same amount of time it used to take us to commute from Welmont to Boston (if the weather was good, if there weren't any accidents, and if the Red Sox weren't in town). Everyone there has been understanding of his need to leave the office early to help with me and the kids. He's usually home by 4:00.

The elementary school here is wonderful. The class sizes are half what they were in Welmont, and the teachers in the special education program are working really well with Charlie. He can't wait to start snowboarding with the school's team this winter. Lucy likes her new teacher and loves Hannah, her new best friend. And Linus has adjusted without a hiccup to his new day care. Bob drives him there every morning before work, and either Chris or Kim from NEHSA brings him home for me at 2:00.

I miss Heidi. She promises to bring her whole family to Cortland over February vacation for a week of skiing and snowboarding.

I miss Starbucks. B&C's is still closed. At least we have the Impressa.

I miss being able to do simple things easily, like reading, typing, shaving, getting dressed, cutting paper with scissors, putting a pillowcase on a pillow, fixing a shirt that is inside-out.

I miss driving and the independence that goes with it. Bob drives me to Mount Cortland in the mornings, and Mike or someone from NEHSA drives me home, but I miss being able to come and go without being someone else's passenger.

A small percentage of people with Left Neglect do eventually recover enough to drive safely. Still unwavering in his encouragement, last Monday, before work, Bob pulled into the empty church parking lot and told me to give it a try. After switching places, I buckled my seat belt (something I never could've done six months ago), shifted from Park to Drive, and eased my right foot from the brake to the gas. We only traveled a few feet before Bob yelled, *Stop!* I hit the brake, panicked but not understanding why. *Look LEFT,* he said. At first, I didn't notice anything at all, and then there it was—the driver's side door, wide open. So I guess I'm still not ready to drive. Someday.

I miss walking. I'm still cane, step, and dragging with my granny cane, but with much more confidence and a lot less drag, and I hope to progress to a regular cane soon. Hope. Progress. There is still both of those.

But of everything that I miss, I miss my mother most of all. What if I hadn't won the shoot? What if I hadn't banged my head? What if I hadn't needed her help? What if she hadn't offered it to me? I'm so grateful that I had the chance to know and love her before she died.

I lift the lid off the unwrapped box. My heart swells with emotion, and tears spill down my smiling cheeks.

"Oh, Bob, it's beautiful."

"Here, let me attach it for you."

He reaches across the table and holds my left hand in his.

"There," he says.

I waggle my shoulder and hear the jingle of my charm bracelet at my left wrist. Look left, scan left, go left.

I find my diamond ring and wedding band. Me and Bob. Look left, scan left, go left.

I find my pink, plastic watch. My good friend, Heidi.

Look left, scan left, go left.

I find my silver charm bracelet and the three dime-sized discs. Charlie, Lucy, and Linus.

Look left, scan left, go left.

I see my gift from Bob. My new charm. A silver hat adorned with a single, bezel-set ruby. My mother.

"Thank you, honey. I love it."

Our waitress brings us a bottle of Shiraz and asks what we'd like for dinner. We both order Caesar salads and the pumpkin ravioli. Bob pours the wine and lifts his glass.

"To a full life," he says.

I smile, loving him for changing with me, for going where my Neglect has taken us, for getting the new me. Because while I still hope for a full recovery, I've learned that my life can be fully lived with less.

I look left again and find my hand, clad in beautiful symbols of me and Bob, our children, my friend, and now my mother. With every ounce of focus I can gather, I lift my wineglass high with my left hand.

"To a full life," I say.

We clink glasses and drink.

I'm riding the quad chairlift to the summit of Mount Cortland. My mother is sitting next to me, to my right, her favorite place to position herself so I can be sure to see her. She's wearing a red knit shawl over a white sweater, black elastic-waist pants, black boots, and a huge Victorian tea hat covered with red flowers.

"Mom, you're not dressed appropriately."

"I'm not?"

"No. And you don't have skis or a snowboard. How are you going to get down the mountain?"

"I'm only here to see the view."

"Oh."

"And to spend time with you."

"You should learn to snowboard."

"Oh no, it's too late for me to be doing that kind of thing."

"No, it's not."

"It is. But I've enjoyed this ride with you."

I look up and see that we're approaching the end of the lift. I raise the bar over our heads, turn my board, and edge forward on the seat.

"Remember to look left," says my mother.

I turn my head to the left and gasp. Nate and my father are sitting next to me.

"Oh my God. Where did you come from?" I ask.

"We've been here the whole time," says my father, smiling at me.

My father and Nate are both wearing red ski jackets and black pants, but they don't have skis or snowboards either.

We reach the top, and I slide down the ramp. Nate, my father, and my mother walk ahead and board another lift without me. I watch their chair ascend and dissolve into sky.

"Hey."

I turn my head to the left. It's Bob.

"You're all here," I say.

Linus is sitting in a child carrier strapped to Bob's back, Lucy is standing next to Bob on her skis, and Charlie is ahead of them on his board.

"Of course. We're waiting for you."

I look ahead at the untouched trail before us, at the snow-covered valley below, at the Green Mountains in the distance, enjoying the feeling of the warm morning sun against my cold cheeks. In the stillness of the summit, I hear nothing but the sound of my own breath.

"Let's go," I say.

I turn the toe of my board and lean downhill.

Slide, turn, slide.

I am peaceful.

Slide, turn, slide.

I am whole.

Slide, turn, slide.

Hush.

AUTHOR'S NOTE

Left Neglect, also known as unilateral neglect and hemi-spatial neglect, is a real neurological syndrome that occurs due to damage to the right hemisphere of the brain, such as might follow a right-hemisphere stroke, hemorrhage, or traumatic brain injury. While the average man or woman has most likely never heard of Left Neglect, patients with this condition are commonly seen by health care professionals in rehabilitation hospitals. Patients with Left Neglect are not blind, but rather their brains ignore information on the left side of the world, often including the left side of their own bodies. The people I came to know with Left Neglect are at varying stages of recovery and have adopted many standard and creative strategies for adapting to life without a conscious awareness of the left. They all continue to hope for further recovery. As of the writing of this story, the neurological processes that underlie Left Neglect are not well understood.

New England Handicapped Sports Association (NEHSA) is a real organization headquartered at Mount Sunapee in Newbury, New Hampshire (and not the fictional town of Cortland, Vermont). Their mission is to "bear witness to the triumph of the human spirit by helping people with disabilities and their families enrich their lives through adaptive sports, recreation, and social activities." They serve people living with many kinds of disabilities, including amputations, autism, Down syndrome, traumatic brain injury (TBI), spina bifida, muscular dystrophy, multiple sclerosis, balance problems, and stroke.

For more information about this amazing organization, go to www.nehsa.org or email info@nehsa.org.

ACKNOWLEDGMENTS

Thanks first go to the many people living with Left Neglect who generously shared their experiences and stories with me, giving me a real and human insight into this condition that simply can't be found in textbooks.

Thank you, Annie Eldridge, Lynn Duke, Mike and Sue McCormick, Lisa Nelson, Brad and Mary Towse, and Bruce and Aimy Wilbur.

A special thank-you to Deborah Feinstein, who passed away while I was writing this story, and to her family for inviting me into their lives at such a personal and uncertain time. Thank you, Dr. Ali Atri for introducing me to Deborah and her family, for taking the time to bring me in, and for trusting that my quest for knowledge would be respectful.

A special thank-you also to my friend Julia Fox Garrison (author of *Don't Leave Me This Way*). You are truly an inspiration.

Thank you to the many health care professionals who took the time to meet with me or talk on the phone, who helped me to better understand the clinical presentation of symptoms, rehabilitation, accommodation, and recovery.

Thank you, Kristin Siminsky (physical therapist), Kimberly Wiggins (neurology RN), Patty Kelly (occupational therapist), Jim Smith (assistant professor of physical therapy at Utica College), Tom Van Vleet, PhD (research neuropsychologist at the University of California, Berkeley), and Michael Paul Mason (author of *Head Cases: Stories of Brain Injury and Its Aftermath*).

Thank you to everyone at Spaulding Rehabilitation Hospital in Boston: Dr. Ron Hirschberg (physiatrist), Lynne Brady Wagner (director, Stroke Program), Becky Ashe (occupational therapist), Melissa DeLuke (occupational therapist), Paul Petrone (occupational therapy practice leader, Stroke Program), Dr. Randie Black-Schaffer (medical director, Stroke Program), Varsha Desai (occupational therapist), Jena Casbon (speech-language pathologist), and Joe DeGutis, PhD (research scientist).

Thank you to everyone at the Rehabilitation Hospital of the Cape & Islands: MaryAnn Tryon (RN), Carol Sim (RN, CEO), Stephanie Nadolny (VP of clinical services and recreational therapist), Jan Sullivan (inpatient speech therapist),

Scott Abramson, MD (physiatrist), Allison Dickson (inpatient rehab aide), Deb Detwiler (inpatient rehab aide), Colleen McCauley (inpatient physical therapist), David Lowell, MD (medical director, neurologist), Dawn Lucier (senior physical therapist, neuro specialty), Sue Ehrenthal, MD (physiatrist), Jay Rosenfeld, MD (physiatrist), Heather Ward (outpatient physical therapist), and Donna Erdman (outpatient occupational therapist).

Thank you to Sarah Bua for giving me insight into life at Harvard Business School.

Thank you to Susan Levine, vice president at Bain Capital, and Stephanie Stamatos, former senior vice president of human resources at Silver Lake, for helping me better understand Sarah's professional life and the juggle of family and career.

Thank you to Jill Malinowski and Amanda Julin for educating me about Attention Deficit Hyperactivity Disorder.

Thank you to Tom Kersey, executive director of New England Handicapped Sports Association (NEHSA), for showing me the miracle of NEHSA and how it would help Sarah.

Thank you to Louise Burke, Anthony Ziccardi, Kathy Sagan, and Vicky Bijur for believing in this story before even reading a word of it, and thank you again to Kathy and Vicky for making this story better through your editorial feedback and guidance.

Thank you to my beloved early readers who read each chapter as I wrote it, encouraging me along from the first words: Anne Carey, Laurel Daly, Kim Howland, Sarah Hutto, Mary MacGregor, Rose O'Donnell, and Christopher Seufert.

Thank you to my village of family and friends who helped me with child care and finding the time and space to write this story, especially Sarah Hutto, Sue Linnell, Heidi Wright, Monica Lussier, Danyel Matteson, Marilyn and Gary Seufert, my parents, and my husband.

Thank you to Chris, Alena, and Ethan. Your love makes this all possible.

Read on for an extract from
Lisa Genova's bestselling novel

STILL ALICE

Also available from Simon & Schuster UK

SIMON &
SCHUSTER

London · New York · Sydney · Toronto · New Delhi

A CBS COMPANY

Even then, more than a year earlier, there were neurons in her head, not far from her ears, that were being strangled to death, too quietly for her to hear them. Some would argue that things were going so insidiously wrong that the neurons themselves initiated events that would lead to their own destruction. Whether it was molecular murder or cellular suicide, they were unable to warn her of what was happening before they died.

Alice sat at her desk in their bedroom distracted by the sounds of John racing through each of the rooms on the first floor. She needed to finish her peer review of a paper submitted to the *Journal of Cognitive Psychology* before her flight, and she'd just read the same sentence three times without comprehending it. It was 7:30 according to their alarm clock, which she guessed was about ten minutes fast. She knew from the approximate time and the escalating volume of his racing that he was trying to leave, but he'd forgotten something and couldn't find it. She tapped her red pen on her bottom lip as she watched the digital numbers on the clock and listened for what she knew was coming.

"Ali?"

She tossed her pen onto the desk and sighed. Downstairs, she found him in the living room on his knees, feeling under the couch cushions.

"Keys?" she asked.

"Glasses. Please don't lecture me, I'm late."

She followed his frantic glance to the fireplace mantel, where the antique Waltham clock, valued for its precision, declared 8:00. He should have known better than to trust it. The clocks in their home rarely knew the real time of day. Alice had been duped too often in the past by their seemingly honest faces and had learned long ago to rely on her watch. Sure enough, she lapsed back in time as she entered the kitchen, where the microwave insisted that it was only 6:52.

She looked across the smooth, uncluttered surface of the granite countertop, and there they were, next to the mushroom bowl heaping with unopened mail. Not under something, not behind something, not obstructed in any way from plain view. How could he, someone so smart, a scientist, not see what was right in front of him?

Of course, many of her own things had taken to hiding in mischievous little places as well. But she didn't admit this to him, and she didn't involve him in the hunt. Just the other day, John blissfully unaware, she'd spent a crazed morning looking first all over the house and then in her office for her BlackBerry charger. Stumped, she'd surrendered, gone to the store, and bought a new one, only to discover the old one later that night plugged in the socket next to her side of the bed, where she should have known to look. She could probably chalk it all up for both of them to excessive multitasking and being way too busy. And to getting older.

He stood in the doorway, looking at the glasses in her hand but not at her.

"Next time, try pretending you're a woman while you look," said Alice, smiling.

"I'll wear one of your skirts. Ali, please, I'm really late."

"The microwave says you have tons of time," she said, handing them to him.

"Thanks."

He grabbed them like a relay runner taking a baton in a race and headed for the front door.

"Will you be here when I get home on Saturday?" she asked his back as she followed him down the hallway.

"I don't know, I've got a huge day in lab on Saturday."

He collected his briefcase, phone, and keys from the hall table.

"Have a good trip, give Lydia a hug and kiss for me. And try not to battle with her," said John.

She caught their reflection in the hallway mirror—a distinguished-looking, tall man with white-flecked brown hair and glasses; a petite, curly-haired woman, her arms crossed over her chest, each readying to leap into that same, bottomless argument. She gritted her teeth and swallowed, choosing not to jump.

"We haven't seen each other in a while. Please try to be home?" she asked.

"I know, I'll try."

He kissed her, and although desperate to leave, he lingered in that kiss for an almost imperceptible moment. If she didn't know him better, she might've romanticized his kiss. She might've stood there, hopeful, thinking it said, *I love you, I'll miss you.* But as she watched him hustle down the street alone, she felt pretty certain he'd just told her, *I love you, but please don't be pissed when I'm not home on Saturday.*

They used to walk together over to Harvard Yard every

morning. Of the many things she loved about working within a mile from home and at the same school, their shared commute was the thing she loved most. They always stopped at Jerri's—a black coffee for him, a tea with lemon for her, iced or hot, depending on the season—and continued on to Harvard Yard, chatting about their research and classes, issues in their respective departments, their children, or plans for that evening. When they were first married, they even held hands. She savored the relaxed intimacy of these morning walks with him, before the daily demands of their jobs and ambitions rendered them each stressed and exhausted.

But for some time now, they'd been walking over to Harvard separately. Alice had been living out of her suitcase all summer, attending psychology conferences in Rome, New Orleans, and Miami, and serving on an exam committee for a thesis defense at Princeton. Back in the spring, John's cell cultures had needed some sort of rinsing attention at an obscene hour each morning, but he didn't trust any of his students to show up consistently. So he did. She couldn't remember the reasons that predated spring, but she knew that each time they'd seemed reasonable and only temporary.

She returned to the paper at her desk, still distracted, now by a craving for that fight she hadn't had with John about their younger daughter, Lydia. Would it kill him to stand behind her for once? She gave the rest of the paper a cursory effort, not her typical standard of excellence, but it would have to do, given her fragmented state of mind and lack of time. Her comments and suggestions for revision finished, she packaged and sealed the envelope, guiltily aware that she might've missed an error in the study's design or interpretation, cursing John for compromising the integrity of her work.

She repacked her suitcase, not even emptied yet from her

last trip. She looked forward to traveling less in the coming months. There were only a handful of invited lectures penciled in her fall semester calendar, and she'd scheduled most of those on Fridays, a day she didn't teach. Like tomorrow. Tomorrow she would be the guest speaker to kick off Stanford's cognitive psychology fall colloquium series. And afterward, she'd see Lydia. She'd try not to battle with her, but she wasn't making any promises.

ALICE FOUND HER WAY EASILY to Stanford's Cordura Hall on the corner of Campus Drive West and Panama Drive. Its white stucco exterior, terra-cotta roof, and lush landscaping looked to her East Coast eyes more like a Caribbean beach resort than an academic building. She arrived quite early but ventured inside anyway, figuring she could use the extra time to sit in the quiet auditorium and look over her talk.

Much to her surprise, she walked into an already packed room. A zealous crowd surrounded and circled a buffet table, aggressively diving in for food like seagulls at a city beach. Before she could sneak in unnoticed, she noticed Josh, a former Harvard classmate and respected egomaniac, standing in her path, his legs planted firmly and a little too wide, as if he was ready to dive at her.

"All this, for me?" asked Alice, smiling playfully.

"What, we eat like this every day. It's for one of our developmental psychologists, he was tenured yesterday. So how's Harvard treating you?"

"Good."

"I can't believe you're still there after all these years. You ever get too bored over there, you should consider coming here."

"I'll let you know. How are things with you?"

"Fantastic. You should come by my office after the talk, see our latest modeling data. It'll really knock your socks off."

"Sorry, I can't, I have to catch a flight to L.A. right after this," she said, grateful to have a ready excuse.

"Oh, too bad. Last time I saw you I think was last year at the psychonomic conference. I unfortunately missed your presentation."

"Well, you'll get to hear a good portion of it today."

"Recycling your talks these days, huh?"

Before she could answer, Gordon Miller, head of the department and her new superhero, swooped in and saved her by asking Josh to help pass out the champagne. As at Harvard, a champagne toast was a tradition in the psychology department at Stanford for all faculty who reached the coveted career milestone of tenure. There weren't many trumpets that heralded the advancement from point to point in the career of a professor, but tenure was a big one, loud and clear.

When everyone was holding a cup, Gordon stood at the podium and tapped the microphone. "Can I have everyone's attention for a moment?"

Josh's excessively loud, punctuated laugh reverberated alone through the auditorium just before Gordon continued.

"Today, we congratulate Mark on receiving tenure. I'm sure he's thrilled to have this particular accomplishment behind him. Here's to the many exciting accomplishments still ahead. To Mark!"

"To Mark!"

Alice tapped her cup with her neighbors', and everyone quickly resumed the business of drinking, eating, and discussing. When all of the food had been claimed from the serving trays and the last drops of champagne emptied from the last bottle, Gordon took the floor once again.

"If everyone would take a seat, we can begin today's talk."

He waited a few moments for the crowd of about seventy-five to settle and quiet down.

"Today, I have the honor of introducing you to our first colloquium speaker of the year. Dr. Alice Howland is the eminent William James Professor of Psychology at Harvard University. Over the last twenty-five years, her distinguished career has produced many of the flagship touchstones in psycholinguistics. She pioneered and continues to lead an interdisciplinary and integrated approach to the study of the mechanisms of language. We are privileged to have her here today to talk to us about the conceptual and neural organization of language."

Alice switched places with Gordon and looked out at her audience looking at her. As she waited for the applause to subside, she thought of the statistic that said people feared public speaking more than they feared death. She loved it. She enjoyed all of the concatenated moments of presenting in front of a listening audience—teaching, performing, telling a story, teeing up a heated debate. She also loved the adrenaline rush. The bigger the stakes, the more sophisticated or hostile the audience, the more the whole experience thrilled her. John was an excellent teacher, but public speaking often pained and terrified him, and he marveled at Alice's verve for it. He probably didn't prefer death, but spiders and snakes, sure.

"Thank you, Gordon. Today, I'm going to talk about some of the mental processes that underlie the acquisition, organization, and use of language."

Alice had given the guts of this particular talk innumerable times, but she wouldn't call it recycling. The crux of the talk did focus on the main tenets of linguistics, many of which she'd discovered, and she'd been using a number of the same slides for years. But she felt proud, and not ashamed or lazy, that this part of her talk, these discoveries of hers, continued to hold true, withstanding the test of time. Her contributions mattered and propelled future discovery. Plus, she certainly included those future discoveries.

She talked without needing to look down at her notes, relaxed and animated, the words effortless. Then, about forty minutes into the fifty-minute presentation, she became suddenly stuck.

"The data reveal that irregular verbs require access to the mental . . ."

She simply couldn't find the word. She had a loose sense for what she wanted to say, but the word itself eluded her. Gone. She didn't know the first letter or what the word sounded like or how many syllables it had. It wasn't on the tip of her tongue.

Maybe it was the champagne. She normally didn't drink any alcohol before speaking. Even if she knew the talk cold, even in the most casual setting, she always wanted to be as mentally sharp as possible, especially for the question-and-answer session at the end, which could be confrontational and full of rich, unscripted debate. But she hadn't wanted to offend anyone, and she'd drunk a little more than she probably should have when she became trapped again in passive-aggressive conversation with Josh.

Maybe it was jet lag. As her mind scoured its corners for the word and a rational reason for why she'd lost it, her heart pounded and her face grew hot. She'd never lost a word in front of an audience before. But she'd never panicked in front of an audience either, and she'd stood before many far larger and more intimidating than this. She told herself to breathe, forget about it, and move on.

She replaced the still blocked word with a vague and inappropriate "thing," abandoned whatever point she'd been in the middle of making, and continued on to the next slide. The pause had seemed like an obvious and awkward eternity to her, but as she checked the faces in the audience to see if anyone had noticed her mental hiccup, no one appeared alarmed, embarrassed, or ruffled in any way. Then, she saw Josh whispering to the woman next to him, his eyebrows furrowed and a slight smile on his face.

She was on the plane, descending into LAX, when it finally came to her.

Lexicon.

LYDIA HAD BEEN LIVING IN Los Angeles for three years now. If she'd gone to college right after high school, she would've graduated this past spring. Alice would've been so proud. Lydia was probably smarter than both of her older siblings, and they had gone to college. And law school. And medical school.

Instead of college, Lydia first went to Europe. Alice had hoped she'd come home with a clearer sense of what she wanted to study and what kind of school she wanted to go to. Instead, upon her return, she'd told her parents that she'd done a little acting while in Dublin and had fallen in love. She was moving to Los Angeles immediately.

Alice nearly lost her mind. Much to her maddening frustration, she recognized her own contribution to this problem. Because Lydia was the youngest of three, the daughter of parents who worked a lot and traveled regularly, and had always been a good student, Alice and John had ignored her to a large extent. They'd granted her a lot of room to run in her world, free to think for herself and free from the kind of micromanagement placed on a lot of children her age. Her parents' professional lives served as shining examples of what could be gained from setting lofty and individually unique goals and pursuing them with passion and hard work. Lydia understood her mother's advice about the importance of getting a college education, but she had the confidence and audacity to reject it.

Plus, she didn't stand entirely alone. The most explosive fight Alice had ever had with John had followed his two cents on the subject: *I think it's wonderful, she can always go to college later, if she decides she even wants to.*

Alice checked her BlackBerry for the address, rang the doorbell to apartment number seven, and waited. She was just about to press it again when Lydia opened the door.

"Mom, you're early," said Lydia.

Alice checked her watch.

"I'm right on time."

"You said your flight was coming in at eight."

"I said five."

"I have eight o'clock written down in my book."

"Lydia, it's five forty-five, I'm here."

Lydia looked indecisive and panicky, like a squirrel caught facing an oncoming car in the road.

"Sorry, come in."

They each hesitated before they hugged, as if they were about to practice a newly learned dance and weren't quite confident of the first step or who should lead. Or it was an old dance, but they hadn't performed it together in so long that each felt unsure of the choreography.

Alice could feel the contours of Lydia's spine and ribs through her shirt. She looked too skinny, a good ten pounds lighter than Alice remembered. She hoped it was more a result of being busy than of conscious dieting. Blond and five foot six, three inches taller than Alice, Lydia stood out among the predominance of short Italian and Asian women in Cambridge, but in Los Angeles, the waiting rooms at every audition were apparently full of women who looked just like her.

"I made reservations for nine. Wait here, I'll be right back."

Craning her neck, Alice inspected the kitchen and living room from the hallway. The furnishings, most likely yard sale finds and parent hand-me-downs, looked rather hip together—an orange sectional couch, retro-inspired coffee table, Brady Bunch–style kitchen table and chairs. The white walls were bare except for a poster of Marlon Brando taped above the couch. The air smelled strongly of Windex, as if Lydia had taken last-second measures to clean the place before Alice's arrival.

In fact, it was a little too clean. No DVDs or CDs lying around, no books or magazines thrown on the coffee table, no pictures on the refrigerator, no hint of Lydia's interests or aesthetic anywhere. Anyone could be living here. Then, Alice noticed the pile of men's shoes on the floor to the left of the door behind her.

"Tell me about your roommates," she said as Lydia returned from her room, cell phone in hand.

"They're at work."

"What kind of work?"

"One's bartending and the other delivers food."

"I thought they were both actors."

"They are."

"I see. What are their names again?"

"Doug and Malcolm."

It flashed only for a moment, but Alice saw it and Lydia saw her see it. Lydia's face flushed when she said Malcolm's name, and her eyes darted nervously away from her mother's.

"Why don't we get going? They said they can take us early," said Lydia.

"Okay, I just need to use the bathroom first."

As Alice washed her hands, she looked over the products sitting on the table next to the sink—Neutrogena facial cleanser and moisturizer, Tom's of Maine mint toothpaste, men's deodorant, a box of Playtex tampons. She thought for a moment. She hadn't had her period all summer. Did she have it in May? She'd be turning fifty next month, so she wasn't alarmed. She hadn't yet experienced any hot flashes or night sweats, but not all menopausal women did. That would be just fine with her.

As she dried her hands, she noticed the box of Trojan condoms behind Lydia's hairstyling products. She was going to have to find out more about these roommates. Malcolm, in particular.

They sat at a table outside on the patio at Ivy, a trendy restaurant in downtown Los Angeles, and ordered two drinks, an espresso martini for Lydia and a merlot for Alice.

"So how's Dad's *Science* paper coming?" asked Lydia.

She must've talked recently with her father. Alice hadn't heard from her since a phone call on Mother's Day.

"It's done. He's very proud of it."

"How's Anna and Tom?"

"Good, busy, working hard. So how did you meet Doug and Malcolm?"

"They came into Starbucks one night while I was working."

The waiter appeared, and each of them ordered dinner and another drink. Alice hoped the alcohol would dilute the tension between them, which felt heavy and thick and just beneath the tracing-paper-thin conversation.

"So how did you meet Doug and Malcolm?" she asked.

"I just told you. Why don't you ever listen to anything I say? They came into Starbucks one night talking about looking for a roommate while I was working."

"I thought you were waitressing at a restaurant."

"I am. I work at Starbucks during the week and waitress on Saturday nights."

"Doesn't sound like that leaves a lot of time for acting."

"I'm not cast in anything right now, but I'm taking workshop classes, and I'm auditioning a lot."

"What kind of classes?"

"Meisner technique."

"And what've you been auditioning for?"

"Television and print."

Alice swirled her wine, drank the last, big gulp, and licked her lips. "Lydia, what exactly is your plan here?"

"I'm not planning on stopping, if that's what you're asking."

The drinks were taking effect, but not in the direction Alice had hoped for. Instead, they served as the fuel that burned that little piece of tracing paper, leaving the tension between them fully exposed and at the helm of a dangerously familiar conversation.

"You can't live like this forever. Are you still going to work at Starbucks when you're thirty?"

"That's eight years away! Do you know what you'll be doing in eight years?"

"Yes, I do. At some point, you need to be responsible, you need to be able to afford things like health insurance, a mortgage, savings for retirement—"

"I have health insurance. And I might make it as an actor. There are people who do, you know. And they make a hell of a lot more money than you and Dad combined."

"This isn't just about money."

"Then what? That I didn't become you?"

"Lower your voice."

"Don't tell me what to do."

"I don't want you to become me, Lydia. I just don't want you to limit your choices."

"You want to make my choices."

"No."

"This is who I am, this is what I want to do."

"What, serving up Venti lattes? You should be in college. You should be spending this time in your life learning something."

"I *am* learning something! I'm just not sitting in a Harvard classroom killing myself trying to get an A in political science. I'm in a serious acting class for fifteen hours a week. How many hours of class a week do your students take, twelve?"

"It's not the same thing."

"Well, Dad thinks it is. He's paying for it."

Alice clenched the sides of her skirt and pressed her lips together. What she wanted to say next wasn't meant for Lydia.

"You've never even seen me act."

John had. He'd flown out alone last winter to see her perform in a play. Swamped with too many urgent things at the
time, Alice couldn't free up to go. As she looked at Lydia's
pained eyes, she couldn't remember now what those urgent
things had been. She didn't have anything against an acting
career itself, but she believed her daughter's singular pursuit
of it, without an education, bordered on reckless. If she didn't
go to college now, acquire a knowledge base or formal training in some field, if she didn't get a degree, what would she do
if acting didn't pan out?

Alice thought about those condoms in the bathroom.
What if Lydia got pregnant? Alice worried that Lydia might
someday find herself trapped in a life that was unfulfilled, full
of regret. She looked at her daughter and saw so much wasted
potential, so much wasted time.

"You're not getting any younger, Lydia. Life goes by too
fast."

"I agree."

The food came, but neither of them picked up a fork.
Lydia dabbed her eyes with her hand-embroidered linen
napkin. They always fell into the same battle, and it felt to
Alice like trying to knock down a concrete wall with their
heads. It was never going to be productive and only resulted
in hurting them, causing lasting damage. She wished Lydia
could see the love and wisdom in what she wanted for her.
She wished she could just reach across the table and hug her
daughter, but there were too many dishes, glasses, and years
of distance between them.

A sudden flurry of activity a few tables away pulled their
attention from themselves. Several camera flashes popped,
and a small crowd of patrons and waitstaff gathered, all focused on a woman who looked a bit like Lydia.

"Who's that?" asked Alice.

"Mom," said Lydia in a tone both embarrassed and superior, perfected at the age of thirteen. "That's Jennifer Aniston."

They ate their dinner and talked only of safe things, like the food and the weather. Alice wanted to discover more about Lydia's relationship with Malcolm, but the embers of Lydia's emotions still glowed hot, and Alice feared igniting another fight. She paid the bill and they left the restaurant, full but dissatisfied.

"Excuse me, ma'am!"

Their waiter caught up to them on the sidewalk.

"You left this."

Alice paused, trying to comprehend how their waiter might come to possess her BlackBerry. She hadn't checked her email or calendar in the restaurant. She felt inside her bag. No BlackBerry. She must've removed it when she fished her wallet out to pay.

"Thank you."

Lydia looked at her quizzically, as if she wanted to say something about something other than food or weather, but then didn't. They walked back to her apartment in silence.

"JOHN?"

Alice waited, suspended in the front hallway, holding the handle of her suitcase. *Harvard Magazine* lay on the top of a pile of unclaimed mail strewn on the floor in front of her. The clock in the living room ticked and the refrigerator hummed. A warm, sunny late afternoon at her back, the air inside felt chilly, dim, and stale. Uninhabited.

She picked up the mail and walked into the kitchen, her

suitcase on wheels accompanying her like a loyal pet. Her
flight had been delayed, and she was late getting in, even according to the microwave. He'd had a whole day, a whole Saturday, to work.

The red voice-mail light on their answering machine stared her down, unblinking. She checked the refrigerator. No note on the door. Nothing.

Still clutching the handle of her suitcase, she stood in the dark kitchen and watched several minutes advance on the microwave. The disappointed but forgiving voice in her head faded to a whisper as the volume of a more primal one began to build and spread out. She thought about calling him, but the expanding voice rejected the suggestion outright and refused all excuses. She thought about deciding not to care, but the voice, now seeping down into her body, echoing in her belly, vibrating in each of her fingertips, was too powerful and pervasive to ignore.

Why did it bother her so much? He was in the middle of an experiment and couldn't leave it to come home. She'd certainly been in his shoes innumerable times. This was what they did. This was who they were. The voice called her a stupid fool.

She spotted her running shoes on the floor next to the back door. A run would make her feel better. That was what she needed.

Ideally, she ran every day. For many years now, she'd treated running like eating or sleeping, as a vital daily necessity, and she'd been known to squeeze in a jog at midnight or in the middle of a blinding snowstorm. But she'd neglected this basic need over the last several months. She'd been so busy. As she laced her shoes, she told herself she hadn't bothered bringing them with her to California because she'd known she wouldn't have the time. In truth, she'd simply forgotten to pack them.

When starting from her house on Poplar Street, she invariably followed the same route—down Massachusetts Avenue, through Harvard Square to Memorial Drive, along the Charles River to the Harvard Bridge over by MIT, and back—a little over five miles, a forty-five-minute round trip. She had long been attracted to the idea of running in the Boston Marathon but each year decided that she realistically didn't have the time to train for that kind of distance. Maybe someday she would. In excellent physical condition for a woman her age, she imagined running strong well into her sixties.

Clustered pedestrian traffic on the sidewalks and intermittent negotiations with car traffic in street intersections littered the first part of her run through Harvard Square. It was crowded and ripe with anticipation at that time of day on a Saturday, with crowds forming and milling around on street corners waiting for walk signals, outside restaurants waiting for tables, in movie theater lines waiting for tickets, and in double-parked cars waiting for an unlikely opening in a metered space. The first ten minutes of her run required a good deal of conscious external concentration to navigate through it all, but once she crossed Memorial Drive to the Charles River, she was free to run in full stride and completely in the zone.

A comfortable and cloudless evening invited a lot of activity along the Charles, yet the grassy area beside the river felt less congested than the streets of Cambridge. Despite a steady stream of joggers, dogs and their owners, walkers, Rollerbladers, cyclists, and women pushing babies in jogger strollers, like an experienced driver on a regularly traveled stretch of road, Alice retained only a vague sense for what went on around her now. As she ran along the river, she became mindful of nothing but the sounds of her Nikes hitting the pavement in syncopated rhythm with the pace of her breath. She didn't replay her argument with Lydia. She didn't acknowledge her growling stomach. She didn't think about John. She just ran.

As was her routine, she stopped running once she made it back to the John Fitzgerald Kennedy Park, a pocket of manicured lawns abutting Memorial Drive. Her head cleared, her body relaxed and rejuvenated, she began walking home. The JFK Park funneled into Harvard Square through a pleasant, bench-lined corridor between the Charles Hotel and the Kennedy School of Government.

At the other end of the corridor, she stood at the intersection of Eliot Street and Brattle, ready to cross, when a woman grabbed her forearm with startling force and said, "Have you thought about heaven today?"

The woman fixed Alice with a penetrating, unwavering stare. She had long hair the color and texture of a teased Brillo pad and wore a handmade placard hung over her chest that read AMERICA REPENT, TURN TO JESUS FROM SIN. There was always someone selling God in Harvard Square, but Alice had never been singled out so directly and intimately before.

"Sorry," she said and, noticing a break in the flow of traffic, escaped to the other side of the street.

She wanted to continue walking but stood frozen instead. She didn't know where she was. She looked back across the street. The Brillo-haired woman pursued another sinner down the corridor. The corridor, the hotel, the stores, the illogically meandering streets. She knew she was in Harvard Square, but she didn't know which way was home.

She tried again, more specifically. The Harvard Square Hotel, Eastern Mountain Sports, Dickson Bros. Hardware, Mount Auburn Street. She knew all of these places—this square had been her stomping ground for over twenty-five years—but they somehow didn't fit into a mental map that told her where she lived relative to them. A black-and-white circular "T" sign directly in front of her marked an entrance to the Red Line trains and buses underground, but there were three such entrances in Harvard Square, and she couldn't piece together which one of the three this was.

Her heart began to race. She started sweating. She told herself that an accelerated heart rate and perspiration were part of an orchestrated and appropriate response to running. But as she stood on the sidewalk, it felt like panic.

She willed herself to walk another block and then another, her rubbery legs feeling like they might give way with each bewildered step. The Coop, Cardullo's, the magazines on the corner, the Cambridge visitors' center across the street, and Harvard Yard beyond that. She told herself she could still read and recognize. None of it helped. It all lacked a context.

People, cars, buses, and all kinds of unbearable noise rushed and wove around and past her. She closed her eyes. She listened to her own blood whoosh and pulse behind her ears.

"Please stop this," she whispered.

She opened her eyes. Just as suddenly as it had left her, the landscape snapped snugly back into place. The Coop, Cardullo's, Nini's Corner, Harvard Yard. She automatically understood that she should turn left at the corner and head west on Mass Ave. She began to breathe easier, no longer bizarrely lost within a mile of home. But she'd just been bizarrely lost within a mile of home. She walked as fast as she could without running.

She turned onto her street, a quiet, tree-lined, residential road a couple of blocks removed from Mass Ave. With both feet on her road and her house in sight, she felt much safer, but not yet safe. She kept her eyes on her front door and her legs moving and promised herself that the sea of anxiety swelling furiously inside her would drain when she walked in the front hallway and saw John. If he was home.

"John?"

He appeared in the threshold of the kitchen, unshaven, his glasses sitting on top of his mad-scientist hair, sucking on a red Popsicle and sporting his lucky gray T-shirt. He'd been up all night. As she'd promised herself, her anxiety began to drain. But her energy and bravery seemed to leak out with it, leaving her fragile and wanting to collapse into his arms.

"Hey, I was wondering where you were, just about to leave you a note on the fridge. How'd it go?" he asked.

"What?"

"Stanford."

"Oh, good."

"And how's Lydia?"

The betrayal and hurt over Lydia, over him not being home when she got there, exorcised by the run and displaced by her terror at being inexplicably lost, reclaimed its priority in the pecking order.

"You tell me," she said.

"You guys fought."

"You're paying for her acting classes?" she accused.

"Oh," he said, sucking the last of the Popsicle into his red-stained mouth. "Look, can we talk about this later? I don't have time to get into it right now."

"Make the time, John. You're keeping her afloat out there without telling me, and you're not here when I get home, and—"

"And you weren't here when I got home. How was your run?"

She heard the simple reasoning in his veiled question. If she had waited for him, if she had called, if she hadn't done exactly what she'd wanted and gone for a run, she could've spent the last hour with him. She had to agree.

"Fine."

"I'm sorry, I waited as long as I could, but I've really got to get back to the lab. I've had an incredible day so far, gorgeous results, but we're not done, and I've got to analyze the numbers before we get started again in the morning. I only came home to see you."

"I need to talk about this with you now."

"This really isn't new information, Ali. We disagree about Lydia. Can't it wait until I get back?"

"No."

"You want to walk over with me, talk about it on the way?"

"I'm not going to the office, I need to be home."

"You need to talk now, you need to be home, you're awfully needy all of a sudden. Is something else going on?"

The word *needy* smacked a vulnerable nerve. *Needy* equaled weak, dependent, pathological. Her father. She'd made a life-long point of never being like that, like him.

"I'm just exhausted."

"You look it, you need to slow down."

"That's not what I need."

He waited for her to elaborate, but she took too long.

"Look, the sooner I go, the sooner I'll be back. Get some rest, I'll be home later tonight."

He kissed her sweat-drenched head and walked out the door.

Standing in the hallway where he'd left her, with no one to confess to or confide in, she felt the full emotional impact of what she'd just experienced in Harvard Square flood over her. She sat down on the floor and leaned against the cool wall, watching her hands shake in her lap as if they couldn't be hers. She tried to focus on steadying her breath as she did when she ran.

After minutes of breathing in and breathing out, she was finally calm enough to attempt to assemble some sense out of what had just happened. She thought about the missing word during her talk at Stanford and her missing period. She got up, turned on her laptop, and Googled "menopause symptoms."

An appalling list filled the screen—hot flashes, night sweats, insomnia, crashing fatigue, anxiety, dizziness, irregular heartbeat, depression, irritability, mood swings, disorientation, mental confusion, memory lapses.

Disorientation, mental confusion, memory lapses. Check, check, and check. She leaned back in her chair and raked her fingers through her curly black hair. She looked over at the pictures displayed on the shelves of the floor-to-ceiling bookcase—her Harvard graduation day, she and John dancing on their wedding day, family portraits from when the kids were little, a family portrait from Anna's wedding. She returned to the list on her computer screen. This was just the natural, next phase in her life as a woman. Millions of women coped with it every day. Nothing life-threatening. Nothing abnormal.

She wrote herself a note to make an appointment with her doctor for a checkup. Maybe she should go on estrogen replacement therapy. She read through the list of symptoms one last time. Irritability. Mood swings. Her recent shrinking fuse with John. It all added up. Satisfied, she shut down her computer.

She sat in the darkening study awhile longer, listening to her quiet house and the sounds of neighborhood barbecues. She inhaled the smell of hamburger grilling. For some reason, she wasn't hungry anymore. She took a multivitamin with water, unpacked, read several articles from *The Journal of Cognition*, and went to bed.

Sometime after midnight, John finally came home. His weight in their bed woke her, but only slightly. She remained still and pretended to stay asleep. He had to be exhausted from being up all night and working all day. They could talk about Lydia in the morning. And she'd apologize for being so sensitive and moody lately. His warm hand on her hip brought her into the curve of his body. With his breath on her neck, she fell into a deep sleep, convinced that she was safe.